MARKED BY MAGIC

AN URBAN FANTASY ADVENTURE

TRACKING TROUBLE
BOOK 1

LINDSAY BUROKER

FOREWORD

Thank you for picking up *Marked by Magic,* Book 1 in my new Tracking Trouble urban fantasy series. The stories feature Arwen, a wilderness-loving, half-dark-elf tracker first introduced in my Legacy of Magic series. She was raised on a farm by her human father and is a little (a lot) out of place in the big city. Also in small cities. Also in crowds of more than two people. People, in general, tend to make her uneasy. Crowds of bad guys that she can shoot with her bow are okay, though!

If you're a new reader, welcome. You can jump in without any familiarity with this world (basically, it's Seattle with dragons, shifters, and other magical beings). If you've already read my Death Before Dragons and Legacy of Magic series, you'll recognize some old friends. Either way, I hope you'll enjoy this adventure.

Thank you for reading, and thank you to my editor, Shelley Holloway, and my beta readers, Sarah Engelke and Cindy Wilkinson. Also, thank you to my cover designer, Gene Mollica Studio, and my audiobook narrator, Vivienne Leheny.

1

Rocket, the golden retriever, bounded through the grassy clearing toward a towering Douglas fir on the far side. His tail oscillated like a fan on the fritz.

Arwen Forester started to smile, certain he'd found another truffle, but the faintest musky scent in the air made her pause. Instead of reaching for her foraging knife, she wrapped her fingers around her bow. Had an ogre passed this way?

She stretched out with her magical senses, sniffing the air as well. Her half-elven blood—half-*dark*-elven blood—gave her the power to detect the auras that all magical beings emanated to varying degrees.

"Another one?" Sigrid Thorvald, her mushroom-hunting partner for the morning, pushed her long gray braid over her shoulder as she watched the dog. "We'll feast tonight."

Arwen's free hand strayed to the quiver of arrows on her back, many imbued with magical powers. She selected one called Swamper. It was enchanted to work well against trolls and ogres, beings that came from worlds filled with jungles and bogs.

"Or did you want to save the rest of what we find to sell at the farmers market? Our Pacific Northwest truffles aren't as lucrative as the European versions, but they go for a fair bit. You said your father's property taxes are going up this year, didn't you?" Sigrid, noticing that Arwen had nocked her bow, stopped and arched her eyebrows.

"*Way* up." Arwen scanned the muddy trail for prints different from the usual human and animal tracks. "We just found out our farm lost its agricultural designation and will now be taxed as residential land. It's a *huge* difference, one I'm not sure how we'll cover. My pies and pickled vegetables don't make us rich."

"What about your goat truffle butter? I'd pay a fortune for that. If I *had* a fortune."

Well aware that Sigrid's daughter helped pay her bills, Arwen would never charge Sigrid for anything. "You might want to get Rocket."

"What did you see? Or, did you, uh, *sense* it?" Sigrid waved her leash at her temple before heading toward the dog.

"Smelled. I don't sense any ogres in the area, but..." Arwen shrugged, not lowering her bow.

"It pays to be cautious out here." Sigrid clipped Rocket's leash to his collar, though he didn't want to be pulled away from the roots of the tree. "I *thought* I was getting a quiet cabin in the woods on the edge of civilization." She waved up the path in the direction of the forested neighborhood where she lived on an acre lot that backed up to state land. "I should have known that if I moved anywhere within fifty miles of my daughter, the *Ruin Bringer*, I'd encounter trolls, ogres, shifters, and other trouble on a daily basis."

"A lot of magical beings from other worlds have taken refuge in the Seattle area these past few years."

"I'm aware. You might be able to make some extra money tracking criminals for the police or even that Army colonel that my daughter works for." Sigrid waved vaguely toward the forest.

"Your father trained you well, and you're good at it. Almost as good as Rocket." She managed to look both fondly and with exasperation at the dog as he tugged at his leash, wanting to be rewarded for having found a prize.

"The authorities have their own trackers." Arwen had been called in to help out a few times, but she wasn't that comfortable hunting people down for money.

"Maybe you could *become* one of their trackers. It has to pay better than Search and Rescue."

"We volunteer at Search and Rescue."

"Hence why you'd make more if you were hired somewhere. There might even be gigs in the private sector." Sigrid shrugged. "Val would know."

Something with an unfamiliar aura twanged at Arwen's senses, something *much* more powerful than the ogre she'd expected.

"What is *that*?" she whispered, looking toward the cloudy sky.

"You'll have to tell me." Sigrid, with her fully human blood, couldn't sense magical beings. Fortunately, despite being in her seventies and wandering the woods barefoot like a peace-loving hippie most of the time, she wasn't defenseless. She opened her jacket to rest a hand on the butt of her Glock 17.

"I... think it's a dragon."

Sigrid groaned. "Not Zavryd. He and Liam do *not* get along. Besides, he's got his own sauna now. Why does he still want to put his naked shape-shifted butt in mine?"

Arwen shook her head. "It's not Val's mate. I've seen Zavryd enough times to recognize his aura. This isn't a dragon I've sensed before. I'm not even sure it *is* a dragon. There's something... elven about him."

"Are you sure it's not an elf *riding* a dragon?" Sigrid also peered toward the sky, but the moss-draped trees rising on all sides of the clearing limited their view.

"There's only one aura."

"Come on." Sigrid tilted her head toward the trail. "We'd better get back to my place and call Val. If there's a new threat in the area, she and her boss will want to know about it."

Arwen nodded, but a black-scaled dragon flew into view before she'd taken a step.

Sleek, muscular, and emanating great power, the majestic being made her breath catch. From below, she shouldn't have been able to see his face, but his head tilted to the side as he flew, one violet eye visible as he scanned the ground.

Looking for something? Looking for *them*?

A jolt of fear went through her at the possibility, but Arwen couldn't imagine why a dragon would want her. Most of the magical community avoided her, even when she promised them that she didn't follow the vile demon-worshipping ways of her mother's people.

Her fingers curled tighter around her bow, but, even if the dragon did something aggressive, would she dare point a weapon at him? It wasn't as if she had an arrow designed to be effective against their kind. An enchanter would be suicidal to even consider making such a thing. Dragons, the most powerful species on all the worlds in the Cosmic Realms, responded to any slight against their kind from a *lesser species* without mercy.

After the dragon's gaze skimmed over them, he kept flying, soon soaring out of view over the trees. Arwen sagged in relief.

"He's not as big as the other dragons I've seen," Sigrid said. "You said you sensed something elven about him? That's strange. Elves can't shape-shift into other beings. Though they can appear to be other things by using illusion magic."

"That wasn't an illusion. It was—" Arwen halted, sensing that the dragon was banking and turning around. "Uh oh."

Should they run? Stand their ground? Unfortunately, none of her arrows had the power to magically camouflage her. Oh, she could hide in the forest better than most people, but a dragon would sense her aura even more easily than she sensed his.

Rocket whined and clenched his tail between his legs. The dragon flew back into view, soaring low over the treetops this time. He descended toward the clearing with *both* of his eyes locked onto Arwen.

She swallowed. "Take Rocket back to your cabin, Sigrid, and call Val. Maybe she knows who this guy is."

"You want me to leave you here alone with him?"

"There's nothing you could do, but Val can, if her mate is around."

Sigrid bristled, no doubt hating to be told she couldn't do anything to help, but she had to know it was true. A mundane human gun wouldn't pierce the scales of a dragon. Arwen doubted even her magical arrows would.

"All right. But be careful." Sigrid backed away with Rocket as the dragon tucked his wings and landed twenty feet from Arwen.

This close, his aura was even more noticeable, his power tangible and terrifying. He might not be as big as Val's mate, but Zavryd was a good dragon—one who obeyed the laws of his people and didn't kill without provocation. Not all dragons were like that.

Even with all four limbs on the ground, this fellow towered over Arwen. With those violet eyes locked on to her, she couldn't keep from shivering. Sweat made her grip on her bow slick. She kept it at her side, not wanting to provoke him.

Maybe he was lost and needed directions.

She almost laughed at the ludicrousness of the thought. He was way too interested in her to be a lost tourist visiting Earth.

In front of her eyes, the dragon's outline blurred, his scales turning to flesh, and his size diminishing as he rose up on his back legs. Soon, a human being stood before her. No, not a human. An *elf*.

The points of the ears poking up through his shoulder-length black hair were unmistakable, but Arwen again dismissed the idea that he was an elf who'd been using an illusion. Even if his powerful aura hadn't been too great to belong to one of their kind, his angular face had a fearsome, predatory aspect that brought to mind the dragon he'd just been.

He wore a dark-brown tunic with forest-green trousers and leather boots and was armed with a sword in a scabbard on his back and daggers sheathed at his waist. Rolled-up sleeves revealed lean and muscled arms. He looked like someone who would be good to have at one's back in a fight—and someone one definitely didn't want to *face* in a battle.

"You have the blood of a dark elf," he stated. His voice had a haughty timbre with an accent but not an accent she'd ever heard before. Not from *Earth*, it said.

And what an odd greeting. It sounded like an accusation.

"*You* have the blood of a dragon," she said.

"Yes."

"I'm Arwen. Do you have a name?" A name she could give to Val and Zavryd if they came by later...

Her instincts told her this guy was trouble, that he wasn't on Earth for any *good* reason.

Without answering, he prowled in a slow circle around her, looking her up and down and considering her from all sides. Like he was sizing up an enemy.

Arwen did not want to be that, but she wouldn't grovel or placate him either. After all, when predators sensed weakness, they attacked.

His lips twitched in dismissal or maybe mockery as he took in her five-foot-nine-inches, her slender build, and her red-blonde hair that was, as usual, pinned behind her head by ornaments she'd fashioned from gnarled sticks. Outwardly, she appeared fully human, with her freckles, fair skin, and green eyes linking her openly to her father. Nothing of her mother's albino-skinned, red-eyed, light-hating people came through on the surface. Thankfully. Only her blood gave that away—to those who could sense the magic in it.

"You wear the garments and accoutrements of a native of this world," he stated.

"Yes, because I *am* a native of this world."

"Your bow and arrows came from elsewhere. Many are magical. Did you steal them?"

"Of course not."

"Respectable crafters would not sell their wares to one with dark-elven blood."

Arwen clenched her jaw. She was starting to dislike this guy. "I traded for some of them and won others in battle."

"Meaning you slew the owners and *took* their belongings."

"I highly doubt the yeti I got my Swamper arrow from was the original owner. He was chasing pigs around Mark Zuber's silos and stabbing them with it."

"A silo is—" he paused as if dredging information from his memory, "—a large cylindrical structure for the bulk storage of food items such as grain."

"Actually, most silos around here are for storing silage."

"Silage," he mouthed.

"Green foliage crops that are compacted to ferment and acidify."

He considered her. "Acidified feed sounds unappealing."

"It kicks ass if you're a cow."

"Cows are... the domesticated ungulates in the fields by the waterway to the west of this locale, yes?"

"Yes."

"*They* are appealing."

"Humans think so too." Arwen shook her head, not sure *what* to make of the conversation. Or him. He sounded like an alien who'd read up on Earth before coming down for a visit. Maybe he wanted to abduct her.

He started a second slow circuit around her, still considering her.

"Can I help you find something?" Arwen asked.

Again, he didn't answer. His gaze lingered on her right arm, and she resisted the urge to make sure her sleeve was pushed down. It was, but he looked right at the location of a spider tattoo on her forearm, as if he could see it through her shirt. Her mother had forced that on Arwen long ago, a supposed sign of her obedience to Zagorwalek, the spider demon, one of the quasi deities in the dark-elven religion.

Though he couldn't have seen the tattoo, something told Arwen he'd *sensed* it somehow. But why would he care?

"If you're looking for some tasty ungulate, there's a barbecue restaurant in Duvall." Arwen pointed in the direction of the nearest town. "They have brisket and corned beef that you'll love. Get the horseradish barbecue sauce to go with it."

For a moment, his eyes grew a touch speculative, but then he shook his head, as if remembering his mission. He pinned her with his gaze. "Where are your people?"

"My people? My father and I have a farm, but it's not around here." Arwen had no intention of sharing her address with a possible enemy.

"Your *dark-elven* people."

"Those aren't my people, and I have no idea where they are. They left the area a long time ago." Well, two years ago at least. That was when Val and Zavryd had driven the only clan of dark elves in the area away. They'd been plotting to make volcanos erupt and to overthrow humanity, something Val's Army employer frowned upon. Arwen, who'd done her best to avoid her mother since she and her father had escaped the clan twenty-three years earlier, didn't know if she'd been part of that or not.

"You protect them? They inspire that much loyalty in you?"

"They don't. They're just not here."

"You protect them with your lies," he said. "Were your people elves or even dwarves, I would understand, but there is no honor in protecting dark elves."

"I'm not—"

He stepped closer, looming six inches taller than she, and Arwen tensed.

"Is there a price at which you would tell me where to find them?" he asked.

Her conversation with Sigrid popped into her mind, the uncomfortable financial situation she and her father now found themselves in. How much was the new property-tax bill? Nearly twelve thousand dollars, she recalled, and that was only for one year.

Right away, she pushed away the thought of giving this guy fake information in exchange for money. Even if she could have ensured there wouldn't be repercussions, it wouldn't have been honorable. She would find a legitimate way to earn that money. Besides, dragons who came to Earth didn't bring chests of money with them, certainly not US currency.

"I don't need anything," she lied.

"No? You and the human spoke of denuding the forest floor of the mushrooms that grow in this area. To *sell* them, not to enjoy them." His lips twisted in a haughty sneer.

Arwen would have been shocked that a dragon cared about truffles, but she was too busy realizing that he'd been in the area before she'd sensed him—before he'd *allowed* her to sense him?— and had been spying on them. That sent another chill through her. How long had he been stalking them and eavesdropping? And why?

"This is state land out here," Arwen said. "There's no law against foraging and selling what you find."

"Humans are overly preoccupied with coin."

"We need it to live." She and her father were more self-sufficient than many, but there was no getting away from needing at least some money to survive in the modern world.

"It is a strange world that I find myself on."

"Yeah, sorry about that." Arwen was on the verge of suggesting he leave. With his power, he had to be able to create magical portals to other worlds.

Before she could voice the thought, an itching sensation started under her skull. It was almost painful. Only rarely had she encountered powerful telepaths who'd tried to read her mind, so it took her a moment to realize that was what he was doing.

"*Where* are the dark elves?" His eyes bored into her, flaring violet as his power enveloped her, as he sought an answer in her thoughts.

"I... don't... know..." she bit out, afraid of what he would do if he couldn't get what he wanted.

Chin up, he lifted a hand toward her head, and she realized she was about to find out.

2

BEFORE THE STRANGER'S OUTSTRETCHED HAND REACHED HER, THE pain grew sharper. Arwen gasped as his attempt to read her mind intensified. It felt like talons raking through her brain.

"Leave her alone," Sigrid called from the trail.

Arwen had thought she'd left. Arwen had *wanted* her to leave, so she would be safe, and held up a hand, hoping Sigrid wouldn't do something foolish. A glance back showed her leaning out from behind a tree, her Glock in hand. Damn.

The pain lessened as the dragon-in-elven-form looked over at Sigrid, but his presence didn't leave Arwen's mind. He stood close enough that his power subsumed hers, his aura crackling all about him and making her skin buzz.

"My daughter is married to Lord Zavryd'nokquetal," Sigrid called, "and he's on his way here. Arwen is a friend of his. You'd better not hurt her."

Arwen hadn't spoken more than three words to Zavryd and wasn't positive he knew her name. Still, she looked hopefully at the dragon, hoping the statement would deter him from doing more than reading her mind.

"You lie, human. Unlike *this one*—" he flicked a finger at Arwen, "—your thoughts are easy to discern."

"He *is* her husband," Sigrid said.

"But not on the way here."

"He could be. They come by *often* and unannounced. That heat-craving dragon can't stay away from my sauna." Sigrid managed to sound indignant, though she had to be worried.

The dragon's eyes narrowed as he considered her. Arwen knew Zavryd *did* visit often. Whether Sigrid truly believed he might show up this morning, Arwen didn't know.

"A dragon goes where a dragon wishes," the powerful stranger stated.

"Tell me about it," Sigrid grumbled.

He focused again on Arwen, and the attempt to read her mind intensified once more. Her knees weakened, and she couldn't keep from gasping, the temptation to lift her bow coming to her again. Anything to stop this.

Surprisingly, she got a sense for his thoughts, or at least his feelings. A sense of desperation emanated from him. He *had* to find the dark elves. Because... because why?

A gun fired, making Arwen jump.

Fire flashed in the air above the dragon's head. It took Arwen a second to realize that had been Sigrid's bullet—and he'd incinerated it.

Irritation flared in his eyes, their glow brightening as he stared at Sigrid. "You *dare* fire at me, human?"

"Leave her alone, or I'll shoot again, and *at* your head, not above it." Sigrid didn't acknowledge that her bullet wouldn't have reached him, no matter where she'd targeted. Her voice held a quaver, though her grip remained steady on the gun.

Flames burst from Sigrid's hand. She cried out in alarm and dropped her gun. It disintegrated in the air, smoke wafting up as ash trickled down.

This time, Arwen did raise her bow. She stepped back and pointed her arrow at the stranger's chest. Attacking a dragon was suicidal, but she couldn't let him hurt Sigrid.

Showing no hint of concern, he looked back at her. "Your mind is strangely difficult to read, considering your mongrel blood."

She'd heard that term before. Full-blooded magical beings liked to use it to describe those like her with human or another unmagical species mixed into their heritage. "I can't say that I'm sorry."

He glanced at her forearm again, her shirt still covering the tattoo. Magic crawled unpleasantly over her skin as he used his power to push up her sleeve. She grabbed it to keep the tattoo covered, but she was too slow. He saw the illustration of the spider demon, the eight legs curling around her forearm, the ugly black carapace darkening her skin, two red eyes visible.

The unwanted gift was nothing Arwen had ever requested, even as a girl, but others saw it as a mark of the dark-elven cult, a sign that she was a loyal member.

"I'm not one of them," she said firmly. "The tattoo doesn't mean anything to me."

He watched her intently, not commenting on her words. "I did catch a few of your thoughts."

"I hope you saw that I not only don't know where the dark elves are living but that I'm positive they're not in this area."

As soon as the words came out, Arwen realized that wasn't entirely true. It was *mostly* true, but the year before, a dark-elf priest had approached her, wanting to mate with her because there were so few full-blooded, fertile female dark elves left. He'd been willing to accept the taint of her human blood in the hope that they would produce offspring. The offer had been as flattering and appealing as roadkill, so she'd rejected it, threatening to put an arrow through his chest.

"They *are* here. If you won't tell me, perhaps another will." The dragon put an image in her mind of her father and the farm, the manufactured home that he lived in and the cozy cob cottage she'd built for herself on the back of the property.

Fear ricocheted through Arwen. He'd learned where she lived —where her *father* lived—from her thoughts.

"Yes," he said softly and stepped back. "Your father is human. His mind will have no protections."

"You stay away from him." Arwen had never shot someone who looked human—or *elven*—before, but to protect her friends and family, she would.

"Like the *sayasha* storm lily when rain comes, he will unfurl his thoughts for me."

She drew her bow to fire. Again, he showed no alarm at her weapon, but he did raise an invisible magical barrier around himself. "If he knows where the dark elves are, I *will* question him. Those dishonorable cowards will not evade my wrath. As the great general of centuries past, Mysolysar, said, taunt not the enemy that has the power to destroy your troops."

"I promise he doesn't know anything more than I—less. He hardly ever leaves the farm, and he's—" Arwen caught herself before blurting that he struggled to live with the trauma of his past —the horrible memories that plagued them both from their time when they'd been prisoners of the dark elves. She'd been so young that much of it was a blur, but he'd been an adult, and he remembered it all. That was not information her father wanted her announcing to strangers, especially *dangerous* strangers. "He doesn't know anything about where dark elves live today."

"We shall see." He blurred, shifting back into the dragon form.

"*No!*" Arwen loosed her arrow.

As she'd feared, it bounced off, not piercing the barrier.

The dragon flew off but not before looking back. *Perhaps,* he spoke telepathically into her mind, his voice booming with its power, *you should read the works of General Mysolysar.*

Perhaps you should screw yourself, Arwen thought back, fury overriding wisdom.

He banked and headed south—in the direction of her father's farm.

3

ARWEN SPUN TOWARD SIGRID. "I HAVE TO GO HOME. HE'S GOING TO question my father. I'm afraid he'll do *worse* than question him."

"I understand." Sigrid eyed the small pile of ashes on the ground, all that remained of her gun.

"Where's Rocket?" Arwen *thought* the dragon had been focused on her, but what if he'd done something to the dog?

"He pulled away and ran into the woods. Back home, I hope." Sigrid managed a worried smile. "He's smarter than I am."

"Thanks for sticking up for me." Even though Arwen had wanted her friend to run and be safe, that information about Zavryd might have been what had kept the dragon from making more attempts to read her mind.

"You're welcome." Sigrid started down the trail. "We're almost back to my cabin. Let me drive you."

Arwen hesitated. She didn't have a car and usually walked everywhere, but it was miles by forest path—and even farther by road—to the farm.

"It'll be faster than going on foot," Sigrid pointed out.

"All right. Thanks."

Bow in hand, Arwen took the lead and jogged up the trail, almost missing a hint of magic in her path. *Ogre* magic. She'd forgotten about the original trouble.

She halted inches before running into a concealed tripwire. Angry with the situation and that her father was in danger, she smacked it with the tip of her bow instead of avoiding it altogether. A trap triggered, and a leaf-covered net swept off the trail while bundling up everything on top of it. That had almost been Arwen.

"What are ogres trying to catch out here?" Sigrid murmured. "Rabbits?"

"I doubt it."

Rocket ran out of the woods toward Sigrid, leaves and needles stuck to his damp, muddy leash as it trailed behind him. She grabbed it and didn't berate the dog for running off. Arwen wouldn't have blamed anyone for running from a dragon either.

Though she hated to delay, she made herself continue forward slowly so she could spot anything else suspicious on the trail. She triggered one more trap, then led Sigrid and Rocket through a stream instead of using a narrow bridge that might have been tampered with. When they splashed past it, they spotted sawn support posts.

Once they returned to the trail, large ogre boot prints were visible in the muddy spots. Again, Arwen caught the musky scent of their kind, and, this time, she detected them with her magical senses as well. They'd probably scattered when the dragon entered the area, but he was gone now, so the ogres had nothing to worry about.

"Except me." Arwen almost longed for a reason to shoot someone full of holes. Someone without the power to deflect arrows with magic.

With the fresh ogre trail in front of him, Rocket tried to go into hunting mode. But Sigrid kept him on the leash, and they made it to the first of the houses in her wooded neighborhood without encountering more trouble.

Until a crash filtered through the trees, an inhuman roar following it. Were the ogres destroying someone's home? *Sigrid's* home?

Arwen broke into a run, wanting to reach it first, especially since Sigrid had lost her gun. Aside from a werewolf who lived across the street, most of Sigrid's neighbors were normal humans and had no means of defending themselves against enemies with the hulking brawn of ogres.

A thud sounded, then wood cracked as Sigrid's modest cabin came into view through the trees. At first, Arwen didn't see the ogres, though her senses promised they were in the area. More wood cracked, and someone squealed in pain.

One of Sigrid's neighbors? That high-pitched cry hadn't sounded human, but there were other intelligent species that lived out here.

Arwen wanted to check on her father, not get involved in a fray, but she might not have a choice.

The first hulking brute came into view, a massive spiked club raised over his shaggy yellow-haired head. Clad in hides that did little to hide his muscled tree-trunk arms, the eight-foot-tall ogre smashed that club down, not onto Sigrid's cabin but onto a barrel-shaped sauna in the yard. The alarmed squeal sounded again, turning into a cry for help. Whoever it was had been trapped inside.

"Stop right there!" Arwen cried, aiming her bow at the towering intruder.

Her instincts weren't to shoot to kill, not when she didn't know what was going on—if some heinous enemy to the ogre clan was hiding in the sauna, did she have the right to interfere? But she couldn't let someone destroy Sigrid's property or take anyone's life.

A second ogre stomped into view, wearing chest armor made

from rib bones and enchanted with magic. He ran toward Arwen. "Dark elf, you will die!"

"I'm not a dark elf." Arwen shifted her aim to him. "I'm half *human* and the protector of the people and homes in this area." Technically, she didn't have the authority to protect anything except her father's farm, but the ogres wouldn't know that. "Get off this property."

With his yellow eyes gleaming and his club lifted, the ogre stomped closer, yelling in his own tongue. Arwen had encountered their kind often enough to catch the gist.

"Your puny weapon will not pierce my magical armor!"

"No? Meet *Swamper.*" Arwen thought the arrow would go through his chest armor, but, to play it safe, she aimed at his unprotected thigh.

The head flashed silver as it sailed into its target, sinking deep. Bellowing, the ogre threw back his head and dropped his club. He fumbled for the shaft, trying to yank it out. The tiny barbs on the head bit in, but he managed to yank the arrow free, tearing a chunk of his flesh out with it. Amid more enraged bellows, he hurled the projectile into the woods.

Opting for a simple aim-enhancing arrow, Arwen fired again. Though she was tempted to target his heart, she instead struck the ogre in the other thigh. She wasn't a law enforcer, and she didn't know what was going on.

"Help!" came another high-pitched cry from the sauna. "Save me, save me!"

Now that Arwen was closer, she sensed a goblin trapped inside. His aura was less powerful—and therefore less noticeable —than those of the ogres. She doubted a goblin counted as an enemy of an ogre clan, unless he had stolen some of their junk to use in a project.

"Get the dark elf!" The ogre she'd shot staggered, grabbing his thigh with one hand and yanking out her second arrow with the other.

Why did everyone want dark elves today? And think she had anything to do with them?

"My sauna!" Sigrid cried, coming up behind Arwen, Rocket's leash gripped in her hand. The dog barked uproariously, equally affronted by the vandalism. Tail rigid and hackles raised, he wasn't as intimidated by these foes as he had been by the dragon.

"You will come with us, dark elf." The other ogre waved his club in the air as he squinted at Arwen.

"No, I won't, but satisfy my curiosity. Why do you want me?"

His squint deepened. He looked confused. Not an atypical state for ogres.

With another arrow already nocked, Arwen pointed it at his chest. But he also wore armor—chainmail under a vest—so she shifted her aim lower.

His squint shifted to it. The arrowhead was glowing white.

"This one is called the *Cockseeker*," Arwen said. "I'll let you guess what it likes to target."

His mouth formed an O.

Something flew out of the half-destroyed sauna and landed on the ogre's foot. A wooden bucket for ladling water onto the rocks.

The ogre roared and glowered at the goblin, then at Arwen's bow. Finally, determining the odds against him, he ran away, a scrap of litter fluttering out of a pocket. The remaining ogre also hobbled awkwardly away as he gripped his thighs. They headed out the gate and turned toward the state land at the end of the street.

"Is that really the name of that arrow?" Sigrid asked.

"No. It's an elven compass arrow that glows when it's pointing toward the North Pole. It's also supposed to be lucky in the forest and help with foraging."

"So, very dangerous to ogre genitalia."

"*All* of my arrows are that." Arwen walked toward what she'd thought was litter, but it was a crumpled hundred-dollar bill. "That's weird."

"That ogres make more money than we do?"

"I was going to say that they usually barter for things and don't use much of our currency, but it *is* a denomination I rarely see at the farmers market. When I do see it, it's usually from someone driving a BMW, wearing expensive sunglasses, and wanting me to make change for a three-dollar item."

"That's awful, Arwen."

"Some people are oblivious."

"I meant that you're selling three-dollar items," Sigrid said. "No wonder the farm is in trouble."

"Ha ha. You can't charge much for medicinal ointments."

"If they're made from the magical herbs you grow, you can."

"Humans can't sense the magic in things." Arwen offered her the bill, feeling it belonged to Sigrid since it had fallen on her property. "They call you *woo woo* if you start talking about such things."

"If your ointment heals their hammertoes and hemorrhoids, they'll have no trouble believing in your magic. Trust me. Charge more." Sigrid waved for her to keep the money and headed for the cabin. "I'll grab my car keys."

"Thank you." Arwen wondered if she'd forgotten about the goblin in her sauna.

Or maybe it wasn't that odd for Sigrid to find goblins in there? After all, it was catnip to dragons.

The rumble of a vehicle came from the street, and Arwen sensed more beings with magical blood approaching. Considering how far Sigrid's home was from town, this area was bizarrely busy today.

"Not someone else looking for dark elves, I hope."

A black SUV rolled into view, the word *SHERIFF* painted

across the doors. But were those shifters in the front seats? A cougar and a tiger?

Arwen had never heard of their kind being employed by the authorities. Usually, the police, military, and other government institutions didn't acknowledge that magical beings existed. Only the special Army unit in Seattle that Val worked for interacted with and, when necessary, stopped crimes committed by their kind.

Arwen willed the SUV to drive past, to have nothing to do with her or Sigrid. She wanted to check on her father, not have hordes of shifters breathing down her neck. She struggled with crowds under any circumstances, but many of the oversexed shifters she'd met stood too close. Worse, some got handsy with her.

The SUV turned onto the property and parked at the gate —*blocked* the gate. The cougar shifter at the wheel rolled down his window and pointed at Arwen.

She groaned. This day kept getting worse and worse.

4

ANY HOPE ARWEN HAD FOR SIGRID COMING OUT WITH THE KEYS TO her Subaru, waving for Arwen to leap in, and them roaring out past the SUV was quashed by her voice floating out an open window. Was she calling someone? Arwen's father didn't have a working phone anymore, so it couldn't be he. Maybe she was updating Val on everything.

Arwen couldn't blame her. They couldn't have left with the SUV deliberately parked to block the gate anyway.

Both shifters were looking out the open driver-side window at her now. And conferring with each other. One glanced more than once at her bow.

Not sure what to think of the shifters, Arwen eased into the trees to collect the arrows the ogre had yanked out and thrown away. It had taken her years to collect the magical projectiles, and she didn't want to lose any. One arrow had a chunk of ogre thigh stuck to it. Grimacing, she pried it off, then looked around for a place to throw it. The garbage bin? Her father usually composted everything—*everything*—on the farm. The year before, attacking yetis had ended up being turned into fertilizer for the beets and rutabagas.

As Arwen passed, a green-skinned and nude goblin peered out of the smashed-in front of the sauna.

"Who are you?" she asked.

The shifters in the SUV hadn't gotten out yet, but they were both still considering her. A feeling of too many people present— too many people *looking* at her—crept over her like ants crawling on one's skin.

The urge to flee into the woods swept over Arwen, but she rooted her feet to the ground. She couldn't go anywhere except in Sigrid's car to check on her father.

"I'm Nuknuk from the Water Clan." The goblin waved toward the woods. "I heard that my people may use this delightful hot box if they perform repairs while they're here."

Arwen eyed the smashed sauna. "Repairs?"

Sigrid stuck her head out the window, first peering at the shifters and then toward the sauna. Still on the phone, a land line with a coil dangling from the handset, she seemed to be describing the situation. Arwen hoped she learned something useful about the dragon.

"I didn't do this," Nuknuk said. "The ogres came before I'd finished my helpful customizations. I was adding a toilet facility so one need not leave the luxurious heat of the hot box to attend to biological necessities."

Sigrid must have heard that because she groaned. "I never should have left Oregon."

She ended the phone call and came outside, leaving the dog in her cabin. She eyed the SUV on the way to join Arwen near the sauna. Her keys were in her hand, but she must have also realized they couldn't go while the shifters blocked the driveway.

"Why *did* you leave Oregon?" Arwen wiped one of her palms as the passenger-side door of the SUV opened. The shifters hadn't so much as glanced at Sigrid, so Arwen guessed they were here for her. But how could they have anticipated that she would be at Sigrid's home? Surely, word hadn't gotten out that she'd had plans to make magically-infused truffle butter here this afternoon.

"To be closer to my granddaughter," Sigrid said.

"But not to your daughter?"

"Val is a pain in the ass."

Arwen had only heard about and not met Sigrid's blunt-tongued teenage granddaughter, Amber, but, from what others said, Arwen might have been inclined to put her in the *pain-in-the-ass* category too. She didn't say so, instead drifting closer to Sigrid's Subaru. Hopefully, whatever the shifters wanted wouldn't take long.

"You like to be closer to your family when you get older and wake at night to the cold kiss of mortality on the back of your neck," Sigrid added.

"Are you sure that isn't Rocket's tongue?" Arwen smiled, not liking the thought of Sigrid passing from old age any more than from an ogre's club.

"He does take a lot of room in bed, but he usually keeps his tongue to himself at night."

"Considerate."

The passenger door shut, and a tall, broad-shouldered, and red-haired shifter in a suit strode up the driveway. That was not a sheriff's uniform. Maybe these guys had stolen the SUV.

Though he appeared fully human, the shifter oozed the menace and power of a dangerous predator. Not as much as the dragon had but a substantial amount. He didn't openly carry a weapon, but, as Arwen well knew, if he took his tiger form, he would *become* a weapon.

The cougar shifter slid out of the driver's seat, revealing that he wore a county sheriff's uniform. Huh.

He withdrew a huge modified rifle that emanated magic. Were

those tranquilizer darts loaded into it? If so, they appeared large enough to take down an elephant.

The tiger shifter eyed the sky, and Arwen abruptly amended her thought: large enough to take down a *dragon*. At least going by dosage. Arwen was skeptical the weapon's magic would be strong enough to pierce a dragon's armored scales. And that barrier he'd had around him? It would take a very powerful weapon to launch anything through that.

"What fresh hell is here to ruin the day?" Sigrid asked as the suited shifter walked toward them. She reached for her empty holster, seemed to remember the gun was gone, and propped her fist on her hip.

In the cabin, Rocket put his paws on a windowsill and barked at the stranger, doubtless sensing he was a predator. Arwen wanted to bark too. Between the goblin, the visitors, and Sigrid, she felt hemmed in.

A memory flashed into her mind of being trapped in a light-less tunnel as a girl, hooded dark elves on all sides, chanting for a ceremony. Someone gripped her arm painfully and reminded her to engage in the prayer, the call to the Soul Gatherer, one of the demons they worshipped. She'd been unable to run, unable to escape.

The goblin noticed the shifter, squeaked, and disappeared back into the sauna. Arwen pulled her mind back to the present. She needed her wits about her since the shifter kept his cool amber gaze on her. Why everyone was so interested in her today, she didn't know, but it worried her. She preferred not to be noticed at all and certainly not to be sought out.

The shifter considered her bow for a long moment, then smiled at her, as if to say, *We're all friends here; no need to wave weapons about.*

Yeah, right.

Arwen didn't lift her bow, but she mentally selected the arrow she would grab if he turned hostile, one that had an affinity for shifters. The troll hunter who'd bartered it to her had said it could veer around trees and other obstacles to hit its desired target. Not many shifters came out to her rural farm, so she hadn't yet tested that.

This guy halted five feet away and looked Arwen up and down, his gaze taking in her secondhand clothing and muddy moccasins. Tensing, she tugged her sleeve down to make sure it hid the spider tattoo and waited for a comment on her heritage. Like all shifters, he would be able to sense the magic in her blood. But it was her bow that drew his eye back, his gaze lingering there. He also considered her quiver thoughtfully.

Arwen raised her eyebrows. Her weapons were all magical, but the bow didn't have a lot of power. As far as she knew, the dwarven enchantment on it only made it resistant to magic and more difficult to break than the wood and bone segments it was made from suggested. It wasn't anything that could down dragons or wyverns or other powerful creatures. Some of her arrows had notable power, but most had specific enchantments. She did wonder if he could tell that she had an arrow designed to be effective against his kind.

"You are Arwen Forester." There was no doubt in his tone, though they'd never met. "A tracker."

"That's right," she said.

"And you are half dark-elven." A sneer curled his lip, but he soon smoothed it.

"I am." Arwen made herself hold his gaze, though she always wanted to shrivel up and hide when someone brought up her heritage—and stated or implied that it was despicable.

"Dark elves aren't known as archers."

"My father taught me the skill."

"And to track?"

"Yes."

"I'm surprised you have a reputation for it. Dark-elven magic also isn't known to give one an affinity for nature."

Why had the shifter been looking up information about her and her *reputation*? Arwen hadn't been aware that anyone outside of Washington State Search and Rescue knew about her.

"Do you track a person through their soul or blood instead of by communing with the earth and trees the way an elf—a *real* elf —would?"

Arwen's jaw tightened at his assumptions. Though she *did* know how to soul track, she hated using any magic that her mother's people favored, always afraid she might come to like it too much. Using such power could supposedly draw one closer to the demons the dark elves worshipped.

When Arwen followed a trail, she did her best to use her magic the way a surface elf would, letting it flow into the ground and flora around her to see what they'd recently seen. It didn't come as naturally for her as it would for one of their kind, but she'd learned over the years to twist her gifts to do the work she wished. Work for the greater good, not to appease a demon.

"Why do you want to know about me and my magic?" Arwen asked, reluctant to explain anything to a stranger, a stranger who might be an enemy.

When his mouth parted in a smile, it revealed canines far sharper than those of a human. "I'm Ebonclaw Tigris, and I want to hire you." He looked again toward the sky. "To track down a half-dragon criminal who is hiding here on Earth. His name is Azerdash Starblade."

5

HALF-DRAGON? THAT WOULD EXPLAIN THE CONFUSION IN WHAT Arwen had sensed, but...

"Dragons can't breed with other species," she said. "There isn't any such thing as a half-dragon."

Tigris's cool amber eyes closed to slits. Why, because he thought she was lying?

Arwen spread her arms, bow still in hand, though if the shifter wanted to hire a tracker, he might not be a threat to her. Yet... something didn't add up. Shifters were usually excellent trackers themselves. These guys had found *her* here, after all. How? If they'd gone to the farm first, her father wouldn't have told strangers where she was. He was protective of her, and she couldn't imagine him uttering a betrayal even under duress.

She squinted back at Tigris. The shifter had better *not* have put her father under duress. She already worried what the dragon— the *half*-dragon?—would do to him and itched to hurry to the farm. All the delays grated on her.

"Some half-dragons *do* exist," Tigris said, "thanks to an elven mage-scientist who used his power to mingle elven and dragon genes together to create offspring."

Sigrid lifted her head and opened her mouth, but Tigris continued his story before she could interrupt.

"Centuries ago, the half-dragons were raised and trained by generals to be powerful wizards and warriors, to go into battle on behalf of the elven people."

"Centuries ago?" Arwen knew elves—and dragons—could live a long time, but to her thirty-year-old self, the idea of someone surviving for centuries boggled the mind. When he'd been in elven form, the half-dragon had appeared to be her age.

"Yes. For much of that time, these half-dragons—deemed criminals by the dwarves the elven people were at war with when they were created—were imprisoned in stasis chambers and did not age. Recently, someone let one of them out." Tigris's eyes narrowed again. "I believe you know Matti Puletasi."

The way he said her name made Arwen believe he considered Matti an enemy, and she replied warily. "Yes, but not well. She gave me some leftover barbecue from her party last fall, and my father gave her some of our farm's jam and honey."

A furrow creased the shifter's brow. He couldn't know that Arwen and Sigrid had helped track down some bad guys to rescue Matti's mother, could he? That had been how Arwen had first met the half-dwarf enchanter. And Sigrid's daughter, Val, too.

Tigris kept eyeing her suspiciously.

It made Arwen nervous, and she found herself uttering inane information he hadn't asked for. "Matti invited me to her party too, but I find crowded events stressful." Panic-attack–inspiring was more like it. "Also, there were dragons there. Real full-blooded dragons. They're also stressful. Maybe you should ask *them* about the half-dragon."

"They believe he's dead. I know he is not. He's been making a pest of himself in downtown Bellevue." Tigris's cheek twitched, and he clenched his jaw for a moment before continuing. "I want Starblade. You will find him for me."

Yes, Arwen loved the idea of taking orders from strangers. "I only track people on occasion for the authorities."

"*We* are authorities in this county." Tigris spread his arm toward the SUV, the driver leaning against the door with his rifle, letting his colleague do the talking.

"Will you show us your badge?" Sigrid asked.

Arwen nodded.

"I can show you ten thousand dollars," Tigris said.

"That's not proof of anything," Sigrid said.

"It is proof that I have the funds to hire a tracker." He pointed at Arwen. "*You*. I must have the best. Someone armed and capable of getting close to a half-dragon." He glanced at her quiver again.

Arwen didn't have any *dragon* arrows.

"You want to pay Arwen ten thousand dollars to track down the half-dragon?" Sigrid gave Arwen a significant look.

Why, because they'd been discussing tracking for money? That *would* be almost enough to take care of the tax bill for the year, but Arwen didn't like the shifter. She liked the idea of working for him even less.

"Yes." Tigris smiled, again showing off his sharp canines.

"You'd pay that much just to have him found?" Sigrid asked. "Arwen is capable, as you can tell, but it would be suicidal of her— of anyone—to go after a dragon."

"A *half*-dragon," Tigris said, as if Starblade hadn't radiated supernova power while incinerating Sigrid's gun with a flick of his thoughts. And if he'd been raised from birth to be a super powerful warrior and mage, tangling with him *especially* did not sound good for one's health.

Still... if he was at the farm, it would be easy enough to find him. Assuming Arwen could get there in time. And if Starblade was a war criminal, maybe it wouldn't be wrong to help someone take him out. It wasn't as if he had endeared himself to her. Tigris hadn't shown her a badge yet, but if he *was* working with the authorities, maybe this would be the right thing to do.

"I will give you the ten thousand dollars if you track him down and tag him. You needn't get in a fight with him."

"*Tag* him?" Arwen asked. "Like an antelope?"

"With this." Tigris opened his suit to pull a small triangle from an inner pocket. "This tracking device uses an anti-dragon magic that I paid dearly for. If you're able to strike his scales with it, barbs will automatically deploy. Their magic will allow the tracker to embed itself." He tapped one of the flat sides, and the promised tiny barbs sprang from the edges, making Arwen jump. When he tapped it again, they retracted, and he held it on his palm toward her. "The size is perfect to be fastened to an arrowhead."

"You want me to shoot him," Arwen said numbly.

She would happily prong Starblade with an arrow if he was harassing her father, but doing so for payment sounded unappealing. And risky. Tigris said she didn't have to *get in a fight* with him, but how would she avoid that after shooting him?

"To tag him, yes. Such minor stings won't kill a dragon, just irritate him."

Just what she wanted to do. Irritate someone with the power of a dragon.

"Here." Tigris waved for his buddy to come over. "I will give you something that will assist you with your goal and protect you from reprisal."

His comrade drew a tranquilizer dart from an ammo pouch. The tip glowed slightly, emanating magic. Enough to pierce dragon scales?

Tigris directed his colleague to give it to her. "Use it the same way. Attach it to one of your arrows and fire it at him. The tranquilizer was made by a powerful alchemist and has the ability to knock out even a dragon for a time."

"You not only want me to shoot him but to shoot him *twice*." Arwen shook her head.

Even though she found fighting for her life less daunting than activities such as strolling along crowded sidewalks, going to a mall, or starting conversations with strangers, she didn't have a suicidal streak. She enjoyed her existence and wanted to keep living. She'd written numerous goals in her journal that she still hoped to achieve, like winning the Washington State Pie Baking Contest with berries from her father's farm and finding her first honest-to-goodness boyfriend. She refused to count the half-goblin neighbor boy who'd kissed her on a dare when they'd been twelve.

"The tranquilizer is optional," Tigris said.

Goodie.

"Why do you want him?" Arwen asked.

Tigris delved into his pocket again and pulled out a phone. After bringing up video footage of a fight, he turned it toward them.

The small screen made it hard to see exactly what was going on, but Arwen could pick out a restaurant with huge wolves—werewolves?—flying through the air before crashing into and destroying tables and chairs. Flames burned, and food on plates and in Styrofoam containers tumbled everywhere. One wolf shattered a window as it tumbled through it and into the street. A blast of fire streaked out after him, searing him in the back when he landed. Shrieking, the wolf raced into the night and out of view.

The person at the center of the chaos was the same person she'd encountered not a half hour ago. Starblade in elven form. Just as they had when she'd seen him, his violet eyes glowed when he looked toward the camera.

His handsome face was harder, as if chiseled from stone, and held no remorse as he stalked toward two men using an upturned table for cover and firing at him. Their rifles shot magical bullets that flared orange as they streaked toward Starblade, but they never reached him. Those violet eyes flared brighter, and the bullets disappeared. Incinerated. The rifles followed, disappearing in fire and smoke, suffering the same fate as Sigrid's gun. The men jerked their arms away, releasing the hot ashes and skittering back from the table as it too went up in flames.

Fur sprouted from their arms as they leaped away from the fire. Before they fully turned into their lupine forms, Starblade thrust an arm outward, striking them with magical power. They smashed into the walls like wrecking balls before tumbling to the floor. They didn't rise or even move again.

Starblade glared around the room, including giving the camera a long icy stare. It sent a shiver through Arwen and made her want to look away—and to make sure he never had a reason to look at *her* like that.

When he stalked out, he left the restaurant in flames.

"That is—*was*—one of my establishments," Tigris said, "a peaceful restaurant that caters to the magical community. As I said, the half-dragon is a criminal, wanted by many. Azerdash Starblade, once *General* Azerdash Starblade, is a menace wherever he goes. Now that he's on Earth, he's a threat to humanity—and all those in the magical community who are taking refuge here." Tigris touched his chest. "I trust that your decision to live here instead of in a dark-elf-infested tunnel implies you care about the people of Earth." He squinted at her again.

"I do," Arwen said.

Did the *shifter* care? Or was he only peeved that Starblade had destroyed his restaurant?

"Excellent. Like I said, all I need is for you to track him and tag him. We will handle the rest. Despite his penchant for showing up and destroying things, he's not easy to find. He disappears shortly after he's spotted. His magic is powerful enough for him to camouflage himself when he wishes, but he doesn't always do so. In addition to demolishing my restaurant, he was recently spotted flying over Marymoor Park. I understand the herons that nest by the river there made quite an uproar. An up-squawk." Tigris smiled sourly.

"I imagine so."

"When he's in dragon form, his scales are black, and he's not as large as his full-blooded kin. If you need a starting place, he was spotted by a quarter-gnome caddy at Glendale Country Club earlier this morning."

Arwen didn't mention that she'd already seen Starblade. "Maybe he wanted to practice his putts."

"If he's a frequent visitor there, he should be easy for you to find." Tigris nodded at her, pointed at the barbed tracking device, then handed her a business card. The name Tigris was all it said, with a QR code instead of a phone number, and it emanated faint magic. "Contact me when you've accomplished the mission, and I'll arrange payment."

"I don't have a cell phone." Arwen had heard of and seen QR codes before, but she wasn't sure how to use one. Her experience with smartphones was limited.

Tigris twirled his finger for her to turn over the card. A seal on the back held the image of a fang and was the source of the magic. "I can also be reached telepathically. That will aid you should your native power be insufficient to reach me at my home in the city." His eyebrows rose. In a challenge?

Arwen barely resisted the urge to throw the card back at him. She *could* use telepathy and had decent range, the presumptuous bastard. Only the fact that it would be nice to be able to help her father pay that tax bill kept her from snubbing him.

"Let's see the money," Sigrid said.

"What?" Tigris looked dismissively at her. He'd barely acknowledged her since he'd arrived.

"The ten thousand dollars."

Arwen expected him to say that he didn't carry such sums around, but he walked to the SUV, fished in the glove compartment, and returned with an envelope of bills. He opened it, thumbing through it to show her the stack of hundreds inside, then closed it. Whether it added up to ten thousand, Arwen didn't know, but if he owned restaurants, he probably *did* have that kind of money.

Whether he could pay or not wasn't her primary concern. It was whether she should take the gig.

"If you're a decent tracker, I'll expect to hear from you soon," Tigris said.

Arwen clenched her jaw again as he and his buddy strolled back to the SUV.

After they climbed into it and backed out of the driveway, Sigrid jangled her key chain. "I called one of your neighbors, but they didn't pick up. We'd better head to the farm. Afterward, you might want to visit Matti and Val. Now that I've heard the name Starblade and gotten the description of what he is, I believe Matti knows something about that half-dragon."

"Oh?"

"You'll have to talk to her. I've only heard snippets of her life from Val. But she may know where to find him."

"If he's at the farm, *I* know where to find him." Arwen just hoped they weren't too late.

Before they'd stepped toward Sigrid's Subaru, a squeaky voice came from the sauna.

"I've heard about Azerdash Starblade." The goblin peered out. "He lives on Earth now, in this very area." His expansive gesture might have meant the neighborhood, greater Seattle, or all of the

West Coast. "Some of my people have seen him. They say he's very powerful. And grumpy."

"The video would have attested to that even if we hadn't met him. I'm ready to go, Sigrid."

"Okay."

As they drove off, Arwen eyed the tranquilizer and tracking device and contemplated again the wisdom of taking a shot at someone powerful and grumpy with dragon blood.

6

ROCKET MILLED ON THE BACK SEAT AS SIGRID DROVE THROUGH Carnation and headed out toward the farm.

Bow between her legs, Arwen peered out the windows and stretched out with her senses, not sure if she wanted to detect Starblade or not. If he was in the area, he would be easier to tag, but his presence would mean he was questioning her father. She hated that she'd been delayed so long at Sigrid's and also that the car had to stick to the meandering rural roads instead of going direct. This was faster than walking but not much.

Behind them, Rocket alternated which half-open window he sniffed out. More than once, his fluffy golden tail whacked Arwen in the head. As the pavement disappeared, and they turned onto gravel roads, he wagged it vigorously and whined.

"He enjoys your farm." Sigrid glanced at him in the rearview mirror. "Especially the cranberry-peanut-butter dog treats you make there."

"I started baking those for one of our CSA clients. She has an older dog who has urinary issues." Something flapped past above them, and Arwen squinted, but it was only a falcon. A much *smaller* predator than she was worried about.

"Rocket doesn't have any problems in that area, as all the trees along the trail behind the house can attest, but he loves your treats. Everything you make is wonderful. I'm surprised you don't sell a lot more of your food at the farmers market."

"My father and I aren't good at business and marketing. Or, uhm, people." If they were, maybe she wouldn't have felt compelled to accept a possibly suicidal job to tag a dragon.

"I can understand that."

Sigrid turned at the Wild Berry Creek and Honey sign and headed up the gravel driveway. Thyme, lavender, and other herbs grew along the side, with blueberry bushes behind the herbs and fruit trees behind them. Bees buzzed through the air on the way from their hives to flowers and back.

Thanks to Arwen's work, magic emanated from almost all the growing things, protecting them from frost, infusing them with health, and helping them draw nutrients and water more efficiently from the soil. It was the type of magic surface elves often used, their kind finding it easy to invigorate plants and trees, but it had taken Arwen years to figure out how to turn her powers toward such things. As a teenager, she'd found a book that elves had left on Earth decades earlier. Not able to read the text, Arwen had traded canned tomatoes, jam, and homemade cornbread to a half-gnome linguist who'd translated the chapters on plant magic for her.

Near the hives, chickens clucked and pecked at the undergrowth, not concerned by anything. That might mean Starblade hadn't shown up. It could also mean he'd already come and gone.

"Any sign of the half-dragon?" Sigrid asked.

"I can't sense him, but I didn't sense him earlier until he chose to reveal himself."

"Right."

Sigrid parked in front of Father's manufactured home, grape, kiwi, and goji berry vines meandering up trellises attached to the siding and lingonberries growing from a few inches of earth on the roof. Her father's ancient truck was parked out front. Rocket woofed.

Since Arwen's father was a mundane human, she couldn't sense him the way she could beings with magical blood. She flung open the door and ran inside to check on him. Horus, their old rooster, crowed at what he always considered unnecessary hustle.

Her father, wild gray-and-brown hair tied back by a leather thong, sat in front of the coffee table in the living room. A recording of *Jeopardy* played on the television while he cleaned a disassembled rifle, his bore brush scouring away carbon. When he looked up, his eyebrows raised in inquiry, he didn't appear disturbed in the least.

"There was a complementary and alternative medicine category on this," he said in his gruff voice as he nodded at the TV. "You would have known all the answers."

"Did a powerful half-dragon come by to question you?" Arwen blurted, though her father was in such a typical position that she had a feeling nothing atypical had happened.

"Uh... what?"

That sounded like a *no*. Arwen slumped against the door frame in relief before realizing Starblade might have been delayed —maybe he'd spotted deer and veered off to hunt—and still intended to come here.

"What happened?" Her father stood, his faded black Eagles T-Shirt rumpled, the cut-off sleeves showing his old Army tattoos. He glanced out the window. "Is that Sigrid?"

A woof came from the car.

"And Rocket?" he asked dryly.

"Yes. She gave me a ride because... Well, I was worried." Arwen summed up her meeting with the half-dragon, hoping her father believed her. Despite all the magical beings that had shown up in the Seattle area these past few years, a lot of normal humans refused to accept that they existed. Since her father had battled ogres and yetis, shooed kobolds out of the corn crib, and spent years with her as a prisoner to dark elves, he wasn't exactly *normal*. But dragons had only recently started visiting Earth, and she didn't think he'd ever seen one.

"Why did this half-dragon want to know where the dark elves were?" was all he asked. His voice remained calm, but he reassembled his rifle quickly.

"He didn't say. He was more into demanding answers to his questions than volunteering anything to me." Of course, she hadn't asked why he wanted to find the dark elves. "I admit I was too nervous to think about questioning him on important things."

"With luck, he'll forget about you, and you'll never see him again."

"Actually, I need to find him."

"Why? Everything I've heard about dragons says they're best avoided. Like a plague. With fangs."

"I know." Arwen hadn't mentioned the shifters or the possibility of earning ten thousand dollars. Her father was proud, and she knew he wanted to find a solution to the money problem on his own. If she hadn't been there when he'd opened the mail with the tax bill, she doubted he ever would have told her about it. "People are looking for him, and I'm a tracker, so..." She shrugged, hoping he wouldn't press her.

"Washington State Search and Rescue is looking for a dragon?"

"No. Other people."

He squinted at her, but instead of questioning her further said, "It doesn't sound wise, but if you want to find him again, you've got to bait a trap with something he wants."

"I don't know what he wants, besides dark elves, and I don't know where they are."

"We don't *want* to know where they are."

"I agree."

Starblade had, Arwen recalled, been interested in mushrooms —or at least affronted that she might sell them. Did he like truffles? Dragons were known for being carnivores, but if he was also half-elven, he might have different dietary preferences. She imagined setting a jar of her goat truffle butter on a bear trap in the woods.

She snorted at herself. Sure, that would work.

Seeking inspiration, Arwen walked into the large kitchen, the dining room long ago sacrificed to expand the space to fit two ovens, a commercial refrigerator, extra cabinets, and all her canning equipment. Though she didn't know if they would work as bait for a half-dragon, she grabbed jars of jam, honey, and pickled vegetables from one of the cupboards.

"He's not hunkering in the pantry," her father said from the doorway. "I promise."

"I know. I'd sense him if he were that close."

"I'd like to think *I'd* be able to sense him if he was standing between our canned tomatoes and spaghetti sauces."

"If he was in his dragon form in the house, you wouldn't miss him. Even if he's not as big as a full-blooded dragon, he definitely wouldn't fit in the pantry." Arwen struggled to imagine even the haughty black-haired elf standing in something as pedestrian as her pantry. Even though he hadn't worn a uniform, he'd had the bearing of an aristocratic military officer accustomed to giving orders, and she could imagine him on an elven riding bird leading an army. Hadn't Tigris said he'd been a general?

"You don't think dark elves are back in the area, do you?" her father asked more quietly, his humor gone.

"I haven't heard of anyone around here sighting them."

When Arwen had seen the dark-elf priest the year before, she hadn't mentioned him—or his loathsome proposition—to her father. Hopefully, that hadn't been a mistake. But it only would have worried him. Between the taxes and dealing with his traumas and getting older, he had troubles enough without needing to glance over his shoulder constantly, wondering if the dark elves were coming back for him. Besides, after all these years, they shouldn't be. Arwen didn't even know if her mother was still alive.

"I hope nothing has changed," she added.

"They put seven years into raising and training you, into molding you to be theirs." Her father glanced toward her forearm. "I'm glad that didn't stick. Even so, I've always worried that they would learn I staged our deaths during our escape and come looking for you."

"I'm nothing special. Just a mongrel to them, my blood tainted with, uhm." Arwen paused, not wanting to offend him.

He snorted. "Mine? Yes, the dreadful taint."

"You know *I* don't think that. I wish I was full-blooded human and didn't have any of their kind in me." Actually, when Arwen had been a girl, she'd wished she were half-*elven* or even *all* elven. Though she hadn't met any elves, even half-elves, until she'd been an adult, she'd heard and read about them and had always felt a kinship toward their kind. From the day she first escaped those tunnels, she'd loved the forest and the mountains and all of nature. "I never understood why she bothered taking you and putting time into raising me."

As he always did when she brought up that concern, her father only shrugged. A *who knows* shrug.

When she'd been younger, she hadn't thought anything of his response—she'd never had any trouble believing that her mother had used her father and kept him prisoner for her own whims without ever confiding in him. And when she'd been a teenager, and another girl had thought her father was hot—"you know, for an old guy"—Arwen had thought it might simply have been his looks that had drawn her dark-elven mother to capture him. But in the past years, she'd either grown more perceptive or her father had gotten worse at lying to her, and she'd started to sense that he knew more than he'd let on. She suspected he had, if not back when it happened then at some later point, figured out why the dark elves had wanted them.

"I need to go into the city to talk to Val—Sigrid's daughter— and her friend Matti. Will you be okay here alone?" Arwen bit her lip, looking out the windows, worried that Starblade might still be coming. "Maybe you should head out to one of your bolt-holes for a bit."

"You know I've got to defend the farm if there's a threat."

"I doubt the half-dragon will be a threat to the *farm*. Horus can watch the place."

Her father snorted. "That rooster *would* stand up to a dragon."

"I'm more worried about Starblade questioning you. It's... not pleasant." Arwen touched her head, the memory of the mind-reading rearing up.

"He hurt you?" Father clenched a fist.

"Nothing permanent. I'm not even sure he knew it hurt. He was using magic to read my mind. Or trying to. He didn't seem to find what he wanted. So..." She extended a hand toward him.

"I'll keep an eye out and hide if I see anything larger than a crow flapping its wings in the sky."

Arwen hesitated, afraid that wouldn't be enough, that a half-dragon would have the power to find even a mundane human who didn't emit an aura. Even without his magic, Starblade would have the keen senses of a predator.

But her father did know how to track and hide. He'd taught her, after all, and he could disappear into the woods in a way that even trained people couldn't find him.

"Okay." She hugged him. "Be careful."

"I will. And *you* be careful. Don't go tracking trouble." He squinted at her. "You have a tendency to do that."

"Sometimes, trouble finds you whether you track it down or not."

He shook his head. "If the dark elves have come back, and they know where we are... we'll have to move. We can't handle trouble like that."

Arwen blinked. "*Move*? Leave the farm?"

"Yes."

"But you've—*we've*—been working on it for years. *Decades.* Some of the trees are just now at their maturity and producing the most fruit. And the hazelnuts. The crop is going to be amazing this year. Everything will be if the weather stays good. And you love this place." *Arwen* loved this place.

"I know, but even before this..." He tilted his palm toward the ceiling. "You were there when I opened the tax bill from the county. We do well enough to sustain ourselves and pay for the utilities and truck and supplies, or we did, but we can't come up with so much extra money each year. We may have had to move anyway. Farther away from the city, I guess." During his life, he'd faced countless dangerous enemies and escaped the dark elves, but at this oppressive onus from the government, defeat lurked in his eyes. "When I first picked this place, Carnation was only a sleepy little town far away from Seattle and its influence. Bellevue wasn't much more than a suburb. Now, all the tech workers with their money buy the land out here and the prices have gone up so much. The taxes have gotten astronomical..." He shook his head, his face more tired and grizzled than usual. He almost looked like he *had* been worked over by a dragon.

"It's a mistake that they changed the designation of our land. It must be. Maybe it's because our farm is so wild, with everything growing everywhere, the way it would in nature, and we don't have silos and barns and herds of livestock. Someone could have mistaken it for—" Arwen flung her arm out vaguely. She didn't know what. Anyone who came by would see the chickens roaming and the beehives along the driveway, and they had the sign out front and the booth at the farmers market.

A soft knock sounded at the front door. Arwen had left it open, and Sigrid stood on the threshold.

Father winced, probably because he didn't want other people hearing about their financial problems and not because her approach triggered flashbacks for him. It was usually only strangers that bothered him, at least from what he'd admitted to Arwen. For years, he hadn't admitted anything, always wanting to be strong and stoic for his daughter, but when she'd complained of nightmares, he'd said he had the same issues. Nightmares that came in the dark and flashbacks that popped up during the day. Since their symptoms were so similar, Arwen sometimes wondered if her mother had done something to them to ensure they would never have peaceful lives if they escaped.

"I didn't mean to listen in," Sigrid said, "but Rocket insisted I ask about the cranberry dog treats, and I wanted to see if you need a ride over to see Val and Matti, Arwen."

"I..." Arwen hesitated, second-guessing herself about leaving her father alone.

"Matti has a real-estate-agent friend," Sigrid added, "and she works in the industry too. She could be a good person to ask about the process for having the zoning for your land changed back. It might be as simple as showing them your business documentation to prove that you are indeed a farm."

"We don't have business documentation," Father said. "I've always filed as a sole proprietor for taxes. We don't make that much, and I... I'm not one to go into offices to hire accountants. That's for the bigwigs."

"We could show them our jars of honey and jam." Arwen imagined walking into some stuffy office full of men and women in suits and trying to convince them she was a legitimate farmer by describing her bees and her methods for improving the crops.

Sigrid smiled. "That might work."

"Really?" Arwen asked skeptically.

"You may just have to prove that you're using the land for agricultural purposes. Talk to Matti. She'll have a better idea or put you in touch with someone who will."

"That's the half-dwarf girl who solves her problems by beating the crap out of things with her big hammer?" Father asked.

"Don't judge," Arwen said. "You solve your problems with your gun."

"She's in construction," Sigrid said. "I believe a big hammer is the appropriate tool for many jobs in that field. And also for dwarves in general."

Arwen nodded, though she hadn't met many dwarves, either full- or half-blooded. "I'll ask about it when I talk to her about the half-dragon."

"We don't need other people getting involved in our money problems." Her father frowned at her, oozing independence and pride.

"Asking someone a question about real estate isn't getting them involved." Arwen smiled and patted him on the arm.

He only oozed *more* independence and pride. "I'll look into it myself. It's getting late, and there's asparagus to cut for the market in the morning. The white is ready, and you know how well that does at the stand."

"I know. This won't take long, and I'll be back to help."

Her father gave Sigrid a dark look, as if a seventy-something grandmother might be a bad influence on his daughter.

"I'll grab the dog biscuits." Arwen patted her father's arm again before rummaging in another cupboard. She wanted to say it would be a good idea for them to skip the market until the half-dragon problem was resolved, but she doubted that suggestion would fly.

"Rocket thanks you," Sigrid said.

"I'll thank *him* for not chasing the chickens," Father said.

"He knows better than to do that now."

Father leaned out the door as Rocket ran past, chasing not a chicken but a wild rabbit. They were all over Western Washington these days, breeding like, well, rabbits, so Arwen doubted her father would object to a dog culling the population. The coyotes seemed to be slacking on the job.

"We're still working on squirrels and rabbits," Sigrid admitted with a sigh.

"I'll be right out." Arwen grabbed a few more items, in case she *did* have to show jars of honey and jam to suited office people. She loved the farm and didn't intend to leave, not because of dark elves, half-dragons, *or* taxes.

7

"THERE ARE EVEN MORE COGS, CHAINS, AND GEWGAWS HANGING OFF that house than before," Sigrid said as she drove her Subaru slowly down the residential street where the half-dwarven enchanter Matti Puletasi lived across from Val and Zavryd.

Before reaching those homes, Sigrid paused in front of a Craftsman that had been decorated in the goblin aesthetic, a new development since Arwen had visited the area the year before. Her senses told her that numerous of their kind resided inside. Fifteen? Twenty? It was a lot. She wondered if dragons and goblins had ever before on Earth—or anywhere in the Cosmic Realms—lived within one hundred yards of each other.

Zavryd wasn't home, at least not that Arwen could detect, and she let out a sigh of relief. The big black dragon had never threatened her or acknowledged her in any way—which was fine with her—but he had a tremendously powerful aura and always made her nervous. Like all dragons, he could read minds. Would he see into hers more easily than Starblade had? Would he learn that she'd agreed to track down someone with dragon blood? And be offended by the prospect?

"I don't sense Matti or Val either," Arwen mused after Sigrid parked at the curb in front of her daughter's remodeled Victorian, a pair of magical dragon-shaped topiaries guarding the walkway leading to the covered porch. "I do sense a vampire in the basement and a full-blooded elf across the street." Arwen pointed at Matti's house. "The assassin, Varlesh Sarrlevi."

Arwen had met him briefly a couple of times, and he'd only gazed coolly at her. He hadn't insulted her or brought up her dark-elven heritage, but those cold looks had left her little doubt that he found her mother's people distasteful and was predisposed to believe she was as bad as they.

Just like everyone else. She shook her head glumly.

"He'll know where Matti is," Sigrid said.

"Did you call and ask if I would be welcome?" Arwen hesitated to get out of the car. "Or at least accepted long enough to ask questions?"

"You helped Matti find her parents. I'm certain she'll *accept* you any time you wish to come over. So will Val."

The curtains stirred on Matti's house, another remodeled Victorian, though hers had a lot more vines—vines that exuded elven magic—twining up the siding and meandering across the roof, leaves fluttering in a soft breeze.

"Sarrlevi might not." Arwen knew he was the one looking out, and even though she couldn't see his face, she had no doubt he was giving her that cool assessing stare.

"Maybe not, but he's haughty and uptight with almost everyone. I'm not sure why I said *almost*." Oddly, Sigrid looked a little wistful as she gazed toward the house. Maybe she realized her expression didn't match her words, because she shook her head and explained. "I spent a summer with elves who were visiting Earth. That's how Val came to be."

"I'd heard that. The, uhm, elven king, right?"

"He wasn't that at the time. He was just... wonderful."

A little ache blossomed behind Arwen's breastbone as, not for the first time, she wished she knew what it was like to be with someone wonderful—and someone who thought *she* was wonderful too. Maybe it was delusional to want that when she came from such tainted blood. Dark elves weren't wonderful in any sense of the word.

"Perhaps Sarrlevi can answer questions about the half-dragon," Sigrid said.

The curtains closed, and the front door opened. Sarrlevi strode out, his short blond hair tousled, two sword hilts poking over his shoulders, and a magical bag gripped in one hand. Was he heading out on an errand? Arwen took a deep breath and made herself get out of the car so she could meet him at the sidewalk.

"Mataalii is not here," he stated, not looking like he wanted to stop to chat. Not with her.

"I know. I mean I sensed that she isn't." Arwen waved at the house. "I have a question for her, but perhaps you could answer it."

"I must turn in this chimera head to the human military leader who occasionally employs me to dispatch the magical riffraff that preys on humanity while taking refuge on this wild world." Sarrlevi held up the bag, then took a step, as if to stride past Arwen, but he paused to regard her.

She braced herself, expecting a comment on her heritage. As she'd told Sigrid, he'd never said much to her, insulting or otherwise, but he was handsome and fully elven, and people like that so often *did* bring up her heritage. Either with wariness or dismissal. Always with the implication that she wasn't welcome.

"I must also acquire deep-fried pickles, salt-and-vinegar pistachios, and *dokdok* cheese. The latter is a normal request, but the two former may be what has been explained to me as *pregnancy cravings*. Thorvald said those should have abated for Mataalii now that she grows nearer to the birthing time, but it is possible some females find such dubious foods desirable during the entire process." Still regarding her, Sarrlevi arched his eyebrows.

It took Arwen a moment to realize he might be asking her opinion. Because she was female?

"I've never been pregnant. I've never even—" Arwen paused, warmth flushing her cheeks as she stopped herself from blurting to a near stranger how little sexual experience she had, or complaining that no one appealing who knew what she was had demonstrated any interest in being with her. She didn't get a lot of interest from people who *couldn't* sense her heritage either, though that might have to do with her tendency to avoid all crowds and places where crowds might spontaneously form. Still, the way he gazed at her, as if he expected more, flustered her, and she caught herself adding, "I've only ever been propositioned about children by an odious dark-elf priest who wanted to breed with me because the dark elves aren't fecund and have been dying off here on Earth —maybe everywhere. He thought my human blood, though not desirable, would make me more fertile." She grimaced at the memory of the insulting conversation.

Sarrlevi gazed impassively at her. Right, he'd only wanted to know if deep-fried pickles were normal for pregnant women.

"I make a sea-salt concord jam that has a unique briny taste that many people find appealing." Arwen didn't have any of that with her, but she did have a few other items that might do. She removed her pack and drew out a jar of pickled carrots and parsnips. "If she's craving tart things, she may also like these." She'd heard Sarrlevi often brought treats of exotic foods from around the Cosmic Realms for Matti. Maybe he would think more kindly of Arwen if she helped him with that endeavor. "They're good to snack on, and the jam pairs well with an aged goat cheese made by a farmer we know in the valley." Now that she'd talked it up, Arwen wished she had thought to grab some of the jam.

Sarrlevi's eyelashes drooped thoughtfully as he considered the carrots and parsnips. "Those are root vegetables, yes?"

"Er, yes."

"Matti, due to her dwarven heritage, likes root vegetables." Amusement twinkled in his eyes.

Arwen felt like she was missing a joke but nodded encouragingly.

"You are offering these items?"

"Yes, here." She thrust the jar toward him. "I can bring the jam next time I come too. And some of the goat cheese."

After accepting the jar, Sarrlevi considered it for a moment, then nodded. "Do so."

"Uhm, would you happen to know anything about a half-dragon named Starblade?" Arwen asked, trying not to feel like she'd offered the food as a bribe in exchange for information.

"He was in a battle with dragons on the elven home world." Sarrlevi spoke indifferently, as if he might have offered what he knew *without* a bribe. "He's believed to be dead."

"Oh, he's alive. And, ah, throwing werewolves through windows in restaurants in Bellevue."

Sarrlevi tilted his head. "That is unexpected."

"If you thought he was dead, I suppose so."

"The *dragons* believe he is dead."

"What do *you* believe?"

"That Mataalii will enjoy these root vegetables and may also find the salty jam desirable." Sarrlevi inclined his head toward her, then walked into the street and disappeared from her sight as well as her magical senses.

Arwen scratched her jaw. That conversation hadn't been what she'd expected. She had little experience interpreting the facial expressions and tones of elves, but she thought Sarrlevi knew more than he'd told her. Was it possible he was looking out for

Starblade? Keeping his secrets? Or at least respecting his desire to remain hidden?

If so, why? Because Starblade was half-*elven* as well as half-dragon?

But if he was a criminal, would Sarrlevi protect him? Of course, Sarrlevi might not care one way or another about criminals. He had been an assassin for most of his life. It was only recently that he'd given up that career to come live on Earth with his mate.

"I think I need to wait for Matti, Sigrid." Arwen hadn't learned as much as she'd hoped, and Sarrlevi wouldn't have been the one to ask about property-tax designations anyway. "You can go if you want. I'll find my way back to the farm later."

"You don't have a car, and you don't even have a phone to call a taxi."

Arwen didn't point out that Sigrid didn't have a phone either. "I usually walk everywhere."

"It's twenty-five miles back to Carnation."

Arwen shrugged. "We've done numerous long hikes, and didn't you say you've walked all the parts of the Pacific Crest Trail?"

"The Pacific Crest Trail goes through the wilderness. It's refreshing and appealing. Walking down fume-choked streets and highways is not."

Arwen didn't disagree, but Sigrid had already gone out of her way to bring her here, and her daughter wasn't even home for a visit. Arwen didn't want to inconvenience her further. "I'll be fine. I need to stop in Bellevue to look for Starblade anyway."

"You should have offered the elf your truffle butter. He's the hoity-toity type. Maybe that would have gotten you more information."

"I'll keep that in mind if I see him again."

Sigrid considered the intersection ahead, then looked back. "I need to run a few errands."

Rocket woofed from the back seat.

"Yes, picking up dog food is among them. I'll come back and check on you after I'm done." Sigrid held up a hand before Arwen could object. "May I offer a piece of advice before I go? In the context of asking a near-stranger for information on another near-stranger, I don't believe your fertility should come up."

"I know. I get nervous and overshare sometimes."

"You're a good girl. If you want to find a nice man, you should go to places where they hang out."

"Like a bar?" Arwen wilted at the idea of walking into such a crowded place.

"I've heard people recommend the produce section of the grocery store. You can advise men on finding fruit at the correct stage of ripeness. Since you're a farmer, that should be right in your wheelhouse, right?"

Grocery stores could be as crowded as bars, and Arwen shuddered at the idea of sauntering into one and walking up to strange men probing cantaloupes. Why could she leap into battle with hordes of enemies but not bring up fruit ripeness with cute guys?

"I will keep your advice in mind." Arwen had no plans to shop for men in the produce section any time soon, but avoiding discussing fertility with elves was doable. Though Sarrlevi *had* brought up the topic first, in a manner of speaking.

Sigrid waved and drove off.

Arwen eyed a porch swing near Matti's front door and wondered if she was on the list of people welcome to cross through the wards to visit. Maybe it would be safer to wait on the sidewalk.

While she pondered that, a dented red hatchback turned onto the street, the driver slightly magical. A quarter-blood?

The car rolled to a stop in front of Val's house where the driver, a young woman with long blonde hair, eyed the dragon-shaped topiaries, then drove around the corner and parked in front of a different house before stepping out.

Elven blood gave her the faint magical aura, and it and her hair color and height—she had to be six feet tall—reminded Arwen of Val. Was this her daughter? Amber? She had a distinctly different fashion sense than Val, who usually wore jeans, tanks, and a leather duster, not to mention her sword harness and gun holster. The girl didn't carry any visible weapons and, dressed in a floral mini skirt, sleeveless crochet top, and sandals, looked like she might have come straight from school.

Despite parking farther from the house than necessary, she strolled up to the topiaries and didn't hesitate to get close to them. Their eyes didn't glow menacingly the way they did when strangers approached the property.

If this was indeed Val's daughter, perhaps she would know how to reach her mother. Val, Arwen suspected, would know where Matti was. Maybe she would also know about the half-dragon. Neighbors shared important news with neighbors, right? Mrs. Zuber always told Arwen when her dogs were in heat and her arthritis was acting up.

The logical thought made her nod, but she promptly grew nervous. The thought of approaching a stranger and striking up a conversation always made her feel awkward and uneasy.

When Arwen approached Amber, her bow on her back and her arms spread so she wouldn't appear threatening, Amber looked at her without concern, even lifting a hand to wave. That was surprising. As a quarter-elf, she wouldn't be that sensitive to magic, but she ought to be able to detect Arwen's aura. She might not have familiarity with dark elves, however, and be able to tell the difference between her and a half-surface elf.

"Just the vampire home, huh?" Amber turned the wave into a vague point toward the covered windows of the basement.

Arwen hadn't met the vampire alchemist who lived down

there, but she'd heard about Val's interesting roommate. "I do sense him, yes."

"Are you here to see Val? Do you know if she'll be back soon? I want to show her my new ride." Amber pointed proudly toward the hatchback.

Arwen hesitated. *Was* this Amber? She matched the description Sigrid had given, but would Val's daughter call her by name?

"I'm not certain if she will be back soon. I came to speak with Matti—" Arwen pointed across the street, "—but only encountered her mate."

"Sarrlevi? He's super hot, isn't he? I wish some of the guys at school looked like that."

"Handsome elves are also infrequent out on my farm. I'm Arwen."

"The tracker, right?" The girl looked Arwen up and down, gaze lingering on her dusty jeans and moccasins as well as the sticks twisting Arwen's hair back. Her lips didn't curl in derision, but they did twitch.

It wasn't the first time Arwen's preferred attire had gotten that response. It bothered her a lot less than people drawing back in horror because of her dark elf-ness.

"Yes. Are you Amber? I work with Sigrid sometimes, and she's mentioned you and how she'd like—" Arwen paused, realizing it might be rude to share the wistful comments Sigrid had made about how she wished Amber liked hiking and being out in nature and would come to visit more often. "She's mentioned you."

"Yeah, I need to drive out and see her, but gas is a fortune. I had to pay for half of the car myself, so I'm broke. That was the deal Dad made with me. He'd pay for half if I came up with the money for the other half. I *wanted* a Mercedes convertible, but I would have been carrying bags of cement mix for Matti until I'm fifty to afford even part of one of those. She does *not* pay me enough for that work or value my unique skills. She uses me like a hulking high-school dropout who killed all his brain cells by smoking pot. As if."

"What are your unique skills?" Some of Arwen's neighbors had kids with experience gardening and raising livestock, but she hadn't met many teenagers from the city with abilities that would be useful on a farm.

"I'm a fashionista." Amber turned and posed, gesturing at her clothing as if it would demonstrate her extreme talent in this area. "Is this outfit snatched, or what?"

Arwen thought she looked cute but had no idea if the skirt, top, and sandals would be considered fashionable. And what was *snatched*?

"I keep trying to get Val or Matti to hire me to be their personal shopper. They both *totally* need my help. Have you seen their wardrobes?" Amber eyed Arwen and *her* wardrobe again, which prompted more lip twitching.

Arwen made sure her sleeve covered the tattoo she hated, thinking of the time she'd tried to have it removed. The magic inherent in it had destroyed the laser machine that had attempted to do the work.

"I don't suppose *you'd* like a personal shopper?" Amber asked.

Arwen gaped in horror as she imagined the girl dragging her through a crowded mall, mobs of people carrying bags and coffees jostling innocent passersby.

"That's not in my budget," Arwen said. "I go to Goodwill or sew my own clothes."

"That can be cool if you've got skills, but, uhm, don't take this the wrong way, Arwen, was it? But your look is really Davy Crockett for a girl. For *anyone*. There's not a coonskin cap in your car, is there?"

"I don't have a car." Arwen could barely drive. Her father had taught her the basics, but they'd never felt comfortable enough to deal with the swarms of people at the DMV to get her a learner's permit or license. She wasn't even sure she was a legal citizen since she'd been born off the grid. *Way* off the grid. "The last thing I drove was Frodo."

Amber blinked. "Frodo?"

"Our tractor. It's a small one. We do permaculture farming and don't tear up the earth very often, so it's all we need. Most of the time. I'm on a tracking mission right now, tracking in the *city*, so it's a little unfortunate that I don't have a car, I'll admit."

Amber touched her chin, a speculative glint entering her eyes. "What I hear you saying is that you need a *driver*. Matti's not doing as much construction right now since she's *super* pregnant, so I've been thinking of picking up a side hustle. I need to pay for gas and insurance now and still save for clothes—I can't do my college interviews in last year's clothes. But you have to be eighteen to become an Uber driver, and Dad said he wouldn't let me pick up sus randos anyway, which is so lame. It's not as if I can't take care of myself. I have a sword and work out with Val. I can kick major ass."

"Really?"

"Absolutely. I would only charge fifteen dollars an hour for my services. No, twenty. I'd need to cover gas. And maintenance. I could take you anywhere though and wait for you while you do things. Like your own personal taxi."

Arwen shook her head, bemused that Amber thought she had the kind of money to hire someone to do *anything*. "I think Matti is a better bet as an employer. She's a successful businesswoman."

"She's *stingy*. She only pays me two dollars above minimum wage. And I had to break a nail and get mud permanently wedged into the soles of my boots—and other more delicate crevices—to earn *that* raise from her."

"If you can relay a message to your mother for me, and know how to let Matti know that I'd like to see her, I actually do need to go to Bellevue next." Arwen might not have much money, but she would feel better about paying someone rather than letting Sigrid waste her time driving her all over for free. "I could do twenty dollars."

"An *hour*."

"Bellevue isn't a full hour away."

"Traffic might be bad. And then I need to drive back."

Arwen was fairly certain people didn't pay for a taxi driver's return trip.

"And you might need me to wait, right?" Amber pulled out her phone. "While you track things. What's your message for Val?"

"Among other things, that ogres and shifters are being problematic over in Duvall."

"Ogres and shifters are *always* problematic."

"They attacked Sigrid and me at her home and destroyed her sauna."

"Oh, that's messed up AF if they went after Grandma. And her sauna. Savages. I'll tell Val. Then I can drive you to Bellevue. I *love* driving. It's such freedom." Her eyes gleamed with unbridled teenage enthusiasm.

"How long have you had your license?" Maybe Arwen should have asked that first.

"Almost three weeks. I'm a pro. Don't worry."

"Of course not," Arwen murmured.

8

"YOU DON'T NEED TO WAIT FOR ME WHILE I TRACK." ARWEN DIDN'T have much experience seeking trails in the city and worried that even with her magic, she would struggle. Soul tracking might work, but she was hesitant to use dark-elven ways. "I don't have enough money to have a driver wait for me." She also couldn't imagine anything more boring for a teenager than sitting in the car for what might be hours.

Amber, who'd insisted on the fast lane on the freeway—and weaving in and out of traffic like a race-car driver—wrinkled her nose. "You can use Venmo or Zelle, if you want. I don't really want physical currency anyway."

"I don't have a phone or a bank account."

"You don't have a *bank* account?" Amber managed to gape over at her at the same time as she veered across three lanes of traffic toward the downtown Bellevue exit. "Are you a criminal or something?"

"No. Just off the grid. My father and I believe in self-sufficiency —and he always wanted... He didn't want anyone to track me down and use me. For my magic." Arwen didn't want to go into detail with a sixteen-year-old she barely knew.

"Like Matti's dwarf-enchanter mom was used? What can you do?"

"Other than using my magic to track people, I mostly help plants grow better."

"So, what? You're afraid Archer-Daniels-Midland will kidnap you?"

"I don't know what that is."

Amber rolled her eyes. "It's a huge publicly traded agricultural company. They're a dividend aristocrat."

"I... don't know what that is either."

"Geez, you really are off the grid. Nobody's going to kidnap you. Trust me."

Arwen bristled at the insult, but she wasn't sure she wanted to argue. Why would she *want* to be kidnapped? Still, she couldn't resist the urge to point out that her skills had value.

"Marie Goodwin always tries to wheedle my marionberry pie recipe out of me when she comes to visit my father. She doesn't realize that the secret ingredient is the magic I infuse the canes with to make the fruit extra healthy and delicious."

"You're weird." After taking the exit, Amber stopped at the first light. "I don't know why Val can't have any *normal* friends."

Arwen decided that pointing out that Amber's mother was *weird* too, at least by full-blooded human standards, wouldn't be polite.

"Which way now? And are you *sure* you don't want me to wait? We haven't used up the full hour yet. You're not staying in Bellevue after you track, right? Don't you need a ride home?"

Arwen hesitated as she eyed the people-filled crosswalks and towering buildings, claustrophobia already creeping into her. She *would* prefer to escape the area quickly after she searched for sign of Starblade. As Sigrid had pointed out, this wouldn't be an appealing place to walk, not for someone who preferred peace and quiet.

"I could use a ride home afterward," Arwen admitted. "If this takes more than a couple hours, I could pay the balance in pies and jams." Teenagers enjoyed sweets, didn't they? She always had. She *still* enjoyed them.

"*Pies*? Seriously?"

"Pies are quite serious, yes." Arwen stretched out with her senses, seeking Starblade's aura, though, restaurant vandalism aside, this seemed like a strange area for a dragon, even a half-dragon, to hang out. Should she direct Amber to that golf course? "I sell them for ten dollars apiece at the farmers market, and my customers always come back for more."

"Then how come you don't have any money?"

"Well, I only have three customers. I usually get the stand in the far back corner, because it's less crowded there, and..." Arwen lowered her voice to finish, "you're not the only one who thinks I'm weird."

"It's the Davy Crockett clothes. And the twigs sticking out of your hair. You *really* could use a personal shopper. And stylist. I do hair and makeup too. I'm very versatile." When they came to the next red light, Amber squinted at her. "How much do you get paid to track people?"

"Usually, it's only volunteer work. Right now, I'm looking for someone magical and dangerous though, so it's a little different."

"A little different in that you'll be paid? Like Val? She and Matti get huge envelopes of money from Colonel Willard when they stop criminals."

Arwen wished she were working for someone as reputable as an Army colonel. She had reservations about those shifters. Many reservations. "If I find this person and tag him, I'll earn ten thousand dollars."

"Wow, that's a lot."

"I'm not certain I'll be successful. I'm not that experienced with finding people in cities. Or... being in cities at all." Arwen eyed a looming skyscraper as they drove past. She hadn't realized Bellevue had grown so populous and had such tall buildings.

"I like cities. And I know all about them. Where the good shopping is, where the best restaurants are, where you can dance or swim. I used to compete over here at Bellevue Athletic Club. Maybe I can help you track this guy down." The calculating gleam entered Amber's eyes again. "And you could cut me in instead of paying by the hour."

"I don't think a half-dragon will be at an athletic club," Arwen said.

"Still, I know the city. And I have a car. Ten percent, and I'll help you all day. Except for when I'm in school. Or doing home-work. Or out with my friends."

"So an hour or two a week?"

"Maybe up to four. I'm free for the rest of the afternoon and this evening, though, if you want to find this guy today."

That would be nice. Arwen looked wistfully out the window, her senses stretched to their fullest.

Among the hundreds of people nearby, she could pick out the occasional man or woman with half- or quarter- elf, troll, or orc blood, though they appeared fully human. To those without the ability to sense magic, most blended in with society, few realizing they had attributes such as extra strength or agility or could heal quickly, gifts from their non-human ancestors. None of that was unusual though.

It wasn't until they drove slowly past Bellevue Square, with Amber casting longing looks toward the stores, as if they might track someone down while shopping for purses and shoes, that Arwen picked out something different.

"Turn right, please."

"Ten percent?" Amber asked.

"What?"

"Of what you earn for tracking. You just got a look on your face like you think we're close."

"For ten percent, you'd need to hold him down while I tag him." Arwen smiled to make sure Amber knew it was a joke. She didn't want Val's teenage daughter to get involved and possibly be hurt. Maybe Arwen shouldn't even have accepted the ride, but she doubted she would find her target today.

"How about I flirt with him? Or ask him for directions while you sneak up from behind and club him on the back of the head?"

"You don't need to do either. You can drop me off when you see a place to pull over. We're close to... something. Not a dragon but a lot of magic. I sense numerous artifacts and enchantments. It might not have anything to do with my target—it *probably* doesn't —but I'll start looking there."

"Where?"

"That way." Arwen pointed.

They drove around a corner, and, at the end of the street, surrounded by a grassy park-like expanse with maple trees casting shadows, a sleek twenty-story building stretched toward the sky. Its facade appeared to be made entirely from black-tinted windows that gleamed in the afternoon sun. The building gleamed even more strongly to Arwen's senses because magic emanated from all sides of it and even from the ground around the base. There was something familiar about that magic, though she'd never been to this part of the city before.

The tattoo on Arwen's forearm itched.

Startled, she pushed up her sleeve to look at it. Though she'd always been able to sense faint magic embedded in her skin there, the tattoo had never itched or otherwise drawn her attention.

"Is that a *spider*?" Amber stared.

Cheeks warming, Arwen shoved her sleeve back down. "Yes."

"You're even weirder than I thought."

"I didn't choose it."

"Did a boyfriend talk you into it or something?"

"Or something, yes." A memory of being a girl in the lightless dark-elven tunnels sprang to mind. Supposedly, her mother had been raising Arwen to be one of them, but even her earliest recollections had been of their cruelty, of feeling like a slave being trained for some purpose, not of being a daughter.

Blinking away the dark memory, Arwen pointed to the curb. "Why don't you let me out here and head home?"

She didn't have a purse and had to fish into a few pockets to find the twenty-dollar bill she'd promised. She still had the hundred the ogre had dropped but doubted Amber could make change. Besides, she wanted to give that to her father to put toward the tax bill.

"I thought you wanted me to wait?"

"I did, but this place looks and feels dangerous. I don't want you to get into trouble."

"But it's only been forty-five minutes. I can't charge you for the whole hour."

Surprised by the honorable notion from the money-hungry teen, Arwen handed her the twenty. "A tip for good service. I'll give Sigrid a pie to share with you as well."

"All right."

As Amber reached for the twenty, Arwen sensed a new aura, one that was heading in their direction and belonged to a magical being instead of an artifact. The owner was familiar and flying high over the skyscrapers.

"That's him." Arwen leaned forward to peer through the windshield, trying to spot him. Had she truly lucked across her target that quickly? "Not that I can tag him from down here unless he flies right over us."

Maybe he would. She grabbed her bow and quiver out of the back seat.

"You're going to shoot a dragon?" Amber asked dubiously. She must also have sensed his aura. "Is *that* who you're tracking? Dragons are kickass and have magical defenses. Haven't you ever *met* one?"

"He's a *half*-dragon, and I just need to tag him."

"Uh, all right." Judging by Amber's skeptical expression, she doubted that would work.

Arwen didn't know if it would either. She'd attached the tracking device to her most powerful arrow, but would it slice into dragon scales?

To have a chance, she would have to catch Starblade off guard so he didn't have a defensive barrier up. She hoped there was so much magic coming off that building that it would drown out her aura and he wouldn't notice her. She didn't want to endure another mind-reading attempt. Or worse.

As Starblade flew closer, his power grew more noticeable, and Arwen second-guessed herself. Meeting him when he hadn't had anything except her blood against her had been bad enough. Did she want to make an enemy of someone who could crush her with a flick of his magic?

Maybe it would be enough for the shifters if she learned where he was staying. If he was coming to this building, was it possible he considered it or some part of it his lair? Maybe he had a cave on the rooftop.

Arwen reached for the door handle, intending to get out, but she was tempted to wait until she saw where he went. So far, he hadn't flown into view. She only sensed him circling the area.

"I can stay and help you with him." Amber leaned into the back and pulled out a gym bag and a sheathed sword that emanated faint magic. "I'm supposed to practice with Val later, so I'm prepared."

"You must really want that ten percent."

"Hell, yeah, I do. Dad doesn't even give me an allowance

anymore. He says now that I'm working, I can pay for discretionary spending myself. Like gas and insurance and cute clothes are *discretionary*."

Wings spread, Starblade soared into view, black scales gleaming in the sun. Arwen and Amber fell silent. He radiated power and elegance as he flew, and the uneasy feeling that Arwen would be foolish to mess with him returned.

"He looks like a smaller version of Zavryd," Amber whispered.

Starblade had been heading for the magical building, but his head jerked to the side, like a hound that had caught a scent. Abruptly, he folded in his wings and dove toward their street. Arwen swore, afraid he'd detected her—and wasn't pleased about it.

But instead of landing in front of them, Starblade stretched his talons toward a car parked in the spot closest to the building and landed on *that*. Only briefly before he sank those talons into the frame. His tail went rigid, and powerful muscles rippled under his scales as, with a great shattering of glass and wrenching of metal that assailed Arwen's ears, he ripped the roof off the car.

Roaring, he flung it down the street. As it clattered away, he stabbed each tire with his talons, tearing the rubber to shreds. He whirled and knocked over the remains of the frame, then breathed fire all over it.

"Uh," Amber said, "that dragon is seriously salty about something."

Arwen stared, terrified that he would leap toward them and do that to Amber's car. What if he'd meant to from the beginning and missed his target?

"Maybe that someone is tracking him." Amber gave her a significant look.

"He shouldn't know about that."

"*Shouldn't*. Zavryd can read minds. Did you miss the part where I said dragons are kickass?"

"He's only a half-dragon," Arwen repeated.

"I'm sure that car feels so much better knowing that."

Starblade snatched something out of the flaming wreckage—the half-melted steering wheel—and hurled it at the building. It bounced off an impervious window so hard that it flew all the way back to land in the street near Amber's car. She flinched and stared at it as smoke wafted up, then slowly returned her sword to the back seat.

Starblade didn't so much as look toward them. He roared and flew straight at the building. At the last second, he banked so that he didn't hit it, but he smashed his tail against one of the windows. Arwen sensed him hurl magical power along with the tail attack, and she expected the glass to shatter.

But the magic that protected the building repelled him. The window didn't so much as crack.

Again, Starblade roared, then swooped down to take his frustrations out on the remains of the car, further demolishing it. Finally, his anger apparently spent, he calmed down and landed in the street. At first, his back was to Amber and Arwen, but then he turned slowly around to face them.

"Uh oh," Amber whispered.

Starblade met Arwen's gaze through the windshield, his violet eyes glowing as they simmered with fury.

Fear clenched her heart. This had been a bad idea, a very bad idea. If he chose to, he could destroy Amber's car—and the two of them—as easily as he had the other.

But he only stared at Arwen, his eyes accusing. *I knew you had knowledge of where the dark elves were,* he told her telepathically. *As General Sayzelar once advised, deception is inherent in warfare, and the tongue of a female enemy is no exception.*

Arwen licked her lips, but before she could come up with an answer, or think to get out and shoot the arrow with the tracking device at him, Starblade sprang into the air and flew away.

Arwen slumped back in the seat. "You still want to help me track him down for a percentage cut?"

Amber waved the twenty-dollar bill. "A flat hourly rate is fine."

"I thought so."

"I wasn't going to help you track him anyway, just wait in the car while you looked for footprints. Or... air prints? How do you track someone who flies?"

"You don't, unless you can stay close enough to sense his aura. And he *lets* you sense his aura. Dragons can hide themselves with their magic if they want."

Starblade hadn't wanted to hide himself from those in the building. He'd been sending a message. But to whom? *Dark elves?* Arwen shook her head in confusion. Even if dark elves were in the city, they would be in tunnels, not a light-filled skyscraper.

As if to demonstrate the truth of her words, Starblade's aura disappeared from her awareness. Not because he'd flown out of her range. Because he didn't want to be followed.

"Do you want me to try to go after him?" Amber opened the window and stuck her head out, but Starblade wasn't visible to the eye anymore either.

"I think—" Arwen considered the ominous building, "—I'll start by trying to figure out who or what he's so pissed at in there."

"Maybe he's just a cranky bastard who likes destroying random things. Some dragons are asses, you know."

A hub cap rolled away from the wreckage.

"*Most* dragons," Amber added.

"I'm going to check out the building." Arwen opened the car door.

"It's magical and strong enough to ward off dragons. Do you think that's smart?"

"Probably not." Arwen eyed her sleeve, the tattoo continuing to itch.

"But you're going anyway? I thought adults were supposed to know better than to do stupid shit."

"That's a common misconception among teenagers, I believe. Go home, okay? Let Val know about this place."

Bow in hand, Arwen took a deep breath and headed for the building.

9

Signs staked on the manicured lawn around the towering building read *No trespassing* and *Keep out.* The defensive magic emanating from the place told Arwen's senses the same.

Even though the building was only a block from a busy thoroughfare and not far from the freeway, the city noises were muted. The whole *place* was muted. Despite the parked cars, there was nobody in sight on the dead-end street or the sidewalk. Though Arwen preferred it that way, it seemed odd in the middle of busy Bellevue. The still-flaming car bits might have accounted for some of the emptiness, but maybe the mundane humans in the area somehow sensed the menace of the building and were avoiding it.

As she drew closer, Arwen couldn't tell if she approached the front or rear of the skyscraper. The tinted glass was the same on all sides, and she could barely see the outline of a door. There were no signs proclaiming the name of the building or even its address. A single narrow cement path cut through the grass toward the door.

Before heading that way, she glanced at the spot where the destroyed car had been, surprised someone hadn't come out to check on it. If anyone was looking out the windows, she couldn't tell. Their tint hid everything within.

Usually, she could sense what race had applied an enchantment or created a trinket, but a confusing hodgepodge of magic was present in the building and its defenses, everything from gnomish to dwarven to elven. She thought she even detected dragon magic, though their kind weren't known for creating artifacts. Regardless, someone had put a lot of effort into acquiring protection for the place.

Maybe, as a pretext for why she was approaching, she would tell the receptionist—assuming there was one—about the... accident.

With that plan in mind, Arwen strode up the sidewalk. The single glass door had neither a handle nor a button or anything to press. Before she could knock, she halted, her instincts warning her of a threat. She couldn't *see* anything but suspected a barrier. Reaching out confirmed that as electricity zapped her finger, and a savage tingle raced up her arm.

"I wonder if Starblade got his tail zapped when he hit the window," she muttered.

She stepped off the sidewalk and into the grass, intending to see if the barrier extended all the way around the building, and noticed small cameras mounted along the exterior. One swiveled to track her. She waved her bow at it, as if she *wanted* attention, then pointed at the remains of the wrecked car.

Amber hadn't yet driven off. She had her head down, texting maybe. Not wanting to get her into trouble, Arwen willed her to leave.

When nobody came out of the building, Arwen continued across the lawn, checking the ground for signs that would give her clues about the occupants. Despite the grass and numerous trees, there was a dearth of birds, squirrels, and other living things. A honk on the freeway sounded like it came from miles instead of blocks away.

Sprinkler heads dotted the lawn, but the lush grass hid footprints or anything else until Arwen came across tire tracks. They weren't wide enough to have been left by a car—maybe a golf cart or riding lawn mower?—but something had flattened the grass recently.

When she rounded the corner, more cameras on that side of the building tracking her movement, a clink came from a large modern garage door. Pavement led away from it, turning toward a street at what had to be the front of the building. Fancy gold letters over the door read: H&B Insurance.

"An insurance building is armored to the teeth with magic?" Arwen asked.

The garage door rolled up, revealing a dark interior. The faint thrumming of an engine wafted out.

Wishing she had a camouflaging charm, Arwen stepped behind a hydrangea bush and wondered if she could slip inside after the vehicle drove out. But did she *want* to slip in? When all those cameras were watching her?

Headlight beams appeared in the dark garage, and not one but four black vehicles roared out, magic emanating from them. Looking more like fast-moving mini tanks than lawn mowers, they had turrets with swiveling cannons that swept back and forth. Instead of heading toward the street, they turned toward Arwen. They roared over the curb, into the grass, and straight toward the hydrangea bush.

Alarmed, Arwen started to lift her bow, but even magical arrows might ping off the armored tanks. She turned and sprinted away.

Afraid of leading them toward Amber, Arwen raced across the lawn toward a side street. The hairs on the back of her neck rose, instincts warning her an instant before she sensed a surge of magic. One of the tanks fired, the cannon booming.

Arwen threw herself into a roll. Her bow made the move awkward, and she clipped a tree with it, but the maneuver was good enough. The cannonball—the magical *flaming* cannonball—missed but not by much.

She sprang up, darting to the side and around two more trees to make herself a harder target. She expected to hear the cannonball slam into a neighboring building. But when it reached the edge of the grass—the property line?—it disappeared.

As Arwen sprinted away, cannons from three more tanks fired. Again, she dove, rolling as fast as she could to reach cover behind another tree.

The flaming projectiles missed her, but one sped past low to the ground and scant inches to her side, almost close enough to catch her sleeve on fire. The tank had anticipated that she would roll. Something smart was guiding the machines.

If she could reach the edge of the property, maybe she would be safe. She leaped up again and kept running. The four tanks split to go around the trees and try to surround her.

When she reached the sidewalk and raced into the street, she glanced back, hoping her pursuers would stop at the property line. But the tanks kept coming, roaring after her. With other buildings rising up ahead of her, and cars parked along either side of the street, she had less room to maneuver.

Again, the tanks fired, two cannonballs aiming for her back. This time, she leaped upward. A good choice, because the fiery balls came in low—the tanks had expected her to dive and roll.

In the air, she yanked an arrow from her quiver, nocking it before she landed. She turned and fired, aiming for the turret on one of the tanks. Her magical arrow gouged into the metal before bouncing off, but the damage was negligible. Not only did the tanks continue but they sped up, and she dared not run back to collect her arrow.

The next time she glanced over her shoulder, only two tanks were following her down the street. She had a feeling the others had gone another way rather than given up. They moved fast, and they might be trying to cut her off.

Entering a busier area, Arwen looked for a door that she could duck through, but she didn't want to lead this trouble to anyone else. She opted for an alley beside an older brick building. Maybe it would have a fire escape or even a drainpipe she could climb to a rooftop.

Up ahead, almost hidden by a dumpster, a green metal door creaked open. Someone with a magical aura stood inside. A gnome?

"Look out!" Arwen yelled over the roar of her mechanical pursuers.

A surge of magic came from the open door as she kept running in that direction. A gray cloud filled the air. Not sure what it was— more than simple smoke—Arwen held her breath. When she entered the cloud, it crawled all over her skin as it obscured her sight. It even dazed her slightly, making her steps falter as she lost her sense of direction.

The roar of the tanks echoed from the brick walls, and did she hear another one at the far end of the alley? One of her pursuers already poised to cut her off?

"In here," a female voice whispered from the doorway.

Hoping she'd found a good Samaritan, Arwen patted her way through the smoke. Her fist clunked on the corner of the dumpster before she found the doorway.

It was cloudy inside as well, and she didn't realize there were stairs until her foot came down on empty air, and she almost pitched down them. Her bow clattered against a brick wall, but she caught her balance and sensed someone—the gnome—at the bottom.

The door thudded shut as Arwen groped her way down the stairs, the gnome moving back to give her room. The cloud grew less dense as Arwen reached the bottom, the cement floor of a basement. She spotted the gnome she'd sensed, but before she got a good look, something startled her by tightening around both her legs.

Invisible ropes yanked her from her ankles and whipped her upside-down to dangle from the ceiling. The gnome, a red-headed female with spectacles, pointed a magical crossbow at her.

Arwen groaned. Out of the cranberry bog and into the pig wallow.

Though Arwen dangled upside-down from the ceiling by her ankles, she nocked an arrow and pointed it at the gnome. Her father had started training her when she'd been eight, so she'd had more than twenty years of archery practice; this wouldn't be the first awkward position she'd fired from.

The determined gnome with her crossbow, the loaded bolt glowing an ominous red, didn't appear daunted.

Right away, Arwen sensed the reason why. The gnome wore numerous items that emanated protective magic, including something in her overalls that was creating a barrier around her. Further magical contraptions, including the trap that had sprung and ensnared Arwen, were mounted around the basement workshop.

"I thought you were an innocent person," the gnome said, "not one of *them*."

The roars of the tanks sounded in the alley, muffled by the thick door and brick walls. Though tempted to glance back and see if that magical cloud remained—would it keep the mechanical contraptions from detecting the entrance?—Arwen didn't dare take her eyes from the gnome.

"I'm not one of them," Arwen said. "I don't even know who *they* are."

The roars faded. Had the tanks left the alley or stopped to wait for Arwen to come out? Or for the gnome to shoot her full of crossbow bolts and dump her body up there?

"I'm a tracker," Arwen added, "and I was hired to find someone."

The gnome squinted at her. "You are half dark-elven."

A lot of people were pointing that out lately.

"Not by choice. Trust me. If I could have picked my mother, I would have been born to an elf. Or even a human. So I could have been a normal person with a normal life."

"Gnomes are better than either." She straightened to what couldn't have been more than four feet in height and jerked her chin up. "We're magical and gifted but not stuck-up and snooty about it."

"I have no objection to gnomes. They're a handy people. Thanks for helping me out. I owe you one. Uhm, can you let me down?" Arwen couldn't see the magical bonds around her ankles, but she sensed them and doubted her foraging knife would be sufficient to cut them. One of her arrowheads might work, but she needed to make sure the gnome wouldn't shoot her while she made the attempt.

"I think you are tricking me. Dark elves do not like gnomes." She scowled, her crossbow not wavering.

Arwen grimaced. She didn't know if she could dodge from her current position, but she would have to try.

"Except to sacrifice. They would prefer every other species be dead, except those who can make beautiful and valuable magical devices for them." Surprising emotion crept into the gnome's voice, distress mingling with anger. "Even then, they kidnap the makers and torture them to force them to do their work. They do not offer to pay them and respect their person and their freedom like civilized people."

"I'm not like that," Arwen said. "What happened to you? Is someone trapping you here?"

And was it tied in somehow with that building? And Starblade?

"The dark elves had my husband kidnapped." Anguish twisted the gnome's face, and, for the first time, the crossbow wavered. "They have him in that big black building, and I haven't been able to get in. But I'm watching them, and I'll figure out a way to reach him. They won't sacrifice my husband. I'll rescue him first." She jerked her chin toward a low workbench full of tools and boxes and projects, then glanced at a back wall where a map hung, several monitors mounted above it. "I'll find a way."

The monitors showed camera feeds. One was of the alley, the gray haze lingering outside, and others were of the Bellevue skyline including the flat rooftop of the insurance building.

"I have drones recording it," the gnome said. "I've figured out how close they can get before the building's defenses activate and shoot them down. I'm getting lots of footage."

"Did you get any of a half-dragon?" Arwen asked.

"Yes, but... did you say *half*-dragon? Such beings don't exist."

"It's a long story."

"Until recently, I had never seen that dragon, but he flew to the building two different times today. I do not know who he is. He may be working with the dark elves, doing their kidnapping for them." The gnome snarled.

Thinking of the destroyed car, Arwen doubted Starblade was working for anyone in that building. She had no idea who had owned that vehicle, but it wouldn't have been a dark elf. Her mother's people had no affinity for human technology and, regardless, couldn't leave their lightless tunnels and caves, except on cloudy nights.

She still couldn't imagine them being in that building. Her mother's clan had once lived in tunnels nearby, but they hadn't been seen in a long time. That was as much a relief to Arwen as to the rest of the world.

"Are you *sure* dark elves are involved?" Arwen wondered if anyone had actually seen them. Might someone have started a rumor that they were behind things?

"I am certain. One came with several minions in the middle of the night to kidnap my scientist husband from our home in Renton where we worked together, inventing things and building useful devices for humans and the magical community. We were very happy until *they* came."

The gnome lowered her crossbow and flicked a finger, using magic to unbutton her overalls. As they drooped, she lifted her shirt to show a scar running across her abdomen and around her side. It looked like a dagger had torn her open, leaving a wound that must have needed stitches if not a powerful healer to keep her from dying.

"They left me for dead. They didn't need an inventor, only a scientist." Her voice grew tight when she added. "I *hope* they needed a scientist. I have not seen him since that night. It is possible they sacrificed him, but I must believe..." She swallowed. "He is still alive. I am certain of it. I am watching them and gathering as much human coinage as I can so that I can hire assassins to take care of them. Maybe the Ruin Bringer. She battled dark elves once before. Maybe she will do so again."

"I'm sorry your husband was taken and that you were hurt. I know how vile dark elves can be."

"I am certain you do." Suspicion still darkened the gnome's eyes. "You say you owe me for helping you?"

"Ah, yes." Arwen worried about what the gnome might

demand. What if she believed Arwen could get her in to meet the dark elves? "What's your name? I'll try to learn more about what's going on in that building while I'm tracking the half-dragon."

The gnome snorted. "You could not even evade entry-level security devices. A dragon, even a *half*-dragon, would kill you without effort. I see that you have some magical arrows, but you are not suitably protected to battle such powerful beings."

Arwen wished she could argue, but it was the truth. She could hold her own against ogres and yetis, but they weren't foes with great magical power. And her own magic... For all her years above ground, she'd refused to practice the darker arts that her mother's people excelled at, always trying to turn her innate power toward improving life instead of taking it. Unless she could tantalize an enemy with a jar of jam, her magic would be of little use.

"I have some acquaintances who can help me. I could also put you in touch with the Ruin Bringer." Arwen hoped she wasn't promising what she couldn't deliver. Sigrid was the one she knew well, not Val, but Val seemed like someone who would help. Besides, if dark elves *had* returned to the Seattle area, her Army employer might send her after them whether Arwen requested it or not.

"Could you get me a discount on her services? Tell her I am Imoshaun the Inventor and quite well known on the gnomish home world. One day, once I've reunited with Gruflen, we will be well known here too. Together, we will continue our work to invent a device that can hide entire gnomish cities—and even human cities—so that dragons cannot find them and exert their will over the lesser races."

Arwen had no idea how much Colonel Willard paid Val to take care of criminals or what rate she charged for freelance gigs. "I can tell her about you and ask her for help."

"Good, good."

"And I'll help you too if I can. I *do* owe you." Arwen might have been trapped in that alley and pulverized by cannonballs if Imoshaun hadn't offered assistance.

"You do." Looking less suspicious and a touch hopeful, Imoshaun waved a hand.

The bindings around Arwen's ankles released. It was so abrupt that it startled her, but she managed to twist in the air and land on her feet.

"Do not make me regret freeing you," Imoshaun said. "It concerns me to let a dark elf, even a *half* dark elf, wander free. Hurt no gnomes, and do no evil."

"I won't. That's good advice for all, and I will follow it."

"Yes." Imoshaun looked toward the display showing the alley.

The smoke had cleared fully, and the tanks were gone. They'd returned to their garage, Arwen hoped.

"Also, do not cross any dragons or half-dragons. I know little of your quest, but it is clearly foolish."

That was also good advice, but Arwen couldn't give the same response to it. She'd gotten in over her head, but did she have the choice to quit?

"I don't know," she whispered to herself, thinking of her father's tax bill and the farm, the place she felt most secure in the world and the only home she'd known for the last twenty-three years. How could she give that up?

10

Dusk was descending on Bellevue, a smattering of lights on in the surrounding office buildings, when Arwen emerged from the alley. She didn't see or hear the tanks, but she peered warily down the street in both directions before going far.

They'd been smart enough to adjust how they fired at her. Might they also be smart enough to lie in wait?

She didn't know why they would when all she'd done was walk on the grass. There had to be limits to the degree of security permitted in the city. Though if someone inside had detected that she was part dark elf... and dark elves were wrapped up in whatever was going on in that building...

Arwen sighed. *Were* they?

Her skin crawled at the thought that dark elves might not only be in the city but somehow involved with Starblade. And her tattoo itched again. It was as if it believed she was close to her mother's kind, even though she couldn't sense them. She also hadn't sensed, among the hodgepodge of magic protecting that building, any artifacts of the dark-elven variety.

Reminding herself that she had only Imoshaun's words to prove that dark elves were involved, Arwen decided to worry only about her mission for now.

Of course, she'd promised Imoshaun that she would try to help her. She *did* owe the gnome a favor.

"Telling Val about all this should be enough," she assured herself. "She and Willard can figure out what to do if there are dark elves in the city."

Her tattoo itched.

Arwen bared her teeth at it.

As she headed toward the nearest thoroughfare, knowing it would eventually lead her in the direction of her home, she sensed Amber's quarter-elven blood and halted. Had she waited in the car the whole time?

Not wanting to go near the building and risk waking up the tanks again, Arwen walked down a block, cut through an alley, and approached the hatchback from behind. She found Amber in the driver's seat, texting on her phone. She must have sensed Arwen approach, because she rolled down the window.

"You're welcome. And it's been over an hour, so that'll be another twenty dollars."

Too tired to object and point out that she hadn't *wanted* Amber to wait, Arwen climbed into the passenger seat. It would have been a long walk back home.

"I can get it for you when you drop me off. I'm outside of Carnation."

"Carnation?"

"It's on Highway 203."

"Where the hell is *that*?" The car didn't have a navigation system, but Amber typed the town in on her phone. "That's way out in the sticks."

"People live out there and commute to Redmond and Bellevue.

It's not that far." Unfortunately. If it were farther from the metro areas, the property values wouldn't have gone up so much, and Arwen and her father wouldn't have the tax problem.

Amber wrinkled her nose as the phone offered directions. "By the time we get there, it'll be another hour."

"You did say you like driving."

"Apparently." Her nose wrinkled again.

Arwen would wait until they were closer to give directions to her father's farm, which was nowhere near the highway and could fairly be characterized as *in the sticks*. From past experience, she knew that their address didn't come up accurately for navigation systems.

"Did you learn what you wanted about the half-dragon and that building?" Amber drove toward the freeway.

"I didn't learn anything before magical security tanks chased me away while trying to kill me."

"Huh. I wondered what those booms were."

"Cannons firing."

"Are cannons allowed in the city limits?"

"I doubt it. A sign above the garage called it H&B Insurance, but the whole place oozes magic. A gnome inventor said there might be dark elves inside or involved somehow. And that they're kidnapping people." Arwen still didn't know how *Starblade* was involved.

Amber gave her a long look while they waited at the light for the on-ramp. "I can tell being your driver is going to be bizarre. You're as bad as Val."

"And yet you want to work with me."

"I want your ten percent. If things work out, we can be a team, and I won't have to go back to hauling bags of cement for Matti after she pops her kids out."

"That can't be all you do. Doesn't Matti renovate homes?"

"Yeah, she's teaching me about how to install toilets and fix leaky showers, but, Arwen, I don't *want* to learn those things. Fashionista, remember?" Amber gestured at her clothing.

"Fashionistas get leaky faucets too."

"But they hire people to come repair them because they make good money in the business. Especially if they design clothing that becomes popular."

Since Amber had waited for her and was driving her home, Arwen didn't point out that repairing leaks sounded useful and was probably a good skill to have.

Once they were on the freeway heading east, Amber said, "There's no way that's an insurance office. Insurance offices don't have *tanks*."

"I suspected that wasn't common."

"What do you think it's a front for? Something nefarious?"

"Probably." Arwen couldn't think of many things her mother's people did that didn't fit other races' definition of *nefarious.*

"Maybe they're scheming to take over the world. Magical bad guys do that *all* the time in Seattle. Just ask Val."

"The building is in Bellevue."

Amber rolled her eyes. "I'm sure it happens in *all* major cities. You can ask my dad too. He reads comic books and fantasy novels, so he knows all about the aspirations of villains."

"Dark elves can't survive in daylight, so their aspirations are largely subterranean." Not that they couldn't do plenty of damage to cities and their populaces from tunnels below them.

"I can look up that building if you want. That *faux* insurance company. If I can't find anything interesting, my dad probably can. He's good with computer stuff."

"It may have nothing to do with the half-dragon I'm tracking, but..." Arwen thought of Imoshaun, the distress stamping her face. "If dark elves are scheming and intend harm to people, I would feel obligated to help stop them."

She wouldn't *want* to get in the way of their plans, lest it bring their wrath to her father's door, but she *would* feel obligated. She did at least hope that this wasn't her mother's clan. Maybe some other band of dark elves had moved in. When she'd last seen her mother, Arwen had only been seven, but she had plenty of memories of the dark times in those tunnels, of learning the ways of her people, and of hating them but being too terrified to do anything but obey them. If her father hadn't found a way to escape and take her to the surface, she had no idea what she would have become. A monster that someone like the Ruin Bringer would have hunted down and killed?

"I'll look it up," Amber said. "I assume, if you don't have a phone, you aren't that good at researching things."

"We have a set of encyclopedias and numerous manuals on farming practices around the world."

That earned her another eye roll. "Researching things that *matter*. And that are current."

Arwen started to mention that they also had a computer and internet, but she wasn't a wiz online. It didn't help that technological things tended to break when she tried to use them. She didn't know if she was extremely inept when it came to such devices or the magic in her blood somehow cursed everything she used. Even Frodo, the old tractor, was more finicky for her than her father.

"Will your research be included in your ten percent?"

"Naturally. I'm willing to work to earn my cut. We *do* have a deal, right?" Amber arched her eyebrows. "I'll even make you some jewelry—or hair bodkins—so you don't have to use *sticks*." Amber gave her head an aggrieved look. "I'll throw those in for free. In fact, I *insist* on throwing them in."

Giving up a thousand dollars was a lot, but this had already gotten more involved than simply tracking someone down. Arwen might need the help of someone computer savvy.

"If you can find out who owns that building and what they're doing there... yes, it's a deal."

Amber frowned. She'd probably wanted a straight *yes* that wasn't contingent on success. But Arwen didn't know if Amber was capable of what she'd promised, and ten percent seemed a lot to give to a driver.

They passed through Carnation, and Arwen directed Amber down the rural roads that would take them to the farm. No streetlamps brightened the way.

"All right," Amber finally responded. "Deal."

"Good. Turn there."

"Is that a silo?"

"Two of them, yes." Arwen remembered her discussion about silage with Starblade, and, for some reason, a guilty twinge went through her. She wasn't, she told herself firmly, betraying him. He'd read her mind—*painfully*—and threatened to read her father's as well.

"I'm not going to run into any cows out here, am I?"

"Not usually at night, no."

Amber eyed her. "What if I bring you information during the day?"

"It's more of a possibility then. Deer and bears also come through, but they don't usually stand in the road and look blankly at you when you honk."

"I should have asked for twenty percent."

"Possibly." When they made the final turn, Arwen pointed at the gravel driveway, the magic of the orchards guiding her in the dark more than the headlights.

The car lurched into a pothole as it made the turn.

"I didn't know I'd have to go off-roading as part of my driving experience." Amber swerved to avoid the grasping branches of a maple in need of a trim.

"It's a good thing you didn't get a Mercedes. You'd worry about scratches."

"If I had a *Mercedes*, I wouldn't need side hustles. I'd already have enough money to keep my wardrobe properly outfitted for college interviews."

As they approached the house, the door opened and Arwen's father slid out, careful not to let the light silhouette his frame. Even in the dark, Arwen knew he had his gun. She leaned out the window and waved, realizing he would be on edge at having an unfamiliar car come up the driveway at night. Or at all. Visitors out here were few.

"Uh, I'll stop here." Amber had spotted him and maybe the gun too.

"Thank you for the ride."

"One sec." Amber pulled out her phone, tapped rapidly into a website, and then thrust it toward Arwen. "Sign here."

"Sign?"

"A contract for our gig, agreeing to the ten percent, to wit one thousand dollars, delivered promptly upon payment from your employer, assuming I perform my duties adequately and professionally."

"Does the sixty dollars I'm paying you come out of that?" Arwen skimmed through the document, impressed that a sixteen-year-old had thought of a contract. Maybe Amber *was* someone who would do good research.

"No, that's a separate gig that we set up before this. And I'm still waiting for the last forty, FYI." She glanced at Arwen's father.

"Right." Arwen awkwardly signed the phone's screen with her finger. "I'll get that."

While Amber waited, Arwen grabbed her bow and headed for the door, the scents of strawberry and lilac blossoms teasing her nose. In another month, they would have fresh berries, and farmers-market season would be in full swing. Things around the farm would get busier, so she hoped she could finish this side project before then. If she succeeded, maybe there would be enough money to buy a new printer to make more professional labels for her jam jars.

"Everything okay, Arwen?" Her father eyed the unfamiliar car suspiciously. "You don't usually accept rides from strangers." He left unspoken the implied, *I taught you better than that.*

She knew his words came only out of concern for her.

"That's Sigrid's granddaughter, and I'll tell you about everything in a minute." She would, but she might leave out mention of the possible dark elves. That would worry him, and she didn't yet have proof that they were involved. "I need to grab a few things and trade you a hundred for two twenties, please."

"That's fine—an oddly good deal—but are you in trouble? Is this about your new tracking assignment?"

"I'll be okay. Don't worry. I can take care of myself. You made sure of that." Arwen smiled while hoping none of her clothing was singed from those fiery cannonballs. As she slipped past him, she tried not to think about how Imoshaun had pointed out her lack of armor or anything useful besides her bow and arrows.

Her father grumbled under his breath but told her to take the money and not worry about the hundred. They earned most of their money together, and he wasn't stingy about giving her some when she needed it, but he paid for everything for the farm, so she always assumed he needed it more than she and rarely asked for anything.

"How am I going to send you what I'm able to research if you don't have a phone?" Amber asked when Arwen came back outside.

"We have a computer that my father uses for bookkeeping and taxes. You can email me." Arwen gave her the address.

"You have internet out here?" Amber looked around the dark farm, only a couple of outdoor lights on near the house, unless one counted the solar-powered butterfly lamps staked along the driveway. Arwen had traded someone pies for them the summer before last. "In the Davy Crockett savageness?" Amber added.

"We just call it the farm, and we have a satellite dish. We got it two years ago."

Amber looked toward the manufactured home, but the roof held only berry crops.

"It's on the corn crib." Arwen pointed. "There was a better unimpeded view of the night sky there."

"Oh, yeah, of course. Corn cribs are known technology hubs. All right. I'll send what I find."

"Thank you. I appreciate your help." Arwen offered a couple of the jars she'd grabbed.

"What are those?" Amber eyed them as if they were poison— or maybe as if they might be unappealing vegetables that were *good for your health.*

"Blackberry jam and vanilla-bean-coffee pickled cherries."

"Pickled cherries?" Amber curled a dubious lip.

"They're one of my most popular things. Most people love them. They're sweet but with a bit of a kick. Vanilla bean, brown sugar, coffee, red chili flakes, and my secret spice blend. Oh, and I slipped in some turmeric. It has health benefits, you know. It's an anti-inflammatory as well as an antioxidant that may help reduce arthritis pain, keep blood sugar steady, and lower the risk of heart disease."

Amber looked blankly at her.

"Never mind. Some of my clients like to know about such things, so I've studied everything we grow. I make tea with turmeric for Sigrid."

"You said there's sugar? And coffee? I like those things."

"Yes. The cherries are good in cocktails, but you can also eat them by themselves like a dessert." Arwen didn't imagine that sixteen-year-old Amber had a lot of cocktails, not if her parents kept an eye on her.

Amber popped the lid and sniffed the contents. "They smell okay."

"Yes, I strive to deliver *okay* food to people."

Missing—or ignoring—the sarcasm, Amber popped a cherry into her mouth and chewed. Her eyes brightened. "Oh, that's straight fire."

Arwen frowned. Had something gone wrong with the batch? "The sweetness should counteract the spice from the chili flakes."

"No, I mean they're *good*." Amber stuck another one in her mouth, then two more, then fastened the lid and held the jar to her chest. "I'm not sharing with Nin and my dad."

"I... don't require that." Arwen didn't even know who Nin was.

"Okay, good. Uhm, maybe next time you pay me for a ride, we could barter for some other stuff." She looked curiously at the jam jar, a blackberry drawn on the simple label. "Is that good on croissants?"

"It's good on everything. I promise."

Amber considered the cherry jar. "I believe you."

Even though Arwen had other concerns on her mind, it always pleased her when people liked her food.

After tucking away her new prizes, Amber put the car in reverse, then seemed to realize backing down the long driveway in the dark would be challenging. She did an awkward seven-point turn, running over a lavender bush and the garden hose in the process.

Arwen stepped forward, about to offer guidance, but as soon as the nose of the car was pointed in the right direction, Amber peeled out, as if in embarrassment.

"Learning to drive may be more difficult than I realized."

Arwen turned, intending to give her father the details she'd promised, but a magical being abruptly registered on her senses. A *familiar* magical being.

She looked up in time to see a dark dragon shape gliding low over the house on its way to land in the driveway with her.

11

THE TRANQUILIZER AND TAGGING DEVICE WERE ATTACHED TO arrows in Arwen's quiver, which she'd left in the house with her bow when she'd gone in to get Amber's money. Starblade hadn't registered to her senses until right before he'd appeared, so there hadn't been time to run in and grab the weapons. He'd also landed between her and the front door.

A whisper of magic wafted from him, and Arwen crouched, reaching for the foraging knife sheathed on her belt. As if *that* would be any defense against someone so powerful.

Had Starblade come to question her father? After being distracted by the need to thrash the car parked at the Bellevue building? Or... had he come because of her? To again accuse her of lying to him.

She *hadn't* lied, but she hadn't told him the entire truth either.

Black scales blurred, and Starblade shifted into his elven form, facing her with a sword already drawn. She swallowed. Maybe he'd come to do *more* than accuse her of lying.

The power he exuded promised he wouldn't need the blade to kill her, and he glanced dismissively at her knife.

There weren't many outdoor lights, but, with the way he stood, the side of his face was illuminated by the porch lamp. Strong, handsome, and hard as steel. His violet eyes weren't glowing, but Arwen well remembered that they could.

"Do you still claim there are no dark elves in the area?" Starblade asked.

"I've recently learned from a gnome inventor that there might be."

"You were hunkered in a driving conveyance outside the building that houses their lair."

"I was sitting, not hunkering, and I didn't sense any dark elves."

He scoffed. "Then the abilities you should have inherited from your mother's people are weak. As Commander Aylida Alonsha once said, it is a great failing to underestimate one's enemy, but tragic results may also come from *over*estimating him." His eyes narrowed. "Or her."

"Listen, we don't have to be enemies."

"Your own Sun Tzu said, 'To secure ourselves against defeat lies in our own hands, but the opportunity of defeating the enemy is provided by the enemy himself.'"

"I didn't know dead Earth generals got quoted in the Cosmic Realms."

"They do not, but I am educating myself on the history of this world and the government structure of the nation in which I find myself a refugee."

"I heard you were a war criminal, not a refugee." Arwen glanced toward the window, surprised her father hadn't come out. Ideally, he would come out *with* her bow and quiver...

Starblade jerked his chin up. "I am *not* a criminal. I fought nobly and with honor during the war between elves and dwarves until I was captured and imprisoned for centuries in a stasis chamber. It is not *my* fault that the elves and dwarves have since reconciled their differences and find my existence—" his lip curled, "—inconvenient."

Arwen hesitated. Was that true? She wished she'd gotten an opportunity to speak with Matti to find out what she knew about Starblade.

"Nor is it my fault that the dragons of this era have decided that our kind are abominations, embarrassments that should be destroyed. Never did I attack or even slight their kind, not until this past year when they attacked *me*. At the time of the war, they were busy with political infighting of their own and indifferent to the battle between elves and dwarves."

Since Arwen hadn't heard of any of this—the history of the Cosmic Realms wasn't a big topic of study on Earth—she didn't know what to say.

"I am *not* a criminal," Starblade repeated, "but if I were, would I not have the right to defend myself and speak my case to my accusers? That is the elven way, or it was once. And is it not the way of your people to hold a justice-seeking session before condemning someone? Your Constitution, the Sixth Amendment, promises a citizen the right to a speedy and public trial before an impartial jury. I understand that I am not a citizen of your nation, but one would expect to be treated fairly until one's guilt is proven. I do not even stand accused, insofar as I know, by your kind." His eyes closed to slits. "Nor have I committed a crime against the dark elves. As far as the shifters... They have earned my wrath. Through *their* actions."

Arwen had a feeling he not only knew the shifters were after him but that they'd hired her.

"You've read the Constitution?" she asked to buy herself time to think.

"I have. When we came to this wild world, believing we could hide from dragons and be forgotten, since they have little interest in this place, I vowed to study the natives so that I could fit in. I am reading books on your history and government."

"If you want to fit in, it would be more plausible if you *didn't* know anything about those subjects."

Starblade cocked his head in puzzlement. "On what more important subjects would a native of this nation be knowledgeable?"

Uh, good question. Arwen wasn't exactly representative of the common man. "I think Taylor Swift lyrics, which celebrity is hooking up with which other celebrity, and what sports team is the odds-on favorite to win whatever finals or playoffs are occurring soon."

The puzzlement faded, and irritation crept onto his face. His eyes glowed. "I believe you seek to distract me with inanity."

"I'm trying to advise you on how to pass as a human. Tip number one, don't do that glowy thing with your eyes."

Starblade walked toward her, the sword still in his hand. The tip pointed toward the gravel driveway instead of at her, but that didn't keep her heart from hammering. She glanced toward the front door again, wondering if she might rush past him and reach her bow. Where *was* her father?

The magic she'd sensed earlier intensified, flowing toward the house. Whatever it was affected Arwen as well, and an unnatural weariness came over her. Her knees weakened, and she had to fight to keep them from giving way. What was this? A sleep spell?

"I came to question your father," Starblade said, stopping scant feet in front of her, "about the dark elves, about what he knows, and where they can be found outside of their protected structure."

"He doesn't know. I told you the truth."

"You told me there were no dark elves, and we both know better."

"I didn't know, not until I found that building today. I wasn't even looking for them. I was looking for—" Arwen caught herself. On the off chance he didn't already know, she didn't want to admit she'd accepted an assignment to track him.

But his brows drew down, and she feared he'd already figured that out. The inside of her skull itched, and she curled her fingers into fists, wanting to punch him. But she let him see the truth in her mind.

"You remain protected, your thoughts difficult to read." Starblade glanced at her forearm.

Her sleeve hid the tattoo, but it didn't matter. He knew it was there.

"I suppose, being unaware of any grievous crime you've committed, and not having ensured that *you* received a trial, I would be out of line if I chopped off your arm so the dark-elven mark could no longer protect you." He eyed her sleeve wistfully.

Arwen stepped back. "Yes, you would. If you're not a criminal, like you claim, that wouldn't be appropriate behavior."

"I am not. I am a warrior. A commander. I was trained from birth to lead my people in battle. Never have I committed a crime. Those I've killed have been in battle, in *war,* a war that began before I was born. A war that—" He lost his anger and finished softly with, "A war that ended long ago. But I am not a criminal. I was not then, and I am not now."

She thought about mentioning the restaurant footage and that she'd watched him destroy a car today, but she wasn't sure the latter crime was unjustified if its owner worked in that building. All she'd been doing was walking across the grass, and the security tanks had tried to *kill* her. There was no way that was legal.

"I am no longer a commander either, not with my last troop missing and the others having all passed." Starblade's eyes sharpened as he seemed to remember she was there. His focus returned to her. "None of this is your concern, mongrel dark elf. All I ask of you is how to find some of your people who are not ensconced behind protection that even a half-dragon cannot thwart. Who were you going to see in that building today?"

"No one. Look, I'd help you if I could. I don't like the dark elves any more than you."

"You'd help me?" Starblade scoffed again and took a step closer, his sword lifting slightly. "Even if you did not have dark-elven blood, I would find this unlikely, based on your actions thus far. And your intent."

Again, Arwen glanced toward the house, but the magic-induced weariness affecting her muscles also made her drowsy. She doubted she could dart past him.

"Is this what you seek?" The front door opened, and Starblade stretched his hand toward it without looking at her.

Before she could answer, her bow and quiver floated out.

She might have lunged for the weapons, but she imagined him levitating them higher, taunting her as he kept them out of reach.

Using only his magic, he dumped the contents of the quiver on the gravel, including the arrows with the tranquilizer and tracking device attached to them. Swallowing, she made herself look at him instead of them, hoping he couldn't tell their exact purpose. If her tattoo *was* somehow keeping him from reading her thoughts, she hoped it would continue working, though she hated the idea that something her mother had inflicted on her might be helpful.

"You wish to destroy me, the same as everyone else," Starblade stated.

"That's not true."

He raised frank eyebrows.

"I'm a simple farmer, not a dragon slayer. I'd be foolish to attack you."

Very foolish.

"That may be the first truthful thing you've said. You—" His nose turned upward, as if he'd caught a scent. Like a hound, he lifted it higher, nostrils twitching.

"What odor do I detect?" he asked.

"There are all kinds of things blooming on our farm."

"It is not natural. It smells of... vinegar and something sweet."

Arwen glanced toward where Amber's car had been parked. "Someone opened a jar of my pickled cherries not long ago."

"Pickled?"

"It's a method we use for preserving food. You pour an acidic brine of vinegar and salt and sometimes sugar and spices over vegetables or fruit so they last longer. It's from the times before refrigerators."

"Silage," he said.

She snorted. "Not exactly. Pickled stuff is good. Do you want to try some?"

He shook his head, but his nostrils twitched again. With... interest?

"I could get you a jar of the cherries. To take with you when you go."

Which he would hopefully do soon...

Starblade drew back. "I am not a fool who lets his taste buds tempt him to ruin. Not like Yen— not like someone else."

"I'm not trying to ruin you, just get you to leave my father and our farm alone."

"So you seek to bribe me."

"I'd call it a gift."

"With crafty words, the enemy manipulates you where bluntness would fail."

"Is that another quote from a dead general?"

"An elven playwright. He is, in fact, dead." Starblade stepped back. "I do not wish your food. It would be poisoned, and when I crumpled unconscious at your feet, you would drive those arrows into me."

"Why would the food in my kitchen be poisoned? It's not like I knew you were coming. I certainly didn't invite you." Arwen folded her arms over her chest and attempted to appear indignant, though the arrows at her feet made her feel she was in the wrong. At the least, *he* believed she was.

"No," Starblade said softly. "Nobody invites the outcast half-dragons."

Arwen lowered her arms, not knowing what to say. As someone who'd always felt like an outcast herself, she had no snarky words for him.

His gaze shifted toward the house. Contemplatively. More magic trickled from him. "He has no knowledge of the dark elves. As you say."

Arwen tensed. "You read my father's mind? Did you hurt him?"

"It is not painful."

"The hell it isn't."

He tilted his head, as if he didn't believe she'd experienced pain. It hadn't been extreme agony, but it had definitely been unpleasant.

"Perhaps we have a different definition of pain. For me, a mind scouring is uncomfortable but negligible compared to the various wounds I've received in battle. Regardless, he slept, so he felt nothing. I will depart." His voice grew icy when he added, "If I learn that you are allied with the dark elves and in any way assisting with their plot, I will return and destroy you." Starblade turned and took several steps, then crouched, as if to shift into his dragon form. He paused, however, and squinted back at her, then lifted a hand. A jar of pickled cherries floated out of the house.

She might have laughed if not for the chilling threat he'd delivered. "You're accepting my gift?"

"Your *bribe*?"

"Call it what you like. They're amazing on ice cream. I promise."

"I do not know what that is."

"You're *definitely* not going to fit in with the natives if you don't learn about the important things."

His squint turned suspicious. Maybe he didn't believe knowledge of history and government were less common among humans, at least in this country, than awareness of pop culture and food.

Starblade sheathed his sword and shifted into his dragon form, the jar of cherries disappearing along with his clothes and weapon.

Her bow and arrows lay on the ground where he'd dropped them. Arwen might have snatched them up and fired quickly enough to catch him off-guard, but she waffled with indecision. She might not get another chance to fulfill her mission, to collect that ten thousand dollars, but was he really a bad guy? A criminal? Or just a haughty jerk?

Did it matter? She'd agreed to the assignment and signed that contract with Amber. And she'd *seen* Starblade tear up the shifter's restaurant for no apparent reason. It sounded like dark elves had wronged him, but that shouldn't have prompted him to destroy the shifters' property.

It is most certainly not a gift, Starblade spoke telepathically into her mind, his long dragon neck turned so that he'd caught her staring at her arrows, *if you fantasize about driving weapons into the recipient's heart after giving it.*

Arwen jerked her gaze up but refused to feel abashed, not after he'd threatened to kill her. Instead, she glowered at him. *From this position, the only thing I could get a weapon into is your back end.* She noticed that a magical barrier protected him. Even if she'd grabbed her bow and fired without hesitation, she wouldn't have gotten through that.

I will let you know if your bribe was as amazing *as you believe.*

Starblade sprang into the air, wings flapping and stirring the leaves on the nearby trees.

Arwen had no idea if a half-dragon would like pickled cherries, but she didn't like the insinuation that he would come see her again.

12

ARWEN SLEPT POORLY, PLAGUED BY DREAMS—MEMORIES—FROM HER childhood, her time before she'd escaped her mother's people. The ritual when she'd received the tattoo was something that came to her often, the hilt of a bone dagger her mother had pressed into her seven-year-old hand, wanting her to drive it into the heart of a sacrifice for the spider demon.

Usually, the dream was the same, but this time, it morphed into a new variation. As she raised the dagger, Starblade stomped into the underground chamber in dragon form, his tail thrashing about and knocking religious paraphernalia to the ground as he sprang at dark elves. He crushed their magical defenses with his power as he snapped his jaws to bite them in half. Blood flowed everywhere, and the spider demon laughed.

Arwen woke in a sweat with her blankets tangled around her waist and the wide neck of her nightie off her shoulder. Sunlight came through the windows of her two-room home, diffused by the leaves of trees and bushes growing around them.

She swept out with her senses, afraid the dream had been a warning that Starblade had returned, but she didn't detect him.

She wiped her brow in relief before climbing out of bed. The amount of daylight filtering into the home promised she'd slept later than usual.

"I wouldn't have minded *not* sleeping in and experiencing those dreams." Arwen pushed her tangle of hair back from her face, attempting to push the memories away as well.

The night before, it had taken twenty minutes before her father had woken from the magic-induced sleep Starblade had left him in. She'd found him on the floor in the living room. He hadn't remembered anything, neither experiencing pain nor seeing the dragon approach. Arwen hoped he was all right, that he wouldn't suffer any ill effects from the magic. She didn't know what to make of Starblade and what he'd told her, but she didn't trust him.

She was about to take a shower and dress when she heard the crunch of a car coming up the gravel driveway. Sigrid? Other than a handful of longtime buyers from the farm, few people came to visit.

Worried trouble had shown up, Arwen only jammed on her jeans and tucked her nightie into the waistband before grabbing her moccasins and bow and quiver and rushing outside. As she jogged up the path and around the corner of her father's home, she sensed two familiar auras. Val and Matti.

Her father's truck was gone—he must have gone to the market without her—and she didn't recognize the SUV parked in its spot. A mundane human woman with dark skin was in the driver's seat. Oh, that had to be Colonel Willard.

Matti rode in the back, maybe munching on some of the items Sarrlevi had acquired. As Arwen put on her moccasins, she reminded herself to grab a jar of the sea-salt concord jam for her.

"Hey, Arwen." Val waved out the window of the passenger seat. "Amber told me an interesting story last night."

"Interesting," Willard said in a Southern drawl as she opened her door. "Right."

They all stepped out of the car, Willard in her military uniform and Val in her duster and jeans. Ready for action? The very pregnant Matti eased slowly out, looking more beleaguered than enthused to have been brought along. Arwen decided to throw in homemade lavender chocolates to go with the jam. Despite her rounded abdomen, Matti drew her magical war hammer out with her.

Arwen hoped they knew about the building and possible dark elves and could advise her on Starblade. She glanced toward where he'd stood the night before, as if some sign might remain of him, but the gravel didn't hold tracks, so there weren't any talon marks on the ground.

As her visitors approached, Arwen made herself smile and tamped down the urge to skitter back, though it was always hard not to feel hemmed in with so many people walking up. These were allies, she told herself, not enemies who would sneak around her back and attack.

"Hi, Arwen." Matti, perhaps sensing her discomfort, stopped several steps away.

"Ms. Forester," Willard said.

Arwen didn't think she'd ever spoken to the colonel and definitely hadn't passed along her surname to her, but she wasn't surprised that Willard knew about her.

"I heard you're looking for the half-dragon Starblade for some reason." Matti frowned.

In disapproval of Arwen?

"He's been destroying property and throwing shifters through restaurant windows. I saw the footage. Someone, a feline shifter who goes by Tigris, hired me to track him and tag him."

"*Tag* him?" Val mouthed.

"With a magical device so he can be found again."

"Uh," Matti said, "Starblade doesn't *want* to be found. He's on

Earth hiding out from all the dragons who would prefer he be dead. Are you *sure* he was destroying a restaurant?"

"Is that even a crime?" Val looked at Willard. "Matti used to destroy restaurants on a weekly basis, and you hired her."

"It wasn't *weekly*," Matti said, "and I was *stopping* crime."

"Funny how much gets utterly devastated when you stop crime with a giant war hammer."

"Ha ha."

Willard cleared her throat. "I actually *have* heard of a dragon— or possibly a half-dragon—who's been appearing in Bellevue and taking out restaurants and bars owned by a shifter family that has established a number of businesses there. The female werewolves who run that winery in Woodinville reported it to one of my informants. They were concerned that the dragon would come after them."

"Why would he?" Matti asked.

"They thought he might be after shifters in general."

"Are Tigris's buildings the only ones he's been attacking?" Matti asked. "Maybe he wronged Starblade somehow."

"How did they find him to wrong him?" Willard asked. "Hasn't he been holed up in that goblin village up north?"

"He's adjacent to the goblin village but within the borders of the sanctuary my mother enchanted, yes. Given that dragons would attack him if they found out he's still alive, I don't know why Starblade would have left."

"Maybe he got antsy," Val said. "Those woods up there aren't that exciting."

"Hasn't he had enough excitement lately?" Willard looked at Matti. "Your report mentioned the explosion of their mountain base—and the entire mountain—on the elf home world."

Matti nodded.

"He is coming off that five-hundred-year nap," Val said.

"Would anyone like to give me more details?" Arwen raised

her eyebrows, hoping that was why they'd come. Though Starblade had alluded to a stasis chamber, she wouldn't take his words as truth, not when he'd scraped his magical mental talons through her and her father's minds.

Matti hesitated and looked at Val.

"Matti is a little protective of him," Val said. "He's the one who freed Sarrlevi's mother—and eventually her mother too."

"Out of the goodness of his heart?" Arwen asked skeptically.

"Well, I freed him first," Matti said, "somewhat accidentally from a dwarven stasis-chamber prison where he was stuck after being captured in a war between the elves and the dwarves many centuries ago. The dwarves considered him a war criminal. They considered *all* the half-dragons to be war criminals though. I'm not sure they actually were that so much as the annoyingly powerful guys on the other side of their battles. Either way, I don't think Starblade would be making trouble if he hadn't been provoked."

"Who here would provoke him?" Val asked. "And why?"

"He's irked about dark elves right now." Arwen summed up Starblade's questioning of her and also mentioned the gnome inventor and her missing husband.

"Reports of dark elves are what prompted me to join the caravan headed out here today." Willard waved at Matti and Val, though she'd been the driver. "I thought you might know something, Forester."

Arwen grimaced. Someone else coming to her for information about dark elves. But *she* was the one who needed information.

"There have been rumors that they're back in the area," Willard continued, "and a few other magical beings have been reported missing—this time in Bellevue rather than Seattle, though I'm not aware of any tunnels there that dark elves could have moved into."

"Imoshaun—the gnome inventor—believes they're in a glass

skyscraper protected by magic. H&B Insurance." Arwen shrugged. "If some of the windows are blocked—*very* blocked—I suppose it's possible, but they're not known for visiting above-ground locales."

"H&B Insurance?" Willard asked. "That rings a bell. I think one of my goblin informants mentioned their building has grown very magical of late."

"Yes, with intelligent security tanks that shoot fiery cannon-balls at trespassers."

"I'll see if I can get some more details on it," Willard said.

"Just don't walk across the lawn," Arwen said. "It's well-defended. I suppose if you're with a dragon, you might be okay. The tanks didn't go after *Starblade*. Though they should have. He's the one who destroyed a car parked there and tried to get in."

"*Tried* to get in? But couldn't?" Val exchanged looks with Matti. "That guy is pretty powerful."

"He thwacked the windows with his tail and threw some magic at it," Arwen said, "but the building resisted."

"That's concerning," Willard said. "The only person I'm aware of who's been on Earth and can enchant things to resist dragons is Matti's mother, the dwarven princess Rodarska."

"I don't think she enchanted anything in Bellevue, but I can ask the next time I visit," Matti said.

"Dark-elven magic is powerful," Val said.

Arwen touched her sleeve, thinking of Starblade's claim that her tattoo protected her.

"Maybe I'll see if Zav is interested in doing a little sightseeing in Bellevue," Val added.

Willard held up a hand. "If you go by, do it at a distance. If there *are* dark elves and they've been kidnapping people, we might not want to make them nervous by snooping openly. We don't want them deciding their prisoners are a liability and should be killed."

"Knowing dark elves and their penchant for sacrifices," Val said grimly, "anyone they kidnapped might already be dead."

"Let's hope not."

Thinking of Imoshaun, Arwen nodded.

"It sounds like Starblade might have more information on them and their plot than we do," Matti mused. "Maybe we should visit him. I never did take him a housewarming gift."

"He would consider a gift a *bribe*," Arwen said. "I offered him pickled cherries and some of the other things I make here, but he was suspicious of it all."

He had *taken* the cherries, but she imagined him performing numerous magical experiments to determine if they were poisoned before popping the lid.

"Does he know you were hired to tag him?" Willard asked. "I'd be suspicious of your food too."

"He knows... more than I'd like. He said he couldn't read my mind, but..." Arwen shrugged.

"Pickled cherries?" Val raised her eyebrows. "Is that what you gave Amber last night? Thad—her father—said she came home with a jar of something but wouldn't share. She was clutching it secretively as she went to her room, like Gollum with the One Ring. Since she'd been out late, he was concerned and thought she might have pot."

"I do occasionally make balms from medicinal herbs we grow here, but that's not something I cultivate." Arwen, reminded of the farm's woes, turned to Matti. "Do you have any idea why someone's property would be changed from agricultural to residential zoning in such a way that it affects taxes owed? Without any warning to the homeowner until the new bill came?"

"The county does rezone things as the population in an area grows," Matti said. "They like to keep space set aside for agriculture and open forest lands and such, but... they also like to collect as much tax revenue as they can."

"We have a legitimate farm that's been in operation for decades."

"I can ask my friend Zadie if she can dig anything up. You might have to call the county and talk to them though."

"Call?" Arwen mouthed with distaste.

"This farm doesn't have a phone," Val said.

"Is it an *Amish* farm?" Willard asked.

"No. We used to have one, but it broke." Arwen shrugged.

"Phones aren't expensive. They probably cost less than a jar of pickled cherries."

"I'll let my father know." Maybe Arwen could buy him a new phone once she was paid for her tracking gig. Though, as things continued to crop up, she questioned her acceptance of that assignment more and more. If Matti was an ally of Starblade's, maybe he would share more information if Arwen showed up with her. And maybe he would tell the truth. She wanted to know whether he was acting as a criminal or if he was being provoked by the shifters, and maybe the dark elves as well. "Matti, would you be willing to take me with you to visit Starblade?"

"That depends," Matti said. "Are you going to try to *tag* him? Or otherwise attack him?"

"I only want to gather information right now." Arwen didn't mention that she'd twice stood by and done nothing when Starblade had appeared. She didn't even know if she *could* tag him.

"Sarrlevi wouldn't be happy with you going off into the wilds in your delicate state," Val told Matti. "I could take Arwen to the spot."

"My state isn't *delicate*," Matti said. "I'm perfectly healthy."

"And seven months pregnant."

Matti waved dismissively. "I doubt he'd let you into his home, Val. You've never talked with him, have you?"

"I've never even met him."

"He'll sense Zavryd's dragon aura on you and won't want anything to do with you."

"Are you sure?" Val rested her hand on the butt of the magical pistol in her thigh holster. "I'm a delight."

"Are you supposed to fondle your weapons when you make claims like that?" Willard asked.

"Of course. An elven general ought to like a girl who handles weapons."

"A girl married to a dragon who would be compelled to report Starblade's presence to his mother, the dragon queen, if he learned of it?" Willard asked.

"Ah, maybe not." Val lowered her hand and looked at Arwen. "Dragons don't like that half-dragons exist. They consider them an abomination."

"He... mentioned that." And that he was an outcast, Arwen recalled. She tried to push aside a twinge of sympathy.

The rumble of a truck came from the street. A neighbor? Arwen's father returning? She didn't know what he would say about all these visitors.

But she sensed magical beings and groaned.

"Shifters?" Val must have sensed them too.

"The tiger shifter and others I don't recognize." Arwen faced the driveway as a black truck drove up, Tigris at the wheel.

Four more shifters lounged in the open bed, all feline in nature, though they felt like cougars rather than tigers. Several carried rifles, and fresh mud spattered the side of the truck and wheels, as if they'd come from a safari. Hunting for a half-dragon?

"I recognize them as trouble," Val said.

"You've met them before?" Willard asked.

"Nope, but I know their kind." Val drew her pistol.

"These the people who hired you, Forester?" Willard asked.

"That one is, yes." Arwen pointed at the driver. "I haven't met the others."

"Did you tell them where you live?" Val's tone suggested it would have been foolish if she had.

"No," Arwen said. "They showed up at your mother's house after we had a run-in with ogres. And Starblade."

Val winced. "They know where my mom lives? Great."

"They seem well connected." Willard watched them approach without concern, though she was only a mundane human and didn't have any weapons—at least none visible. "I'm surprised they didn't already know where they could find Starblade."

"If he's still living inside the boundaries of the goblin sanctuary," Matti said, "they would have a hard time locating the place even if they *did* know where it was. My mom hid it well."

The truck stopped, and Matti rested her hammer on her shoulder.

"Why don't you wait in the car?" Val told her, giving her belly a significant look. "In case this turns into more than a chat?"

Matti rested a hand on her abdomen. "I won't jump into a fray, but I'm not hiding. My doctor said I can do low-impact exercise right up to the birth."

"You don't think brawling with shifters counts as *high*-impact?"

"Maybe for them." Matti patted her hammer.

Tigris stepped out of the truck, a rifle in hand, and he gave Val an unfriendly stare. She might not have recognized him, except by type, but he appeared to know the Ruin Bringer. He looked more briefly at Matti and Willard before turning his amber eyes on Arwen. The other four shifters remained in the truck bed, but they could vault out at any moment.

"She's kind of hot for a dark-elf mongrel," one whispered, openly checking out Arwen.

"Sexy nightie," another said with a snicker.

Arwen blushed, wishing she'd taken the time to put on a regular shirt. The nightie wasn't sheer, but it was more revealing than her typical clothes, and the wide neckline had fallen off her shoulder again. She shoved it into place and drew an arrow. She didn't, however, nock it. The shifters hadn't lifted their weapons yet, and it was probably bad form to threaten one's employer.

"Not as hot as the tall one. I'd do her in a second."

"You'd do the Ruin Bringer? Are you suicidal?"

"I could take her."

"She's mated to a dragon."

"I don't mind if he watches."

"He'd flambé you, dumbass."

"You find that half-dragon yet?" Tigris asked Arwen, ignoring the commentary from the truck bed. "He destroyed one of my bars last night. *Another* one."

"What did you do to piss him off?" Matti asked.

"Nobody's talking to you, fatty," one of the shifters in the truck said.

"Fatty?" Indignation flared in Matti's eyes, and she lifted her hammer to throw it.

Willard stepped closer to her and raised a hand. "Let's not start the day out with vigilante justice."

"I spotted the half-dragon," Arwen told Tigris, "but wasn't able to tag him."

"Why not?"

"He levitated my weapons away from me." Actually, he'd levitated them to the ground three feet from her, but she hadn't had the chutzpah—or maybe the stupidity—to grab them and shoot. "I don't know if you were aware, but he inherited some dragon power."

"We guessed," Tigris said grimly.

"He's got a *lot* of dragon power." Hand still on her hammer, Matti smirked at them. "You should challenge him to a duel. He'd like that."

"I don't want to duel him. I want him tagged and captured.

You, human soldier." Tigris pointed at Willard. "Do you not send your assassins after criminals when they appear here?"

"It's *Colonel* Willard, and I'll look into the half-dragon. And also your clan."

"Our *clan* has done nothing wrong. We are respectable businessmen in the area, and some of my brothers work for the county sheriff's department."

"We'll see," Willard said.

Tigris stepped closer to Arwen, towering over her. She made herself stand her ground and raise her chin, though she envisioned how she would spring back and lift her bow if he tried to grab her.

"We have a deal," Tigris said softly, the words for her alone.

Val, gun in hand, stood ready to come to Arwen's aid.

"I know you need that money," he added without looking at Val.

Arwen clenched her jaw.

"It would be a shame if anything happened to your farm—or your father."

He hadn't spoken loudly enough for a normal human to hear, but Val's half-elven blood made her ears sharp. She said, "If anything happens to either of them, we'll hunt you down, flay you, and stretch your fur hides out in front of our fireplaces."

"The Ruin Bringer only hunts down criminals," Tigris said without looking away from Arwen. "And we are not that. As you will find out, we are respectable members of the community and break no human laws. *We* are the victims here."

"Respectable members of the community don't threaten people's families and farms," Willard said.

"You defend a mongrel dark elf? With that blood, she must have committed many, *many* more crimes than any of our kind." Tigris stepped back, pointing a finger at Arwen. "Dark elves cannot help themselves. They crave the souls of those weaker than they. The demons they worship like gods require such sacrifices."

Arwen started to object, but if he believed she was dangerous, maybe he would be less likely to mess with her—and her father.

"You should leave before I deem you my next sacrifice," she told him.

"We are not weak or easily cowed, mongrel. Don't forget our deal. I've already set aside money for your payment, and maybe I'll even throw in a bonus. Enough to take care of the taxes on your farm for years to come." After giving her an icy smile, Tigris turned his back on them and climbed into his truck.

As the shifters departed, Matti flexed her arm, her hammer still in hand. "I'm disappointed. I was hoping for some low-impact exercise."

"Me too." Val looked at Willard. If her boss hadn't been here, would she have attacked them?

"You tell them the details of your tax situation, Forester?" Willard asked.

"No."

"Their knowledge is disconcerting then."

"Everything about this situation is disconcerting."

13

WHILE SHE WAITED FOR HER FATHER TO RETURN FROM THE FARMERS market, Arwen harvested the white asparagus from the shady ditches where it grew. She lamented that she hadn't woken early enough to gather some for him to take with him, but one of them would go again the next day. Probably. With the shifters growing more threatening, Arwen was tempted to reiterate her suggestion that her father hang out somewhere else for a while.

The sound of a vehicle arriving made her grab her bow and head for the driveway. What now?

Matti had said she would come get her and take her to the sanctuary, but that wasn't supposed to be until later. Willard had wanted to go back and research the building *and* the shifters before anyone took action against them—or did their bidding. Not that Arwen wanted to do that anymore, not after Tigris kept threatening her. If not for the money situation, she never would have agreed to his proposition originally.

"Money really is the root of all evil," she muttered. "Or maybe it's the fact that we need it to get by."

Amber's hatchback rolled into view, and Arwen set her weapons aside.

After parking, Amber stuck her head out the window. "Are those *bees*?"

She peered at the wooden hives in the field of medicinal plants near the driveway. By night, the bees weren't that noticeable. This morning, they were flitting from flower to flower, buzzing loudly enough to be audible once the engine was off.

"Yes. They help improve the crops, and I harvest some of their honey to sell. I plant a lot of their favorite forage to encourage their good health. Right now, they're enjoying the hawthorns and hollies." Arwen waved to the May-flowering shrubs to one side of the house. "They're doing wonderful work with the raspberries and currant bushes too. My black-currant jam is a favorite. Even the bees like it. Sometimes, in seasons with lower nectar levels, I'll leave jam out for them."

Amber scrunched her forehead. "So, the answer to my question is, *yes,* those are bees."

"Yes." Arwen shrugged. "I thought you might be interested in them. Did you know that an established hive can provide up to a hundred pounds of harvestable honey? Of course, I don't take that much. You have to leave them plenty to get through the winter. Bees don't hibernate. When it gets cold, they hunker down in a cluster and vibrate their bodies and wings to create warmth to keep the queen warm."

"What should I ask about if I *don't* want an encyclopedia's worth of information on insects?"

Arwen hesitated. "I don't have much knowledge on fashion, sports, or anything found on a television or computer screen."

"Well, I'm not asking you about fashion." Amber climbed out of the car. "And I came to give *you* information. Didn't you get my email? I sent it hours ago, but you didn't answer." She raised her eyebrows frankly at this great failing.

"Sorry. I've had some visitors, and then I was harvesting the asparagus."

"Do you pickle that too?"

"Not the white and purple—those sell well fresh—but I do have a recipe I use on the green. You're welcome to try some the next time I make a batch."

"Hm, maybe. Or I could try some more of the cherries. You know, if you have too many."

Arwen smiled, remembering Val's description of Amber's antics with the jar.

"Anyway, about the building," Amber said. "It's been occupied by that insurance company forever, but it recently changed its hours to *by appointment only*. When I called to make an appointment, they said the boss was out of the office and hung up on me. Arwen, that's weird. Insurance agencies want your money. Trust me. They are for-profit businesses. *Very* for-profit."

Though Arwen didn't know if her teenage assistant was worldly enough to know all about insurance agencies, that did sound like a true statement.

"Something fishy is going on, but get this. They're hiring. A secretary. It's not on any of the big job sites, but I found it on this little board that Val mentioned once—she's gotten gigs there before. It's where you look if you want to hire someone with magical blood—and magical abilities. Willard probably knows all about it, but I don't know if *she* would have thought to look up the insurance company there." Amber looked smug until a bee flew past. She leaped back, eyes wide, as if it had meant to sting her.

"They're very placid," Arwen assured her.

"I'm not that into flying bugs of any kind. What do you think of my plan?"

"Your plan?"

"You should try to get the company to hire you. *You* have magical blood. Once you're whoever's secretary, you could snoop around and figure out what's *really* going on inside that building. It would be perfect."

A job as a secretary? In an *office*? An office full of *people*? Arwen struggled to tamp down the panic threatening to swallow her.

"I'm sure I don't have the right kind of magical blood," she said as calmly as she could. "Besides, there were security cameras, so someone must have seen me walking across the lawn before the tanks came out. They would recognize me."

"Whoever monitors the security cameras isn't the person in charge of HR. *Trust* me."

Arwen scratched her jaw, noting that Amber said that a lot.

"Besides, you'd have to change up your style for a job interview. You wouldn't look the same *at all*." Amber curled a lip at Arwen's *Davy Crockett* attire.

At least she wasn't wearing the nightie anymore.

"I can help you out," Amber promised. "I can create a résumé to send in for you too. Guess I'd have to put my phone number on it since you don't have one. Or get some burner number online. But seriously, Arwen, don't you think you should remedy your lack of a phone?" Without waiting for an answer, Amber continued outlining her plan. "Anyway, when they call, I can pretend to be you. We should get a résumé in right away if you want to be considered and invited in for an interview. Once you're hired, you can snoop. Maybe you can even snoop during the interview. That might result in you *not* being hired, but you're probably okay with that. What skills do you have? Secretarial skills, not tracking. Can you type? How many words per minute?"

"I... words?"

"Never mind. Maybe they have dictation software. I'll set everything up."

"Maybe you should apply," Arwen said with a smile, suspecting Amber would be less lost when it came to doing office work. Arwen could count on one hand the number of times in her life that she'd been in an office. But as soon as Amber adopted a thoughtful expression, Arwen shook her head. She couldn't endanger Val's daughter. "Never mind. If I can't find Starblade and learn about the building and the dark elves from him, I'll attempt your ruse."

"We need to get things rolling *now* if you want the option to be invited in. I'll send your résumé today. After I create it. Don't worry. I'm including this in with my ten percent. I am going to exceed your expectations and prove myself a valuable partner in your tracking endeavors." Amber gestured magnanimously. "And if there are *more* tracking endeavors down the road that require research and a driver, then you might want to work with me again, right?"

"Of course." Arwen tried to smile instead of grimace, but she already had doubts about doing that shifter's bidding. If Willard found out Tigris and his cronies were bad guys, Arwen definitely couldn't do it.

Feeling guilty, she considered voicing the possibility that the gig wouldn't be completed and there wouldn't be pay, but getting invited into that building *could* be valuable. Not only did she owe the gnome Imoshaun a favor, but, as she'd been thinking, if dark elves were hurting people, she would feel obligated to help stop that.

"Excellent. I need speakers for my car. So badly. I suppose you don't have makeup or professional clothing?" Amber looked dubiously through the window of the manufactured home. "Is that a gun rack? And... a moose head?"

"It was a thirteen-point elk, actually. My father and I got him together on my first big hunt, and we enjoyed the meat for months. He doesn't usually taxidermy the animals he kills, but he did that one since it had meaning to us. And I learned how to make an onion elk-roast stroganoff that's to die for."

Amber rested a hand on her car for support, a stricken expression twisting her face.

Arwen thought about pointing out that her father had originally taught her to track so that she could hunt game and be self-sufficient, but maybe Amber was a vegetarian and found such activities distressing. Arwen would stick to giving her gifts she tracked down on fruit trees.

"Never mind on the clothing. I'll pick some out for you. What are you? About a size four?" Amber waved her hands in the air, making measurements of a sort. "I'll bring my makeup. And I'll find clothes. I don't suppose you have a credit card I could use to go shopping?"

"I don't have a credit card at all."

"Wow, do you ever need my help." Amber shook her head. "You're super lucky you found me."

"Of that I'm certain."

"I'll update you when I hear back about the job." After a last stricken look through the window at the elk head, Amber opened the car door. "Don't forget to check your email."

"Wait." Arwen held up a hand, then jogged inside. She grabbed a couple of cans of her maple and bourbon roasted peanuts, another jar of the cherries, and one of strawberry jalapeño jam. That was another favorite at the market, adored by those who enjoyed a spicy kick with their sweet preserves. Amber seemed the type for such things. "Here."

This time, Amber didn't balk at taking the items, and her eyes lit up at the cherries, in particular.

"I hope you enjoy them." Arwen also hoped she could find a way to pay the girl for her time. With more than canned goods.

After giving a thumbs-up, Amber drove off, managing not to run over anything this time. She was improving.

14

ARWEN HAD NEVER BEEN ON A MOTORCYCLE AND DEFINITELY NEVER on a Harley behind a pregnant half-dwarf with a tendency to speed. Though Matti kept catching herself and slowing down, maybe remembering her *delicate state*, as Val had put it.

Not wanting to be judgmental, Arwen didn't ask if one was supposed to ride a motorcycle while pregnant. But maybe Matti sensed the question—or could read minds—because she addressed it.

I scrounged my funds, and a bank loan, to buy a new truck for the business, Matti said telepathically after they took the Arlington exit and slowed down, heading east. The roar of the Harley made regular conversation difficult. *But the truck flattens a lot more foliage when you drive it off-road up to the sanctuary. I didn't use to care about such things, but then I married an elf. He has acerbic comments about foliage-flattening. Trucks also tend to scare the goblins, on account of the hunters who used to drive through these forests, shooting at them. That's why my mom and I enchanted everything, to make it hard for assholes like that to find them and bother them.*

Do the hunters also go after half-dragons?

They'd be suicidal to do that, but Starblade should also be lying low. The whole point of telling him about this place was to help him disappear. You see, he staged his death so the dragons, elves, and dwarves would stop hunting for him. He wouldn't want the word to get out that he's alive and hiding out on Earth. He shouldn't. *That's why him popping up in Bellevue and destroying things doesn't make sense.*

Has Colonel Willard learned anything about the building or the shifters yet? Arwen debated if she should mention the job opening that Amber had dug up and was in the process of applying for on Arwen's behalf.

I only got a quick update from Val, but it sounds like the shifters— led by Tigris—haven't committed any crimes that Willard's people know of, and they run legitimate businesses. They serve the magical community and also regular humans who like such foods as raw steaks and bone-in haunches of meat. The werewolves at Wolf Winery said they're capitalistic money-grubbing furry dicks, but they also vouched for them. Oh, and Tigris's two cousins do work for the sheriff's department.

Meaning I would have gotten in trouble if I'd clubbed him in front of Willard?

I don't know about you, since he was trespassing on your property, but I definitely would have. Matti shook her head. *Sometimes, it's annoyingly constraining being employed by the authorities.*

Arwen sighed. She would have preferred it if the shifters had been criminals. This didn't bode well for Starblade being innocent.

Matti slowed the motorcycle down, turned off the paved street, and headed up a gravel road that soon turned to dirt. It climbed, switchbacking through a logging area. Some spots had been clearcut in recent years and others were jammed with Douglas fir, the trees about ten years old. The permaculturist in Arwen always cringed at seeing mono plantings, whether on a farm or in a forest.

Seemingly at random, Matti veered off between the trees,

weaving carefully over roots and around ferns. Now and then, Arwen thought she sensed a goblin in the woods nearby, but their auras disappeared as soon as she detected them. A foraging or scouting team operating outside their protected sanctuary?

They entered an area of older and more natural growth. Arwen didn't sense any magic ahead of them, but between one eye blink and the next, that changed. Abruptly, she detected dozens and dozens of goblins. An entire village. There were magical items —no, magical *dwellings*—as well. Attractive cedar-shingled tiny houses on wheels with durable metal roofs.

A few cook fires burned in pits near the homes, but Matti didn't head toward them. She waved to a couple of goblins, maybe communicating with them telepathically, then pointed to the north. After skirting the village, she drove slowly onto a path that meandered around bushes and up a slope.

We're heading to what used to be the dark-elf priest's laboratory, she said. *Did you ever come out here?*

No. It was distressing enough that he came to see—to proposition— me. Arwen had already told Matti that story.

I'll bet. The last I saw this place, our half-dragon had taken it over and grown elfy stuff all over the dead ground and stumps and bones.

Elfy stuff?

Trees, green things. Matti waved a hand. *Nature. It looked* much better.

Is it your human blood that makes you appreciate nature? Or has being married to an elf prompted that?

Some of both, I suppose. I always liked nature from an artistic point of view, and I've now learned to appreciate elven repair vines and other handy things created with their magic. Matti glanced back as the motorcycle crested the hill. *Is it* your *human half that makes you like nature and being out in it?*

It must be. Dark elves aren't known for that. It could also be that I was so stubbornly determined to be nothing like my moth-

er's people that I embraced anything that was the opposite. Arwen didn't think that was *all* that had drawn her to the forests and being outside in them though. Since she and her father had escaped the dark elves, she'd felt drawn to and comforted by the wilds. It had been a balm for the nightmares that plagued her—and the *day*-mares too. The daylight filling the forests had seemed to promise that no dark elves would approach her, their eyes too sensitive for such environments.

Matti stopped the motorcycle and turned off the engine. She pointed across a tree- and fern-filled gully toward a higher hill on the far side. A tingle of magic emanated from the ground all around the top of it. Elven magic.

"It looks like he's done more than grow trees and ferns in the six months since I was last here," Matti said aloud. "Is that a window?"

Frowning, Arwen looked left and right for sign of a dwelling. Usually, her eyes were sharp, and she picked things out of a forest quickly, but she couldn't see anything that would qualify as a *window*.

"Where?"

"At the center of all the magic." Matti pointed at the hill.

"I... don't see anything."

"No? Oh, there's a camouflaging enchantment mixed in. A localized one, not the one my mother applied to cover the whole area. I wonder why I can see through it. Maybe Starblade decided he didn't need to hide his home from me—or figured it wouldn't work anyway since I already knew where it was."

Arwen shifted on the seat at the reminder that Matti was something of an ally to him. Arwen had her bow as well as the arrowheads crafted to tranquilize and tag. Just in case. She'd told Matti she wouldn't attack Starblade, but if he got perturbed when she asked him about the crimes, she *would* defend herself.

"I don't know if this will work, but..." Matti turned enough to rest a hand on Arwen's arm.

A little tingle of magic came from her fingers.

The gully remained the same, but the hill changed, with gaps visible in the undergrowth. Calling them *windows* seemed generous. The holes, with magic applied to keep out the rain, might qualify as skylights. If there was a cave underneath them, Arwen couldn't tell. She didn't see a door.

"You used to go in from the top." Matti waved for Arwen to slide off the motorcycle, then climbed off after her. "I don't know if that's still the case. There was a boulder pile up there and a trapdoor that led into a chamber—the priest's laboratory."

Arwen frowned at the idea of visiting a dark-elf laboratory. Memories of what one found in such places flitted through her mind: magical artifacts to alter and torment, deadly potions, devices for experimentation on prisoners....

"Let's see if he's home," Matti said. "I don't sense Starblade, but that doesn't mean much."

"No." Arwen again thought of how close he'd flown to her before she'd known he was there.

"Do you know what you're going to ask him?"

"I want to know how he's tied in with the dark elves, that building, and the shifters, but he wasn't forthright with me before. Maybe *you* could ask him."

"He's not overly forthright with me either. He'd be more likely to respond to Varlesh, I think, though he's bitter toward elves too. He's pretty bitter toward everyone."

"If his people created him and now don't want him, that's understandable." In a sense, that had happened to Arwen as well, but her mother *had* wanted her for some reason. Arwen had been the one—Arwen and her father—who hadn't wanted to stick around and find out what exactly.

A little shiver went through her as she imagined running into her mother after all these years. And being captured and dragged back into a dark-elf subterranean complex and forced to swear allegiance to demons.

They climbed down the gully and up the other side, pausing to peer through one of the skylights. The magical barriers over them were translucent, but they somehow obscured what was on the other side.

A ring of boulders rested on top of the hill, too precisely placed to have occurred naturally. A stone bench sat in the middle. Its position offered a beautiful view of the surrounding forest and, through a gap in the trees, the distant snow-capped Cascade Mountains.

"Think he sits up here to enjoy his coffee?" Matti turned a circle. Looking for the trapdoor she'd mentioned?

"Do elves like coffee?"

Arwen tried to imagine an espresso machine set up on the floor of a cave. It was hard even imagining an *elf* on the floor of a cave. From what she'd read, they built their homes in trees and were uncomfortable with earth over their heads. But since Starblade was half-dragon, maybe he liked subterranean dwellings.

"Coffee plants don't grow on their world, but I've gotten Varlesh addicted. Oh, he assures me he's *not* addicted, since an assassin, even a former assassin, would never allow his body to become reliant on a drug, but he's down there first thing every morning, guzzling from my coffee maker. Excuse me, the fancy Barista Express that he insisted we get after realizing the drinks from the Coffee Dragon packed more punch than what came out of my ten-year-old machine."

Arwen had heard of but never visited the shop that Val jointly owned with a couple of other people with magical blood. It was in the heart of Fremont, a part of Seattle that had *far* too many people per square mile for Arwen's taste. Further, she'd heard the coffee shop thrived, serving hordes of goblins, orcs, ogres, and shifters. That was the kind of dreadful overcrowded place that she avoided.

"We also have to pony up for the special blends custom-roasted for the Coffee Dragon." Matti prodded at the ground with the toe of her shoe. "Folgers isn't acceptable to elves. Let me warn you that if you ever get romantically involved with one of their kind, they're extremely snobby. About everything."

"You didn't find that a detractor in a mate?"

"Well, have you *seen* Varlesh?" Matti smiled like a besotted teenager. "Even if he wasn't drop-dead gorgeous, he stands at my side in battle, brings me exotic cheeses from around the Cosmic Realms, and didn't kill my mother even though my aunt hired him to."

Arwen's jaw dropped. She hadn't heard all the details of *that*.

"Those are good qualities in a man. I can put up with some snobbery." Matti cupped a hand around her mouth and raised her voice. "Hello? Anyone home?" She repeated the question telepathically, broadcasting the mental words in all directions.

Nobody answered.

"Maybe he's moved closer to the city to more easily destroy restaurants, bars, and pummel people's cars," Arwen said.

"Could be." Matti sat on the bench and yawned. "I get tired more easily these days. I'm carrying a lot of extra weight around." She looked at her hammer. "No, I'm not talking about you. It's always an honor to carry *your* weight."

Arwen arched her eyebrows. "Does your hammer speak to you?"

"Yeah, telepathically. It's sapient. And sarcastic." Matti shrugged. "My mom made it."

Arwen scratched her jaw. Since she'd never met Matti's dwarven mother, she didn't know if that explained sarcasm from a weapon or not.

"Your bow doesn't talk to you?"

"No. It's not nearly as powerful as your hammer." Arwen's senses told her that. She'd always found the weapon more than adequate, especially with the magical arrows she'd been able to acquire over the years, and she was glad to have the bow.

"My mother could probably spruce it up if you want it to have more capabilities."

"Like... sarcasm?"

"Definitely sarcasm. That's an elite power that I'd be bereft without."

A soft drizzle began falling, dampening their cheeks. Matti stood and tried calling telepathically again. Once more, they didn't receive a response.

"Guess this was a big waste of time." Matti waved back to her motorcycle. "Ready to go?"

Arwen hesitated, reluctant to leave without gaining the information she sought. She crouched and touched the ground, letting a trickle of her power flow into it, asking the nearby trees if they'd seen Starblade.

Sometimes, such magic could help her find those she tracked, whether prints were visible or not, but she met resistance. The earth grew closed and unresponsive. Unwilling to reveal its secrets. Protective. Maybe that made sense if Starblade had enchanted this place.

"Be careful." Matti must have detected what she was doing. "He might have some defenses that'll zap you."

"I suppose. Go ahead and go back. I'll wait here." Arwen waved at the bench.

"If he doesn't come, you'll have a long walk home. Assuming you're not planning to hitchhike on I-5. I wouldn't recommend that. You've got the kind of cute-and-innocent face that makes creeps want to prey on you."

Arwen could handle run-of-the-mill creeps, but she wouldn't hitchhike regardless. The thought of being packed into a car with one or more strangers and not being able to escape before it reached its destination... She shuddered. "I'm used to long walks. I like them."

"If you say so. If you're not home in three days, I'll come back to look for you. Or at least send some leftover barbecue this way."

"Thank you." Arwen smiled. "I *did* appreciate the barbecue you shared with me last fall."

"Food is the best way to befriend people."

"Possibly true, but I haven't thus far had any luck winning Starblade's comradery with offerings of food."

"Did you try meat? Dragons are way into meat."

"I told him about a barbecue restaurant, but I gave him pickled cherries."

"Uh, I couldn't imagine Zavryd eating that."

"There's coffee and sugar in the brine."

"Oh, well, coffee. Maybe Starblade's elf side will dig them then. As long as you didn't use Folgers." Matti winked and waved, then ambled toward her motorcycle.

The sun sank below the horizon as Arwen walked around the ring of boulders, investigating everything and prodding the ground with the tip of her bow. She was about to expand her search to the slopes of the hill when she noticed a small hole beside one of the rock legs of the bench. When she slid her bow tip inside, a tingle of magic ran up it, flowing into her hand and up her arm. The skin around her tattoo seemed to vibrate. An unpleasant sensation.

A warning? The magic hadn't hurt, but it was forbidding enough that she had no problem imagining it intensifying and knocking her on her ass—or across the gully.

Arwen knelt, wishing she had a light to shine into the hole, then eased one of her arrowheads into it. It just fit, but the warning tingle ran up it to her again, centering on her tattoo. Somehow, the defensive magic not only conveyed that dark elves weren't welcome but this was a keyhole and she wasn't using the right key.

"Maybe something enchanted with elven magic?" She drew one of her favorite arrows, one of the first she'd acquired years earlier. "This is called the Heartseeker in Elven, I understand. A door seeker might be more useful, but we'll try it."

Bracing herself for backlash, Arwen slid the arrowhead into the hole. It sank deep, and a thrum of energy different from the irritated buzzes ran up her arm. Yellow light flashed in the hole, and a rumble and a creak came from beside the bench.

Not sure if this was an invitation to come in or she'd triggered the security system, Arwen sprang to her feet with her bow ready. Fortunately, no tanks or other magical constructs appeared. A trapdoor swung downward, revealing a square hole with a gentle green glow seeping out.

Arwen crept forward to peer inside. Stairs carved from the earth descended, its railing made from wood and wound with vines sprouting green leaves. Plants shouldn't have been able to survive underground without sunlight, but magic emanated from them—from everything—and the air smelled of loam and growing vegetation, like a greenhouse.

"Guess this is the entrance." Arwen looked in the direction Matti had gone, but she and her motorcycle had disappeared. "Time to see if I'm allowed in without an escort—or at all."

After taking a bracing breath, Arwen headed down the stairs.

15

Arwen left Heartseeker in the keyhole, afraid the door would swing shut and trap her inside if she removed it. After drawing another arrow, she descended the earthen stairs with her bow ready.

Even though Starblade hadn't attacked her during any of their meetings, he *had* threatened her, and he might not appreciate her entering his home uninvited. Maybe she should have waited outside for him to return, but the answers she sought—the answers he hadn't been willing to give—might be inside.

At the bottom of the steps lay a flagstone floor with moss growing in the gaps. Chairs, a table, and what might have been a wardrobe or pantry occupied the chamber, the furnishings made from a mixture of wood and foliage, all magical to her senses. More than one piece appeared to be growing up from the flagstone floor, the legs like roots that anchored into the ground. A washbasin was fastened to a wooden slab mounted to one rock wall with a few plates stacked on open shelves above it.

She spotted the jar of pickled cherries on the slab, and

curiosity prompted her to investigate. Had he tried them? Or had he been too certain they would be poisoned?

The lid was loosened, and a few had been taken out. He must not have been as smitten with them as Amber. Too bad. It would be nice if one could win the allegiance of a half-dragon with food.

A few trays of soil and straw held mushrooms, though Arwen didn't recognize the species. Were the gills glowing a faint orange, or was that her imagination? The stalks were thin and bent, as if holding up the cap was almost too much for them. She had no idea if Starblade was growing the mushrooms for food or medicine—he *had* been interested in truffles, after all—but they didn't appear to be doing well.

"Might need a better substrate," she murmured.

An archway supported by gnarled wood led down a tunnel to a smaller room where a platform bed hung from vines that grew down from the dirt ceiling. Shelves dug from the walls held numerous books, some with titles in languages she couldn't read, but many were in English. *The History of the Ancient World, Napoleon the Great, The History of the Peloponnesian War, The Art of War, The Guns of August.*

"No wonder he doesn't know anything about sports and music if those are his sources on humanity."

A couple of titles didn't fit into the war category with the rest: *Stronger than a Hundred Men: A History of the Vertical Water Wheel* and *A History of Engineering in Classical and Medieval Times.* Arwen had no idea if the tomes represented interests for him or were what he'd found on the discount table at a secondhand bookstore.

Another chamber off the bedroom was surprisingly spacious with mats scattered over the flagstones and what might have been gym equipment along one wall. Different-sized bags filled with sand or something similar had handles and were perhaps the equivalent of kettlebells. A rack held practice swords, shields, and staffs. On the far wall, a doorway led to another bedroom.

Arwen blinked. She had assumed Starblade lived here alone. Maybe because Matti had mentioned only him, not an encampment of half-dragons. Or did Starblade have a lover? No, that probably wasn't it. If he did, they would sleep together, wouldn't they?

She admitted most of her knowledge about intimacy came from books, and she'd never invited a man to stay at her home, nor had any invited her to stay at theirs. Those times she'd been propositioned, it had always been by someone who wanted a fling rather than a relationship. She assumed such things didn't involve people living together.

A tunnel to one side of the exercise chamber descended deeper into the hill. Surprised by how large the place was, Arwen stepped into it to continue her investigation.

Inside, the smell of vegetation grew stronger. Not mold or mildew, as one might expect in a dark environment, but pleasant greenhouse scents. She spotted berries growing from one species of leafy vine covering the wall.

A couple of the skylights they'd seen from above broke up the earthen ceiling. By day, they would allow sunlight in, but she couldn't imagine it would be sufficient to grow plants.

"Magic," she whispered, in awe of all Starblade could do with it. She'd struggled for years to figure out how to use her limited power to make things thrive on the farm. There was no way she could coerce anything to sprout in a cave.

Warmth wafted up from below, the air growing humid with a new scent mixing in. Eucalyptus? Something similar? The gurgle of water also reached her ears.

Maybe she'd left the bounds of Starblade's home without realizing it and was heading into a natural grotto. But his vines still grew along the walls, and magic emanated from everything, so he had to have claimed this area. Maybe he'd even created it along with everything else. Thus far, Arwen had seen nothing of the dark-elf laboratory Matti had said was once here.

The tunnel ended in a chamber with a high ceiling and a pool with steam wafting from it. There were even bubbles here and there, making her think of hot tubs with jets, though this was nothing so vigorous. The eucalyptus scent was stronger in the chamber, and she sensed magic mingled with it. Did it have soothing properties?

The flagstones created something like a pool deck, and there were two lounge chairs made from wood and vines, the same as the other furniture.

"Definitely more than one person living here." Arwen picked up a towel draped over one chair.

It was dry, so maybe it had been a while since Starblade had been here. Underneath where the towel had lain, a green loincloth hung, and she flushed in embarrassment. She hadn't chanced across many pairs of men's underwear in her life.

She doubted she would find the answers she sought here; all she was doing was snooping and invading his space. She hurried to drape the towel back over the loincloth, then turned to leave.

But she couldn't resist kneeling to stick a finger into the water. It was the perfect temperature for a soak, and that eucalyptus scent wreathed her face, so pleasant that she had the urge to shuck off her clothing and slip into the water so it could caress her bare flesh.

"Not a good idea." Arwen knelt back, blushing at the idea of getting naked in a stranger's home. A stranger who didn't even like her.

Abruptly, she sensed Starblade. And he was close.

With his powerful aura, she should have detected him from miles away, but he must have been camouflaging himself. He already stood on the hilltop, maybe staring at his door and wondering why it was open to the night. And, damn, she'd left her arrow in the hole. She might as well have written a sign announcing that she was inside snooping around.

Arwen lurched to her feet and jogged toward the tunnel, doubting there was a back way out and sure he already sensed her anyway. At the least, she would hurry up to a less private section of the home, one not decorated with loincloths. Maybe that would seem less intrusive.

But as soon as she stepped into the tunnel leading from the pool, some of the vines growing along the wall detached and barred the way. Though startled, she drew her foraging knife. Would a mundane blade cut through a magical elven vine? She lifted the knife but hesitated. This was his home. If she started hacking his plants to pieces, he wouldn't be pleased.

Instead, she ducked and lifted her knee, trying to slip between the vines. As if intelligent, they shifted to block her. Not only that but one wrapped around her wrist, immobilizing her arm. Before she could pull away or reconsider trying to cut the vines, another gripped her ankle. Yet another wrapped around her bow.

"Not *that*." Arwen yanked on it even as she tried to wriggle free herself.

As she twisted and pulled, her arrow fell free, and the vines tightened around her. One slipped around her waist. Tiny pricks assailed her everywhere they touched bare skin. What the hell were those?

Panic set in, and she caught herself thrashing, claustrophobia taking over her rational mind. Her shirt came off her shoulder, and she couldn't lift a hand enough to push it back into place. That made her pause, afraid she would end up half-naked when Starblade showed up.

Caught like a fly in a spiderweb, she used her senses to check on Starblade's location. He must have shifted into his elven form, because he was descending, heading in her direction.

"Damn it."

16

HAD THE SMALL FRUITS BEEN POISONED, STARBLADE'S TELEPATHIC voice spoke into Arwen's mind as she stood, entrapped by his vines, *I would have assumed you'd come to take advantage of me, weakened and dying from their taint, so you could sacrifice me to your demons.*

That's my mother's religion and her *demons, not mine, and that's not why I came.* Arwen wished Matti had stuck around and could have vouched for her. Why hadn't Arwen thought to look for keyholes *before* she'd left?

The green glow emanating from the earthen walls shifted from nightlight dim to daylight bright, so Arwen had no trouble seeing Starblade walk into view. His sword wasn't in hand—yet—but maybe that was because his vines held her fast. He knew she wasn't a threat.

For some reason, he gripped his side, his jaw tight. With anger, she thought at first, but then spotted blood on his hand and realized he'd been wounded.

"Are you okay?"

What foe had been strong enough to harm him?

"I would be better if the way to my healing grotto weren't blocked." Starblade eyed her bow, the arrow on the ground at her feet, and her bare shoulder.

Arwen flushed, glad *more* of her shirt hadn't jerked free. Oh, hell, part of her midriff was on display too. She was lucky the things weren't suffocating or completely crushing her, like boa constrictors.

"These are *your* vines," she said, flustered.

"Yes, but your presence triggered them." Starblade raised his eyebrows, glancing at her shoulder again. "Were you armed with fewer weapons, I would wonder if you sought me for a sexual encounter."

"Of course not. I'm not even— you're not—" What did she want to say? That he wasn't her type? Was that even true? She had no idea. He was handsome and powerful and alluring, so she suspected he was *most* women's type. But that certainly wasn't why she'd come.

His eyebrows climbed higher.

"Your trapdoor opened and let me in," she settled on. "It seemed like an invitation to explore."

"Interesting. That is typical behavior for uninvited guests on this world?"

"I was looking for you because I need to talk. I want to know..." Arwen stopped herself from finishing with *if you're a criminal.* He'd already told her he wasn't. "I want to know what's going on with the dark elves, shifters, and that building, and I think you know. I understand that you don't owe me anything and are predisposed to dislike me because of my blood, but I'm willing to barter for information." She flexed against the vines. "Also to be released from your prison."

Starblade considered her for a long, silent moment, the vines not shifting in the least, though blood trickled through his fingers.

That wound was fresh. Didn't he want to move his security plants aside and hurry into his *grotto* to heal himself?

"I desire more of your fruits," he finally said.

"In exchange for information?"

He smiled faintly. "In exchange for freeing you. Usually, I let the vines eat trespassers."

"You're lying. Elven magic isn't cannibalistic. I've read all about it."

Admittedly, only in the *one* book, but elven grimoires were hard to come by on Earth.

"Indeed?" The glint in his eyes suggested he might have caught that thought—maybe her tattoo couldn't protect her from mind reading in his magical abode. "Are you as well versed in *dragon* magic?"

"No," she had to admit. "I have no problem giving you more of my food. I even brought some along in the pack by the bench up there."

"I know." The smile returned.

"How? You snooped inside it?"

"As you were snooping inside my home." His gaze shifted past her shoulder.

Her cheeks heated even further as she worried he would know she'd found his underwear. Not that it mattered, but it seemed far more intimate an invasion than peeking in a bag for pickled sweets.

"What will you want in exchange for the information I need?" Arwen asked to distract him from reading her mind or whatever he was contemplating.

"We'll see." Starblade stepped closer.

Arwen tensed, but the vines loosened, slowly releasing her from their grip and resuming their position along the walls. When the one around her waist let go, her weight returned fully to her legs, but they were surprisingly weak. Her knees buckled, and she flailed, almost dropping her bow as she sought the support of the wall.

Starblade had moved close enough to catch her by the arm and keep her upright, his powerful aura electric in the air around her. The energy sent a weird little zing through her, and she grew aware of the heat of his hand through her sleeve, the heat of his whole body.

"The security vines seep a sedative into their prisoner's skin. Since you weren't held for long, it should wear off soon, but if you'd come with the intent to harm me, I would have let them keep you entangled for longer." His violet eyes bored into hers. "I trust you know how unpleasant it is to be tranquilized and helpless before an enemy."

Her mouth went dry. He knew about the tranquilizer arrow. And the tagging device too. She was certain. Maybe he knew all about her deal with Tigris.

"You *are* easier to read here," he stated.

Wonderful.

"I don't think it has anything to do with my magic. Perhaps that of the dwarven enchanter. Princess Rodarska, knowing the remains of the priest's laboratory was here, may have sought to nullify dark-elven magic." He looked down at her sleeve.

Since he was supporting her and still gripping his wound— didn't he need to go find some Band-Aids?—Starblade didn't have a hand free. That didn't keep him from using his magic to push up her sleeve, revealing her spider tattoo.

Arwen clenched her jaw. He'd already looked at it once. What more did he want to see?

One of his eyebrows twitched as he met her gaze again. "You say you *don't* worship the demons of your mother's people?"

"No, I do not. My mother forced me to get the tattoo. She forced me to do everything until my father and I escaped when I was seven."

"Did she also *force* you to sacrifice an innocent to the demons at their marking ceremony?" The way he asked the question made her certain he already knew the answer. He might know more about her people's religion than she did.

Memories of that night came to her, the dark tunnel brightened only by fiery braziers, a helpless orc female strapped to a stone slab of a table with the Web Spinner statue leering down at them, the demon it represented watching, demanding the dark elves give her a sacrifice.

"She forced me to do everything then," Arwen whispered around her dry tongue. "I had no choice." Remembering the background he'd shared—and what Tigris had told her—she responded defensively. "Weren't you forced to become a warrior? To kill on behalf of the elves? It's not that different, is it?" It was, and she knew it. What she'd done back then still gave her nightmares, even if her mother's power had guided—forced—her hand.

"We fought capable warriors," Starblade said coldly. "We didn't sacrifice innocent females."

"Maybe your people aren't as much of assholes as mine."

At first, he said nothing, but then he snorted. "The elves are also *assholes*." He said it like it wasn't a familiar term, a reminder that he hadn't been on Earth long. "In their own way."

He pushed her over to the wall so she could lean on it for support, then walked past her toward the pool. Near the chairs, he opened a box that she hadn't noticed before and pulled out two moist green pads. Magical elven healing bandages. She'd read about them but had never seen one.

"What do you want to know?" Starblade glanced over his shoulder before gingerly removing his tunic.

If not for the blood soaking the clothing and smearing his abdomen, she might have admired his lean, muscular physique. She did *notice* it, blood notwithstanding, and decided he had to spend a lot of time in that exercise room training. She also noticed a silver dragon tattoo on his left pectoral. Something he'd chosen? Or had he also been inked by his people? His tattoo was far more exotic and appealing than hers. It also emanated a hint of magic. Elven magic?

"Why are you looking for the dark elves and, uhm, why are you irked with them? Beyond the usual reasons people don't like them." Her gaze fell to four garish slashes in his side, the source of all the blood. His body had to have powerful regenerative abilities, but the wounds still looked painful. And recent. Had his enemies found this sanctuary? "And why are the feline shifters after you? And vice versa?"

"I am not *after* them."

"You ravaged their restaurant. I saw footage."

"When we were targeted by the dark elves, and they then disappeared before I could strike back, I learned of the shifters and that they worked with the law enforcers of this world. Since the dark elves were committing crimes, I thought we might both consider them an enemy and work together. But the reason I'd encountered them in the first place was because they were—they *are*—complicit in the kidnappings. They go where the dark elves cannot, into the light. I do not know if their subservience to them is voluntary or they are compelled—" Starblade touched his temple to indicate magic, "—but I *do* know that the shifters betrayed me."

"So you lashed out at them?"

"I sought to use force to pull the dark elves' location from their minds."

"By throwing them through windows?"

Starblade looked darkly over his shoulder at her. "I did not believe that giving them jars of fruits would be sufficient."

"Pickled meat might work better than pickled cherries on them."

"Neither would sway them if they are, as I believe, being magically compelled. Dark elven power is greater than that of shifters."

"I know they kidnapped a gnomish scientist, but was there someone else?" Arwen glanced at the two chairs.

"The dark elves have taken *many* magical beings with useful talents or blood worth exploiting."

"Including someone close to you?"

He didn't answer right away other than to glower at the pool.

"You lost a friend?" Arwen asked quietly. "Or a lover?"

"My brother in arms, Yendral. The last half-dragon besides myself who survived being attacked by dragons, dwarves, and elves, and having a mountain collapse on us." Starblade scooped some of the water from the pool to clean his wound.

"Do you want help with that? I've had basic first-aid training."

"I do not know how they caught Yendral," he said without responding to her offer. "I do not even know if he is still alive. But I will find out. I am not surprised the dark elves would want to study our kind. Maybe they seek to replicate what the elven scientists did centuries ago and find a way to mingle dragon blood with theirs to create half-dragon dark elves." His voice grew soft as he added, "It would not be the first time. Perhaps they learned of Gemlytha and know it is possible." He didn't expound on who that was.

"Are you sure dark elves are behind everything?" Enough people had brought them up that Arwen was starting to believe it, but she hadn't yet seen proof. Unless the itching of her tattoo counted. "I don't doubt that they could have that interest, but they haven't been seen around here for a couple of years."

"It is they. Now that I know of the building they have commandeered, I have no doubt. Among other types of magic, some of *theirs* is infused into it, especially at the base."

Arwen hadn't detected that, but a half-dragon would have much greater sensitivity for identifying magic than she.

"Had only artifacts crafted by lesser species defended the building, I would be able to tear through their magic and gain entrance, but dark elves have power enhanced and twisted into something alien by the demons they serve. It is difficult to deal with, even, from what I've heard, for full-blooded dragons." Bitterness twisted his lips as he added, "Not that those dragons would speak with me and tell me anything of use. They are too busy wanting me dead."

"Because you're... an abomination?" Arwen remembered the word he'd used and voiced it before she could think better of it.

Another dark look came her way. She should have been more tactful.

"So they say." Starblade laid the two green pads over his wounds, and they stuck of their own accord. "The dragons do not matter right now, other than that the shifters have threatened to tell them that I exist if I don't leave the dark elves alone. They are a nuisance, but my priority is the dark elves. I must get my comrade back. I am not certain who on this world might assist me against them. My studies have not progressed far, and your books say nothing about magical beings."

"A lot of humans are unaware of them or pretend they don't exist. Up until recently, there weren't many on Earth."

"Regardless, I know little of how many dark elves are present and what alliances they claim. Surprisingly, there is dragon magic defending that building as well. I could alert your authorities to the threat, but humans would be insufficient to combat dark elves, especially if the shifters are aligned with them. It's possible more than magical compulsion motivates those felines. The dark elves may also be bribing them with coin to do their bidding." Starblade sneered.

"Some people are motivated by that," Arwen murmured, hating that she was, at least right now. Before the farm had been in jeopardy, she hadn't minded that she didn't have much money.

She'd never believed she *needed* much, but, now, she had to accept that there were times when it was useful.

"*Many* people on this world, it seems." Starblade leveled another cool look at her.

As Arwen groped for a response—could she promise that she wouldn't go through with Tigris's mission now that she understood more?—Starblade removed his boots, trousers, and loincloth. All conscious thought dumped out of her mind, and she caught herself gaping.

It wasn't so much that she hadn't seen naked men before—admittedly, few had been this attractive to look at—as that she was shocked he had undressed in front of her. But if this pool was for healing, she couldn't blame him for wanting to climb right in. And he did exactly that after draping the rest of his clothing on the chair. He slid into the pool and submerged fully for a long moment before rising to stand hip deep, facing her and pushing his damp hair out of his face as water ran down his torso.

Arwen told herself to look away, *definitely* not to stare, but his hard, delineated muscles were captivating. *He* was captivating, and more than her cheeks flushed with heat.

When he opened his eyes to look at her, she managed to jerk her gaze aside.

"When I was flying over the forest where I have collected mushrooms, I sensed you," he said, "and I smelled your blood, the dark-elf running hot in your veins."

"Only *half* hot," Arwen said, her voice oddly raspy. What did that even mean? "I'm much more like my father than my mother, my *human* father."

"You have a strong aura for a half-blood, and it radiates *dark-elven* power."

Arwen couldn't deny it, but she wished she had *elven* blood running through her veins and that her aura radiated magic of the forest and nature. Not... whatever it looked like to him. Something ugly and twisted, she had no doubt.

She didn't want to meet his gaze, and not only because he stood naked in that pool, the water level low enough to reveal more than those bandages and the taut muscles of his abdomen. She didn't want to see the sneer twisting his lips, the disgust in his eyes. She didn't want him to think her unworthy to stand here in his presence.

"I sought you out," Starblade continued, "because I thought you might have information about the dark elves. At the time, I didn't yet know where they were. And I didn't know for certain what they wanted with Yendral. I *still* have only guesses. Do they only need his blood? Or do they intend to sacrifice him?"

"Let me help you," Arwen caught herself saying. She forced herself to look into his eyes. Whatever his expression had been a moment before, it was masked now. "I promised Imoshaun—the kidnapped gnome's mate—that I would help her. I owe her since she gave me a place to hide from those tanks. And... I can help you too. I think we have the same goal."

"*Help* me? When you have already told those shifters that you will track me down for coin?"

"No. I mean, yes. I mean..." Arwen swallowed, nervous and flustered once more. "That was a mistake. I didn't know you at the time."

He snorted. "You do not know me now."

"Well, I've seen you naked."

"That is not *knowing*."

"No. I know. It was a joke."

He'd smiled earlier, but he didn't give any indication now that he felt amusement at her attempt at humor. Maybe it had been a horrible joke. Nobody had ever accused her of being smooth with men. Or anyone. That was why she loved the woods. The trees always offered their support and never judged, merely welcomed her with the soft rustling of breezes stirring their leaves. In the forest, she always felt at home and comfortable.

"Place your food items in my kitchen, and then leave. I have answered your questions." Starblade turned his back to her and sank low into the water, pushing his hands through his hair again.

The dismissal stung.

Why she would have expected anything more when she was the one in the wrong, she didn't know, but she wanted to make amends. If he could read her thoughts here, couldn't he see that?

17

As Arwen lined up jam, hazelnut butter, elderberry honey, and pickled asparagus in the kitchen area, she eyed Starblade's trays of sickly mushrooms and debated ways she might convince him to let her help him. Yes, he'd dismissed her and told her to leave, but she wasn't ready to give up.

Admittedly, she believed he could help *her* as much as she could help him. Oh, she did feel guilty that she'd accepted the tracking gig and wanted to make amends for that. But getting to the bottom of the dark-elf scheme and finding Imoshaun's husband would be more achievable with the aid of a powerful half-dragon. Not to mention dealing with the shifters. Tigris had made it clear that he would take his anger out on her father and the farm if Arwen didn't do his bidding. Getting him and his clan to leave her alone would be easier with an ally—an ally who didn't mind kicking shifter ass.

The last item she removed from her pack was a jar of tea that she made for camping trips and enjoyed herself. As a non-Earth-native, Starblade might not know about tea and how the bags worked. She would explain them. And maybe he would appreciate mushroom-growing tips. His glowing orange fungi needed help.

Nodding to herself, Arwen headed back toward the underground pool.

A few of the vines on the walls undulated as she passed, and she eyed them warily. Had Starblade reset his home-security system? To make sure he wasn't disturbed during his soak?

When she neared the spot where the vines had leaped out at her, she called, "I've left food in your kitchen, and I have some bags of honey-herb-lemon tea for you too. Do elves have tea? Do you know how to make it?" She hadn't seen anything in the kitchen for boiling water, but she hadn't poked into all the nooks hollowed from the earth.

Starblade didn't answer.

With a final glance at the vines, Arwen crept the rest of the way down the tunnel. They didn't attack.

Starblade was in the same spot in the pool, and he watched her approach through slitted eyes. "You have not departed."

"No. Because of the tea bags." Arwen smiled and held up the jar. "I want to make sure you know what to do with them."

"Elves do have such a drink, and I'm aware of the need to steep the herbs in hot water before consumption."

"Oh, okay."

He closed his eyes and turned his head away, as if saying the conversation was over.

"You should try it when you get out," Arwen suggested. "The herbs are ginkgo and ginseng. We grow them on the farm. They're believed to help with cognition, inflammation, and even erectile dysfunction." As soon as she said that last, she wished she'd held that factoid back.

His eyebrows flew up, and he stared at her. "I do not have *dysfunction* in that area."

"That's good. I'm glad."

"It is very adequate," he said.

Arwen made a mental note about this subject being the best way to inadvertently offend a male...

"Yes. I'm sure," she said. "I just meant— Well, I was sharing the benefits. I, uh, tend to do that. I mostly meant that you might find the tea helpful for healing your wounds. Though I suppose you could benefit from the cognitive support, since you're... Well, the shifter said you're centuries old."

"My cognition is also sufficient. Dragons and elves are long-lived by nature. I am not *old*."

"Of course. I can see that." Arwen waved toward his mostly submerged naked form. "You seem very, er, fit."

His eyes closed to slits. "If you have lingered because you wish to proposition me for sex, this is an odd way to do it."

"That's not what I want."

"Excellent. Then my rejection will not disturb you."

"No." She resisted the urge to ask whether he was rejecting her because of her blood, because she'd been willing to track him for money, or because he found her completely unattractive and off-putting. Whichever of those reasons it was—and maybe it was all of them—it would only hurt her feelings. "I only wanted to make sure you knew how to make the tea. Oh, and your mushrooms aren't growing well. I *am* a farmer, and I know about such things if you want some tips."

He regarded her through his still-slitted eyes, nothing in his expression suggesting an interest in her advice.

Doggedly, Arwen pushed on. "I assume you're growing them for medicinal purposes or to eat. They're not from Earth, right? Do they usually grow on logs in their native environment? If so, they may prefer a hardwood sawdust substrate to straw. Some like soy hulls mixed in. Our button mushrooms *love* composted manure."

His eyes slitted even further. Maybe women didn't usually discuss manure with him.

"You could also try my secret ingredient." Arwen paused and raised her eyebrows, hoping for a hint of interest from him.

"Which is?"

"Used coffee grounds. Oyster mushrooms thrive with a little of that mixed in, and your fungi remind me of them. Except for the orange glow."

"Where does one acquire *coffee* grounds?" The way he said coffee suggested he wasn't familiar with it. That was hard to believe, especially if he was attempting to learn how to blend in with the natives.

"They're left over after making coffee. I can bring you some if you like."

"Hm."

That *hm* didn't sound that hopeful or speculative.

"I do not fear one as weak as you," Starblade said, "nor do I believe your modified arrows can pierce my defenses, but you are scheming."

"I'm scheming to improve your mushrooms. I hate to see such sickly specimens."

"And you are an expert in this area."

"Not an expert but certainly a mycophile. Who do you think inoculated the woods around Sigrid's neighborhood with all those truffles?"

Starblade stared at her. With interest? In disbelief?

She couldn't tell. At least he was listening.

"And I admit it: I *am* scheming. I've realized I was foolish to contemplate tracking you, especially for those shifters."

"*Very* foolish."

"When I accepted the assignment, I also didn't know anything about the dark elves and what was going on in Bellevue. Now that

I know, I think we should help each other. I have a plan for getting into that building to snoop around." Technically, *Amber* had a plan, but if it could get Arwen through the door without tanks firing at her, it was worth trying. "You originally came to me because you wanted information on the dark elves. I don't have it now, but if I could *learn* it..."

"You no longer seek the money the shifters offered to pay you for tagging me?"

"I... need it, yes, but I won't take it from them. I shouldn't have said yes to their mission in the first place." Arwen almost added that she *wouldn't* have if Starblade had been friendly when he first approached her, and that their first meeting had made her *want* to stick an arrow in his ass... but reminded herself that she was trying to sway him to her side.

"No," he agreed. "You believe the dark elves will invite you in because you share their blood?"

"No, because they need a secretary. I'm going to apply for the position." Arwen had no idea if a half-dragon military officer would know what a *secretary* was. Did elven armies have such positions?

"You are qualified for this role?" was all he asked.

"I'm... hoping they believe I am. And that there aren't a lot of other applicants."

That building was forbidding, and they'd wanted someone with magical blood. Those things ought to cut way down on the number of interested parties.

"Perhaps you should discuss cures for erectile dysfunction with the person responsible for hiring." Was that a joke? His expression didn't change.

"If the topic of medicinal herbs came up, I would be very capable of answering related questions, but I believe secretaries answer phones, make appointments, and..." And what? Arwen didn't know much about what secretaries did. Didn't software do most of those things, these days? What would happen when she sat down in the office, and her magic prompted the computers around her to stop working? That might not happen, but her experience with technology suggested it was a possibility. She imagined sitting in an interview while smoke wafted up from tablets and monitors all around the office.

"Should you be awarded this position, you would spy on the occupants and snoop throughout the building, as you did my abode?"

Arwen wanted to object, but she *had* been snooping... "Yes, but I wouldn't leave my favorite tea for anyone inside. They sent magical tanks after me. They're obviously despicable people."

"Yes, I wish the dark elves *inflamed,* not anti-inflamed."

"Inflamed or *in* flames?"

A savage look crossed his face. "That latter would be particularly acceptable."

"While I'm in the building, you could wait outside. I bet I could find a way to let you in, and then we can work together to find the kidnap victims. While, uh, flaming anyone who opposes us."

He smiled slightly, probably imagining dark elves on fire. Arwen didn't want to burn her mother's people down—or start a war with them—but if they had kidnapped Starblade's friend, she couldn't blame him for desiring that.

His eyes narrowed again as he focused on her. "If the dark elves hire you to be a secretary, will you not then feel loyalty to them instead of me? They will have purchased your services. Perhaps you would work together with them and, as with the shifters, be willing to conspire against me."

He really didn't trust her, did he?

Arwen sighed, aware that he had a reason for that feeling. "I'm not going to be compelled to give them my loyalty. Besides, they won't offer to pay a secretary ten thousand dollars up front."

"Your loyalty can be purchased, but only for a price?"

"No." Why had she even joked about that? "Look, money makes the world go around. That's a saying here, and it's true. I don't like it, but people need things that can only be bought with money, and you have to trade your labor for it. Don't elves and dragons have money?"

"Dragons, no. If they need something, they take it."

"That sounds brutish."

"Elves have a currency and trade with gold. That is what my soldiers were paid with." Starblade lifted his chin. "I never received payment. I was expected to perform honorable duties out of obligation to those who brought me into the world. My loyalty could not be purchased."

"I'd rather have coin than be *obligated* to anyone," Arwen muttered, then realized she was reaffirming his negative suspicions of her.

Before she could correct herself, he sighed and said, "It does not bind one in the same way, that is certain. When will you attempt to gain access to the building through this subterfuge?"

"Soon. My, ah, research assistant is making a résumé for me now. She might already have emailed it in." Arwen wondered what ridiculous list of abilities and experiences filled the document. Maybe it would be better not to know. Then she would feel slightly less dishonest going into the interview, assuming she got one.

"Very well. When you enter the building to snoop, I will wait nearby in case you are able to let me in. I dare not get too close, though, as the magic around the building can knock out my camouflage when I approach it. As you saw."

"Ah." That would make it hard to sneak him in through a side door. "I'll come up with something once I'm inside and see what we're dealing with."

"Is gold acceptable coinage on this world?"

"I think you can trade it for dollars at a pawn shop."

Starblade stood, the water lapping at his waist, and she looked away, lest he again think she'd come to *proposition* him. He pushed himself out of the pool, stirring the scent of eucalyptus in the air, and she couldn't keep from glancing at the interplay of his powerful muscles, wet and gleaming as the water dripped down his body.

He strode toward her. Startled, she had to fight the urge not to skitter back. Instead, she thrust the jar of tea bags toward him, though she doubted that was what he wanted.

He took the jar but only to set it down before stepping close and gripping her forearm. This close, his aura subsumed hers, and that electric charge crackled around her again. His fingers didn't tighten with crushing force, but his nearness—everything from the breadth of his shoulders, the strength of his body, and his height above her—made her nervous. She kept from looking down—barely.

A tingle of magic flowed from his fingers, wrapping around her forearm and centering on a spot on top. The other arm held her tattoo, so she couldn't imagine what he was doing. His magic heated her skin, not painfully so, but it was intense, and she grimaced, thinking of cattle-branding irons.

"What are you doing?" Damn the squeak to her voice. She'd fought ogres, trolls, and yetis. Why was she so nervous around him?

"Marking you."

She mouthed the words, as if confused, but she grasped the meaning right away. The branding-iron thought had been apt. He had to be tagging her, the way Tigris had wanted her to tag him, so he could locate her later.

Her tattoo throbbed, as if it knew what was going on and found it unacceptable.

Starblade smiled tightly. "I can sense you from many miles away, since you do not use any camouflaging magic, but this will make it easier for me to locate you through the many types of power protecting that building. I will also know where you are when you're *not* inside the structure, even if you acquire a camouflaging charm."

The heat on her forearm didn't keep a chill from going through her. "Why do you need to track me? You already know where I live."

"This way, I will be aware if you are meeting with my enemies." He thrust an image of Tigris's face into her mind.

The uneasy chill turned to a lead weight of fear settling into her stomach. "I don't have any plans to meet with him, but he keeps showing up where I am. It's not my fault."

Starblade watched her intently. "You will make it clear to him that you are no longer interested in his coin."

"I'm *not* interested." Arwen licked her lips. "But Tigris hinted that my father and our farm could be in danger if I don't work with him. I'd prefer he not know that I've changed my mind about tracking you. Not until we've rescued everyone, and the dark elves... Well, I hope they'll go away once their plan is thwarted."

"They will not go away. Once I'm inside, I will *kill* them."

Arwen swallowed. Though she didn't like the dark elves and maybe even hated them, did she truly want them annihilated?

"Not only did they kidnap my subordinate—my *friend*—but they are a vile scourge on this and other worlds." Starblade looked past her as he spoke, his voice growing softer. "Perhaps if I get rid of this clan, the dragons will realize that I deserve to live. That I have value."

"Do you care that much about what they think?" Arwen looked up at his profile, his jaw tight, his face hard.

"I want them to leave me be so I don't have to stay on this backward wild world forever and so that I can't be *extorted* by any magical being who learns my location and threatens to tell the dragons where I am." He'd implied the shifters had done that, hadn't he? "It is bad enough that *I* am marked so they can find me whenever they're close."

She looked at his pectoral, at the tattoo she'd thought exotic. It was a way for his kind to track him?

"Yes," she murmured. "It's tedious to be marked without your permission."

Starblade snorted softly. "Should you do what you say you will do, and we are successful, I will remove this mark."

With a final surge of his power, the heat intensified, almost making her gasp and arch toward him, but it quickly abated, the sensation disappearing before it grew painful.

"This is how half-dragon commanders ensure the obedience of their troops?" Arwen almost asked if he'd marked his friend.

"The compliance of those they don't trust. Your ancient Earth commander Sun Tzu said, 'Keep your friends close and your enemies closer.'"

"Yeah, I've heard that one." Arwen shook her head sadly. She didn't want to be his enemy. She wanted... Oh, she didn't know. Just for him not to believe that she was dark-elven scum whose loyalty could be purchased with a few dollars.

"The elves have another saying. The wise commander will gain everything he wants from his troops by rewarding them with everything *they* want."

"That seems a better policy than marks and threats."

"Indeed." Starblade bent closer, his lips brushing her ear. A tingle shot through her, all the way to her core, and the urge to step closer to him, to press herself against his taut hard body came over her. But he only whispered, "Come with me. I will give you what you want. In advance."

"Uh, okay." Her voice came out raspy, and her heart pounded as she anticipated what he might think she wanted. To have sex with him? She didn't want that, despite her body's weird reaction to having him close and *marking* her. But what if he *thought* she did? What if he assumed *all* females wanted him?

"Come," he repeated, releasing her and heading for the tunnel, not bothering to put on any clothes or even grab a towel.

Trying not to feel like an enraptured female eager to do his bidding, Arwen paused to take a long steadying breath before walking after him. As she trailed him up the tunnel, she looked at the vines and the skylights, anything but his naked butt, but her gaze kept being drawn back. He was far more aesthetically pleasing than his tunnel.

Without looking over his shoulder—he assumed she would follow—Starblade passed through the gym and into the first bedroom. *His* room.

Nervous, she wiped her palms on her jeans. She couldn't keep from glancing at the platform bed dangling from vines, thick furs spread across it, still concerned about what he believed she wanted. What if he flung her onto the mattress and mounted her like some stag in the forest?

Starblade stopped not at the bed but at a bookcase. Reminded that he was able to read her thoughts here in his sanctum, she dashed notions of sex from her mind. He *wasn't* going to mount her.

And she was right. He shifted a stack of books aside and drew out a blue velvet bag. Heavy coins clinked within it.

Starblade turned to face her. "How many ounces of gold are equivalent to your ten thousand dollars?"

Arwen blinked. He meant to pay her? That was why he'd asked if gold had value on Earth?

"Uh, five or six, I think. I'm not sure on the exchange rate right now, but you don't have to give me any gold."

"It is what you desire." One of his eyebrows twitched, and he glanced toward the bed. "*One* of the things you desire."

Embarrassment scorched her cheeks. He *had* read that thought. Just as bad, he thought she wanted a handout. The gold probably meant little to him—with his power, he could earn—or take—such wealth easily. For him, this might be like giving a dollar to a homeless woman begging on a street corner.

"It's what I need to help my father pay the taxes on the farm, but I want to earn it, not be given it as a bribe."

"It is a reward, not a bribe. As we discussed."

Yes, yes, he was thinking of her like one of his troops.

"A reward is for something someone has already done," she said.

"Perhaps true. This, we shall call an obligation." He smiled tightly again, bringing to mind their other conversation, and counted out five coins and placed them in her palm. "I will give you another five once you've let me into the building. I will not make the rest of your reward contingent on my success. Just find a way to allow me to gain entrance." His face grew grim and determined. "I'll do the rest."

The coins were cool and heavy in her hand. Pride made her want to thrust them back at him, but he'd already returned the bag to the shelf and turned his back on her. Besides, this was the answer to her problem. If he paid her twice what the shifter had offered, her father could take care of the taxes for two years, not only one. And she'd wanted to get into that building regardless. This was a good deal.

When Starblade turned back, satisfaction lurked in his violet eyes, and she realized he was manipulating her. He'd figured out what she needed and offered it to ensure her compliance. Her *obedience.*

"Fine," she said. "I'll let you know when I find a way to let you in."

"Yes, you will." He glanced at her freshly marked arm.

After nodding curtly, Arwen strode toward the exit. Neither he nor any of his security vines stopped her.

Only when she stood outside under the night sky did she think to push up her sleeve and examine the mark he'd left on her. A dragon's head in profile glowed violet on her pale skin.

"Wonderful," she muttered.

18

ARWEN WOKE WITH A START BEFORE DAWN. HER HEART HAMMERED in her chest, as it so often did when she had nightmares, but she hadn't been dreaming of her past or anything scary. No, she'd dreamed about Starblade in his underground pool, naked, handsome, and... arguing with her about mushroom substrates. She was fairly certain dreams about naked men were supposed to turn erotic, but maybe her inexperience in that area meant her subconscious mind didn't have enough to work with. Or maybe something had woken her before things could go in that direction.

Not that she *wanted* to have erotic dreams about an overpowered half-dragon who didn't trust her. They would just be an improvement over her usual nightmares.

A whisper of something plucked at her senses, and she sat up, listening and stretching out with her awareness. Maybe her hammering heart hadn't had anything to do with dreams.

As she groped to pinpoint what she'd felt, she checked the time. 3 AM. She'd intended to get up early to cut kale and arugula to go with the asparagus she'd harvested for the market that day, and she needed to weed the greens, but it wouldn't be light for a couple more hours.

The hint of magic came again, something feline, something dangerous.

The shifters?

Shit.

She sensed Tigris on the road in front of the farm, and she didn't think he was alone, though his buddies were using their magic to cloak their auras.

Arwen rolled out of bed, Starblade's words coming to mind, his promise that he would know where she was—and if she was chatting up his enemies.

"It won't be by choice," she said.

Though she hurried to dress, she did pause to look at her forearm, hoping the dragon tattoo had been a part of her dreams. Hoping that whole conversation had.

No. It glowed violet on her arm. His mark.

Her spider tattoo had never glowed, and it didn't now, but she again had the feeling that it didn't approve of this new competing mark.

"Let's hope the shifters don't want to tattoo me too."

What *could* they want? Why come in the middle of the night? To threaten her father again? Or her? Could they know she'd made a deal with Starblade? How? It had only been a few hours, and she was positive *he* wouldn't have told them.

Well, no. If they'd come after him, he might have. Maybe he'd smugly informed them that he'd convinced her to switch sides, and she was working for *him* now.

"I hope not."

As soon as she dressed, stuffed her feet in her moccasins, and pulled her hair into a ponytail, she grabbed her bow and quiver. Her senses told her Tigris was coming up the road along with another shifter, both in feline form. True to his name, Tigris had turned into a tiger. His buddy was a lion.

Arwen ran out the door, afraid they would go to her father's house first. He would wake up if they made any noise, she had no doubt, but since he was fully human, he didn't have the ability to detect magic. He wouldn't *sense* these guys approaching.

When she rounded the house, Arwen found them sitting on their haunches in the long driveway near her beehives, staring at her. Only a half moon was out, but she had keen enough night vision to see their amber eyes. They were oddly glazed, and she wondered if the shifters had been drinking or were on drugs.

She does not wear the baggy nightdress that was half-falling off, the lion said telepathically, his mouth open in something like a silent laugh. *A shame.*

Yes, he'd been one of the shifters in the truck bed the other day.

You have interest in mating with a human female while you are in this form? Tigris cocked his head as he studied Arwen.

Not in this form, no, but my other *form remembers being interested. Her blood is tainted.*

Yeah, but she's kind of hot. And not dangerous like real *dark elves.*

Arwen clenched her jaw. No, she wasn't like *real* dark elves, but that didn't mean she wasn't dangerous. And she could certainly defend herself.

She nocked her bow and pointed Tangler, her arrow with an affinity for shifters, at Tigris's chest. *I don't have any updates on the half-dragon for you. Please, leave my property.*

She opted for telepathy since her father would hear if they spoke—thus far, everything had happened in silence—and she didn't want him to run out with his gun. If they hadn't come here intending to attack, that might escalate the situation, and she didn't want her father to be hurt. He was a good fighter, but the shifters had magic and preternatural speed and power on their side. Not to mention that she was sure there were more of them in the road.

No updates? Are you certain? Tigris looked pointedly at her sleeve.

It hadn't fallen back, so he couldn't have seen Starblade's tattoo, but she wasn't surprised that he sensed it.

You were not only in his presence, but he left his mark on you. Did he claim you?

Uh, no. What the hell was claiming? Something sexual? Arwen almost pointed out that he'd had zero interest in that, but that was none of their business. Nor anything she wanted to announce. *He doesn't trust me. He knows you hired me, so he's keeping an eye on me.*

Why did he not slay you?

I gave him fruit.

The lion shared his toothy smile and weird laugh again. *You have not given us fruit.*

For a moment, Arwen thought they might leave if she brought out jam or pickled cherries for them, but that had probably been an innuendo.

The rumble of an engine reached her ears, and the headlights of a truck came into view before the vehicle did. She could just see it on the road through the trees and berry bushes. Abruptly, she sensed two more shifters, one in the driver's seat and another in the truck bed.

You will come with us, Tigris said.

I'm fine here, thanks, Arwen replied. *I've got veggies to harvest this morning.*

It is not a choice. You have failed to be of use to us, but another wants you.

The lion's tongue lolled out, and he laughed again, but his eyes remained glazed.

Who? Arwen asked.

Who do you think?

Starblade had implied the shifters were working for the dark elves, doing their kidnapping for them. Could that be who he meant?

Fear ran cold through her veins as she imagined her mother's people not only being aware of her but *wanting* her for some reason. After all these years, had they learned she still lived?

Collect her, Grayson. Tigris looked toward his comrade. *It's clear you want to handle her.*

Yes. The lion blurred, his fur turning to flesh as his body changed, shifting into human form. A shirtless man with shaggy blond hair and six-pack abs soon crouched in the driveway. He retained his predatory aspect as he leered at her.

Arwen shifted her aim toward him, but Tigris bunched his muscles to spring. Would he try to bowl her over first?

Go with them, a female voice whispered into Arwen's mind from a distance. *They were supposed to collect you days ago, but they feared your arrows.*

The words startled Arwen. They were in a language she hadn't heard for twenty-three years. Dark Elven.

Tail rigid, Tigris locked his eyes onto her arrow. Grayson took a step toward her.

Arwen opened her mouth, on the verge of shouting out, realizing she might need her father's help after all, especially if the other two rushed in to join Tigris. Then a great roar came from over the trees, from the property opposite the farm.

Against the clouds, the black-winged form wasn't easy to pick out, but she abruptly sensed him. Starblade.

Tigris and Grayson glanced at the road as the half-dragon soared toward their truck and the two shifters in it. His cold violet eyes met Arwen's across the distance, and she realized he hadn't come to help her but because he thought she was betraying him, still working with the shifters.

Get her and camouflage afterward, Tigris barked to his buddy, whirling back toward Arwen. His eyes sharpened, and he sprang.

"Father!" Arwen shouted as she shifted her aim again, loosing an arrow at Tigris.

He twisted in the air, and it thudded into his shoulder instead of his chest, but it sank deep, and he yowled. His momentum carried him toward Arwen, his claws slashing toward her head. Ducking, she dove to the side, rolling to put distance between herself and him.

A heavy foot crunched in the gravel, warning her as her senses did that the lion shifter was reaching for her. Even as she finished rolling, she whipped her bow toward him, deflecting his grasping hands. The bone of the staff cracked hard on his knuckles, and he jerked back. That gave her enough time to leap to her feet.

The lion shifter might have reached for her again, but the front door of the house banged open. Arwen ducked, certain her father was rushing onto the deck with his rifle.

The weapon boomed, proving her right, and a bullet slammed into the lion shifter's bare chest. He kept coming, his magic giving him greater resilience than a typical human, but she had time to catch him off-guard and smack him in the side of the head with her bow. She leaped away before he could grab her, nocking another arrow as her feet hit the ground.

By then, Tigris had recovered, using his maw to yank out her arrow and spit it to the gravel. The lion was closer and more vulnerable in human form. Eyes glazed, despite the adrenaline that had to be surging through him, Grayson tried to grab her again.

Only their supposed link to the sheriff's department kept her from aiming between his eyes. Instead, she opted for a non-lethal target and shot him in the thigh.

Her father might not have known about that link, or, with his daughter in danger, didn't care, because he fired again, hitting the lion shifter in the chest. The arrow and the second bullet were enough to slow Grayson, and he stumbled back, a hand clasped to his chest.

"Damn you, Tigris," he bellowed, dropping to one knee. "*You* get her."

Still in his feline form, Tigris crouched to spring again, but a wrenching noise came from the road, along with a cry of pain. Something flew all the way up the driveway and landed in front of him. One of the side mirrors off the truck. He glanced toward the road in time to see a shifter fly almost as far before striking a tree with bone-crunching force.

Violet flashed as Starblade's glowing eyes turned toward Arwen's confrontation.

Tigris snarled and glanced at her as if he might still try to reach her, but when the half-dragon roared, he whirled and ran toward the side of the property. From a hundred yards and more away, Starblade blasted power at him. Arwen didn't see anything, but she sensed it, a battering ram of magic that slammed into Tigris. With a feline screech, he flew through the air, clipping several trees before landing and slinking off.

The lion shifter, blood running from his wounds, turned to follow, but his cheek twitched, and he jerked back to face Arwen. He dropped a hand to his belt and yanked out a knife, then walked jerkily toward her, like a poorly manipulated marionette.

"Who *are* these thugs?" Father demanded, stepping up to the railing with his rifle. "You try to touch her again, and I'll shoot you into the next town."

The shifter's lips rippled, blood leaking from his mouth, though nothing but a wheezing sound came out. His amber eyes remained glazed.

With little choice, since he kept advancing, Arwen aimed her bow again. She wished she could break whatever magic was compelling him to risk his life to reach her. Tigris had given the order to get her, but she had little doubt that someone else was behind their attack. Whoever had spoken telepathically to her. A dark elf. She shuddered.

Another shot came from the deck, the bullet taking the shifter in the throat this time. Still moving, still compelled to do so, Grayson raised his dagger to throw it at Arwen's father.

She loosed her arrow, driving it through the shifter's palm. Again, her father fired, the final bullet hitting him between the eyes. Finally, the shifter pitched to the ground, the weapon falling from his grip.

"Not sure I want to hack up that crazy bastard for the compost," Father said. "Whatever brain disease he's got might make the crops sick."

Arwen smiled without humor. "He was compelled by magic. Powerful magic."

Her father started to comment but instead whipped his rifle toward the driveway.

Now in human form, Starblade strode toward them. Fortunately, he wore all his clothing, though Arwen's mind had no problem conjuring the memory of him naked.

Without slowing, Starblade passed the downed lion shifter and came to stand at Arwen's side. He gazed without concern at her father and his mundane rifle for a long second before looking down at her.

"*Some* allies are more reliable than others," he stated, glancing dismissively at the shifter.

Oh, she had no doubt about that, but she was positive he hadn't shown up because he wanted to show her his reliability.

"You came because we're allies now? Not because you were suspicious of me talking to them?"

As if she'd had a choice.

"I came to ensure I was not being betrayed to the dark elves."

"How'd you get here so quickly?" Even if the mark had alerted him across the miles that she was in proximity to the shifters, he couldn't have flown here that fast. That sanctuary was fifty miles to the north. Even if he'd made a portal, her understanding of those was that people had to take them to another world before they could return to another point on the original world. They couldn't pop from place to place in seconds. "Are you stalking me, now?"

Her father growled, his grip tightening on the rifle, and his glower deepened. The road and truck weren't visible from the front door, so he might not have seen Starblade arrive, and might not realize he was different from the shifters. *Very* different.

Arwen held out a palm toward her father.

"It is you who came to *my* abode when I was gone, let yourself in, and snooped all about the premises," Starblade said. "You left your scent even on my loincloth."

Her father's mouth dropped open. Was that *horror* in his eyes?

"I accidentally found that," Arwen blurted. How the hell had he known? How much *scent* could she have put on his undies in those two seconds? She hadn't even *touched* them.

"Of course."

She glanced at her father and whispered, "You're a jerk," to Starblade.

He stepped back from her and bowed. "You are most welcome for my assistance with the cat-overpopulation problem in this area." He surprised her by also bowing to her father.

After taking a couple more steps from her, he shifted into his dragon form again. Her father's rifle—and his jaw—drooped as Starblade sprang into the air and flew over the roof of the house and off to the north. Jaw still dangling, her father turned to watch until he was out of sight.

"Guess it's a good thing I didn't shoot that one," he said.

"It wouldn't have mattered. Between his scales and his magical defenses, he should be impervious to regular bullets."

Her father slanted her a sidelong look. "That's *why* it's good I didn't shoot him."

"Ah. True."

He lowered his rifle, turning his gaze toward the dead shifter. "Your life has turned interesting of late. Want to catch me up?"

"It'll be light soon. I was going to pick some greens for the market."

"You can pick and talk at the same time," he said sternly, though his voice softened when he added, "I'm worried about you."

Remembering the dark-elven voice that had spoken into her mind, Arwen sighed. "I am too."

19

THAT AFTERNOON, ARWEN GOT A RIDE FROM HER FATHER TO THE Coffee Dragon in Fremont, a terribly busy neighborhood full of foot traffic. Most of the people passed by the coffee shop without noticing it. Thanks to a magical illusion that encouraged mundane humans not to see it, they opted for the adjacent ice cream parlor or the psychic's office, leaving the converted house to quarter-, half-, and full-blooded magical beings.

Arwen had never been interested in visiting the busy neighborhood or the crowded coffee shop, but four hours into selling at the farmers market, she'd received a summons from a dragon. Not Starblade—he hadn't reached out to her since the shifter incident. The unexpected voice of Lord Zavryd'nokquetal had rung out in her mind.

You will attend a meeting with the human military leader and my mate at the Coffee Dragon as soon as possible, he'd stated from across Bellevue, Lake Washington, and most of Seattle. *And you will acquire a human communications device so that a powerful and important dragon need not lower himself to deliver messages.*

It had seemed like a good idea to obey that summons, especially since Arwen wanted to report everything she'd learned to Val and Willard. Fortunately, she and her father had sold most of their produce by then, so they weren't losing money by leaving early. She'd told him a lot about the last two days, but she hadn't mentioned the gold coins Starblade had given her. She felt uneasy about having accepted them, about allowing him to not only buy her allegiance—her *obligation*—but *mark* her. Not that she could blame anyone but herself since she'd foolishly gone back to him after he'd told her to leave.

"You're sure this is the place?" her father asked from the driver's seat of the truck. "I don't see anything. Is it in the alley?"

"No. There's a building right there with an illusion camouflaging it from normal humans."

Father grunted but didn't deny the possibility. By now, he'd seen so much of the magical world that he couldn't doubt its existence.

"When I named you after an elf," he said, "I should have known you'd get involved in magical trouble."

"It was a fictional elf," Arwen pointed out.

"Yeah, but by then, I knew *real* elves existed." He lowered his voice. "And dark elves. Goblins. Dwarves. Dragons. I'm still waiting to see a hobbit."

"A gnome might be as close as you get." Arwen thought of Imoshaun and opened the door to get out. "You don't need to wait."

He looked like he wanted to but said, "I suppose. Gotta take care of those shifter bodies before they get ripe."

Not only the lion shifter had passed in the fighting the night before, but the other two hadn't made it either. Starblade had destroyed them *and* their truck.

"And before the authorities show up to look for them," Arwen said grimly.

They'd used Frodo to drag the pieces of the truck to her

father's shop to break down and turn into planters or whatever he decided on, and the bodies were also out of sight, but Tigris had escaped and knew what had happened. If his cousin worked for the sheriff's department, what story might he tell the authorities? Not the truth, she was certain, that *they'd* trespassed and had tried to kidnap her. Arwen vowed to explain to Willard her side and hope she could keep any misplaced justice from falling upon the farm.

"I don't believe those thugs had anything to do with the authorities," her father said.

Arwen shook her head glumly.

"Be careful. Lot of people here." He waved to her and drove off, though she suspected he would return instead of leaving her to find a ride back on her own. That was probably for the best. It would be a long walk home, and, unlike Val, she didn't have a dragon to fly her around. She snorted as she imagined Starblade offering to let her ride on his back.

"Not likely."

"We're in here, Arwen," Val called, waving from the doorway. "Thanks for coming."

"Your mate didn't make it sound like it was optional." Arwen didn't sense the dragon present, but she had to veer around ogres, orcs, goblins, and all manner of mixed-blood humans as she followed Val to a corner table where Willard already waited.

Around them, overly caffeinated goblins bounced between the seating areas, and raucous laughter flowed down from the loft. Animated ogres engaged in an argument thumped their fists—and clubs—down on display cases full of enchanted gizmos made from scrap metal. Fortunately, the cases were as enchanted as what they contained—they had to be to protect their wares against such brutish patrons.

Arwen's skin crawled at being close to so many people, and she gripped her bow like she might need to defend herself at any moment. When she sat, it was on the edge of a chair and with her back to a corner, her chest tight as the walls seemed to grow closer, the voices of all the patrons battering at her eardrums.

"I thought you might like to see the place," Val said, watching her, "but maybe Willard's office would have been better."

Arwen took a deep breath and attempted to smooth her face, to hide the panic that always threatened in such close quarters.

"Willard's *office*," Willard said, both hands gripping a coffee mug for support, "has been inundated today with shifters complaining about a rogue dark-elf mongrel killing upstanding members of their clan. That Tigris himself came by with his cousin who's with the sheriff's department to file a formal complaint with me." Willard raised her eyebrows, inviting an explanation.

Arwen started with, "I'm sorry for the trouble," then hurried to decant everything, including Starblade's belief that the dark elves were controlling the shifters.

"We believe you." Val looked at Willard. "We do, right? Arwen's a good kid. She helped Matti find her parents."

"I'm aware," Willard said. "I read your brief and insufficient report on that and saw the base where they were held. I'm not inclined to believe those shifters, but, as we discussed, some of them *do* work for and assist the sheriff's department with crimes. Someone over there decided to stop ignoring the fact that magical beings exist—and cause trouble—and recruit a few to work for them, just as the Army has. It puts me in a bind insofar as taking action against them, or those allied with them, goes. We're supposed to work *with* the local authorities, not against them."

"They weren't attacking Arwen on her farm because the sheriff's department sent them," Val said. "I'm *positive*."

"I know. But it sounds like they aren't the main problem, that these dark elves are."

"I hate those guys." Val gave Arwen an apologetic look. "Sorry, not you."

"I know. I prefer to avoid them as well. When they disappeared from the area, I was relieved. If they're truly back..." Arwen stared bleakly at the table.

"You think they're in that insurance building?" Willard asked.

"Starblade does," Arwen said.

"*Starblade* isn't a reliable resource."

"Please, Willard," Val said, "you don't even think Sarrlevi is a reliable resource, and he's an elf noble."

Willard snorted. "One who was an assassin and as noble as gum on your shoe when we first met him. You might recall that he tried to kill you."

"And now he's my across-the-street neighbor and besties with the elf king. The world evolves." Val waved airily.

"Uh-huh. Ms. Forester." Willard turned her focus to Arwen. "I understand that you might not be enamored with dark elves or want anything to do with them—"

Arwen nodded vigorously.

"—but none of my operatives are as inextricably linked to them and that building as you are." Willard glanced at Arwen's forearm, the one with the spider tattoo.

With her sleeve down, Arwen didn't know how she'd learned about it. As a mundane human, *Willard* shouldn't be able to sense its magic. But if she had spies and operatives all over the greater Puget Sound area, maybe someone else had mentioned it.

"I also understand that you have a plan to get into what has proven to be a well-defended building," Willard added.

"*Very* well-defended," Val said. "When Zav and I flew over there, not only did we sense that the defenses were so powerful that his magic might not be able to break through them, but something went off that only he could hear. Or maybe sense. He tried to describe it to me, and I gathered it was like a magical dog whistle for dragons. He said it was extremely painful to him."

"Hell, if you find one of those," Willard said, "I'll take a dozen."

"It sounds like shifters are harrying your office, not dragons," Val said.

"True. Maybe an actual dog whistle would work on them." Judging by Willard's wistful expression, the shifters were being a huge pain in the ass.

Arwen couldn't help but feel she'd brought that trouble to the colonel's door.

"My reason for calling you here," Willard told Arwen, "is to see if you can and are willing to try to get into that building and verify if dark elves are there and responsible for the kidnappings. I've now learned of a number of magical beings who have gone missing in the last couple of weeks. I'd like to get a better idea of what we're dealing with over there, and you might have an easier time of it than Thorvald."

"If I can get in, I will, but the plan is dependent on a few things that are out of my control. And it's actually more Amber's plan." Arwen nodded toward Val.

"Your teenage daughter is masterminding things?" Willard asked her.

"She's a smart and creative girl," Val said.

"Who's not previously shown much interest in assisting our office with its work—or even attending your sword-training lessons without complaint."

"Well, I assume Arwen is paying her for her help." Val arched her eyebrows at Arwen. "Probably in more than pickled cherries, unless I miss my guess. I know Amber pretty well these days."

"She made me sign a contract to give her ten percent of what I earn from tracking down and tagging Starblade. Though, uhm, now that I've had more encounters with him, I'm not planning to do that anymore."

Willard stared at her. "That you were *ever* planning to do that suggests some naiveté on your part."

"You can always trust Willard to be blunt," Val told Arwen.

"No, she's right."

Val's phone rang. "Speaking of the mastermind." She held up a finger and stepped away from the table, Amber's name on her phone.

"Had I known Thorvald's *daughter* was tied up in this plan, I would have quashed it already," Willard said. "I thought this was something Thorvald and Puletasi came up with."

Arwen could only shrug.

"When did you *encounter* the half-dragon?" Willard asked. "Puletasi said he wasn't home."

"I figured out how to let myself into his house, and he returned while I was looking around." Arwen rejected the word snooping and did not mention loincloths.

"You're lucky he didn't kill you."

"He did mark me." Arwen pushed up her other sleeve to show the glowing dragon tattoo.

"Hell," Willard said as Val returned. "Thorvald, did your dragon ever mark *you*?"

Val studied the tattoo. "No, but he claimed me and did something to my aura to let other dragons know I was his." Val squinted at Arwen in consideration. Examining *her* aura?

"He didn't do that. He doesn't want me. Just to make sure he can track me down when he needs to."

"So, you failed to tag him, but he tagged you?" Willard asked.

"Like a national park researcher studying the migratory patterns of antelope," Arwen said glumly.

"I'm not sure if that's better or worse than being claimed." Willard looked at Val.

She only shrugged and held up her phone. "Amber says you're in, Arwen."

"In?" Arwen asked.

"Your job interview is at ten tomorrow morning. It's a school day for Amber, but she says if you come by her house early, she'll help you get ready."

"Get ready?" Arwen imagined setting up targets on the farm and getting in some shooting practice.

"Dress nice, comb your hair, and put on makeup," Val said dryly.

"Oh." Arwen slumped back in her chair. She would rather have target-practiced.

"She looked less daunted when we were talking about tagging dragons," Willard noted.

"Rough-and-tumble girls like us aren't naturals when it comes to makeovers. Or getting gussied up, as you Southern types say." Val smirked at her.

Willard eyed Val's wardrobe. "We also say you can't make a silk purse out of a sow's ear."

"Ouch. We've been insulted, Arwen."

"I think that was more for you than me."

Willard nodded and sipped from her coffee mug.

20

"I DON'T USUALLY VISIT MY GRANDDAUGHTER BEFORE SCHOOL HOURS on a weekday and during rush-hour traffic," Sigrid said after a harrowing bumper-to-bumper drive from Duvall to Edmonds. She took the Subaru down a steep road before turning into a neighborhood called Emerald Hills, with houses perched to overlook Puget Sound from a distance. Rocket, who rode in the back seat, whined until Sigrid rolled down the window. He must have recognized the neighborhood.

"I'm sorry. Amber is going to attempt to turn me from a sow's ear to a silk purse." Arwen wiped her palms on her buckskin trousers, already nervous, and the interview was two hours away.

"So you told me." Sigrid slanted her a long look. "Are you sure this is a good idea?"

"I'm positive it's not, but I seem to be the best candidate." Arwen had shared *most* of the previous days' events with Val and Willard, but she hadn't mentioned the voice that had spoken into her mind when the shifters had attacked. A part of her thought it might have been her imagination or that she'd misremembered. A larger part of her thought the dark elves knew she was around and wanted her for some reason. Delivering herself to their building, if they *were* there, was not a good idea. But, if not her, who else could go? Who else could stop the dark elves from whatever evil they were doing?

"Do you have any experience with job interviews?" Sigrid asked, unaware of Arwen's whirling thoughts.

"No, but Amber said she'd coach me." When Arwen had returned home the evening before, there had been an email from Val's daughter with more details.

"The only job *she's* gotten has been through nepotism."

"She said they coached her on the basics during Career Day at her school."

"Thus making her a professional."

"It's more experience than I have. I've only ever worked for my father, unless you count volunteering for Washington State Search and Rescue."

"I do not. They *like* people who dress in buckskins and moccasins there. I'm less certain that will be the case with someone looking for a secretary."

"We checked the address, and the interview is at the building, *inside* it. Even if I don't get the job, it'll give me a chance to look around and learn a few things. Hopefully, I can figure out if dark elves are really there and what they're up to."

"From all you and your father have said, I didn't think you wanted to find them." Sigrid pulled into the driveway of a two-story house with impeccably tidy landscaping. Never had shrubs been so perfectly rounded as the two placed to either side of the walkway that led up to solid-wood double doors.

"I don't, but... if they're up to something that hurts people, I feel obligated to stop them." Arwen glanced at her forearm, though her sleeve covered the new tattoo, and her discussion with Starblade about obligation came to mind again.

"You're not their keeper, and if your mother is involved, that can't be good. Didn't you once say she might want you and your father—especially you—back?"

"I did say that, but I'm not sure she still wants me. It's been a long time. I'm not even sure why she wanted me to begin with, why she took my father and forced him to— Well, I gather their joining wasn't voluntary, that my father wasn't looking for a half-dark-elf daughter." Not that he'd ever acted like he didn't love her. The rest of his close family had passed years ago, so they only had each other. That and the farm bonded them tightly together. Arwen knew he would do anything for her.

"If she's there, you might find out, whether you want to or not."

"I'm hoping she's not there, that this is some other clan, maybe some dark elves that the priest got together." Not that Arwen wanted to see him again either. "Even better will be if Starblade is wrong, and dark elves *haven't* come back to the area. Maybe someone less inimical got ahold of some of their magical artifacts."

Sigrid turned off the engine. "I'm not sure whether to wish for you to succeed today or not."

Rocket stepped onto the armrest and licked Arwen on the cheek.

"He's less ambivalent and always offers encouragement," Sigrid said.

"I appreciate that."

Rocket wagged his tail.

"It's why people like dogs more than humans," Sigrid said.

"Yes."

Sigrid, who presumably visited the house often, got out, opened a gate in the fence, and let Rocket race into the backyard. A squirrel chattered, either in welcome or alarm.

Arwen removed her bow and quiver and waited, wanting to let her knock. It was only seven in the morning, and Arwen didn't know if Amber's father was expecting her.

The door opened, and Amber answered, a croissant in her mouth. "The blackberry jam *is* delicious. It zings in your mouth. Is that magic? It's especially good on croissants. And scones. And toast. Oh, and I put it on crackers last night." She waved Arwen and her grandmother in. "The cherries are sadly gone. Did you bring more?"

"I didn't, but I can if I survive the job interview."

Amber wrinkled her nose, maybe not deeming the odds of that to be favorable. "If you die, can I have what's in your kitchen?"

"My father would need to sell everything in there to pay for my funeral. Unless he cremates me and adds me to the compost to nourish the orchard."

That prompted a horrified expression from Amber and a concerned one from Sigrid.

"I wouldn't mind. It's the circle of life." Arwen, perhaps wisely, did not mention that the shifters who'd attacked the day before would soon head to that fate.

"It's the circle of Grim and Ghoulish as Hell," Amber announced. "This way. There are more scones in the kitchen, Grandma."

"How come she calls you *Grandma* and Val by name?" Arwen asked as they followed her in.

"Val stayed out of her life for a decade, so they barely knew each other when they started talking again a couple of years ago. It was for Amber's own good, Val always said, since her life was so dangerous, but..." Sigrid spread an arm, maybe deciding she didn't want to speak ill of her daughter, and headed for the kitchen.

The voices of a man and woman came from inside—Amber's father and a lady friend? Or had he remarried? Arwen didn't know, nor did she venture in that direction. She didn't want to run into Amber's father ambling about in a robe. It had been bad enough encountering *Starblade* naked. Well, that hadn't exactly been *bad*, but she'd been flustered the entire time. She had no idea what the appropriate etiquette on the elven home world was when someone wandered around naked in front of a near stranger. For that matter, she wasn't sure what it was on Earth either.

Amber had disappeared down a hallway and into a bedroom, but she leaned out and waved for Arwen to join her. "This way."

Though the house wasn't as ostentatious as Arwen had expected for the neighborhood, the rooms were large, and Amber had her own bathroom and walk-in closet. Both were almost as big as Arwen's entire cob home. Of course, Arwen didn't need much. Her wardrobe wasn't extensive, and she didn't have a lot of hobbies that required bulky gear. Her sewing machine and projects took up one corner of her bedroom and sometimes spread outward, but that was it. She did all her baking and canning in her father's house.

"In here." Amber led her past a four-poster bed and pale-blue walls decorated mostly with posters of boy bands and hunky sports stars, though portraits of an older man and woman in matching frames stood out. Relatives? If Arwen hadn't met Amber's grandmother and heard of her elven grandfather, she might have guessed the pictures represented them. Maybe they were her grandparents on her father's side.

"That's Warren Buffet," Amber said, noticing Arwen's gaze, "who I trust needs no introduction. And Geraldine Weiss. She was a super amazing *female* stock investor who wrote books about dividends. My dad makes me save some of what I earn for college, but I'm also investing ten percent in the stock market. I learned *all* about the eighth wonder of the world, and I'm preparing to be rich."

Arwen looked blankly at her. There were eight wonders of the world? When her father had been homeschooling her, she remembered reading about *seven*.

Amber rolled her eyes. "Compound interest. Einstein supposedly called it the eighth wonder of the world, but I don't know if that was really him. He gets attributed with a lot of stuff because dumbasses can't remember who really said or invented something, and he's the only dead famous math guy they know." Amber took Arwen's hand and led her to a makeup vanity in the bathroom, gesturing her to a poofy blue and gold stool in front of a huge mirror. "You should look up Geraldine Weiss. She was one of the most successful female investors in a male-dominated industry."

"I'm not that into investing." Arwen let her makeup artist settle her onto the stool facing the mirror.

"*Everyone* should be into investing. Are these leaves?" Amber plucked something out of Amber's hair. "And twigs? Didn't you shower and wash this... nest this morning?"

"I did shower. But then I walked through the woods to Duvall so I could get a ride over here from Sigrid."

"Did you drag your *hair* along the trail?" Shaking her head, Amber fished out another leaf and grabbed a brush and comb.

"It wasn't light yet, and the branches can claw at you. There aren't any direct trails, so sometimes I have to clear the way."

"With your *head*?"

These criticisms made Arwen wonder what she'd looked like when she'd been in Starblade's home. Her life didn't take her past many mirrors, so she didn't think to check on her appearance that often. Had there been twigs sticking out of her hair? Maybe it hadn't been her dark-elf heritage that had made his lips curl with distaste.

"I should have had you come earlier." Amber glanced at the time on her phone. "We'll have to do the best we can. I've got an outfit you can borrow. It's from my college-interview collection, and I haven't even worn it yet, so don't drag it through the woods." Amber pinned her with a glare before walking into the closet and pulling out a forest-green jumpsuit with wide legs. It looked professional as well as elegant and feminine.

Arwen stretched a hand out to touch the flowing material. "It's pretty."

"Yes, it is. I can't believe I'm lending it to..." Amber groped in the air, fingers waving vaguely toward Arwen.

Arwen smiled sadly. "Someone who isn't pretty?"

"A *project*. Your looks are fine. I think it's impossible for a half-elf to be anything but beautiful, but the saying diamond-in-the-rough is super apropos here. But don't worry. I'm a miracle worker. You'll see. You'll be gorgeous when I finish with you. Once you see your face in the mirror, you'll be more confident in yourself too."

"I'm not *un*confident. I'm just a little out-of-place in the city. Or around crowds. Or groups. More than two people at once, really." Arwen grimaced. She was perfectly confident in the woods, firing at ogres and yetis.

"Uh-huh. Every time I see you, you look like Bambi on the verge of flight."

After setting aside the outfit, Amber finished combing Arwen's hair, then swept it back into a loose braid, pulling out a few strands to artfully frame her face. Since Arwen never cut her bangs, they hung down to her chest. Without asking, Amber whipped out scissors and trimmed them to chin-length. The shortened strands tickled the sides of Arwen's face, and she could see them in her peripheral vision.

Grimacing again, Arwen reached up to tuck them behind her ears.

Amber swatted her hand. "Don't touch."

"But—"

"Don't touch, or I'll prong you with these scissors." Amber waved them menacingly.

Arwen lowered her hands.

"*Project*," Amber repeated, then had Arwen strip down. "You're a couple of inches shorter than I am, but I think the outfit will work. The cuffs aren't dragging on the floor. That's a plus. I don't think my heels would fit your feet."

Arwen shuddered at the idea of fighting or even walking in high-heeled shoes.

"Do you have trouble finding clothing that fits?" She sometimes struggled at five-foot-nine, and Amber was almost as tall as Val, easily six feet.

Amber uttered a passionate, "*Yes*. A lot of my stuff is custom-made. It's why I have to make so much money. To afford a quality wardrobe."

"And have enough left over to invest?" Arwen pulled on the jumpsuit.

"*Obviously*. I'll send you a book on investing and compounding. Since you're half-elven, you'll probably live for centuries. You and my mom both. It's ridiculous for you not to be taking advantage of all those years you'll have to grow your wealth."

"I've never had a lot of wealth to invest." Arwen thought of the gold coins Starblade had given her, but those would be for her father's taxes. Better to have land and a home than anything else.

"Then you're the perfect person *to* invest. I'll send you two books. And some YouTube videos."

"Are you as..." Arwen rejected the word *abrasive* in favor of, "quick to give advice to your peers as adults twice your age?"

"I'm blunt, but I want to help. People can be better than they are, and they *should* be. For their sake *and* mine. People are annoying when they're ultra lame. Others either appreciate my wisdom or avoid me in the halls. Here." Amber handed her a sash to complete the outfit.

Did that go around the waist like a belt?

Amber nodded at her.

As Arwen tied it on, she wondered if she could tuck the sheath for her foraging knife into it, or would it slip through? And what about her bow and quiver? Would she be allowed to take her weapons inside the building? She would feel naked without them, but the tanks might roll out if she approached the front door armed.

Amber made a few adjustments to the outfit, then opened boxes filled with brushes, powders, jars, and tiny tools Arwen couldn't name. Once everything was spread out on the vanity, she felt like she was in an alchemist's lab.

"I emailed your résumé to the address of who I assume is the HR person," Amber said as she selected a brush and opened a circular container of packed powder, "but I've got a printout for you too. And you can use my cute little leopard-print briefcase. But I want it back. And don't drag *it* through the woods either."

"There shouldn't be a lot of woods between Edmonds and Bellevue."

"I'm sure you can find wetlands or a park if you try." Amber's scowl promised she did not want Arwen to try.

Arwen might have objected to the repeated admonitions, but they seemed fair. After all, she'd arrived with twigs in her hair. There had also been coyote scat on her moccasin earlier, but she'd wiped that off. The woods did tend to be messy.

"There's a cover letter too," Amber said. "Your specialties are spreadsheets and mail merges, and you're a great people person who makes clients feel welcome and at ease."

"I... am not that." Arwen didn't know what a spreadsheet or mail merge was, but claiming to be a people person seemed the far more egregious lie.

"Résumés and cover letters are all about getting you the interview. Everyone fluffs them up. Even my counselor said that. She said that when she wrote her interview for the school, it said exactly that: great people person who makes students feel at ease. You want to talk about bullshit, that's it. Kids would rather see Brutus the Ape than her."

"Is that also a teacher?"

"The PE teacher. He's hairier than a Neanderthal, doesn't shower regularly, wears his socks to his knees, and stumbles over every other word in his mandatory sex-ed lecture. To this day, I'm aggrieved and traumatized that Dad didn't let me go to a private school. He could afford it. *He* knows about compound interest. But he doesn't want me to be spoiled. Can you imagine?" Shaking her head, Amber delved into her makeup kit for more tools. "I put that you're part *elf* on your résumé, okay? I didn't know if *dark* elf would be a selling point."

"I can't imagine that it would be."

It never had been yet.

"Like I told you, they specifically said in the listing that they wanted people with magical blood. It was weird that they were advertising that openly out on a publicly accessible job board. I'm not sure it's legal to discriminate like that."

"I doubt whoever is in charge of that building cares about upholding the law." Arwen was positive it wasn't legal to send magical attack tanks after people who walked on the lawn.

"I guess. I figured we had better comply if we wanted an interview, so your elfness is noted under the Core Competencies header. I didn't really know where to put it, but I don't think your heritage can be categorized as an Achievement."

"Definitely not."

When Amber wasn't looking, Arwen reached up to tuck the dangling strands of hair behind her ears.

Scowling, Amber turned back and lifted a finger, but she paused when she spotted Arwen's bare forearms. The loose sleeves of the jumpsuit had fallen to her elbows. Arwen jerked her hands down.

"You got *another* weird tattoo?" Amber gaped. "What is that? A dragon?"

"Yes. It was not by choice."

"What? You were walking by a tattoo shop, and the artist pounced you with an ink gun?"

"I... was walking inside a dragon's lair, and *he* pounced. With magic."

"What is *wrong* with your life?"

"Recently, a lot." Arwen looked down at the dragon tattoo, then flinched. It was glowing even more brightly than it had when Starblade first applied it. What did *that* mean? Was he using the link at that moment to check up on her?

"At least it's better than the spider," Amber said.

"You think so?" Arwen didn't agree. They were equally unwelcome.

"Yeah, dragons can fly. They're kind of cool when they're not being pompous and stuffy and wandering around the backyard naked."

Arwen blinked and glanced toward a window overlooking Amber's backyard.

"Not *here*. That really would be horrific. Val's mate has a hot tub and sauna in the yard, and he's *always* naked in them. And on his way to and from them. I've seen his twig and berries. It traumatized me."

"Because... they were odd?" Arwen had been doing her best *not* to look at Starblade's genitals, but they had seemed normal, based on her limited experience with such things.

"Because they were *there*. On display for anyone to see. Val hurries to wrap a towel around him if I'm there, but he doesn't get it. Apparently, dragons don't wear clothing. Not even loungewear."

Maybe that explained why Starblade had thought nothing of stripping in front of her.

Warmth flushed Arwen's other forearm, and she frowned down to find the spider tattoo glowing as well. Glowing purple and *throbbing*.

"That is not normal," Amber said.

No, it wasn't. Never in Arwen's memory had the spider tattoo done that. When it had itched by the building, that had been the first time it had done that.

"What does it mean?" Amber asked.

"I don't know."

21

By the time Sigrid dropped Arwen off near the H&B Insurance building, the tattoos had stopped glowing.

"One good thing," she murmured, not sure what had prompted them to start in the first place.

When Arwen had been a girl, she'd entered youth archery competitions, more because she'd hoped to make friends than because she'd cared about earning trophies. There hadn't been a lot of kids to play with in her rural neighborhood. Many of the wooded lots held cabins only used as second homes, and the handful of other farms had been owned by older people whose children had already grown up.

Even though she hadn't cared about winning, Arwen had always been nervous for those competitions, both for how she would perform in front of others and what people would think about her. At first, the mundane humans hadn't noticed anything odd about her, not until her arrows had flown flawlessly into the targets, even when the wind kicked up. That same wind had rustled her sleeves and let someone glimpse her tattoo. After that, the other kids *and* the adults had started avoiding her. A tournament director had asked her to stop coming.

She had the same nervous feeling now as she approached the magically protected building for the second time, its tinted glass hiding those who might be inside peering out at her. Would they recognize her? Sense her dark-elven blood? Unleash their tanks before she reached the front door?

"This is *not* a good idea," she whispered.

I am in the area, Starblade spoke into Arwen's mind.

She stumbled, though she shouldn't have been surprised. He might have been monitoring her all morning.

I am hidden, he added.

Were you in the area earlier when I was in Edmonds?

The domicile near the water? Apparently, Starblade hadn't been on Earth long enough to learn the names of Seattle's suburbs.

Yes.

I did check on your location to see if you were yet engaged in the ruse to gain entrance.

I was preparing to engage in it. Was it you checking on *me that made the dragon tattoo glow?*

Likely so.

My other tattoo didn't like it. All Arwen could assume was that the spider's irritated glow had been a reaction to Starblade's mark emanating power.

Admittedly, its presence irritated her too. She didn't like being *tagged* and that Starblade could tell where she was at any time. She imagined him checking on her while she was sleeping, her arm glowing in her dark bedroom without her knowing about it.

Dark-elf magic likes little that is not dark-elven, was all he said.

Arwen couldn't argue with that.

Starblade didn't say more. She had no idea if he was half a block away or across the lake and perched on the Space Needle. Who knew what counted as *in the area* to someone who could fly?

This time, Arwen approached the building from the front, passing an H&B Insurance sign built into a rock formation near the walkway. Before she reached the tinted glass doors, one opened.

Sensing a troll's aura, Arwen half reached over her shoulder before remembering she'd left her bow and quiver in Sigrid's SUV. Reluctantly. She *had* figured out a way to thread the sheath of her foraging knife through the outfit's belt-sash.

Under her arm, she carried the fuzzy leopard-skin briefcase Amber had lent her, the résumé and cover letter the only items inside. At Amber's insistence, Arwen hadn't stuck any extra weapons in it. The curved foraging knife *might* be able to pass as a letter opener, Amber had said, an item a secretary could plausibly carry. More than that would be suspicious.

As she'd sensed, a blue-green-skinned troll with frizzy white hair stepped out wearing a security guard uniform, one tailored for his seven feet in height. The baton that hung from his belt emanated magic, and he squinted at Arwen with stone-gray eyes as she approached.

If she'd had any doubts that magical beings worked inside, the guard would have put them to rest.

Stopping well back from him, Arwen patted the briefcase. "I'm here for a job interview."

The troll grunted and looked her over. If he recognized her, she didn't get a sense of it.

"You bring weapons?"

"No. Should I have?" Arwen offered him her most innocent smile while hoping he couldn't detect the magic embedded in her arms from the tattoos. *She* couldn't, not unless they started glowing, but a full-blooded magical being would have keener senses.

The troll grunted and waved for her to enter.

"Thank you."

A buzz rippled over her skin as she crossed the threshold. A magical barrier allowing her through.

She hurried inside without asking the troll for directions. Maybe if nobody told her where to go, she wouldn't be blamed for wandering around lost. Or wandering around and *snooping*.

But a marble-floored lobby inside the door held numerous other magical beings—more job applicants?—and a burly human with orc blood, his shoulders bulging at the seams of his suit. With bored indifference, he prodded at a tablet as a male goblin half his size burbled at him while standing on a nearby red-cushioned bench. The goblin was one of *many* people on the long bench.

Gilded elevator doors gleamed behind the half-orc, but he stood so that nobody would be able to get to them without his notice. A couple more security trolls loomed around the lobby, armed not with batons but with huge axes with razor-sharp blades. A quarter-elven human with pink hair chewed gum behind a reception desk, but she was more interested in her smartphone than the visitors on the bench.

Arwen scratched her jaw while she considered those visitors. Suddenly, it made sense why she'd so easily been chosen for an interview. It didn't look like they'd weeded out anyone who applied, anyone who had magical blood anyway.

No fewer than twenty beings waited on the bench, including everything from half- and quarter-blooded humans to a dwarf with a hammer, to two goblins, a kobold, and finally an ogre too large to sit on the furniture. He paced about, grunting to himself and carrying a club and a briefcase large enough that it could also function as a club.

"Is he here for the secretary job?" Arwen murmured, wondering if interviews for more than one position were taking place today.

Since she wasn't close to anyone, she didn't expect an answer, but the half-orc turned toward her. He opened his mouth, starting to speak, but paused and looked her up and down, his gaze shifting from boredom to interest.

Arwen stood still and resisted the urge to dart behind one of the thick support posts tiled to match the marble floor.

"You're next." The half-orc smiled and pointed at her.

"What?" the standing goblin asked. "She cut the line."

"She just *got* here," the kobold said.

"She..." The other goblin squinted at Arwen before his eyes widened. "She's part dark elf."

That prompted every single applicant to look at her. Again, Arwen wanted to hide behind the post. Nobody raised a weapon toward her, but she found observing eyes equally horrifying. Maybe *more* horrifying.

"Yes, she is." The half-orc looked Arwen over again, pleasure gleaming in his dark eyes. He licked his lips. Was that sexual perusal?

Arwen wasn't an expert at reading such expressions. It almost seemed like greed. Maybe he thought he'd found what his employers wanted and that he would be rewarded.

Behind her, the front door opened as the troll ushered in another applicant. One Arwen had met before. She blinked in surprise as Imoshaun, the gnome, walked in with a leather satchel and a metal toolbox.

Their gazes met, but Imoshaun quickly looked away without acknowledging that she recognized Arwen. After taking in the waiting beings, she hurried to the bench and jumped up to sit on it, her shoes dangling above the floor. Had she come for the same reason? To snoop? Probably to search for her missing husband.

The half-orc grunted and waved his tablet. Beckoning Arwen over.

Though all eyes remained uncomfortably toward her, she made herself walk to him. A few hostile whispers, most of the speakers indignant that she was being called in ahead of them, floated across the lobby.

As she neared, the half-orc tilted his head, cocking an ear as if he was listening to something in the distance. Or receiving a telepathic communication? He nodded, then leaned back and pressed the *up* elevator button.

"You others wait here," he told the applicants. "Some of your auras aren't bad. They might have a use for you."

Auras? Arwen had assumed the hiring would be dependent on whether a person could appropriately fill in spreadsheets and do mail merges. She had a hard time imagining that ogre even being able to type with his sausage-like fingers.

"Who's *they*?" Arwen asked quietly.

The half-orc didn't answer.

"Will we be paid for coming down if we're not selected?" the kobold asked.

"You'll be paid if they've got a use for you." The half-orc stepped into the elevator, making room for Arwen.

The interior, including the floor and ceiling, was paneled in gleaming black tiles, and a camera observed from an upper corner.

Arwen looked toward the buttons. The rows labeled for floors 1-20 were innocuous enough, but her breath caught at four purple buttons outlined in silver and set below the others. They weren't labeled with numbers but with symbols, symbols she recognized. One was almost identical to the spider on her arm. The other symbols denoted three of the core demons that the dark elves served: the Soul Gatherer, the Inferno Queen, and Yeshelee.

Were those levels underground? Were dark elves down there now? In a windowless basement?

Not able to keep from staring at this proof that her mother's people had something to do with this building, Arwen almost didn't notice the half-orc stepping closer. His chest brushed her shoulder as he loomed, looking down at her—at her breasts.

"You're pretty," he said.

Arwen stepped back. "Pretty into my own bubble of space."

He grunted and smiled. "You're like me, a half-blood. You've got a strong aura, like them. But if you're like most mongrels here on Earth, you grew up human, don't know anything about your heritage, and can't use your magic."

"I *can* use my magic," Arwen said, in case he was thinking he could molest her because she wouldn't be strong enough to do anything about it. Making her tone as cold as she could, she added, "If you don't want to see what I can do with it, you'll press the button and take me to my interview."

Which she hoped *he* wasn't giving.

The half-orc grunted again, no concern in his dark eyes, and didn't press anything. The elevator wasn't moving yet. "The others can't be touched. Can't even be looked at. They have the power to torture you—or cut your cock off with a flick of their fingers and feed it to their demon gods. You dare not fantasize about them."

"The dark elves?"

"The dark elves."

"Why work for such people?"

"Better to work for them than be killed. Like the others." He waved vaguely toward the building. "And it can be lucrative. With perks. They don't care what you do to those who don't interest them." He smiled and gave her chest another look. "We'll see if you do."

The jumpsuit didn't reveal much skin, so Arwen couldn't imagine why she'd captured his imagination. Prepared to block a grasp if she needed to, she leaned around him to press a button.

Smirking, he didn't move to block her. Because she couldn't know which floor was their destination? That was fine. She pressed the one with a silver flame on it, the symbol for the Inferno Queen.

Startled, he knocked her arm away. "Nobody is allowed down there."

The flame on the button glowed purple, the same purple Arwen's spider tattoo had emitted earlier. She thought it might recognize her magic and accept her touch, but the glow soon faded, and the elevator didn't move.

Maybe someone somewhere in the building sensed her attempt to activate it, because the half-orc paused, his head tilting again. He grunted—he did that a lot—and hit the button for seventeen.

"That's where your *interview* is." He folded his arms across his chest and stared at her.

Well, better than trying to grope her. She'd thought he had that on his mind. But she wasn't that relieved. His strange emphasis on the word *interview* made her suspect nobody was waiting up there to ask her about spreadsheets. What *would* she find on the seventeenth floor?

22

THE ELEVATOR DOORS OPENED ON THE SEVENTEENTH FLOOR, A WIDE hallway tiled in the same black marble. The walls had also been painted black—recently, the smell of chemicals promised. A window at the end of the hall was as tinted on the inside as the out and let in little light. It was still too bright for sensitive dark-elven eyes, but Arwen couldn't help but think their decorating tastes had been taken into account by whoever had remodeled.

The half-orc held the elevator doors open but didn't yet step out. Head tilted, he appeared to be engaged in another telepathic conversation. He and his boss had a lot to say about her, apparently.

Are you able to hear me? Arwen asked telepathically, imagining Starblade's face in her mind.

Since he hadn't been able to breach the building before, she doubted he could help her if she ended up in trouble, but she would ask.

Faintly. Starblade's reply sounded distant in her mind, as if he were across Puget Sound, rather than a few blocks away. *The magic of the building is insulating as well as obfuscating. It blocks communication from outside.*

I figured.

I believe we are able to communicate through the link inherent in the mark I placed on you. Starblade sounded self-congratulatory, like it had been brilliant of him to think of that.

Arwen rolled her eyes.

You may keep me informed about any interesting findings as you snoop, he said.

So far, all I know is that a lot of people were invited for job interviews today. Arwen attempted to share her memory of the lobby with him, including the kobold, gnome, goblins, and ogre.

A gnome was present? Their people make excellent siege engines.

I'm sure that's why the dark elves want them, Arwen replied before remembering the titles on engineering that had been on his shelf. Maybe that was a passion of his.

I haven't observed that dark elves employ machinery to aid them in their endeavors. Dwarves do, but gnomish work has more finesse. Somehow, even through telepathy, Starblade managed to sniff haughtily into her mind.

What about elven work?

Elves are unwilling to build anything that can't be constructed with wood, vines, and magic. One must travel to other worlds if one wishes to acquire a legitimate siege engine.

Everyone should have one.

Every military commander, certainly. Apprise me on what you find.

There's nobody else I'd rather report to.

A tingle spread up her arm from the dragon tattoo. It was probably only her imagination that the response seemed... snarky.

His silent conversation complete, the half-orc ushered Arwen out of the elevator, using his body to encourage her to go first. Not wanting him to touch her, she hurried to walk ahead.

Few rooms in the hallway were open, but she peered into each one that was. Snooping because *she* wanted to, not because Starblade was waiting for her prompt updates.

"What happened to the people who ran H&B Insurance before you took over?" Arwen asked as they passed an empty conference room.

The half-orc laughed shortly, following more closely than she would have liked. "They didn't need the facility anymore. Third door on the right after that intersection."

Arwen walked quickly, not wanting to give him an excuse to bump her, but she glimpsed a bloodstain on a white desk through a doorway on the left and paused. A few voodoo-like dolls scattered the table, and ash and charred wood, the remains of a fire, marred the floor.

A red globe-shaped artifact pulsed from a pedestal in a corner. Arwen could sense dark-elven magic rolling off it but couldn't tell what it did. The dolls weren't anything her mother's people used for rituals, nor did they make fires, so Arwen didn't know what to make of the scene. Maybe some other race had made a deal with her people and adopted rituals like what they believed the dark elves would like? Presumably, a non-dark elf was in charge of the surface portion of the building.

Another bloodstain smeared the doorframe. Had there been sacrifices here? Made to honor the dark elves plotting below? Maybe *that* was what had happened to the insurance employees.

"I *know* you can't use your power," the half-orc said from right behind her, his mouth near her ear, as his body brushed against hers, "if you don't even know the difference between left and right."

"I'm looking for my future office." As she hurried into the indicated room—and away from him—Arwen touched her knife to reassure herself that it hadn't fallen from the flimsy sash. Too bad it was a mundane blade meant for cutting mushroom stems, not appendages off handsy half-orcs.

"Office, sure." He followed her inside and turned off the lights.

The room, empty save for a desk and filing cabinet on the far side, had no windows, so the only illumination came through the doorway. The half-orc sauntered across the hall, plucked the glowing globe out of the other room, and returned, shutting the door behind him.

Now, the only illumination came from the globe, a red glow that painted his face in a demonic interplay of shadow and light.

Not sure what to make of any of this, Arwen kept her hand on her knife hilt. She didn't care if she was telegraphing that she had a weapon. If he thought she could defend herself, maybe he would leave her alone.

He set the globe on the floor and stepped back. Its glow grew stronger, and a wide beam of red light shone from it.

Arwen's tattoo itched. It also recognized dark-elven magic.

Memories came to mind, her mother's people using a pair of globes like this, one in their subterranean lair and one placed above ground. They transmitted to each other, allowing the under-ground person to see what was around the other globe. When the beam shifted to encompass her, she knew without a doubt that a dark elf was looking at her.

Her heart pounded in her ears, and her palms grew moist. What if it was one of her mother's people? Or even her mother?

Her skin tingled under the scan as the device sent back more than a visual representation of her, she suspected. Could it tell what magical items she carried? Or how much power she had?

For a half-elf, she was strong—she'd been told that in the past by magical beings who could gauge such things. Even so, she wasn't nearly as powerful as a full-blooded dark elf. They wouldn't want her for her magic. To them, her abilities were nothing.

The memory of the dark-elf priest returned, of his proposition that they breed. Could these dark elves want that? If so, why had their job listing been so unspecific about what kind of magical being they were interested in? No dark elf was going to breed with an ogre or a kobold. She was surprised her mother had deigned to lure her human father into her lair.

Abruptly, the beam went out, and the glow disappeared, leaving her in pitch darkness with the half-orc. For a few seconds, he didn't move, maybe receiving more telepathic instruction. Her senses told her where he was without the need for eyesight, but she couldn't make out details that way. Even though she could see with less light than mundane humans, she wasn't like full-blooded dark elves, who had no trouble navigating in absolute darkness.

"You don't have power unique enough to make them want you for the experiments," the half-orc said.

The experiments? Starblade's words about his kidnapped comrade came to her, about what they might be using him for. And were they also *experimenting* on Imoshaun's husband?

"But they wish to keep you here for their other purposes," he added.

"Secretarial purposes?" Arwen doubted it.

"I'm told you are recognized."

She'd been afraid of that.

"I'm also told they don't care if I rut with you." He chuckled and stepped closer.

Arwen slipped her knife out of its sheath and attempted to loosen her tense shoulders. Greater speed came when one's muscles were relaxed.

"They said that if you weren't powerful enough to defend yourself from it, you deserved my huge—"

Arwen lashed out with her blade, targeting the hand she sensed reaching for her, though she was tempted to aim lower, to cut off something he used to torment others.

His night vision shouldn't have been any better than hers, but he might have had a charm that compensated for that, because he saw the attack. He jerked his arm away from her slash.

That didn't keep her from springing in, slicing again with the knife, this time aiming for his abdomen.

He twisted, and the blade only cut through clothing. He tried to grab her, faster than his bulk suggested he would be capable of, and she barely ducked under his grasping arm. The accuracy of his attempted snatch reaffirmed her hunch that he saw perfectly in the dark room.

Arwen ran behind him and threw Amber's briefcase. It clubbed him in the back of the head but lacked the heft to do damage.

"Getting me excited, mongrel girl." With a snarl, he whirled and lunged for her.

Arwen danced to the side, again ducking under his grasping fingers, then leaped back in and swung. This time, she was faster than he. Her blade sliced through his clothing and into his side.

It didn't hit a vital target, but his snarl turned into a cry of pain. He jerked his elbow down protectively, giving her time to get around to his back and cut again. She could have leaped onto his shoulders and swiped her blade across his throat, but killing him would put her in hot water with whoever had been watching her through the globe. Probably with everyone in the building.

Instead, she drove her elbow into his kidney, then whipped her leg up to kick him across the room. When he went flying, she ran to the door and grabbed the knob. He'd locked it.

Arwen rattled it in frustration and was about to turn back and prepare for another attack, but her spider tattoo itched. Surprisingly, the lock clicked, as if she'd inserted a key.

Arwen flung the door open, leaped out, and shut it behind her, willing it to lock. It did not. The magic wasn't *that* obedient to her.

When she spun toward the elevator to run, the doors opened, as if in invitation. But the troll in the security-guard uniform stepped out.

Shit. How had Security known so quickly that she'd been forced to start a fight?

Arwen sprinted down the hall in the other direction.

"Hey!" The troll thudded after her, keys and weapons jangling on his belt with each step.

Running, Arwen glanced wildly through open doors, hoping to spot stairs. Buildings like this always had emergency exits in case of fire, didn't they?

"Get that bitch!" came a snarl from the room she'd fled. The half-orc.

Have you completed the interview and been offered employment? Starblade asked as she ran through an intersection.

Not exactly.

Are you snooping and learning about the plans of the dark elves?

I'm fleeing right now. I'll get back to you on their plans.

Arwen turned left at the next intersection, not seeing anything but doors, a drinking fountain, and signs for a bathroom in the other direction. Only after she'd committed to the left, did she glimpse something glowing orange the other way and think that might have been an EXIT sign.

Her pursuers thundered after her, ensuring she couldn't run back to check.

Not only was the hallway she'd chosen short, but it ended with only one option, a door open to a spacious office with numerous windows. Some former executive's suite.

She sprinted inside, shutting and locking the door behind her, but that wouldn't stop a troll or a half-orc. With their bulk, they could knock down doors with ease.

Though the daylight coming through the windows made the suite brighter than the hall, artwork of demons leered at her from the walls. Magical artifacts lined the top of a credenza, and a gauzy crimson cloth was spread across a conference table with a skull resting in the middle. Her spider tattoo itched madly.

"Yeah, I'm sure you like being here with all this stuff."

Something hit the door hard enough to make it shudder. The troll's shoulder, probably.

Other than the windows, there was no way out, and they didn't appear to open. Not that she would consider a window seventeen floors above the ground an appealing escape option. The sleek facade of that building didn't have any ladders, probably not any handholds at all.

She would have to fight past the troll and half-orc and hope she could reach the elevator—and that twenty guards weren't waiting for her in the lobby.

Afraid the foraging knife wouldn't be sufficient, she ran around the conference table and fished in the drawers of a desk, hoping to find more weapons. Explosives would be handy, but she would settle for anything sharp or heavy that she could throw. Hand-to-hand combat wasn't her favorite way to fight. She preferred distance—the better to avoid grabby half-orc hands. Why hadn't she insisted on bringing her bow? The guard had let that ogre in with a club.

A key chain that emanated magic was the lone item in a middle drawer. She almost dismissed it as useless, but maybe one of those keys would open an exterior door so Starblade could get in. Or maybe one could let her *out*.

Another thud sounded, and wood splintered.

"Whose idea was it to reinforce these doors?" one of the males snarled from the other side.

The doorknob rattled.

Arwen grabbed the keys, wishing the jumpsuit had better pockets or that she hadn't lost the briefcase. The drawers didn't hold anything else that caught her eye. Wood crunched under another assault of the door, crunched and *gave*.

Arwen grabbed a stapler and a fist-sized agate paperweight off the desk, the closest things to projectiles. She sheathed her knife and grabbed one item in each hand as the troll and half-orc charged in. Arwen backed away from the desk to give herself room to fight, but when they split up to run around either side of the table, she ran toward it, another thought coming to mind. She hurled the stapler and paperweight, willing her magic to make the items hit hard, then dropped to her knees and scrambled under the table, the gauzy edges of the cloth dangling down on either side.

Thuds sounded when her makeshift projectiles landed, and both sets of legs faltered in their run. She crawled past the troll and half-orc, out from under the table on the other end, and sprinted out the doorway.

You are moving rapidly, Starblade said. *I can sense this through your mark.*

That usually happens when people flee.

The sounds of footsteps promised her pursuers hadn't been deterred by her blows. She raced toward the intersection, hoping for the fire escape stairs she needed. She passed the bathrooms and, yes, there was an orange EXIT sign over a metal door. Fortunately, it wasn't locked. She glanced back as she pushed through it, hoping vainly that the troll and half-orc wouldn't see where she went, but they were already in the hall and charging after her.

The half-orc lifted his arm. To pump his fist and curse her heritage, she thought, but no. He threw a dagger.

Arwen sprang through the doorway but not quickly enough. The blade cut into the back of her shoulder, pain jolting her so badly that she almost tripped. The dagger hilt bumped the doorframe and tumbled free, clattering to the cement floor, but it left an agonizing gouge that made her curse the day.

At least she'd found a legitimate fire escape, the cement stairs offering up and down options. Hoping she could stay ahead of her pursuers—and that those tanks wouldn't be waiting at the bottom to annihilate her—Arwen started down.

Should you be able to flee upward, I could pluck you up from the rooftop, Starblade spoke into her mind.

She skidded to a stop, flailing to catch her balance. She almost ignored the suggestion, but the roof was only three floors away, and there wouldn't be *tanks* up there.

"Hopefully." Arwen surged up the stairs, agony jolting through her shoulder with each arm movement.

Her pursuers thundered into the stairwell after her, their breaths and curses echoing from the walls. And was that a third person she heard?

The door at the top was locked, something she found out when she jammed into it, jarring her wounded shoulder. Fresh pain blasted her, making her cry out and almost bringing her to her knees.

Arwen gripped the bar, willing her tattoo to open this door as it had the last, but she didn't sense any dark-elven magic in the area, and the tattoo didn't do anything.

She fumbled for the purloined keys in her jumpsuit pocket, hoping one would open the door, but there wasn't a hole.

"There she is!" A human male with dwarven blood charged into view on the landing below, wearing tactical armor and carrying a rifle.

Arwen drew her knife, a poor weapon against a gun, and pushed on the bar again. She glowered at her other forearm, wishing the *dragon* tattoo could do something.

To her surprise, a surge of power came from it, and the door blew outward. Startled, she stumbled onto the rooftop. A good thing because the gunman fired, the rifle thundering like a cannon in the enclosed space. The bullet sped over her head as Arwen rolled across the flat roof and away from the exit door.

Right away, she sensed Starblade's aura. He'd been camouflaged earlier but wasn't now. She leaped to her feet and ran in his direction, rain that hadn't been falling before spattering down around her.

His black scales gleamed as he flew back and forth near the edge of the building. He looked like he was pacing, not coming to get her.

With the gray sky and Seattle and Bellevue skylines visible from her high perch, Arwen waved for him to come closer.

Behind her, the gunman burst through the doorway, the troll and half-orc right behind. They fanned out, rage in their eyes as they charged after her.

"Over here!" Arwen cried at Starblade, sprinting toward the edge of the roof, but she soon ran out of room.

The building's defenses keep me from physically encroaching on the premises, Starblade said. *This is as close as I can get. I am unable to land on the roof, nor do damage to it.*

Meaning he would only be able to watch her be killed?

Groaning, Arwen turned to face her pursuers as they approached, her knife ready, but it wouldn't be enough.

The gunman slowed to a stop and raised his rifle. There was nothing to duck behind, nowhere left to run.

23

ARWEN SQUINTED HER EYES SHUT, ANTICIPATING A BULLET TO THE chest.

Instead, a great burst of heat roiled over her head from behind, making her drop to her knees. A twisting gout of flame struck the gunman in the chest.

Screaming, he dropped his rifle. The fire didn't reach the troll and half-orc, but another type of power did. Starblade's magic slammed into them like a tsunami, knocking them halfway across the roof. They landed, rolling hard, and one almost tumbled off on the far side. The gunman, flames all around him, ran back into the stairwell, his clothing on fire, his hair incinerated.

I am able to damage things on *the roof, it seems,* Starblade mused calmly.

"I'm so pleased you made this discovery." Arwen wanted to flop onto her back in relief, but she wasn't out of danger yet.

She staggered to her feet, gasping at the pain in her shoulder.

You are injured, Starblade stated.

She gripped her shoulder. "Uh-huh."

A shout came from the fire escape stairs, someone wanting an update. Great. A whole platoon of security guards would flow out onto the roof at any second.

Leaving blood behind, Arwen shambled as close to the edge as she could. Starblade continued to fly back and forth, dragon pacing. He was about ten feet from the edge. Arwen peered over, the lawn and the trees far, *far* below. She could see traffic backed up on 405. That was *also* far below.

I am unable to levitate you off the roof, Starblade said. *Some of my magic works and other things I try are thwarted. However, if you run and jump, you will easily reach me.*

"Run and jump off a twenty-story building?" Arwen squeaked. "Are you crazy?"

I can catch you with my magic. Or my talons.

Arwen stared at him. She had no doubt that he *could* catch her, but she barely knew him and didn't trust him. He might enjoy seeing her and her mongrel dark-elven blood splat on the side-walk below.

You will not fall. Come. Our enemies have sensed that I am present, and more come to retrieve you and hurl dark-elven magic at me. Starblade looked past her toward the fire escape door where footfalls echoed from the stairwell. He formed a curtain of fire to block the exit. *That will not delay them long. Jump.*

With blood flowing from her wound and pain making her arm numb, Arwen didn't want to jump, didn't want to trust this ally who didn't trust her. She'd failed to learn anything that would be useful to him, so why would he care about helping her? The entire mission had been a waste of time, and she'd already admitted that to him.

But what choice did she have?

They have firearms, Starblade warned her.

They would be able to shoot through the flames with guns.

All right. Inspired, she added, *If you catch me, I'll reward you with more jars of pickled cherries.*

I will catch you, regardless, but I will accept more of your fruit bribes.

She backed up so she could take a running jump.

And the asparagus, he added.

Catch me, and get me out of here, and you can have anything in my pantry.

Excellent. Jump.

A magical compulsion accompanied that last word, and she felt herself running toward him before she'd made the conscious decision to do so. Bunching her muscles, she sprang, willing herself to leap farther than she'd ever leaped.

She needn't have expended so much effort. As soon as her feet left the rooftop, Starblade's power wrapped around her, levitating her toward his back.

Gunfire rang out behind her, and she flinched, certain bullets would slam into her. But Starblade formed a protective barrier around himself that included her. The bullets struck it and disappeared, incinerated.

He settled her onto his back, then flew away from the building, powerful wingbeats quickly carrying them out of range.

The fresh air, heavy with the scent of rain, whipped at Arwen's hair and ruffled her clothing. Exhilaration thrummed through her. Even in pain, she appreciated the magnificence of flying above the city on the back of a dragon.

Only when they'd soared out over Lake Washington and Starblade banked to head north did Arwen realize Sigrid was still parked down there, waiting for her to return. Even though she was blocks away, Arwen couldn't be sure she wouldn't be in danger. Even if she wasn't, it would be rude to leave her wondering where she'd gone.

"I have to go back," Arwen blurted, thrusting an image of Sigrid, the SUV, and her bow and quiver into Starblade's mind.

You require healing.

"Yes, I do, but someone is waiting for me." Arwen didn't say that she would rather go home with Sigrid than Starblade, but it was true.

Maybe he sensed that because his next reply was stern. *You will accompany me for healing, and then you will share everything you learned about the layout of the building and those who occupy it.*

"Does that mean you're not taking me home?" Arwen longed for her bed on the farm and one of her father's poultices for her shoulder. Thanks to her magical blood, her wounds always healed quickly, so she might not need stitches, but he could determine that.

You will come to my refuge on this wild world. There, I can more easily read your mind.

"Oh, goodie. You're not rescuing me; you're kidnapping me."

I am taking you for healing.

"And to read my mind."

Yes. I hope that during your short interlude in the enemy dwelling you learned something.

Arwen grimaced. She hoped she had too, something he would consider useful. He could yet let her drop and splat to the ground. They were even *higher* than twenty stories now.

I have informed the woman in the conveyance that you have found a superior method of transport and do not need her services.

Arwen groaned, not sure how *superior* Starblade was. She hoped he hadn't offended Sigrid. Later, Arwen would have to reconnect with her to retrieve her bow.

You should learn to more properly express your gratitude, Starblade informed her.

"Yes. I'll work on that." Still gripping her shoulder, Arwen let herself slump on his back while wondering if either of them would be able to get anywhere close to that building again.

24

"REMOVE YOUR CLOTHING," STARBLADE SAID.

"Uh." Arwen stood with him by the underground pool in his subterranean abode, the eucalyptus scent wafting invitingly from the warm water. "Maybe you could bandage it through this lovely window the dagger left." She tilted her head toward the wound in the back of her shoulder—and the torn and bloodstained jumpsuit.

Not only had Arwen lost Amber's briefcase, but the special outfit for her college interviews might be beyond salvage. Arwen would take it home and do her best to wash out the blood and sew the rip, but she would have to confess to what had happened. Not that it had been her fault. That had *not* been a job interview; it had been a trap.

She wished she hadn't walked right into it. And what of Imoshaun? Arwen hoped the gnome and the other candidates had been dismissed because they hadn't been what the dark elves were looking for.

"If you refer to that slender rip, it is insufficient. I am not a strong healer, but I have the elven pads of regeneration. I will clean your wound, apply one, and you will soak your entire body in the pool and enjoy its rejuvenating benefits." Starblade opened the box that held the pads and withdrew one.

"I can't rejuvenate with my clothes on?" Arwen didn't object to a nude dip, just a nude dip with a strange male watching her. Would he think her body plain and substandard compared to the females he usually spent time with? Would her tattoo bring the vile dark elves that he hated to his mind?

"You are a strange being."

"I know."

"I am not interested in mating with you. My opinion of your body should not matter to you."

Arwen blushed, hating that he could read her thoughts more easily in his lair. "I know that. And it doesn't."

Or at least it *shouldn't*. Why she cared one iota, she didn't know. She didn't want to mate with him either.

His eyebrow twitched, as if he'd heard the thought and believed it a lie.

She glared at him.

"After you are relaxing, I will extract the information you learned in the building from you. I must see what you saw."

"Fine." Arwen suspected he would be disappointed by what she'd experienced, little more than a half-orc trying to force her to have sex with him. The bastard.

Starblade lifted the pad.

"Fine," she repeated.

She untied the sash and unbuttoned the jumpsuit to ease it off her shoulders, trying not to wince in front of him. Starblade already thought so little of her. She didn't want him to believe she couldn't handle pain.

Her bra had a slice taken out of it too. She was lucky the dagger hadn't cut the strap. Though she wasn't the most substantial woman, running up stairs and dodging bullets without proper boob support wasn't ideal.

Starblade snorted softly. Had he read *that* thought as well?

Arwen bared her teeth at him.

Unperturbed, he waved his fingers at her wound. Magic flowed from them, and tingling heat flushed it. He'd said he would only clean it, but it immediately stopped bleeding and started to scab over. Even the blood smearing her skin disappeared before he laid the pad over the wound. It adhered, its magic conforming to her body as a cool, soothing sensation entered the area. She slumped as some of the pain and tension seeped out of her.

"It is irritating to be lusted after by those who seek only gratification of the flesh," Starblade stated.

Indignation flared in Arwen. She wasn't *lusting* after him. She was—

"I refer to the half-orc," he added.

"Oh."

"It is also irritating to be incorporated into the plans of others, like a piece taken from its case and pushed around the *Thyslysar* board. You have that game on this world?"

"I don't think so."

"It is a strategy game where you seek to outmaneuver another's troops with your own to conquer the enemy nation."

"Sounds like chess. And aren't you the one incorporating me into your plans?" Arwen arched her eyebrows. Even though she'd come to his home to look for him, he'd shown up in the woods where she'd been first. She also felt she'd been the one who ended up sharing information and doing what he wanted.

"My attempt to incorporate the shifters did not go well." Starblade looked toward the tunnel.

"So I was the backup plan?"

"You were not being magically coerced by dark elves."

She'd also been eager to help him once she'd heard his story. Or maybe once she'd seen his bare chest...

She sighed, feeling like a fool.

Clothing floated out of the tunnel and came to rest next to a folded towel on one of the chairs. The button-down shirt and trousers looked like men's garments but were closer to Arwen's usual style than the jumpsuit. If they were his, they would be baggy on her, but maybe she could use the sash as a belt again. Unlike the jumpsuit, it wasn't ripped and bloodstained.

"You will rejuvenate in the pool, and then you may borrow these garments to wear." Starblade stepped back.

Arwen rotated her shoulder experimentally. The stabbing agony had faded to dull discomfort, and the pad continued to seep soothing coolness into the wound. A vast improvement.

With the eucalyptus scent rising from the pool, its promise of healing magic teasing her nostrils, she *did* want to sink into the water. If he wanted to watch her take the rest of her clothes off, so be it.

She eased out of the jumpsuit and slipped off her underwear, then draped everything on one of the lounge chairs. Starblade was looking toward the tunnel and not at her, apparently uninterested in her nudity.

"Another dragon approaches this sanctuary," he stated.

Ah, he was distracted.

"An enemy dragon?" Arwen recalled that he was avoiding them because, if they found out he lived, they would kill him. "Do you need to hide?"

Starblade's chin lifted in indignation. "It is the Stormforge dragon that lives here on Earth and is mated to a half-elf. He has come up here before with his female and the half-dwarf enchanter Puletasi. Sometimes, they check on the goblins and participate in their festivities." A crease to his brow suggested he either thought it was something else this time or such activities irritated him. If he was worried about dragons finding him, she could see why he wouldn't want *any* to visit the area. "I will subdue my aura and hope he is not interested in me."

"Okay." With the magical warm water caressing her body and unknotting her tight muscles, Arwen found that she didn't care about what dragons outside were doing. She could stay in here all day. All week. Already, she felt refreshed and less stiff. "If you're not a healer, how did you build this place? The pool? It's more than a hot tub. I can tell."

"Yes. It is a pool of rejuvenation." Starblade opened the box that she'd thought only held his healing pads and withdrew a green striated marble that emanated magic. "This is a gift I received long ago from a commander I served under before I earned the right of command myself. Most of my belongings, including the Galaxy Blade from whence my name came, were taken from me when I was captured and forced into the stasis chamber, but this was not with me. Though centuries passed during the time of my unrestful forced sleep, it remained in the ruins of the barracks where my troops had once been housed. The barracks were destroyed at some point, but this was deep in the rubble, and I dug it out. Not only is it sentimental because that commander was a mentor, but, as you are now experiencing, it makes magical rejuvenation pools."

"Can you make them anywhere? I'd love one on our farm." How many jars of cherries would she have to bring to convince him to make one there?

"There must be a source of fresh water, and then it takes about three days of meditation linked to the artifact for the creation."

Three days? That might take more jars than she had. Maybe if she traded with their neighbor who had a dedicated orchard and that fancy hydraulic cherry-picking crane...

Starblade must have caught that thought, because he looked over at her with interest. "That is a gnomish device?"

"The cherry-picking crane?" Arwen asked. Sure, he wasn't interested in her nudity, but *that* won his attention. "I think VEVOR makes them. A human company. They do hoists and cranes and such."

"Siege engines?"

"No, there's not a lot of call for those these days. It's mostly agricultural equipment to help with harvesting. We don't have a lot of machinery on our farm though. We're not a big operation."

"Ah." Did he look disappointed?

"There *is* an antique steam-powered apple press in the barn that came with our property. My father has it all fixed up, and we use it in the fall. We make a lot of cider." Arwen envisioned it, gears grinding and apples being smashed, and tried to share the imagery with him. "Fifteen horsepower."

"Fascinating. It is also not of gnomish origin?"

"No, humans are pretty good at making things."

"Magic could infuse such a device with more power. More *horses*."

"It's a shame our people haven't mastered magic."

"Perhaps. Perhaps not. If this world had a great deal of magic, it would have been of interest to dragons, and they would have established rule over it long ago." Grimly, he shook his head. "Your father's kind should be glad they are so feeble."

"Oh, they are."

Starblade left the tunnel and crouched at the edge of the pool next to her.

Arwen eyed him warily and might have tensed, poised to flee, but that was hard with the water soothing her muscles. It would take so much effort to tense and poise... so very much effort.

"I will have your memories of the building now." Starblade lifted a hand. "It is easier if I touch your head."

"From what I've noticed, you haven't had much trouble reading my thoughts in here. Without touching."

"Your surface thoughts, yes. But memories lie deeper."

"Trade me a rejuvenating pool for my thoughts?"

His eyes narrowed. "Should your thoughts and assistance lead me to retrieve my comrade alive, I *will* build you a pool."

"All right." Arwen closed her eyes and attempted to relax her mind as much as her body. Let him see what she'd experienced in there. She feared it would show how incompetent she was and how slow to react or confront someone she had been. She should have battled the half-orc in the elevator, knocked him out, and figured out a way to send it to those lower levels so she could have learned something. Instead, she'd crawled under a table, gotten stabbed in the shoulder, and fled in agony.

Starblade's palm rested lightly on the top of her head. There was nothing erotic or sensual about the gesture, but, for some reason, her body grew abruptly aware of and *interested* in his touch. The hope that he would do more than rest his hand there blossomed. Maybe he would rub her scalp and trail his fingers down to her neck...

Bodies, she decided, were silly, and she willed herself to focus on everything that had happened once she'd walked into the building.

Her worry reignited when she remembered Imoshaun. Later, she would go to the gnome's laboratory and check on her. Hopefully, Imoshaun had already returned there and was fine. Maybe she had even learned something useful during her time in the lobby. Right now, Arwen had nothing but the keys, and she didn't know what they unlocked.

The half-orc was odious, Starblade spoke softly into her mind, *and presumptuous. Assuming you do not know how to use your magic could have been his downfall.*

Not knowing she had a half-dragon waiting outside had been the half-orc's downfall. As to her magic... *He wasn't wrong, unfortunately. I've put so much effort into learning to use my power to help things grow on the farm that I know little about how to defend myself or attack others.*

Of course, she'd distinctly *not* wanted to use her dark-elven magic to attack others. She'd attempted to forget all the lessons she'd received from her mother's people before she'd escaped, desiring nothing to do with their ways. She'd never wanted her magic to hurt anyone. Nor had she wanted to give anyone a reason to hate her for being part dark elf. If she'd been part surface elf instead, it wouldn't have seemed so egregious to learn to use her magic for defense. And everything she'd done with the crops on the farm would have come much more naturally. How she'd longed for that, especially in the earliest days of her experimentation when things had died to her magical touch rather than being enhanced.

Tears pricked at her eyes as she remembered how many failures it had taken before she'd forced her power to do what she wished, not what some demon had long ago twisted her people to do. She wiped her eyes, reminded that Starblade was reading her thoughts, and tried to focus on the building again.

I have never heard of a dark elf who longed to be a surface elf, he said.

She couldn't tell if he was amused or believed her a joke, but the mere thought made her want to shrivel up and disappear under the surface of the water.

I simply observe that you are unusual.

No kidding. Arwen had been hearing *that* her whole life. Only people like her father and Sigrid didn't seem to think her weird.

He scraped his fingers through her hair, a thumb brushing her ear. Maybe he meant the gesture to be apologetic, but it sent a zing of pleasure through her, and her body tingled in response.

As you fled, did you see any keyholes that might be a match to those keys?

Relieved he'd switched subjects, she replied, *I don't think so.*

He stirred her memories, zooming in on doors and cabinets that she'd passed but barely registered.

There were no keyholes in the elevator?

Not that I saw.

Your touch might work on the dark-elven buttons. That may be why the half-orc knocked your hand away.

Maybe, but nothing happened when I pressed one.

You needed more time inside without a brute assailing you.

Yes, it would have been nice if his lust hadn't interfered with my snooping.

Indeed. His fingers pushed through her hair and brushed the back of her neck, just like she'd wanted.

She couldn't keep from leaning her head back into his hand and opening her eyes to gaze up at him, his handsome face looking back down at her. Not at *her* face, but at the water in front of her.

No, not the water. She blushed and sat straight, realizing her position had made her breasts thrust up out of the water.

"That's all I learned there," she said.

Starblade withdrew his hand. That, she told herself, was a relief, not a disappointment.

"Your tattoo had some ability to open doors and access what was likely meant only for dark elves," he said, without commenting on her position shift. "If we could use one of the keys to get in, you might have the ability to open more doors, to get us into the heart of their lair, to where they keep their prisoners."

"I'm not sure about that, especially now that they're aware of me, but I can try."

"Yes." He brushed his fingers through her hair again but only for a second before standing abruptly. "The dragon comes to my lair."

Arwen blinked. "Not to check on the goblins?"

"The *goblins* do not come here." Starblade strode for the tunnel and disappeared into it, the vines rippling on the walls, as if they were as agitated as he.

Arwen stared in that direction even after he disappeared. Was she supposed to stay in his pool to recover? Go out and talk to Zavryd? She doubted he was a threat to her, but was he among the dragons who wanted Starblade dead?

As she debated what to do, Zavryd flew close enough for her to sense. His aura was so powerful that she couldn't have missed it, even Starblade's seeming modest in comparison.

Starblade wouldn't be forced to fight Zavryd, would he? What if, because he'd been here healing her, Starblade had waited too long to hide? Her only strong ally against the dark elves might be pulped by a bigger, full-blooded dragon.

25

WITH AN INJURED SHOULDER, GETTING OUT OF THE POOL WAS harder than getting in. Even though the wound felt much improved after Starblade's ministrations, it still twinged painfully when Arwen pushed herself out and grabbed a towel.

As she dried herself, the pad remaining affixed to her shoulder with its tingling magic flowing into her, a great roar reverberated from somewhere above. The layers of earth muffled it but not so much that she couldn't tell it belonged to a dragon. A pissed-off dragon.

Maybe Zavryd *was* here to kill Starblade.

While grabbing the clothes he'd left, Arwen sensed two people flying with Zavryd. Val and Matti. Since they were half-bloods, like her, they had lesser auras and were easy to miss next to a dragon.

Another angry roar sounded. Arwen only managed to get the shirt on before concern prompted her to run outside to make sure Zavryd hadn't come with murder in mind. She couldn't imagine why Matti and Val would participate in that—Matti had seemed protective of Starblade—but Zavryd sounded like he was on the verge of tearing this lair, and anyone nearby, to pieces.

Arwen hurried through the training area, bedroom, kitchen, and toward the stairs leading up to the hilltop.

You dare lie to me, you half-blood abomination? Zavryd's voice boomed telepathically, broadcast to everyone around, not only the recipient of his ire.

I am not lying, Starblade replied coolly in kind. *You may ask the dark-elf mongrel yourself.*

Dark-elf mongrel. Arwen winced at the condemning label and reminded herself that Starblade didn't care about her. Why would he? Whatever sympathy he'd offered over the half-orc attacking her had only been so she would continue to work for him.

I will ask her and inquire about what crimes you have committed against her since kidnapping *her from the human metropolis.*

Kidnapping? Arwen poked her head warily through the open trapdoor, half-expecting to find the dragons battling in the sky.

I did not kidnap her, Starblade said. *I rescued her.*

Then stole her back to your lair for your nefarious purposes. She is the friend of my mate's mother, and I will challenge you to a duel.

Starblade had shifted into his dragon form and *was* in the sky, flying back and forth as he glowered at Zavryd. If not for their distinct auras and the size difference, with Zavryd almost twice as large as Starblade, it would have been hard to tell them apart. Both had black scales and violet eyes. One might have believed they shared the same father, though Arwen doubted that was possible, especially if Starblade had been born centuries earlier. How old was Zavryd? She didn't know.

"Arwen?" Val called from the other side of the bench, her longsword in hand and a huge magical silver tiger at her side. She looked like she'd been prepared to go into battle with Starblade herself.

Matti stood on her other side and carried her war hammer, but she appeared more confused than prepared to fight.

"Yes. Uhm, I'm fine." Arwen climbed out onto the hilltop, wincing at another twinge from her shoulder.

When Val looked her up and down, uncertainty furrowing her brow, Arwen remembered that she wore neither pants nor shoes.

"I need to apologize to your daughter for losing some of her stuff."

"Like... her pants?" Val frowned up at Starblade, who continued to fly about, maintaining a distance from the also-airborne Zavryd.

Neither seemed to have noticed them talking down below. Zavryd bared his long fangs and slashed at the air with the talons of a forelimb, as if fantasizing about engaging in a duel right now.

"No, I know where the pants are—the whole jumpsuit. They're just a little ripped and bloodstained."

Val frowned. "He didn't bring you back here and try to plant his pole in you, did he? Dragons aren't usually *that* into us mongrels or anyone with human blood." Val looked at Matti, as if *she* had an answer for why such a thing might have happened.

"No, no. I was stabbed by a half-orc." Arwen almost added that *he'd* wanted to plant his pole in her, but that wouldn't do anything to relax Val or Matti. "Starblade brought me back here to heal me and, uh, read my memories of the inside of the building."

Val frowned again. "A mind scour?"

"No, nothing like that. I don't think." The only basis for comparison Arwen had was the first time Starblade had tried to read her mind. That had been borderline painful, but this hadn't been uncomfortable. "He rubbed my head, and it felt okay."

Matti snorted. "I'll bet."

Val frowned at her.

Matti shrugged. "She seems fine."

"I am." Arwen eyed the posturing dragons. Starblade had his own fangs bared. "What made you come here? And why did you think..." She waved toward Starblade.

"My mom said he kidnapped you," Val said.

"Oh." Arwen remembered her concern that Starblade had been rude to Sigrid. Or, at the least, hadn't bothered to explain things fully.

"She was worried. She saw him fly off with you, and, out of nowhere, he spoke telepathically to her and said he was taking you to his lair and she could go home. Mom didn't think you'd voluntarily go anywhere without your bow." Val raised her eyebrows.

Zavryd chose that moment to open his great maw, fly straight at Starblade, and spew a gout of flames.

"No!" Arwen yelled, raising a hand.

As if she could help from thirty feet below.

But Starblade was fast—surprisingly so—and defied gravity as he whipped his body away from the flames. They crackled through the air where he'd been but missed him by ten feet.

I do not wish to duel with you, you pompous blowhard. Despite the words, Starblade opened his maw and returned the attack, his gout of flames as impressive as Zavryd's had been.

Instead of dodging, Zavryd raised a barrier, and the flames split around him, never touching his scales. *Because you know you would lose.*

Because it would be stupid. *Why did you come to my abode to harass me?*

Why did you kidnap the friend of my mate's mother?

Do you even know her name, you arrogant egotist?

It is... Zavryd looked down at Arwen, as if she might be wearing a name tag. *She is the dark-elf mongrel.*

Fool, you do not *know her name.*

You dare call me fool?

They didn't hurl more fire at each other, but they snapped at the air with their powerful jaws and made more slashing motions with their talons.

Val sighed and lowered her sword. "He hasn't gotten to duel with Sarrlevi that often of late. I think he's antsy."

"Sorry," Matti said. "Varlesh is busy splitting his time between finding exotic foods to curb my pregnancy cravings and fulfilling his duties as an elf noble on his home world."

"Your cravings haven't gone away?" Val waved to her belly. "You're pretty far along."

"I *always* crave the exotic foods he finds me. He has excellent taste."

"So I've seen."

As one, Val and Matti looked back to Arwen. Still waiting for an explanation?

"I did want my bow, but the hole in my shoulder also wanted to be healed, and Starblade promised he could help with that." Arwen pushed the baggy shirt collar aside to show them the green pad. "We're kind of working together."

She refused to admit she'd let herself be manipulated by him or that she was voluntarily working for him. After all, he'd paid her. It wasn't as if she was doing whatever he wished because she was infatuated with him.

"To what end?" Val asked.

Arwen hesitated, not sure if Starblade wanted her to blab everything he'd shared with her. Especially when Zavryd was hurling fire at him. But it might confirm to Val that they were all on the same side.

"Someone he cares about has been kidnapped by the dark elves," Arwen said.

"Interesting. I don't think Willard dug that up."

"I doubt Starblade has announced it to many people. He's lying low and trying to learn to fit in as a human so others won't notice him."

Val looked up as Starblade breathed fire at Zavryd. "How's that going?"

"He can quote a lot of our historical military leaders."

"That should help him blend in at a coffee shop. Did you learn anything new for Willard?"

"Maybe a little. I can tell her what I saw in the building."

"Good. She likes information." Val looked at Arwen's bare legs. "She also likes her operatives to visit her office fully clothed."

"Is that *really* a requirement?" Matti asked. "I'm positive I've been there when Gondo wasn't wearing any pants, on account of them being useful in one of his inventions. Remember the flying fans?"

Val touched the side of her head. "Oh, I do. And I didn't say pants were a *requirement*. Just that they're preferred. Willard's formal, you know. It has to do with being a colonel. Right and proper, as they say."

"Does Zavryd want to kill Starblade?" Arwen asked, more concerned with the posturing going on overhead than the colonel's pants preferences.

"His mother, the queen, and many other dragons would like Starblade dead," Val said, "and most even believe he *is* dead. Up until now, Zav has been pretending not to know he's on Earth. That wasn't difficult until Starblade started tearing up restaurants and bars in Bellevue."

"He said the shifters are after him because the dark elves are paying them or controlling them somehow," Arwen said. "It should only be the restaurants and bars *they* own that he's attacked."

"Interesting tactics for a genius military commander," Val said. "Do you think Napoleon regularly brutalized his enemies' pubs?"

"I don't remember my father's European history books mentioning the pubs of the opposition."

"They didn't write down all of the important things back in the day."

Arwen thought about explaining everything she knew about

the shifters and Starblade's entanglement with them but decided it wasn't her story to tell. She also didn't mention that he'd successfully won her over to his side. She didn't know if that indicated his military genius so much as her naïveté and inexperience with the world.

Val's phone rang, and, after glancing up at the dragons, she stepped away to answer it.

"When I invited him to use this sanctuary," Matti said, "it's possible I wasn't thinking that through fully. It's hard to remain hidden from the world—the Cosmic Realms—when one lives within spitting distance of a clan of goblins. Goblins are known gossips and, from what I've seen, communicate with all other goblin clans. I've heard the clientele of the Coffee Dragon mention that a half-dragon lives up here. It may only be a matter of time before more dragons than Zavryd know about Starblade." Matti grimaced. "Hopefully, he can get out of Dodge quickly if he needs to. My mom's enchantments are really good, but I'm not positive even her work could keep him hidden from dragons. At least goblins don't open up dialogues with their kind very often. Dragons don't think highly of them."

"That's a common theme, from what I've seen," Arwen said. "It's interesting that you have a goblin as a roommate."

"*Had.* Tinja has moved down the street to the house she bought and turned into an urban goblin sanctuary." Matti touched her chin. "She does still visit me frequently. *Very* frequently. She's in my kitchen every morning, swilling my coffee and eating my cheese. Truth be told, I'm not one hundred percent certain she's moved out."

"Does she leave a toothbrush at your place?" Val put her phone back in her pocket as she returned. "That's usually how you know."

"She doesn't, but goblins don't brush their teeth, so that's not an accurate indicator for them."

"Does she leave *tools* at your place?"

"Ah, yes."

Val nodded. "Roommate. Willard wants to see me, you, and them in her office before the end of the workday." She pointed to the circling dragons.

Forcing Zavryd and Starblade to occupy the same office seemed like a recipe for disaster.

"Not me?" Matti asked.

"You're on maternity leave. Willard says it's against policy to have you hunt bad guys in your third trimester."

"But it was okay for me to fly on a dragon to come up here?"

"You did that voluntarily. Besides, Zav's flights are smoother than a baby's bottom. You'd be jostled more on a commercial airplane."

"Are you sure? You yourself have complained about his lack of seat belts."

"That's just because it irritates him."

Barely listening to them, Arwen kept her eyes toward the dragons. They hadn't spat fire again, but they also hadn't backed away from each other. They continued to circle with fangs bared, eyes flaring violet.

"Have you explained to them that this was a misunderstanding?" Arwen asked. "That I wasn't kidnapped?"

"I did try," Val said. "Zav is concerned that your womanhood was assailed, due to the lack of pants."

"He's... concerned about my womanhood?"

"Because you're a friend of my mother's."

"Whose name he doesn't know."

"He doesn't know the names of a *lot* of people. Goblins, mongrels, humans. Basically, he considers anyone who isn't a dragon beneath him. But if you're a part of his clan, which now includes my family, since we're married, he'll be loyal to you. It's a dragon thing."

"Huh. If I put on pants and assure him that my womanhood hasn't been assailed, will that reduce his ire?"

"Let's try it."

Arwen was about to head back into Starblade's home when something floated up through the trapdoor. The jumpsuit, her shoes, Starblade's pants, her foraging knife in its sheath, and her underwear.

"I guess Starblade wants to see me dressed too." Arwen assumed he'd been responsible. Maybe he was paying more attention to their conversation than she'd believed.

"Could be," Val said. "Our nudity doesn't excite them as much when they're dragons. Zav only gets horny for me when he takes human form."

Arwen flushed. "Starblade isn't *horny* for me, I'm positive."

"A statement that would be more believable if you hadn't been naked in his home when we arrived," Val said.

"Naked in his *rejuvenation pool* after he bandaged my wound. I was injured." Arwen showed them the elven healing pad again.

"Those are nice," Matti said. "When Varlesh uses those, his wounds heal so well there aren't scars."

"Starblade probably doesn't want any scars detracting from Arwen's looks." Val winked.

Far more mortified than encouraged, Arwen hurried to put on the rest of her borrowed clothing, tying the sash around her waist to keep the pants up. She'd barely slipped on her shoes when levitation magic wrapped around her, lifting her from the ground.

She almost let out a cry of alarm, but Val and Matti were also rising into the air and didn't seem to think anything of it. The three of them floated toward Zavryd, who'd put some distance between himself and Starblade and stopped baring his teeth. He pointedly did not turn his back toward the half-dragon though.

The mongrel dark elf may fly with me if she wishes, Starblade announced.

Your back is too tiny for another to ride upon, Zavryd informed him.

That's not true. She rode up here with me from the metropolis.

No doubt clutched in your talons like the kidnapped prisoner she was. Zavryd settled Arwen, Matti, and Val onto his back.

It *was* broad and spacious, with his magic wrapped protectively about them, but Arwen felt like she was betraying Starblade by not going with him. Which was silly because she hadn't been given a choice.

That is not *true,* Starblade said. *She will tell you herself that I carried her gently and was mindful of her wounds.*

Though Zavryd had already started flying south, his powerful wingbeats carrying them over the forest and toward distant city lights, he managed to turn his head enough to pin Arwen with one violet eye.

"It's true," she said. "And without his help, I wouldn't have escaped the building."

Zavryd's telepathic *harrumph* sounded skeptical.

"Is he always this difficult?" Arwen whispered to Val.

"Oh, yes. It's a genetic dragon trait. Starblade probably has it too."

"Along with elf haughtiness," Matti said. "Also a genetic trait."

"For some reason," Val said, "we're never drawn to men with gnome tinkering abilities and humility."

Reminded of Imoshaun, Arwen asked, "Can we stop in Bellevue on the way to Willard's office? I need to check on someone." Realizing a dragon wasn't likely to ferry her around the Seattle area for no reason, she added something that might sway the others. "A gnome named Imoshaun. She knows more about the dark elves. Her husband was kidnapped by them."

A dragon is not a taxi that flits about at the whims of those he permits to ride on his back, Zavryd said.

Arwen groped for a way to convince him.

"The Brazilian steakhouse is near that area, isn't it?" Val asked Matti.

"I think so."

The eatery where the servants bring all-you-can-eat skewers of meat to the table? Zavryd asked.

"*Servers*, yes," Val said. "Maybe you and I could have an early dinner while Arwen checks on her friend."

That would be acceptable.

"How many all-you-can-eat tickets do you have to pay for when you bring a dragon?" Matti asked.

"Last time, eight," Val said.

"Your mate is an expensive date."

"Don't I know it."

26

ZAVRYD CAMOUFLAGED HIS AURA WHEN THEY FLEW INTO BELLEVUE, his magic also keeping the falling rain from hitting their heads. At some point during the trip, Starblade had also camouflaged himself. Either that, or he'd veered off because he had no interest in a meeting at Willard's office. He hadn't spoken to Arwen for a while, so she wasn't sure.

This gnome is located adjacent to the suspicious building the dark elves might control? Zavryd asked.

"Not adjacent but close." Arwen pictured the alley and what she remembered of the area. Her mad dash from the tanks had distracted her from noticing as much as she normally would.

Zavryd grumbled. Or was that a growl? It reverberated through his body so that Arwen felt it on his back.

It is not wise to announce one's interest in an enemy fortification beforehand, he said. *I will remain camouflaged.*

"Good idea." Val patted his scales and looked back at Arwen. "We won't discuss how we flew by yesterday, and he roared in irritation at the dog-whistle device. Loudly enough for everyone in Bellevue to hear."

The numerous tall structures bristling upward in close proximity to each other offer insufficient landing pads for dragons. Zavryd harrumphed as he banked a few times, flying around buildings as he sought a good spot to alight.

"There should be a code requirement covering that," Val said. "Sufficient room for dragon landing pads in every square mile of the city."

Yes. You will contact your urban planners about this matter, my mate.

"I'll get right on it."

"Given how many times he's squashed the mailboxes in our neighborhood when landing," Matti said, "I'm surprised he's that particular."

"I gather a mailbox crunches nicely under one's scales and doesn't hurt," Val said. "The pinnacle of a skyscraper is another matter."

Zavryd opted for the rooftop above the building where Imoshaun had her workshop. As he levitated Arwen, Val, and Matti off and lowered them toward the alley, Arwen peered about for sign of Starblade. She still didn't see or sense him. He could be sunning himself in Aruba by now, and she wouldn't know it.

I am present, came his dry comment. *I am camouflaging myself as well. If you encounter dark elves, I will join you in an attack.*

Thanks. There shouldn't be any in Imoshaun's workshop.

Because of cleverly designed gnomish defensive machinery. Starblade nodded into her mind.

Since Arwen had been dangled from a ceiling beam by a booby trap when she'd last entered the workshop, she could only say, *Likely so. I'll let you know if I see any siege equipment inside.*

She'd meant it as a joke, but he said, *Yes. Do so. I also enjoy perusing diagrams of war machinery. And reading accompanying literature from the engineer.*

If we're still friends at Christmas, I'll know what to get you.

Are we friends now? Was the purpose of your bribes to engender feelings of kinship from me? Starblade sounded genuinely curious rather than sarcastic. Maybe he was still trying to figure out how native society worked so he could fit in.

They were gifts, *and I'd rather be your friend than enemy.*

Since I am paying you for your assistance, would not our relationship be one of employer-employee?

Whatever keeps you from coming to the farm and mind-scouring my father again.

Now that I know the location of the dark elves, that is unnecessary.

I'm glad.

Will the human military leader send you to infiltrate the building?

If we can figure out how to get back in, maybe. Arwen dug the key chain out of the jumpsuit and slipped it into the pocket of her borrowed trousers. *Though she'll probably send Val and Zavryd.*

It is unlikely she can send *a dragon to do her bidding.*

I think she sends Val, and Zavryd helps her because she's his mate.

I suppose that makes sense. Female dragons outrank males in their society.

Val poked her in the shoulder. "Everything okay?"

Arwen had been standing in the alley and staring at the trash bin while she conversed with Starblade. "Sorry. I'm trying to figure out what to get a half-dragon employer for Christmas."

"Meat," Val said without hesitation.

"He probably eats that, but he also likes truffles and pickled cherries."

"He sounds quirky," Matti said.

"I think so."

The door to the workshop didn't open to Arwen's touch. She tried knocking while sending her senses inward, hoping to pick out Imoshaun's aura. She could detect the magical items that had been inside before, but that was it.

"If you need that door opened," Matti said, "I'm a semi-pro."

Arwen looked toward her—and her giant hammer. "I owe
Imoshaun a favor. She might not consider the destruction of her
front door an adequate way to repay it."

"I have more subtle means," Matti said. "Besides, Sorka gets
disgruntled when I use her to bash down doors, especially doors
that don't lead to an enemy stronghold."

"Sorka? Your hammer?"

"Yes. I think I mentioned she talks to me. Telepathically."

"Oh, right. Your mother enchanted it."

"Yup." Matti patted the hammer fondly.

Arwen kept herself from saying that it must be nice to have a
gifted mother who was a boon to the world—the Cosmic Realms.
It wasn't right to feel bitter about what others had. Maybe a little
wistful but not bitter.

Stepping aside, Arwen gestured for Matti to unlock the door if
she could.

When Matti approached it, she didn't swing her hammer but
rested her hand on the metal.

Zavryd hopped down from the roof, transforming along the
way from dragon to human and landing in a crouch beside Val. "I
am also capable of opening doors."

"Even doors protected by gnomish enchantments?" Val asked.

"Certainly. Gnomes are a lesser species."

"As all are to dragons."

"Yes, my mate." He smiled and nodded at her, as if pleased
she'd finally come to understand that fact.

A trickle of magic flowed from Matti's fingers. Arwen sensed
that it was dwarven magic but not what it did.

A clunk-thud sounded, and Matti stepped back. The door
swung open.

Arwen started for it, but Zavryd strode forward, blocking her
and erecting a barrier around himself. "I will enter first and ensure
no dangerous gnome traps await."

"Dragons can be helpful allies," Val said.

"There's at least one trip wire and trap," Arwen said. "Or there was when I visited last time." Since Zavryd had already headed down the stairs, she added, "Should we warn him?"

"Nah," Val said. "He'll deal with it."

A grunt came from below, followed by the scent of something burning. Frowning, Arwen headed in. If Imoshaun was inside and camouflaging her aura, Arwen didn't want her to be hurt.

She found Zavryd standing in the middle of the windowless laboratory, a few monitors on and shedding enough light to show smoke wafting up from the floor as well as a shattered globe dangling from the ceiling. Traps?

"There may be other security devices," Zavryd said, "but I triggered the immediately dangerous ones."

"Thanks," Arwen murmured, looking around.

One of the monitors displayed a website with a job listing highlighted. It looked like the same one Amber had found for Arwen, that *many* had found and been lured into that building by...

Imoshaun's absence made Arwen worry that she hadn't made it *out* of that building again.

She might be doing nothing more than running errands, Arwen told herself. She set aside the dirty clothes she'd clutched throughout the ride down and searched for clues to suggest the gnome's whereabouts. She peeked through a brick door that had been closed before, blending into the wall so Arwen hadn't known it was there. Only a bedroom lay beyond it, sparsely furnished and decorated. She remembered Imoshaun saying she and her husband usually lived in Renton.

A framed painting rested on a crate being used for a nightstand. It showed Imoshaun and what had to be her husband, a white-haired, bulbous-nosed gnome in overalls. In the picture, they were holding hands and gazing at each other.

"I'm afraid she didn't make it back from the interview," Arwen said when Val peeked into the bedroom.

"It doesn't sound like it was much of an interview."

"No. It was a trap. They were selecting useful people for... I don't know what for."

"We'd better head to Willard's office and see how she wants to handle this. Zav can't get into the building, and I doubt we'd be able to walk up to the front door with a pizza and ask to be let in."

Arwen imagined Val delivering Domino's with her sword on her back and her gun in her thigh holster and figured *most* people wouldn't let her in.

"Just give me a minute." Arwen sniffed the air and looked all about, seeking clues, the same way she would when tracking in the forest.

As the smoke from the traps Zavryd had triggered faded, she noticed the scent of dirt. Since the basement floor was cement and the walls brick, that was odd. It smelled like freshly dug dirt.

Arwen scanned every wall, gizmo, and piece of furniture before stepping back into the main room. A tiny bathroom held no clues, though the composting toilet—or gnomish equivalent—had some scents of its own.

A glint of silver on one of the workbenches caught her eye. When she walked over, she found a single beautiful arrow, the head and shaft enchanted with a power she wasn't familiar with. Her senses suggested it had been made, or at least enchanted, by a gnome, but what was its purpose? Had Imoshaun crafted it for Arwen to use against the dark elves? The gnome had seen her bow and mentioned her magical arrows. Maybe she had anticipated Arwen returning and wanted her to have this.

The thought seemed presumptuous, but how many archers were around who needed magical arrows? Arwen occasionally ran into bow hunters in the woods, but most humans favored their rifles, and they used them to hunt elk or deer, not creatures that required magic to kill.

She rubbed the arrowhead, its power making her thumb tingle. Deciding she would kick herself if she left it behind only to need it later, Arwen took it. When she found Imoshaun, she would return it if it wasn't meant for her.

"Arwen?" Val asked from the stairs.

Matti and Zavryd had already gone back up to the alley. Were they waiting impatiently?

"Sorry, but I smell dirt." Arwen didn't object to going to see Willard, but if it was possible Imoshaun had left clues behind, she hated to leave before finding them.

"Well, it is a basement," Val said.

"Not one with a dirt floor."

"True." Val sniffed but didn't remark on whether she smelled freshly dug earth.

Arwen trusted her nose when it came to such things. She knelt and rested her hand on the cool floor. She couldn't track on cement, not by normal means, but she could, as Tigris had mentioned, *soul* track. It would mean using her dark-elf magic as it was, not twisting it in an attempt to act for the greater good. The idea of it always made her uneasy, as if using it might somehow serve the demons and lure her to want to please them, to fully embrace her mother's heritage.

She shuddered but shook away the thought. That *wouldn't* happen.

"You can go, and I can meet up with you later." Arwen was hesitant to use her power with Val watching, Val who might know she was calling upon dark-elven magic and judge her for it. "I wasn't expecting her to be gone, and I need to try to find her."

"Willard wants you to join us in her office, so we can plan. If you had a phone, I could keep you in the loop that way, but..." Val looked up the stairs. After a pause—for a telepathic conversation?

—she said, "I guess Zav has enough telepathic range to speak with you from afar."

"Yes, he's done so before."

"Expect him to be haughty and grumpy about being used for such a purpose."

"Okay." Arwen didn't point out that her impression of the dragon was that he was *always* haughty and grumpy.

Before leaving, Val said, "You'd better not go near that building without backup. Let us come up with a plan first, all right?"

Maybe she also believed Imoshaun's absence suggested a kidnapping.

"I'm definitely not going to try to get back in without powerful allies," Arwen said.

"Some people might not return to a place where they were chased off by tanks and half-orcs even *with* allies."

"I've been told I'm atypical."

Weird, was the word that came so quickly to people's lips.

"Yeah, I can see that. Willard should hire you." Val grinned. "She's got Matti and even Sarrlevi on the payroll now, not to mention more goblin informants than I can count. Oh, not all of them get full-time pay, like Gondo, but she seems to have a bottomless budget for paying—or bribing—people who can help stop crimes."

"I'm already being employed by someone else." Arwen imagined Starblade perched on a nearby rooftop while glowering over at the magically defended building.

"Your dad at the farm?"

"Among others."

"All right. We'll come back to get you after seeing Willard. You need a ride to my mom's place to get your bow, right?"

"That would be helpful. Thank you."

Val waved and disappeared up the stairs.

When she sensed that Zavryd had taken flight, Matti and Val

with him, Arwen let her magic trickle into the floor, using it to seek the traces that a soul shed when a person passed through an area. Her tattoo tingled, as if eager she was calling upon her mother's magic. It had never done that before, and that worried Arwen, but not enough to stop. She swept the floor with her power.

If more than a day had passed, the soul traces would have faded, dissolving into the ether, but Imoshaun ought to have been there that morning, preparing for the so-called interview. Besides, soul traces tended to be stronger and remain longer in a home or other place where the owner spent many hours a day.

Affected by the magic, Arwen's vision shifted slightly, the room growing darker as spots on the floor appeared to her eyes. They were a faint greenish-white, like ectoplasmic goo left behind by Hollywood ghosts.

The soul tracks ran all over the room but concentrated along paths that went from the bedroom to the eating area to the workstation and up the stairs. Surprisingly, a heavy concentration lingered by a back wall adorned by a cartoon map of Seattle. It was the kind sold in tourist shops that highlighted popular locales and wasn't to scale. In this one, a whale spouted water out in Puget Sound, while a kraken waved its tentacles at a passing ferry.

Arwen walked back and lifted up the map. Nothing but brick lay behind it, but something plucked at her senses.

She pressed her hand against the wall, wondering if there might be another hidden door. The tracks suggested *something* was back there unless Imoshaun spent a lot of time walking to that map and contemplating it.

"Shouldn't have sent Matti away," Arwen murmured.

"You need assistance with a hidden door?" came a voice from the stairs, startling her.

Starblade stood on the steps with her bow and quiver in hand, his sword in a harness on his back.

Arwen blinked. "You went to get my weapons from Sigrid?"

LINDSAY BUROKER258

"I did."

"I thought you were on a nearby rooftop, glowering at the enemy building."

"I glowered at it as I flew by." Starblade walked over to her, not likely seeing the soul remnants or anything different about the room. She didn't know the extent of dragon powers but suspected that only someone using soul-tracking magic would. Starblade held the bow and quiver out to her. "As I returned, I spotted some of those feline shifters walking into the building. I contemplated destroying their conveyance again."

"Is *that* why you annihilated that other car? It belonged to them?"

"Yes. They've gone several times into the building. Presumably to receive instructions from their masters. The troll guard lets them in without question."

"Did they have any recently kidnapped victims slung over their shoulders?"

Starblade looked sharply at her. "I did not see that, but I believe some had already gone inside by the time I arrived, so it's possible. There are certain times of a month when dark-elf ceremonies are more common, are there not?"

"Yes. On this world, the new moon is a time of religious rituals. Also, lunar eclipses." Arwen hadn't looked at the night sky lately but realized it might be about time for a new moon.

"Of course. When it's darkest." Starblade looked not toward the wall she'd been studying but in the direction of the building. "I believe in my heart that my comrade still lives, though I have no way to pierce their obscuring magic and detect his aura, but... I have a hunch that I may not have much time to save him, that once the dark elves have what they need, they will do away with him. He's powerful and dangerous. How they are keeping him prisoner, I do not know."

"I hope he's still alive and isn't being tortured."

Starblade winced. Maybe she shouldn't have brought up that possibility.

"Yes." He offered her the weapons again, and she accepted them, sliding the new arrow into the quiver before slinging it over her back. "Later, I intend to look more closely at the building and attempt to find locks that might match the keys you pilfered. I already flew around it from a distance. The obvious doors do not have such keyholes. They are opened by technological readers that one waves a flat rectangular device before." He outlined a card shape in the air with a finger.

"Not all doors are obvious." Arwen waved at the map to remind him of his offer to help her search for a hidden one.

What she hoped to find back there, she didn't know, but Imoshaun had been studying the building and dark elves longer than she had. Maybe her drones and other magical equipment had helped her draw maps and she'd dug a secret vault to keep them safe. Or maybe she'd learned what lay on the four subterranean levels the special elevator buttons accessed.

"Indeed." Starblade considered the bricks, then waved for her to stand back.

Arwen was about to mention Matti's enchanting power and how it had unlocked the exterior door when a magical barrier formed between her and the wall. Starblade lifted a hand, and his magic flared. Intensely bright fire roared, engulfing the wall, incinerating the map, melting nearby computer monitors, and assaulting the bricks.

Though the barrier protected Arwen—and most of the contents of the room—from the heat, the brilliant light made her step back, squinting her eyes shut and raising an arm to further block it. She was on the verge of pointing out that bricks didn't burn, at least from what she remembered from her science and engineering studies, but thunderous snaps rang out and would have drowned out her voice. Thuds followed, making Arwen fear the ceiling would collapse on them. But the flames disappeared, leaving her blinking as her eyes struggled to adjust to the low level of light again.

A pile of cracked bricks lay before them, jumbled between the wall and Starblade's invisible barrier, and an opening was now visible. It didn't lead to a vault but a tunnel that disappeared as it stretched back into the darkness.

27

"MATTI USED ENCHANTING MAGIC TO UNLOCK HER DOOR," ARWEN
said.

"She possesses dwarven blood." Starblade lifted his chin. "I
possess *dragon* blood."

"Which compels you to incinerate obstacles whenever
possible?"

"Certainly." He smiled a little sheepishly. "It is not always
convenient or desirable, but sometimes the urges from my dragon
half are difficult to resist."

His smile didn't last long, but it was appealing while it was
there, smoothing some of the haughtiness and, for a moment,
almost making him seem boyish.

"It's difficult sometimes being a mongrel," Arwen said,
thinking more of herself than Starblade. Belatedly, it occurred to
her that he might find the term offensive, at least applied to
himself.

"Yes." He didn't sound offended, but his eyes lost their humor
when he added, "I must take care not to draw too often on the
dragon power or spend too much time in that form. I was born an

elf, but the dragon calls to me and wants me to embrace it fully. When I was growing up, one of our kind lost the power—or maybe the will—to shift back to elven form. He must have come to believe he fully *was* a dragon for he attempted to woo a female. The males in her clan tore him to pieces for his presumption—or maybe simply because he existed."

Arwen shivered at the grim tale. "I get that."

His eyebrows rose with skepticism.

"Not being torn to pieces, but I worry about using the power I inherited, even when I'm doing it for noble reasons, because..." She eyed the pile of bricks and shrugged. "I worry that it could be a conduit through which the demons could claim me. And that if I used it to hurt someone, I'd start to like... that I'd become more like my mother's people."

Maybe she shouldn't have admitted that. Starblade already thought so little of her.

And for a long moment, he didn't speak, only considering her with an intentness that made her squirm.

"It is difficult being of two worlds," he finally said, touching her shoulder.

"Yeah." Uncomfortable after revealing such inner concerns, Arwen peered into Imoshaun's hidden tunnel.

How far back did it go? And *where* did it go? She'd expected a vault, not a secret passageway.

"I want to see where this leads." If not for the smoke wafting from the opening, she might already have crawled into it. Though it would be tight. The tunnel was the perfect width and height for a gnome, but for Arwen... "Is it safe?"

"I am unable to ascertain that from this position." His voice was detached, as if he'd also shared more than he was comfortable with.

"I mean, is it safe to touch the edge?" Arwen pointed to the smoke, and were those remaining bricks glowing slightly?

Since Starblade had dropped his barrier, she could feel the heat radiating from them from several feet away.

A whisper of magic brushed past her like an invigorating arctic breeze and swept into the tunnel.

"It is now," Starblade said.

"Thanks."

Taking her bow, Arwen crawled into the tunnel, the smell of excavated earth wreathing her. She wondered where all the dirt had gone. This had been a substantial project, and there weren't mounds piled in the laboratory.

A dozen yards in, the tunnel curved. Sensing that Starblade hadn't moved, Arwen looked back.

Should she invite him to join her? Was there room?

"I am considering checking on the shifters and again looking for keyholes," he said.

"Because you're afraid of confined spaces or you don't want to be alone in a tunnel with a half-dark elf?"

"It is a *small* confined space." He didn't comment on the rest of her question.

"I think there are siege engines back here."

"A tunnel-boring machine would be more likely."

"Yes, made by gnomes. Possibly intriguingly designed with schematics and labels full of engineering text."

"You *want* me to accompany you?" Starblade sounded more amused than annoyed at her attempt to manipulate him.

"The tunnel is curving toward the building, and I told Val I wouldn't infiltrate it—I think that was the word—without back-up." Arwen pointed around the bend, though she couldn't know for certain if it led to the dark-elf lair. Still, where *else* would Imoshaun have tunneled? Maybe she'd found a way in through the basement.

"Oh? Infiltration is a possibility?"

"Maybe."

Starblade crawled into the tunnel after her, his body blocking out the little light that filtered in from the laboratory.

Maybe Arwen shouldn't have encouraged him to come. The tightness hadn't bothered her when she'd been alone, but having someone else in the small passage stirred up her fear of crowds. Two people in a tunnel *shouldn't* count as a crowd, but the knowledge that she wouldn't be able to crawl back out—to escape—easily made a hint of panic creep into her chest.

Perhaps sensing her fear, Starblade paused before getting too close. He also conjured a glowing orange sphere of light and floated it past her shoulder to brighten the way ahead.

"Thanks."

Arwen crawled after it, expecting more twists and turns, but the tunnel continued on straight, except where boulders had been too large to move. In one place, it turned a sharp left at what had to be the cement foundation of a building. Not the magical one. Arwen would have sensed that.

As they skirted the foundation, she marveled at all Imoshaun had carved out down here. An alcove opened to her left, and the scent of metal and oil reached her nose. She almost laughed at what was parked inside.

"There *is* a tunnel-boring machine." Starblade paused behind her to peer into the alcove. "It's so small, and there's no seat. Magic must guide it. Yes, I can sense it. The engine is magical, and there's an artifact under the housing that powers it."

Arwen smiled and continued forward so he could get a better look—and because she wasn't that interested in such things.

His light sphere lingered with him, so she had to pause. By now, they'd moved into complete darkness, the faint influence from the monitors in the workshop far behind.

He didn't seem to notice that she was waiting; he'd opened a panel to examine the innards of the machine. "Are those the thrust jacks? What a clever design. And the conveyor... Ah! That's where all the dirt went. It accesses an inter-dimensional pocket. Is it all automated? Fascinating. The gnome inventor must be powerful." His tone lost its wonder and turned grim when he added, "I'm surprised the dark elves didn't kidnap her. You said it was her mate they selected?"

"A scientist, but they may have her now as well."

Starblade gave the machine a loving caress before lowering the access panel. "We will save them as well as my colleague."

"That is my goal." Arwen pointed to the dark passageway ahead. "If you're still coming?"

"Yes." He nodded firmly and sent his light ahead of her again.

As they continued on, rumbles reverberated through the earth. Traffic, Arwen realized. They were crawling under a street. The street that passed the front of H&B Insurance?

"The tunnel *does* lead to the building." For the first time, Starblade sounded excited. "Hm, but it is unlikely there will be an entrance below ground, correct? Prior to the gnome excavating this tunnel, there would have been nowhere in the basement for the building occupants to exit."

"Maybe Imoshaun *made* an exit. Also known as an entrance for us."

If that were true, however, Imoshaun could have sneaked in and wouldn't have needed to show up for that job interview. More likely, Arwen and Starblade were about to come to a dead end. She hoped there would be room for them to turn around.

Starblade's grunt sounded doubtful, but he continued after her. "I sense the power of the building ahead. Its defenses extend underground."

"What *kinds* of defenses?"

Images of magical tanks rolling down the tunnel toward them came to mind. There would be no room to dodge flaming cannonballs.

"Varied, and I believe there are not as many underground as

above. I can protect us from attacks if necessary. It is the impene-
trable magic shrouding the building itself that I have been unable
to defeat." His voice lowered to a grumble when he added,
possibly only to himself, "I did not expect to find such power on
this magic-bereft wild world." He huffed in irritation.

Arwen had heard numerous times that Earth lacked much of
the native magic that was inherent in the ground of many of the
worlds in the Cosmic Realms, all those claimed by civilizations of
intelligent beings. It was why they'd evolved with the ability to use
it, to draw not only upon their inner power but the magic existing
under their feet. The dearth on Earth was apparently why neither
dragons nor any other race that relied on magic had made an
effort to take it over and claim it as a colony.

"Dark elves aren't originally from this world," Arwen said,
though he had to know that.

"I am aware. I believe the artifacts in use in the building were
made in places where the power available to draw upon is
greater." Starblade sighed. "*My* power was much greater back on
Veleshna Var and elsewhere in the Cosmic Realms. I feel handi-
capped here."

"You incinerated a brick wall."

"A great feat indeed," he said with another sigh. "I used to
smite the armies of our enemies. And shifters feared me. I doubt
even a dark-elf compulsion could have driven their kind to
attack me."

"It must be difficult being only a hundred times more powerful
than everyone else instead of a thousand."

"You are mocking me. That is even more humiliating than the
shifters attacking me. Truly, I have fallen far."

"You could threaten to smite me to cow me to silence. I doubt
that would take much of your power."

Starblade didn't answer right away, and she hoped she hadn't led him to contemplate that. They'd just had a moment of kinship, after all.

"If I did that," he said, "nobody would bring me spicy vinegar-doused cherries."

"Nobody at all? Do your goblin neighbors not provide such offerings?"

"They do not. They avoid the area where I live. *Most* people do."

"Except for cheeky mongrels who like to snoop?"

"Quite."

As Arwen had feared, the tunnel came to a dead end. Starblade's orange light shone upon the rough earth, the marks from the boring machine's bit visible, this portion less finished than the rest.

By now, Arwen could also feel the defensive magic of the building, so close that it made her senses tingle. Disappointment washed through her at the realization that the passageway didn't reach the foundation. Had the tunnel borer been halted by that very magic?

Arwen touched the earthen wall, half-expecting to be zapped. Nothing attacked her, but a crawling sensation made her spider tattoo itch. It knew it was close to dark-elven magic.

"It ends?" From behind her, Starblade couldn't see much besides her butt.

"Yes. Would you like to incinerate the dirt for another ten yards and see if that gets us there?" Arwen trusted that even weakened by Earth's poor native magic, he could do such a thing.

"Let me look at the area." Starblade tapped the sole of her moccasin, wanting to get by.

Arwen squeezed over as much as she could, but there wasn't any more room here than there had been at the beginning. There was less.

When he wriggled up beside her, his shoulders caught

between her hips and the side of the tunnel. He grunted, giving her an exasperated look, as if *she* were the problem.

She flattened herself to the side as much as she could. "It's not my fault you're too big for this little tunnel."

That earned her another look, this one not as easy to read. "My elf half wants me to take your statement as an invitation to respond with a sexual innuendo."

"And your dragon half? What does it want? For you to incinerate me?"

"That *is* a frequent desire that comes from it." Starblade grunted again, pushing himself forward, and made it past her, but not without gouging his sword pommel into her shoulder and dropping his knee on her hand.

"Next time you enter a gnome tunnel, bring lubricant." Arwen jerked her hand to her chest with a grimace.

"I have little interest in squeezing into *gnome* tunnels." The backward smirk he gave her suggested his elf half had won out on the innuendo front.

"And yet you're in one."

"Against my better judgment. Curiosity can be one's downfall."

"Our saying is, *Curiosity killed the cat.*"

Starblade rested his palm on the dirt dead end and probed it with his magic. "General Herathdor the Great is quoted often for saying, *More successful traps have been baited with mystery than meat.*"

"Meat wouldn't entice me that much."

"I believe he referred to ogres. Possibly dragons, though even he wasn't so arrogant about his abilities as to try to ensnare them. The history books, at least, did not record any such events."

"A trap baited with a pie might lure me in. Butter pecan is my favorite."

"I am aware of what butter is, though there are only a few animals similar to your ruminants on Veleshna Var, but what is pecan?" he asked absently, magic more subtle than his flames of incineration flowing into the ground.

"They're nuts, nuts that are amazing smothered with butter and brown sugar. Pecan trees don't naturally grow in Western Washington, since the summers don't usually get hot enough for them to ripen, but I planted a few on our farm and use, uhm, special methods to overcome the climate limitations."

"Special methods such as dark-elven magic?"

"It's *elven* magic."

"Performed by one with dark-elven blood, it would be considered dark-elven magic, no matter what grimoire one took the instructions from."

Arwen stuck out her tongue at the back of his head, deciding she would *not* share a butter-pecan pie with him. Maybe she'd *imagined* that they'd had a moment.

Large clumps of dirt tore free from the earth and floated toward her. Again, she pressed herself to the side.

"Though I am tempted to widen the tunnel as I dig deeper, I will refrain," Starblade said. "I am not a soil engineer and could only guess about the stability here. Further, having heard the conveyance traffic overhead, I prefer to be extremely cautious."

More clumps floated past on their way down the tunnel. Was he piling them up back in Imoshaun's workshop? Or would they disappear into an inter-dimensional pocket?

"The defensive magic *is* slightly less powerful directly ahead of us," he said, "than it is aboveground."

"Maybe Imoshaun knew that would be the case when she started this project."

Arwen Forester, dark-elf mongrel tracker, a familiar male voice spoke into Arwen's mind. *It is I, Lord Zavryd'nokquetal.*

Yes, I rode on your back recently. Arwen had a feeling Val had reminded him of her name before he'd reached out.

A great honor for a mongrel like yourself.

Undoubtedly so.

My mate and I are at the office of the human military leader, Willard. What is your current location?

I'm squished in a tunnel with nothing but a view of Starblade's butt.

A long moment passed, and she worried she'd offended the dragon with her bluntness. Or lack of reverence. Until recently, she'd never interacted with dragons, but she knew they insisted on being treated with great respect and deference by the lesser species.

I am uncertain if that is a reference to a sexual encounter, but, if so, the human military leader will not find that an acceptable reason for not attending her meeting. In the past, the presumptuous female has even dared berate my mate for being tardy due to lengthy interludes with me in our marriage nest.

Though they were speaking telepathically, Arwen found her mouth dropping open as she groped for something to say to that. *It wasn't anything about sex,* she finally managed. *We found a tunnel, and we're digging our way to the building from the workshop to see if there's an underground entrance.*

Is that likely?

The gnome, Imoshaun, must have believed one could gain access this way.

Willard has unearthed more evidence that dark elves are in the area and using the feline shifters to assist in the kidnapping of select victims. Several of what she refers to as powerful people in the magical community—you understand that they, as lesser species, are all quite weak and immaterial compared to a dragon—have gone missing. One of those who went missing only a few days ago was a talented bard who used his magic to please human crowds while occasionally ensorcelling individuals to gain information, information that he sold to her for a price.

Because her spy disappeared, Willard cares more about the dark elves now? Arwen asked.

Until recently, she was unaware of the dark elves.

I don't think they've been advertising their presence.

The shifters complicate the matter, due to their allegiance with the sheriff's department, but Willard has decided that she must put an end to the dark-elf plot and recover the missing people, should they still live. She would like to send my mate to handle this, should she be able to gain access to the building. I would assist my mate, of course. She is very capable, but having a dragon as a partner is extremely useful.

I'm sure. Arwen considered Starblade, whose butt was wiggling as he scooted forward. She looked away, but that meant a clump of dirt almost smacked her in the face when it floated past.

Your current actions will gain you entrance to the building? Zavryd asked.

I hope so.

Excellent. Once you enter, you will find a way to lower the defenses so that my mate and I may also enter. Once inside, we will assist you with the dark elves.

I'll see what I can do.

Should we be successful, Willard said she will reward you. She does not expect you to volunteer your time for this dangerous mission.

The only reward I want is to keep dark elves from hurting people. Arwen glanced toward her itching tattoo, having a feeling she wouldn't find peace herself until she thwarted them.

I have observed that humans and mongrels born on this world are driven by coin.

Sadly true, but Arwen had already been paid.

Starblade scooted farther ahead, widening and heightening the tunnel, despite his earlier words that he wouldn't. Arwen couldn't see much around him but glimpsed what might have been cement rather than dirt. The building's foundation?

A whoosh of power came from Starblade, startling her. She braced herself, half-expecting another blast of flames. But the power dissipated before she could tell what it did. No, wait. The magical defenses had diminished, at least in this area. More power flowed from Starblade, finer and pinpoint.

She said she would pay you at the same rate that she compensates my mate, Puletasi, and the odious elf former-assassin who occasionally does work for her, Zavryd continued.

Was that... Sarrlevi?

Magic flared again, and the smell of burning cement wafted back to Arwen. Would whoever had set the defenses notice someone fiddling with them?

I'll keep that in mind, she replied to Zavryd. *Maybe if you fly over here, the dark elves will be distracted from what we're doing.*

Dragons are not typically used as a distraction. Zavryd seemed to sniff haughtily into her mind. *We are great beings capable of solving problems with our power and wits.*

Except when dark-elf security magic keeps you from reaching your problem?

Hm.

If we get in, I'll try to open a door for you. I'd be very happy to let you use your power on whoever is running the show. Her tattoo warmed and itched, as if in disapproval at her thoughts. No, it probably had more to do with whatever Starblade was doing.

For the first time, he shifted aside and looked back. That allowed her to see the cement more clearly, now with an oval outline burned into it, as if he'd had an acetylene torch.

Instead of appearing proud of his work, Starblade winced. Had he screwed something up? Or was he in pain? He lifted two fingers to his temple, as if he'd developed a headache.

You will *let us in,* Zavryd told her. *We will return to the area and prepare for an assault.*

Okay.

"I will attempt to protect you as I break through," Starblade said, lowering his fingers, "but you may wish to back up in case of traps. I have shifted some of the defensive magic away from this area, but it is elusive. Also, I did not wish to use my full power. It may be a vain hope, but I would prefer *not* to alert those inside that we are attempting to bypass their defenses."

"I'm trying to get a dragon to knock on the front door and distract them."

"What?"

"Never mind." Arwen backed into the tunnel to give him space.

Starblade created a barrier around himself, angling it so that it also blocked the tunnel to protect her from whatever backlash might come from the building. His power whooshed toward the cement oval. He must have already cut most of the way through, because it crumbled inward without resistance.

Before the dust cleared, a creepy black mist swept out of the hole. It doused his light sphere and licked hungrily at his barrier.

Fear swallowed Arwen as she sensed dark power trying to reach her, to smother her as it had the light. A memory tickled the back of her mind of having seen something similar used on prisoners to kill them, to eat away their flesh, organs, and bone, like a powerful acid.

Starblade grunted but poured more power into his barrier. His aura radiated magical energy like a sun, and she worried the dark elves and whoever else was inside would have no trouble sensing him out here, no matter how little magic he thought he was using.

Long seconds passed in silence, the magical mist trying to eat away Starblade's barrier. Sweat dripped down Arwen's face, though *she* wasn't the one battling the nebulous foe. More power flowed from Starblade, and his jaw clenched in concentration.

An unfamiliar voice in the back of Arwen's mind suggested she could help him. If she drew upon her dark-elven power, she might be able to thwart the mist herself. The demons helped those who embraced their heritage.

She shied away from the idea. Starblade could handle it. Wit*hout* demons.

Fortunately, she was right, and the mist soon dissipated.

Starblade didn't lower his barrier as he recreated his light. The orange glow illuminated the hole he'd cut in the thick cement and pitch darkness beyond it.

"We now have an entrance," he said.

"Or is it a trap?" Arwen murmured. "With our enemies aware of us out here and inside waiting to capture us?"

If the dark elves had wanted one half-dragon, they might well want another.

"It could be a trap." Starblade gazed into the inscrutable dark depths.

"Baited with mystery."

"The most treacherous kind, as we discussed. I must go in to retrieve my colleague. If I'm able, I will also rescue the gnomes." Starblade looked back at her. "You do not need to come in."

Arwen hesitated. *Did* she need to go? Zavryd wanted her to lower the defenses for him, but couldn't she ask Starblade to do that?

On the one hand, she felt obligated to help if she could—and not only because he'd paid her. On the other, she did *not* want to irk her mother's people. Bad things might happen to her and her father as a result.

But she worried the dark elves knew they were out here and that Starblade was coming for them. They might be ready for him. He might *need* her help. After all, his comrade had been captured, someone with power similar to what he possessed. The dark elves had great magic of their own and myriad artifacts to assist them.

Maybe it was hubris to believe she could make a difference, but the thought of him being captured and sacrificed filled her with dread. A couple of days ago, she'd thought him a pompous jerk and hadn't cared one iota about him, but now... She wasn't sure what she felt, but she didn't want him to die or be sacrificed.

"I'll go with you. I can be handy." Arwen waved at her quiver of arrows, though her weapons would have been useless against the mist. Hopefully, the next foe would be more tangible.

"Very well." Starblade nodded, as if he approved of her willingness to throw herself into danger.

Hoping she was being brave, not foolish, Arwen followed him into the lair.

28

WHAT HAD BEEN UNCOMFORTABLE ITCHING AND HEAT FROM ARWEN'S tattoo turned cool and soothing as she followed Starblade through the hole he'd made. It probably wanted to be reunited with those who'd long ago placed it on her arm. She missed the days when it had seemed to be nothing but ink under her skin.

The hole led them into a cement corridor that paralleled the foundation wall. The cool air, humidity, and dank smell reminded Arwen of her childhood. Unpleasantly so.

If not for Starblade's glowing orange sphere, there wouldn't have been any light. It allowed them to see an access door farther down the corridor on the inside wall as well as P2 painted opposite it.

"I'll be disappointed," Arwen whispered, speaking softly since it was oppressively quiet, "if we did all that only to find a parking garage full of Hondas and Toyotas."

Starblade frowned at her.

"Cars," she clarified, then added, "Conveyances," the term he'd used earlier.

"The dark elves must have converted the area from its prior use."

"I agree." The magic Arwen sensed promised they'd entered far more than a parking garage.

Still frowning—or was that a grimace of pain?—Starblade strode toward the door. Overhead ceiling lamps might have once brightened the way, but every bulb had been shattered.

He placed his hand on the door but paused to look back at her.

"Are you affected by... whatever this is?" He waved at his head and vaguely toward the air around them.

"I don't feel anything."

"Since opening that hole, I've had an intense headache. Some magic I'm not familiar with is in the air, irritating my senses. Maybe it specifically targets dragons."

"Val did say something about a dog whistle for dragons."

"*Dog* whistle?" Starblade gave her an insulted frown.

"Something designed to specifically hurt dragons. Something only they can sense."

"It does feel like a weapon. Maybe it targets anyone who doesn't have dark-elven blood." Starblade eyed her. It wasn't a look of appreciation, though that might have been because he was in pain.

"Then you're lucky you brought me along. Do you want me to go first?" Arwen pointed at the door but issued a frown of her own at a spider-demon symbol painted near the handle. It wasn't exactly the same as the image on her tattoo, but she had no doubt it meant dark elves had claimed the area.

"Normally, I would refuse to hide behind a subordinate, but that might be logical. You may be less likely to trigger traps."

"Yeah, and I'm not a subordinate. I'm an independent tracker who brought you food and tea."

"You are not my equal in power."

"Maybe not, but I'm at least the equivalent of a delivery person."

"Does that position indicate high rank on Earth?"

"Absolutely. Don't forget to tip me on the way out."

That prompted a forehead furrow. Arwen decided to blame it on his headache and not the dubiousness of her wit.

Easing past him, she tugged at the door handle. It didn't budge, but there was a keyhole below it.

Though it was a long shot, she fished into a pocket for the key chain. "We may need you to burn another hole, but let me try this first."

Starblade nodded. "This inner wall and door are more heavily protected with defensive magic. Forcing my way in from here will be difficult."

"Right."

There were almost twenty keys, and Starblade shifted impatiently as Arwen tried them one by one.

After the first five, he gripped his knees and stared at the floor. "Twenty thousand years ago, surface elves and dark elves interacted on Veleshna Var, sharing the world without trouble. Since the dark elves favored the lightless underground caves and tunnels, they did not compete for resources with the surface elves, who prefer the forests and grasslands, reveling in sunlight." He sounded like he was reciting a passage from a history book. "It wasn't until the dark elves learned to summon demons and other sinister creatures from different dimensions that they grew cruel, developing a religion and culture that catered to their new masters. It's possible the first summonings were inadvertent, but my people don't know for certain. It's also believed that the demons placed a permanent magical compulsion on them, forcing them to acquiesce to their desires, at least early on. As time passed, and their culture and religion grew ingrained in the dark elves, with children being indoctrinated by their parents and the demons themselves, they knew no other way. We believe that their servitude to the demons and desire to eradicate or sacrifice other beings became voluntary. At points in history, elven missionaries visited them and tried to convert them back to a goodly path. They were themselves sacrificed."

"I've read about most of that before," Arwen said as she tried another key. A couple had fit in but not turned, and she was down to the last three. She had a feeling this wasn't going to work. Given her luck lately, she'd probably grabbed the keys to the mail room. "The dark elves have a somewhat different version of the past, and they consider the First One, she who learned to summon demons, as the historical figure who set them on the Distinguished Path."

"I have no doubt." Starblade rubbed his temple. "Pardon the lecture. I'm trying to distract myself."

"Distract away. I don't mind lectures."

"No? Many of my subordinates have found them tedious."

"I like trivia. You may have noticed my propensity for speaking at length on some topics."

"Such as mushroom substrates?"

"Yes. If we both make it out of here, I'll bring you those coffee grounds I mentioned."

"A compelling reason to survive."

The last key slipped into the hole and turned. Startled, Arwen would have dropped it if it hadn't been stuck in the door.

A distant cry came to them, muffled by the walls and floors. It sounded like it was a level or more below them, but that didn't keep the hair on the back of Arwen's neck from rising.

"*I* will not try to convert the dark elves." Starblade straightened and drew his sword, but he paused to consider her before stepping toward the door. His gaze drifted to her bow and grew thoughtful.

"Everything okay?"

"I am debating... If this pain incapacitates me, I will be vulnerable."

"Do you want to turn back?"

Nothing in his expression suggested that, and he shook his head resolutely. "No. I cannot. But let me see your bow. It needs more power, and I believe... I no longer believe you will attempt to tag or kill me."

Arwen was touched that he, he who'd made it clear he didn't trust her, wanted to give her a stronger weapon. Especially when she was walking at his back.

Not sure how to express what that meant to her, she merely lifted the bow and asked, "How can that be done?"

"I am not an enchanter, and I cannot ensorcell it permanently, but I might be able to give it greater power for tonight. Your arrows have varying degrees of magic, as I can sense, and some are quite strong, but they are limited by that which fires them. A bow of great power would enhance how much damage they do—what defenses they can pierce."

"That could be useful in here."

"Yes."

Starblade wrapped his hand around her bow without taking it from her grip, then inhaled deeply and closed his eyes.

She sensed him gathering his power and channeling it into the weapon. A great zing of energy coursed through it, her palm tingling where she held the grip.

The power was appealing rather than threatening, and she found herself gazing enraptured at him as his magic flowed into her bow. The desire to step closer to him and bask in his aura swept through her, and she had the urge to promise to be his ally, whether he gave her gold or not, to stand at his side in all battles.

When Starblade opened his eyes again, her bow glowed silver, as if he'd turned it radioactive. She knew better. She sensed that it could now cast arrows farther, piercing the barriers of enemies, at least for tonight.

He frowned down at her, and she realized she *had* stepped closer, her chest almost against his as she stared at him, drawn by that power and by something else she couldn't put a finger on, a yearning for something—someone—that he could fulfill.

Except he'd made it clear that he didn't want *that*. All he wanted was to make sure she would have his back tonight.

Clearing her throat, Arwen stepped back and nodded to her bow. "Thank you."

Starblade released it. "Use it well."

After they opened the door, his orange sphere floated through first, leading them inside. It shone on a cement floor and posts and also glinted off shattered glass in more broken ceiling lights.

Palm damp where she gripped her bow, Arwen walked slowly after the light. Starblade came behind her, eyes alert, his sword in hand.

Though she disliked her mother's people and should have felt no allegiance to them, the niggling feeling crept over her that she was betraying them by leading an enemy to their doorstep. She tried to shake the notion away. The dark elves had kidnapped Starblade's friend and the gnomes. If trouble found them, it was their own fault.

Magic—or magical beings?—moved in the darkness, beyond the sphere's influence. She couldn't see them but sensed them, nothing she'd encountered before. Whatever they were, they weren't large, perhaps a foot in diameter, and they floated about like frisbees.

"Do you know what those are?" she asked quietly.

"I have read of such creatures, but I am not personally familiar with them."

A couple of times, Arwen caught the faintest hint of a glow in the darkness, but it disappeared before she got a good look. They were like ghosts shifting in and out of their dimension.

Starblade sent his light farther afield, but the magical beings flitted away before it shone on them. Arwen saw little but support posts in the cavernous space of the former parking garage.

A few dusty cars lurked by a wall. Left by the people who'd previously worked in the building?

Though it hadn't sounded like it had been long since the insurance company stopped answering its phones, cobwebs draped the mirrors and stretched from one vehicle to a nearby post. Arwen was too far away to see if any spiders lurked in those webs, but she wouldn't have been surprised.

Crates, bags of food, and other supplies were stacked by one post, with small chests resting next to them. A few words in Dark Elven labeled the contents: ritual and spell components.

Another scream reached them from below. Though still muffled, the sound of someone in pain was impossible to misinterpret.

Jaw set, Starblade sent his light around the garage more swiftly. Looking for a trapdoor or a way down?

As it flew about, the light casting moving shadows, something reflected its orange hue back at them. Metal doors.

"The elevator." Was it the same one Arwen had ridden in before? Were they now on one of the floors that had been marked by the dark-elven symbols? She assumed so.

"It will take us below?" Starblade asked, urgency in his voice. Concern for his comrade.

"I think so."

Perhaps forgetting his agreement that she should go first, Starblade strode past her, heading straight toward the elevator.

Arwen hurried after him, thinking that not all traps were baited with meat or mystery. Some used love and loyalty to lure one in.

Before they reached the elevator, numerous of the magical beings they'd been sensing moved abruptly—flying straight toward them.

Starblade raised a barrier and his sword as he turned to face them. Arwen lifted her bow.

Amorphous pale-blue discs floated toward them. Not much larger than the frisbees she'd imagined, they reminded her of jellyfish without the tentacles. They throbbed and crackled with energy as their speed increased. Could they launch lightning or something similar?

Whatever their capabilities, Arwen knew they meant to attack and believed they had the power to hurt them. Not hesitating, she fired.

Though her aim was accurate, her arrow went right through the blob, as if it were the ghost she'd been envisioning earlier.

Swearing, she more carefully selected the next arrow, one that was supposed to have power against the supernatural. She'd seen little evidence that ghosts existed, at least on Earth, but that hadn't stopped her from buying the arrow and keeping it in her quiver.

As she loosed it, Starblade also launched an attack. They hadn't come within his sword range yet, but he targeted several with a wall of fire. Flames roared from ceiling to floor, their brilliance throwing back the shadows, and swallowed several of their enemies.

Arwen aimed at one to the side of his inferno. This time, her arrow pierced the amorphous glowing flesh. The strange creature throbbed faster, its light intensifying before it exploded. Bits of its glowing body spattered a nearby post and the ceiling. Her arrow clattered to the cement floor.

The group that Starblade had targeted with flames should have been incinerated, but they floated out of the fire, unharmed. Still flying, they accelerated toward him. All the glowing blobs did except the one Arwen had destroyed.

"What power does that arrow have?" Starblade asked.

"It's enchanted to be effective against the supernatural."

He extended his barrier to protect her while levitating the fallen arrow back to her. It slid through his defensive magic to land in her hand. "Do you have more?"

"I'm afraid not." Arwen nocked the arrow as the flock of floating blobs split to encircle them.

"I do not know if these qualify as *supernatural*. If they are what I've read about, they are from the dimension of the demons, vampiric creatures that thrive on the life and power of others."

"Sounds supernatural to me."

The blobs flew into his barrier, and Arwen jumped, afraid their inter-dimensional nature would allow them to slip through. Instead, they splatted into it, amorphous bodies shifting and molding to it like the jellyfish she'd envisioned. They throbbed and hummed.

The barrier held, keeping them at bay without trouble, but Starblade grunted and winced. From the effort? Or because the dog whistle—the *dragon* whistle—was continuing to harass him?

He stabbed toward one creature with his sword. His barrier shifted ever so slightly to allow his own weapon through for the attack, but it didn't matter. As with her first arrow, his sword passed through the creature without hurting it.

"Is your headache worse?" Arwen asked.

"Among other things. As I said, these creatures are vampiric. They're draining the energy from my barrier. I'm debating what type of magic would be effective on them. I've never battled entities from other dimensions and have only cursory knowledge of them."

The humming grew louder, the creatures brightening. Like batteries charging themselves with his power.

Angry magic swelled from Starblade, and wind swirled outside of his barrier as he attempted to knock them away. Bits of refuse and a random shoe skidded across the parking garage floor. The side mirror from a car clattered past. But the creatures remained in place.

Arwen could sense the power of his barrier dwindling, even as the creatures' auras grew more substantial. She lifted her bow but didn't think she would be able to fire through his defenses unless she stepped out from behind them—an unappealing idea.

"Let me see your arrow." Starblade held his hand out.

She gave it to him. "Are you going to reverse engineer it to figure out what magic it uses so you can employ it on them?"

"Something like that."

With an irritated battle cry, Starblade sprang forward, jabbing the arrow at the creature he'd unsuccessfully attacked with his sword. Her weapon sank into it. It shuddered, shrinking in on itself. Before it could back away from the barrier, he stabbed it again. Not hesitating, he sprang after the next one, his barrier shifting with him.

Arwen fingered through her arrow collection, wondering if another type of magic might work on them. He'd tried flame and storm power. What about ice?

With a silver-blue arrow she called Glacier, she fired at a creature that was pulsing menacingly at Starblade. But her projectile went straight through without causing it to flinch.

Sweat gleamed on Starblade's forehead, a testament to the effort required to maintain the barrier while vampire jellyfish slurped up its magic. But he'd found a way to hurt them and was. Two more flew to bits, destroyed by the arrowhead.

The last three creatures realized the danger and released his barrier to fly away. Lowering his defenses, Starblade ran after them, agile as he leaped and jabbed. He used Arwen's arrow like a fencer's foil.

A creature swept around him, attempting to reach his head from behind, but he finished the one he faced and whirled in time to slash the arrow through his attacker. Like the others, the creature exploded into dozens of blobby pieces. They splattered to the cement floor before vanishing. With the glows from the creatures gone, darkness descended upon the parking garage once more.

After releasing a weary sigh, Starblade conjured his illumination sphere again. He walked up to Arwen and returned her arrow.

"That was useful. Where did you acquire it?" Starblade wiped sweat from his brow. "Such things are usually won from enemies or purchased at select shops around the Cosmic Realms that cater to assassins and military commanders of means."

Did that imply he didn't believe she could have acquired such an arrow through legitimate methods?

"Three summers ago, I traded my strawberry popover recipe and twenty pounds of fruit from the farm to a half-gnome weapons smith with a sweet tooth."

Starblade blinked slowly. "You traded food for an invaluable magical weapon?"

"If you'd had my popovers, you would understand. They're sweet, delicious, and have an unexpected kick."

"I see."

"Come by the farm once the strawberries are in season, and I'll prove it."

"You'll bake me one of these creations?" Starblade looked toward the elevator.

"I will. Since you're paying me for this job, I won't even make you bring me an arrow."

"Generous." He headed for the elevator and waved for her to follow. "Let's see if your blood can take us to the lower levels."

They hadn't heard the pained cry for several minutes. Arwen, hoping that didn't mean they were too late, trailed after Starblade.

Vleesha, a female voice whispered into her mind, startling her. *You are remembered.*

Horror filled Arwen, and she froze. At first, she thought it was her mother, because the voice was vaguely familiar, but it wasn't. Her mother had come often to oversee her training and tell her she would have to work hard because her human blood made her weak. Arwen wouldn't have forgotten her voice. Whoever this was, however, knew the name her mother had given her. In the Dark Elven tongue, it meant *useful one*. Over the years, Arwen had done her best to forget that name.

Vleesha, the speaker continued, *this is not the plan She Who Leads had in mind for you, but we have been expecting your return since your thirtieth birthday. You are an adult now. It is time to fulfill your destiny.*

Abruptly, Arwen realized this was the person who'd spoken into her mind when the shifters had come to the farm, the one who'd wanted her to go with them.

We approve that you have brought a half-dragon into our laboratory, the speaker continued. *Since we have the other of his kind to experiment on, we can sacrifice this one. The great demons will be most pleased to nip at the veins of one with such delicious power. Only a full-blooded dragon would be a superior sacrifice, and we might entrap one of those tonight too.* The speaker inserted an image into her mind of Zavryd with Val on his back, flying low as they soared over Bellevue and toward the insurance building.

Starblade touched Arwen's shoulder. He must have noticed that she'd frozen.

Alarm made her heart pound. If he'd caught any of those telepathic words, he would think she'd set him up, that she was intentionally leading him into a trap.

But the speaker had used Dark Elven. Could he understand the language?

Arwen swallowed. Even if he couldn't, he might find it suspicious if he caught her communicating with a dark elf. She didn't reply to the speaker, instead telling him, "They know we're here."

"I would have been surprised if they didn't. We'll have to deal with whatever else they throw at us. I intend to free those they're torturing." His voice grew softer and determined as he added, "I intend to free my comrade."

"I understand." Heart still pounding, Arwen stepped into the elevator.

After Starblade entered, the doors slid shut, magic curling along the seam. Locking them in?

Excellent, the female said. Zyretha. Her name came to Arwen from the depths of her memory. A priestess and one of her early teachers. *Bring the half-dragon to us for a sacrifice.*

Compulsion laced the words, filling Arwen with the desire to do exactly as the dark elves wished.

29

The elevator doors opened without hesitation, and the words, *trap, trap, trap,* floated through Arwen's mind. She opened her mouth to warn Starblade that one of the dark elves had been in contact with her, but nothing came out. She knew Zyretha had put a compulsion on her, using magic to control her, but that awareness didn't make her immune. Fear crept up her spine as she tried to figure out a way to escape the dark elf's clutches.

If Starblade knew, he might have the power to sever the link. But when Arwen switched to attempting to warn him telepathically, a wall kept her words from escaping her mind.

Oblivious to her inner turmoil, Starblade touched the flame button on the panel. Nothing happened.

He looked to Arwen, extending his hand toward the buttons.

She didn't know if this was the same elevator that she'd been in before, but it had the same sets of buttons. She pressed the flame symbol, guessing it was the next level down, what might previously have been parking level 3.

She was tempted to send the elevator straight to the bottom, but it might make more sense to be methodical. Besides, if that was the heart of the lair, the dark elves might all be waiting down there.

At her touch, the button lit up, and the car descended.

Starblade faced the doors, his sword in hand, his barrier wrapped around both of them. Arwen touched the ends of the arrows in her quiver, but none of them would give her extra power against dark elves. It had never occurred to her to seek out a weapon to target her mother's people explicitly.

When the car halted, Starblade grunted in pain, wincing and reaching toward his head. He caught himself and jerked his hand back down.

He is more able to resist the dosk'keyar *than the other half-dragon,* Zyretha told Arwen.

Was she watching their every move? Arwen didn't recognize that word but assumed it referred to an artifact.

It is a device made by dragons to combat dragons from rival clans. We cut a deal for it. There are some of their kind who believe they have a use for dark elves, who do not want to see our kind disappear from the Realms. The device is keeping the full-blood dragon at bay, but if we could entice him in, we would have an even greater prize.

"They aren't opening." Starblade looked from the sealed doors toward Arwen again. "Will your touch work on them?"

Though Arwen didn't see an *open* button, she rested her hand on the cool metal. Faint magic hummed through it, and she willed the doors to part. Her tattoo tingled, but they didn't budge.

"I'll see if I can force them." Starblade nodded for her to step back and slid the tip of his sword into the seam. "I thank you for coming along and helping me, Arwen." That was the first time he'd used her name. "Yendral isn't just a friend and a former subordinate. He's..." The sword wasn't enough to force open the doors, and Starblade applied his magic to the seam while he spoke. "He means a lot to me. We grew up together and trained together, and then we were brothers in battle for a long time. Now, we're all that are left of our kind."

"I understand." Arwen closed her eyes, hating that Zyretha wanted her to betray him. And Val and Zavryd too.

With a grunt and a flush of magic, Starblade succeeded in prying the doors apart. Another dark area waited for them, cobwebs draping everything this time.

The doors only parted a foot before jerking to a halt and trying to close again. Starblade lunged to place himself in the gap to keep them from shutting. One of the webs plastered his cheek and pointed ear, and he grimaced, swatting at it.

"They sure can grow those quickly," he grumbled.

Abruptly, he leaned forward and grabbed his temple, cracking his forehead on the door. The pain must have intensified.

Not sure what she could do, Arwen rested a hand on his shoulder. "I'm sorry."

Starblade drew in deep breaths, tendons in his neck standing out as he struggled.

"Do you want me to go ahead again?" Arwen peered into the gloom, the hazy webs making it impossible to see far, but she could sense magical artifacts on this level.

"No," he rasped, forcing himself to straighten. When the doors attempted to close on him again, he snarled and thrust his palms against them. With muscle and a great surge of power, he shoved them hard enough to break them. "I sense the auras of people here." He looked out of the elevator and toward the left. "Gnomes. A troll... an elf... more."

Arwen sensed artifacts but not people. Strange. Since Starblade was much more powerful than she, he would be able to detect things from farther away, but the parking garage wasn't *that* big. She ought to have been able to sense magical beings.

Starblade sucked in a quick breath. "Is that Yendral's aura?"

Arwen bit her lip, certain she would have caught the presence of a half-dragon if he'd been there. But she neither sensed what Starblade sensed, nor could she detect dark elves on this level, and she was positive some would be present if their prisoners were here.

"I think some of the artifacts—" Arwen started, but the abrupt compulsion to remain quiet swept over her, stilling her tongue.

Starblade glanced at her. "You think it could be a trap?"

She tried to nod but couldn't.

"I'm sure it is." He sighed and looked toward the left again. "But I do not know how to spring it without walking in. If you were an ally of theirs, I could push you ahead of me at sword point, but I now believe you don't have anything to do with them —or want anything to do with them." He smiled briefly at her, though his face remained pained, his eyes full of worry for his friend.

His words would have delighted her if she hadn't been under Zyretha's control. Damn it.

"If we can find the artifact that controls the defenses," she found she could say while waving toward the ceiling.

"Zavryd'nokquetal could come in? I sense him out there, and, yes, he might be useful. Having him distract our enemies might allow us more freedom down here." Starblade swatted at the cobwebs with his sword as he advanced, his orange sphere lighting the way again. Its illumination was muted by the silky strands stretching between the posts and from the high ceiling.

As she trailed him, Arwen eyed the webbing. Those strands were thick. Far thicker than typical from a spider—a *normal*-sized spider. What had made them? She didn't remember any tunnels that had been filled with webs in the underground compound where she'd been born, but tributes to the spider demon were frequent enough that they didn't surprise her.

Though she still didn't sense the auras of people, she could tell they were getting closer to the artifacts. The vibrations of a machine or something else hummed through the cement floor and into her body. Arwen imagined Zyretha smiling into her mind as they walked into her trap. Maybe it wasn't her imagination.

A human-sized crystalline cylinder came into view ahead of them, the hollowed interior glowing a faint red. It was the first of many such devices, all obscured by webs. It had a doorway, reminding her of a freestanding closet. The strands hung thickly over it, draping down like a curtain, and she couldn't tell if anything was inside.

The magic of the cylinders was enticing, inviting one closer.

Starblade headed straight for the first of them.

Arwen tried to blurt a warning, afraid he'd been mesmerized by their power. But the telepathic equivalent of a hand across her mouth stopped her again.

Starblade held up a hand of his own. To stop her? To protect her?

Using his sword, he cut through the cobweb curtain. It was thicker than it looked, but his magical blade sliced it without trouble. The cut section wafted to the floor, revealing a mound of cobwebs inside the chamber. Two coiled glowing cords were attached to it.

It wasn't a mound. Arwen rocked back as, for the first time, she sensed an aura. A *gnomish* aura.

"There's someone in there," she blurted.

"Yes." Starblade had already known.

Sword raised, he eyed the coils. Thinking of trying to slice the gnome free?

Not recognizing the aura, Arwen didn't think it was Imoshaun, but might it be her husband? A panel glowed on the inside of the cylinder, muted by cobwebs. If there were buttons or knobs to operate the device, Arwen couldn't pick them out.

"I don't know much about your people's magic or technology," Starblade admitted.

Arwen winced at being lumped in with the dark elves. They weren't *her* people.

"It's possible this is designed to kill the occupant if we try to cut him free without knowing what we're doing," he added. "We may have to find a dark elf and force her to operate it."

"I agree." Arwen hated the idea of leaving prisoners—freeing them was the entire reason they'd come—but accidentally killing them would be worse.

You have gained entrance to the building, yes? Zavryd spoke into her mind.

Yes.

Find a way to allow us in, and we will deal with the dark elves.

Arwen wanted to free the prisoners, not *deal with* anyone, but, as Starblade had said, accomplishing their mission would be easier with Zavryd inside with them. And maybe he could break Zyretha's link to her. Arwen attempted to warn Zavryd about that, hoping that speaking to him might sidestep the magical compulsion, but she still couldn't utter words about Zyretha aloud or telepathically.

Brushing aside more cobwebs, Starblade moved to the next cylinder. Another prisoner was buried inside, someone larger than the gnome. A half-troll. Again, Arwen detected only the faintest of auras. Did the cobwebs and chambers insulate them? Or were the people barely alive in there, their auras almost extinguished?

A dusty guitar leaned in the cylinder with the half-troll. Was this the missing bard Zavryd had mentioned?

They passed four more cylinders, Starblade cutting down the curtains that hid the occupants but not daring to do more. An elf, a half-elf, a goblin, and—Arwen halted. "That's Imoshaun."

Starblade nodded but continued to the next chamber. He had to be looking for his friend.

Arwen stared bleakly at the cocoon burying the gnome, again eyeing the control panel and cords. She wiped aside cobwebs, searching for instructions. It had been a long time since she'd read Dark Elven, but she had been taught the language as a girl and might be able to make out enough to get the gist. If only she could *find* instructions.

"Have you seen any writing?" she asked.

Starblade didn't answer. He'd moved on and was staring into another chamber.

Arwen joined him and peered inside. It was empty, a few cobwebs on the bottom the only hint that a prisoner might have been there.

"Yendral was here," Starblade said softly.

"How can you know?" Arwen, who could barely sense the people under the cobwebs, couldn't feel anything except the magic of the chamber itself.

"His aura lingers inside."

"They may have taken him out when they realized you were here. Bait for—" As if she'd said too much, the magical vise clamped down on her words, and she couldn't finish.

"My trap, yes. I'm surprised they care about me when they have him. His blood is as good as mine."

"Is it? You were the leader of your people, right? Maybe yours is, uhm, more desirable."

"More likely, they're irritated that I've been attacking their kidnapping team and trying to get into their lair."

Arwen remembered him utterly thrashing that car and trying to thrash the building too.

"I doubt that's it," she said. "They're... mission-driven."

"Oh, I'm aware."

"Do you think he's who we heard..." Being tortured, she couldn't bring herself to say. This time, it had nothing to do with Zyretha's influence.

"I don't know."

"If we can figure out how to get Imoshaun out, she might know where they took your friend."

Maybe if they experimented on the chamber without a prisoner in it, they could figure out how the machines operated.

"The lift buttons suggest two more levels below us," Starblade said.

It took Arwen a moment to realize he meant that they already knew where his comrade was, on one of those two floors.

Abruptly, Starblade bent forward with a hiss. He leaned his elbows against his knees, his sword tip brushing the floor, and a fresh grimace twisted his face.

"If you want to try to free the prisoners from the chambers, you'll have a better chance than I. I need to find... whatever is stabbing my brain like a dragon's teeth. Then I can do more."

"Okay." Arwen rested a hand on the panel of the empty chamber, hoping it would respond to her. She still didn't see any writing, nothing to suggest how to work the devices, but she prodded experimentally with her magic.

After drawing in a bracing breath, Starblade looked toward a few glowing dots flashing slowly, barely visible through more cobwebs. More devices, Arwen's senses told her, then thought of Zavryd's request that she lower the building's defenses. Might they find the thing that could allow the others in on this level?

Yes, Zyretha said into her mind, sending a fresh chill down Arwen's spine. *The dragon wants you to lower the defenses. It would be disrespectful of you not to obey his wishes.*

Arwen swallowed. The dark elves *wanted* Zavryd to come into their lair?

Maybe they believed that whatever was giving Starblade the monster migraine would affect Zavryd as strongly? Or *more* strongly? If a half-dragon struggled under its influence, maybe a full dragon would be even more debilitated.

"That device is made from dwarven magic." Starblade waved

his sword toward the red dots, oblivious to Arwen's thoughts, to the dark elf contacting her. "It might be responsible for the building's defenses. Their people are known for such magic." Starblade took a step toward the glowing dots but paused, lifting his sword. "Something is over there."

"Something... alive?" Arwen eased away from the empty chamber.

She hadn't learned anything from it and kept expecting a trap. Why would the dark elves let strangers root through their prisoner area? It wasn't as if they didn't know she and Starblade were here.

"When defending, spread the caltrops all about, not to stop the enemy, but so you know when he approaches." Starblade sounded like he was quoting one of his generals.

"What are the caltrops in our current predicament?"

Something stirred in the darkness ahead of him. Something large.

"The webs, I believe." Starblade pointed his sword at two new crimson dots shining through the haze. Eyes. They were higher above the floor than his. "I'll deal with this. Try to get around it and find a way to turn off the dwarven device. I believe that controls at least some of the building's defenses."

"I'm not experienced with dwarven devices." Arwen did step to the side of him, but mostly so she could raise her bow and point it toward those eyes. Whatever the creature was, it was huge, and it was also blocking the way to the device. "How do you turn them off?"

"Bashing them repeatedly sometimes works."

Starblade twitched his sword, and his orange light grew brighter. Its illumination reached the creature waiting for them, a towering, dark-blue-skinned, hairy tarantula, its fangs gleaming with saliva. No, not a tarantula. Arwen abruptly recognized it from dark-elven literature.

"A soul *drykar*," she said. "It's as vampiric as the blobs above. If it sinks its fangs into you, it steals not only your blood but your life's energy."

He grunted. "I've heard of them."

"Are you experienced fighting them?"

"Not yet." Starblade raised his barrier, a barrier the *drykar* might be able to destroy with its vampiric fangs, and strode forward. "Get to the device."

"You can be pushy, you know." Arwen took a few sideways steps, in case she *was* able to get past the spider when it engaged Starblade, but she had no intention of abandoning him to fight it alone. She selected the same arrow that had worked on the blobs, wishing she had a dozen more of them in her quiver, especially since that blue hide looked thick. Would her weapons be able to pierce it?

Thus far, the *drykar* hadn't moved, only showing its fangs as it stared at them. But, as the glowing sphere pushed its way closer, the creature screeched, and power pulsed from it.

The spider's attack shattered the magical light, plunging the area into darkness.

"What now?" Arwen almost loosed her arrow, but she hesitated, willing her eyes to adjust to the gloom.

A skittering sound came from ahead—the *drykar* rushing them.

"We fight," Starblade said.

30

"*ERAVEKT*," STARBLADE BARKED INTO THE DARKNESS AS THE *DRYKAR* charged him.

His sword flared with blue light, illuminating the great spider as it reared up, hairy legs pawing at the air. He attacked with magic instead of his blade, a great gust of fire that engulfed the beast in flames.

Not sure that would harm it any more than it had the vampiric blobs, Arwen fired her arrow, aiming for its carapace. She doubted she would hit a vital target, but she didn't want to risk shooting anywhere close to Starblade. As his flames roared, he charged the spider, swinging at one of its flailing legs.

Tiny barbs shot from them. They would have impaled Starblade, but his barrier blocked them. With lightning speed, his sword sliced in, lopping off the tip of a leg.

Flames burned all around the *drykar*, and the air crackled and smelled of roasting meat. Even so, the creature didn't screech or give any indication that the fire bothered it.

Arwen's arrow struck and sank into its carapace but only a few inches. If it did any serious damage, she couldn't tell. She yanked out another arrow as the *drykar* stopped rearing, dropping to its legs again to snap at Starblade.

Unperturbed, he swung his sword, aiming for its fang-filled jaws. His blade struck one of those long teeth but clanged off without damaging it.

When Starblade backed away after the attack, Arwen targeted the *drykar's* brain, willing her magic to help the arrow pierce its skull.

It did not. Instead, it bounced off and hit the cement scant inches from Starblade's darting feet.

He didn't glance at it as he danced in and out, striking while evading the barbed legs and snapping jaws, but he did say, "The defensive device, please."

A second later, his sword lopped off a front leg at the halfway point. This time, the spider screeched. It lunged for him, attempting to crush him with its hulking carapace. Starblade leaped to the side, avoiding it as he slashed again.

Though Arwen hated to give up on helping, his sword had the power to hurt it, and the rest of her arrows probably didn't. He could handle this.

Yes, Zyretha crooned into her mind. Her telepathic voice seemed to originate on the level below them. *Turn off the defenses. Let the dragon believe you are his ally and will allow him in to catch us unprepared.*

That made Arwen want to leave the defenses up, to ensure Zavryd and Val *couldn't* get in, even if it meant she and Starblade had to handle all the dark elves on their own.

But Zyretha repeated, *Turn off the defenses,* and the magical compulsion flooded into Arwen.

As she'd suspected, she had to be close to Zyretha now, for her power was strong, too strong to resist. That didn't keep Arwen from gritting her teeth and trying.

With her motions jerky as she was manipulated like a marionette, Arwen hoped Starblade would notice and understand what she couldn't say, that she was as dangerous to him as the dark elves.

Another leg flew off the spider, skidding past her and weeping blood and ichor onto the cement. Starblade was too busy to pay attention to Arwen.

Grimacing, she made it to the device, glowing domes, buttons, and levers offering no hint about how to operate it. If there were instructions written in Dark Elven or any other tongue, she couldn't see them. Nonetheless, the knowledge of how to shut it down flowed into her.

With her hand guided by Zyretha, Arwen turned a dial, pulled a lever, and rested two fingers on a dome. A blueprint of the building flashed into her mind, as did information on the various defenses, including a two-foot-wide, dragon-shaped artifact on the level below. It was the source of the power being emitted to irritate her scaled allies.

Had Zyretha meant to share all that? Or had the information come from the device Arwen was interfacing with? It seemed to be a control center for all the artifacts working together to protect the building.

Would destroying it turn off all the defenses?

No, Zyretha said, then compelled Arwen to touch a final button.

The defenses around most of the building remained in place, but those protecting the rooftop disappeared. That left an opening for Zavryd and Val. To the dragon's senses, it would seem like Arwen had succeeded, like she'd done exactly what he'd asked.

If only.

Flames roared behind Arwen, and she stepped away from the device. It went dark, as if she'd destroyed it, but she knew it was only a ruse, that most of the defenses remained up. Zavryd was being lured toward a narrow path that he could take to get in. And the dark elves, or, more likely, all the magical beings in the building above who were serving them, would be ready. Arwen hoped they wouldn't be a match for a dragon's power, but if the pain induced by the artifact was worse for him than for Starblade...

The flames died down, the scent of charred meat—charred *spider*—stronger now in the air.

Arwen turned to check for further threats and retrieve her arrow. With half its legs severed, the *drykar* lay on the floor. It didn't twitch when she pulled her arrow out.

With his enemy defeated, Starblade turned his attention toward the dark device, his face still contorted with pain. And frustration. Maybe he could sense that it hadn't been fully turned off, because he gestured for Arwen to scoot back, then blasted it with flames.

Heat scorched the air in front of her, probably turning her cheeks pink. She scooted even farther back. A good thing because the device, engulfed in dragon fire, exploded. Shards of metal and magical bits flew in all directions. Arwen sprang behind a post as they pinged off the ceiling and floor.

"You're a dangerous ally," she said as the fire died down.

She stared at the remains of the device, surprised he'd been able to destroy it. No, surprised the dark elves had *let* him destroy it. But when she swept out with her senses to see if the rest of the building's defenses had dropped, she found they hadn't. Nothing had changed. The rooftop remained accessible but nothing else. Had this device been nothing but a decoy? Or maybe there was a backup somewhere else.

"Yes," Starblade said. "Especially when a headache is making me crabby."

"I think the source of that is on the level below, unless I read things incorrectly—" unless the information Arwen had received had been a lie, "—and the device you just flamed *was* responsible for it."

He hesitated—waiting to see if the pain went away? "No. I still have the headache."

"I'm sorry."

Starblade lifted his gaze toward the ceiling. "Zavryd'nokquetal has landed on the rooftop."

Arwen wanted to ask if Starblade could reach out and warn him that this was a trap. Instead, what came out of her mouth was, "His assistance will be invaluable."

I hate you, Arwen thought to her controller.

Such emotion. That comes from your human half. Dark elves are a rational people.

What are you doing here anyway? Why do you need dragons and half-dragons?

To ensure our longevity and survival as a species, we are gathering and melding their genetic material with ours and will produce new and stronger offspring.

Is that why you took the gnomes too? And other races?

We are taking the best from each species, but it is the dragons that have the power that will make our new offspring strong enough to survive in Realms that detest our kind. First, we must deal with the half-dragon while our servants delay the dragon above. He will be more problematic to capture, and he has that odious female with him. But we will handle her. After all our plans she's thwarted, I will enjoy capturing and sacrificing her.

Arwen swallowed. *Val?*

Zyretha didn't reply, but her presence remained, ensuring Arwen couldn't issue any warnings. Her tattoo throbbed in sync with her heartbeat, and the urge to return to the elevator and descend lower into the lair filled her with each pulse.

Starblade walked about, sweeping his sword through cobwebs, clearing more of the area. Another larger cylinder came into view, this one set apart from the others. He stopped in front of it. It lacked a prisoner, though it was powered on and seemed to be waiting for one.

A dragon?

"Step in, if you like," a female voice said from the elevator, the words in English but heavily accented.

Fear froze Arwen in place as the speaker dropped whatever camouflage had cloaked her, letting them sense her powerful aura. It was Zyretha, her albino skin half-hidden under the hood of a cloak but the shadows not quite hiding her red eyes as she regarded Starblade. She carried no visible weapons, but Arwen sensed numerous magical charms under her cloak in addition to the power she could wield. Zyretha was not unarmed.

"Though that chamber was not meant for you." Zyretha lifted an arm, fingers splayed toward the ceiling.

Now, Arwen could also sense Zavryd up there. In human form so he could fit inside the building, he was fighting his way down with Val. They had to believe they were breaking in instead of being lured in.

Starblade's eyes flared violet with indignation as he faced Zyretha. He masked his features, trying not to show his pain, but the creases at the corners of his eyes betrayed him.

"We will be happy to capture you and draw samples of your blood and soul for our project," Zyretha said, fearless despite Starblade's powerful aura crackling around him and his raised sword, "but our assistant was kind enough to lure a *real* dragon into our clutches, and that chamber is for him."

Starblade had taken a step toward Zyretha, but he paused. "Your... assistant?"

"Of course." Zyretha shifted her spread fingers toward Arwen. "Did you think one with our blood would loyally serve a mongrel dragon? Or any but the great demons?"

Starblade looked at Arwen. His face remained masked, but was that betrayal in his eyes? He couldn't believe Zyretha.

Arwen shook her head vehemently. "I'm not assisting them. I don't even—" She started to say she didn't even know Zyretha, but that wasn't entirely true.

"Long ago, we released the daughter of She Who Leads into the human world," Zyretha said, "so she could infiltrate it and blend in, so she could shop for suitable sacrifices among them. Since she lacks our aversion to the light—" Zyretha eyed Starblade's glowing sword with distaste, "—she could go where we could not. She could find those worthy of our greatest project, one we've been pursuing for many decades now. One that we, with that which we extract from you and the dragon, will finally be able to complete."

"If you had her to work for you, why employ the shifters?" Starblade asked.

Arwen nodded, glad he was skeptical of Zyretha.

"The shifters are greedy and easy to enslave. And they'd found a place among the law enforcers of the humans. That made it a simple matter for them to collect those we wished without repercussions. They kept reports of powerful missing people from going out, to ensure we were at the culmination of our plans before anyone knew we were here in the human city." Zyretha pointed toward Arwen. "Grab the half-dragon."

Starblade snorted, then blasted such tremendous power at Zyretha that Arwen, forty feet away, rocked back.

The gale should have knocked Zyretha into the wall on the far side of the parking garage, if not obliterated her altogether. But one of the trinkets she wore maintained a barrier around her, one Starblade's power couldn't overcome.

Under her hood, Zyretha smiled tightly. After a twitch of her finger, Starblade gasped, his knees almost giving way as he jerked a hand to his head. She hadn't attacked him but increased the amount of power coming from the dragon device on the level below. Zavryd, wherever he was, would be gasping too. And vulnerable to the shifters and whoever else was attacking him?

Arwen stepped toward Zyretha and reached for an arrow. She *had* to stop the dark elf.

But power flowed from her tattoo, locking her arm in place. It traveled farther, winding down her spine and to her legs, rooting her to the floor. Arwen cursed in frustration.

Unconcerned, Zyretha didn't even glance at her.

"You came unprepared to battle our people," Zyretha told Starblade.

"Apparently," he grunted, glancing at Arwen.

In disappointment. That look stabbed her like a dagger. He'd thought he had an ally in her. And she *wanted* to be his ally, not to work for her mother's people.

"I expected more from a battle-hardened general," Zyretha said.

Starblade sighed, as if to say, *Me too.* All he spoke aloud was, "This new era and this world are not mine."

"Your blood does sing with power, and you've more potential, I believe, than you've unlocked. Did your elven masters not wish you to be too powerful to control?"

Starblade frowned and didn't answer her.

"Your potential will be useful to us. Indeed, I am eager to explore it." Zyretha flicked a finger at Arwen. "Capture him. We'll collect his essence before we lock him away."

Still frowning, Starblade pointed his sword at Arwen, though he didn't take his gaze from Zyretha. *She* was the real threat. He had to know that.

Arwen struggled to shake off the compulsion, to free her mind and her body of control. But her hand jerked of its own accord toward her quiver.

She grabbed a particular arrow—the one she'd found in

Imoshaun's workshop, the one she'd thought had been made to use against the dark elves. Only now, as she drew the arrow, did she realize it had been part of the dark-elf trap. They'd been expecting her. They'd sent the shifters to try to get her. Maybe even those ogres. When that hadn't worked, they'd drawn her here. She wagered it hadn't been chance that had brought Amber's car down the right road to discover this building.

"Capture him," Zyretha repeated, holding Arwen's gaze.

Unable to fight the command, Arwen nocked the arrow.

Starblade crouched, his barrier around himself, and prepared to dodge. He could have attacked her with his power, but he didn't. Why not? She would rather have him send her flying into a post and break her neck than be responsible for his death.

His barrier was strong, and maybe he believed it would be enough to protect him. It would have repelled *most* weapons, but, with sinking certainty, Arwen knew that the power he'd infused in her bow would now be used against him and that this particular arrow could pierce that barrier. And she... she never missed.

If she fired. Her hands shook as she fought to keep from doing that.

The spider tattoo sent more power surging through her, an enemy within her own skin. An enemy the dark elves had the foresight to embed in her two decades ago.

Surprisingly, a tingle came from her left arm, from the dragon tattoo. Arwen willed it to help her, to fight the dark-elven compulsion, to free her.

Though she didn't expect that to happen, Starblade's eyes narrowed, as if he knew what she wanted, and he wanted the same. The power of the dragon tattoo grew, and she sensed it sending its magic through her body to battle that of the spider tattoo.

In her hands, the bow shook, the arrow nocked but trembling.

With all of her strength, she tried to shift her aim, to point it at Zyretha.

Zyretha frowned, removed something from her cloak, and threw it at Starblade. A magical smoke grenade.

Though it bounced off his barrier, landing several feet away without doing harm, it spewed noxious fumes into the air. Whether it distracted him or not, Arwen couldn't tell, but Zyretha used the moment to reassert her power. Not only the spider tattoo but Zyretha herself fought against the magic emanating from the dragon tattoo. The combined forces won the tug-of-war.

Arwen's bow jerked back toward Starblade, and she loosed the arrow. As she'd feared, it sliced through his barrier. She'd kept herself from firing at his chest—at his *heart*—but the arrow sank into his thigh.

He cried out and dropped to one knee. Zyretha cackled with triumph.

"I'm sorry," Arwen whispered, horrified. Tears stabbed at her eyes.

He didn't hear her whisper. The embedded arrow oozed a magical lethargy into him, and he dropped fully to his hands and knees. Even they wouldn't support his weight, and he pitched onto his side on the floor.

"We have you now," Zyretha said.

Instead of subsiding, the war between Arwen's two tattoos intensified, the dragon magic again fighting the dark-elven magic. The two forces tore at her from the inside out. Then their power surged, overwhelming her like a lightning strike.

As Arwen pitched to the cement with darkness overtaking her, her last thought was that she'd captured herself as well as Starblade.

31

Arwen woke to a scream.

Starblade, she thought at first, the memories of what happened before she blacked out flooding into her before she opened her eyes. She expected to come to in chains, dangling from a wall or thrown into a cell. But as she focused on a ceiling light with a shattered bulb above her, she realized she lay on her back on a cot. Screams sounded, jolting her fully awake. When she turned her head, she didn't spot Starblade crying out but Imoshaun.

The female gnome hung suspended between two great floor-to-ceiling coils attached to numerous magical apparatuses, their glow providing faint illumination. Behind her, P4 was painted in black on the wall. Arwen had been taken down another level.

One of the apparatuses throbbed as Imoshaun's power—her *essence* was what Zyretha had called it—was channeled out of her and into a globe of swirling red energy. Some kind of magical battery or capacitor? Arwen sensed numerous types of energy within. Gnome, troll, ogre, and even—her breath caught—half-dragon.

Had the dark elves already done this to Starblade? While Arwen had been unconscious? Or had they taken the essence of the comrade that he'd come to save?

People in cloaks and hoods—dark elves—moved about the area, murmuring to each other and carrying blood samples and tiny magical vials. Arwen picked out the words *dragon coming* and *what we've been waiting for* in Dark Elven.

Across the room—the *laboratory*—Arwen sensed Starblade. His aura was still strong. That was one small relief.

"Hurry," a dark elf said, one of several males and females gathered around Starblade. "Slather the nullifier all over him before he wakes up. His power is greater than that of the other half-dragon."

The speaker waved toward a cylinder similar to the cobweb-draped chambers on the level above, but this one was sparkling clean, no hint of web or even dust dulling it. The captive inside was easy to see, a handsome male elf naked but caked in what looked like hardened mud. Arwen's senses told her it was more than that, the dried substance emanating magic while simultaneously dulling the aura of the person inside. If that was Starblade's half-dragon colleague, he should have had a substantial aura.

A bucket of liquid goo rested on the ground by Starblade. Naked Starblade. He lay on his side on the floor. They'd ripped his clothes off while leaving the arrow in his thigh.

Arwen winced at the reminder of her treachery, at her failure to keep from hurting him with the power *he'd* given her. If he hadn't made her bow stronger, she might not have gotten through, even with that arrow. Though she suspected the dark elves had planned everything, and it had been made specifically for him.

Two of them stepped closer to Starblade, chanting and creating magical chains of power that wrapped around him as he stirred. Two more dark elves hurried to dip brushes into the bucket and paint his body with the goo. The nullifier they'd mentioned? Arwen had never heard of such a substance, but Starblade's aura grew less substantial as they covered more of his body with it.

"If we can't handle another half-dragon, we'll have trouble with the full dragon," another dark elf said.

"The defenses have brought the dragon and his mongrel female to a standstill, and the shifters are keeping them at bay." That was Zyretha's voice. "By the time the dragon reaches us, if he does at all, his power will be exhausted. With our weapons and artifacts, we'll capture him as easily as we did the others, and we'll also nullify his power."

"Your arrogance may be our downfall."

"My *arrogance* and willingness to take chances is what will save our people."

"If you call being mutated and mingled with the souls and blood of other species *saving* us," a new speaker grumbled.

"It's better than facing our extinction as a race. And the power of a dragon..." Zyretha risked stepping close to Starblade, though his eyes were open now, burning with fury, and stroked his bare shoulder. "I will not object to it flowing through my veins."

Starblade rose to his knees and jerked an arm up, trying to grab her, but the magic binding him kept him from reaching her. Chuckling, Zyretha stepped back.

Growling, he threw more power at the magical bindings. They flexed, weakening.

Losing her mirth, Zyretha backed farther from him and waved to the paintbrush wielders. "Hurry up, and cover all of him with that. The gnome is almost drained and of little use after that. We'll slip the half-dragon into the *vyarstir* and start drawing his essence. Between him and the dragon, it may be all we need to complete our mission."

Starblade glanced to the side and saw his unconscious comrade in the chamber. Even more fury flared in his violet eyes. He staggered to his feet, raging and writhing, and Arwen sensed how close he was to overcoming the dark elves' ensnarement, nullifying gunk or not.

Surprised she wasn't bound, neither by rope nor magic, Arwen looked around for her bow. She'd had enough arrows left in her quiver for each dark elf in the room. If Zyretha was distracted and not consciously compelling her, maybe Arwen could plant an arrow in her chest. At the least, she might be able to get the dark elves binding Starblade. If she could break him free, he could do the rest, and they could free the prisoners before—

Imoshaun threw her head back and screamed.

Arwen winced. Before it was too late.

What a strange creature you've grown into, Zyretha spoke into Arwen's mind at the same time as Arwen spotted her bow leaning against a rack that contained dozens if not hundreds of vials of blood. The quiver was on top of a counter next to it. *We did not expect your loyalty, not after so many years away, but you do not even flush with excitement at the draining of the life force of another, at the promise of giving the Soul Gatherer what she wishes.*

Yeah, no flushing here. Arwen tensed as Zyretha's cool gaze fell on her. *Why don't you have me chained?*

Maybe Arwen shouldn't have asked that. She should have pretended she didn't hate the dark elves as much as she did and wouldn't take them out if she found a chance.

Zyretha chuckled, glancing at Starblade, who'd noticed Arwen for the first time. The fury in his eyes grew tinged with betrayal and frustration. He glanced at her arm. No, at the spot where his tattoo lay under her sleeve.

If only it had been enough to counteract the spider tattoo. If only she'd never been marked by either.

Chained? The daughter of She Who Leads? Because you are one of us, you are free.

Not very free.

You will learn to embrace your power and serve your mother. Zyretha's red eyes closed to slits. *I will ensure it. I owe your mother this for doubting her when she let you escape all those years ago. But she was right. You will serve us well.* Zyretha smiled at Starblade, saying in English, "The gifts you were able to bring us will be cherished." She looked toward the ceiling.

Reminded that Zavryd and Val were in the building, Arwen stretched upward with her senses, searching for them. They were battling on a middle floor, still far away. Unfortunately, she sensed that the rooftop defenses were back in place.

Yes, we've trapped him inside. Zyretha glanced at the dragon-shaped artifact resting on a pedestal near the elevators some fifty feet away.

It was made from blue crystal that looked like water, and, as Arwen had seen before, was responsible for emitting that painful irritation to dragons. The artifact itself didn't appear that invulnerable. One of her magical arrows might shatter it if she could reach her bow. Her fire arrow might even hit upon its weakness if its base material had something to do with water.

Come, Zyretha said, *you will assist us with the draining. Your mother will be pleased with our progress when she returns to this world.*

Arwen didn't want to assist with anything and certainly didn't want to do anything else to Starblade—he was glaring at her as much as at Zyretha. That stung, but Arwen deserved it.

Her forearm throbbed, and Zyretha asserted her compulsion magic again. Not by choice, Arwen swung her legs off the cot and rose.

That damn tattoo was what was letting Zyretha control her so easily; she knew it. It was as if her people, foreseeing a future where their half-blood daughter might not want to work for them, had stuck it on her to ensure they could control her.

Starblade snarled as more of the nullifier was painted onto him. His muscles flexed, his power flared, and he almost broke the bonds again. But the dark elves whispered prayers to the demons as they poured more of their magic into keeping him still. If not for the nullifier already half-covering Starblade, they wouldn't have succeeded.

The nullifier. Arwen stared at the bucket.

An idea formed in her mind, but she jerked her gaze away, not wanting Zyretha to catch her thoughts. Zyretha had looked toward Starblade when he'd made his escape attempt, so Arwen hoped she was distracted.

Keeping her mind blank, Arwen walked toward Starblade and the dark elves. When Zyretha wasn't looking, Arwen veered to the side to grab her bow and quiver.

You will not raise a hand against one of us. Zyretha smiled with certainty.

Power flared around her, a barrier. All the dark elves were protected by defensive magic.

"You walk freely about in their compound?" Starblade rasped, looking at Arwen, not seeing that Zyretha was compelling her. Maybe if he hadn't been in such pain, he could have sensed the magic, but his naked chest heaved, his face contorted with agony.

Arwen hated the accusation in his eyes and shook her head.

"You *shot* me," he added.

"I am certain she is not the first to have fantasized about doing so." Zyretha smiled at Arwen and stepped over to grip her shoulder, as if they were friends.

"I knew I shouldn't— when I couldn't read your mind... I shouldn't have trusted someone with your blood." Starblade snarled and threw back his head, more angry with himself than with Arwen, she feared.

You can trust me, she wanted to cry, but what evidence did he have to support that?

You should have enjoyed striking him with an arrow, Zyretha said. *The Stormforge dragons cursed us for not obeying their laws, did you know? We believe they are the reason our fertility fell and even deals with the demons haven't been enough to maintain our population. They want us gone; all the other species do. You should not side with one of them.*

"I'm not siding with anyone," Arwen said, "but I don't appreciate being manipulated."

A roar echoed down from levels above. A dragon roar. Had Zavryd found a place where he could shift back into his native form?

"Are you *sure* we can handle that dragon?" someone asked. "Using him wasn't part of the original plan. The equipment—"

"Just get this one subdued," Zyretha snapped.

Magic surged from the not-so-subdued Starblade. A pair of infernos roared into existence, surrounding the two dark elves restraining him. But, as Zyretha had promised, they were sufficiently protected. That didn't keep one from stepping back, instinctively raising her hands against the light that came from the flames. Those painting Starblade with the nullifier also paused, squinting and looking away.

For a second, nobody was paying attention to Arwen.

She leaped back from Zyretha, turning toward the painters.

Zyretha lifted her arms, her barrier strengthening around herself. Arwen plunged a hand into the bucket of magical goo, shoved her sleeve up, and smeared it over her tattoo. Starblade's infernos intensified, the light almost blinding, even to Arwen's less sensitive eyes.

That didn't keep her from seeing Zyretha's eyebrows rise in surprise. Arwen felt the faintest lightening of the compulsion magic and took the opportunity to raise her bow. Zyretha lifted a hand toward her, gathering power for an attack.

Before she could, Arwen loosed an arrow. She didn't fire at Zyretha but at the dragon-shaped artifact by the elevator.

As the arrow landed, knocking the device off the pedestal and cracking it, Zyretha's power blasted into Arwen like a sledgehammer. It knocked her from her feet, hurling her across the laboratory.

Starblade roared and flung his arms up, finding more power. Even though the dark elves had succeeded in half-caking him with the nullifier, he broke the magical bonds and sent those who'd been casting them stumbling back.

Arwen hit a cement post, knocking the air from her lungs as pain blasted her. She tumbled, landing hard on her shoulder and almost lost her bow. But her fingers clenched it with determination. A number of her arrows tumbled out of her quiver.

You dare nullify the power of the mark of the demons? Zyretha demanded, as if that was the most offensive thing Arwen had done. The dragon-shaped artifact had gone dark, its power diminished.

Arwen rolled to her knees and grabbed an arrow. Another blast of power struck her with crushing force. She slammed into the side of one of the coils restraining Imoshaun. It flashed and stopped working, and the gnome fell to the floor.

Though pain hammered her body, Arwen managed to rise to her knees again. She'd only kept a grip on one arrow and didn't even know which one it was. The rest lay ten feet away, scattered about her quiver. Zyretha kicked them as she strode toward Arwen, not sparing a glance for the freed gnome.

Arwen sensed Zyretha was still ensconced behind a powerful barrier but pointed the arrow at her anyway, hoping vainly that it would get through.

Fire that at the half-dragon, Zyretha ordered, compulsion lacing the words.

Arwen's bow twitched two inches to the side, toward Starblade. He'd found his sword and was tearing into the dark elves who'd presumed to paint him. But this time, the spider tattoo on her arm was dormant, covered by the nullifier. Clenching her jaw, Arwen jerked the arrow back toward Zyretha's chest. But how to breach her barrier? Arwen had only one shot. If her arrow was deflected or destroyed, she would be defenseless...

Starblade roared in fury again.

Fire at him! Zyretha ordered with even more compulsion.

Intent on Arwen, on bending her to her will, she didn't notice Starblade behind her. Arwen fired her arrow. If nothing else, it would distract Zyretha so Starblade could attack.

But he raked his hand through the air, as if he were in dragon form and using talons, and his power tore Zyretha's barrier to shreds. With it gone, Arwen's arrow struck, her aim perfect. The arrow slammed into her heart.

Eyes bulging, Zyretha stumbled back, utterly stunned.

You... you dare! She was looking at Arwen, not Starblade.

He sprang on her and slashed his sword into her neck. Her head flew free, white hair flapping.

Though horrified, Arwen slumped back in relief. The laboratory fell silent. Starblade had killed the other dark elves as well.

Sword still raised, blood dripping down the blade, he stared down at Arwen. His eyes glowed violet, and he looked and *felt* like a dragon, not a rational elf.

Arwen swallowed. She'd betrayed him, and she feared he didn't understand that it hadn't been her choice. What if he ended her life just as he'd ended Zyretha's?

Starblade strode forward with his sword raised as if that was *exactly* what he intended. In his battle rage, he might not recognize her. Or maybe he recognized her dark-elven blood and cared about nothing else.

With shaking hands, Arwen pushed up her sleeve, showing him the gunk covering her tattoo as she groped for words to explain that she hadn't wanted to betray him, that Zyretha had controlled her.

The elevator dinged, the sound so mundane that it was ludicrous at that moment.

Val walked out with her huge silver tiger at her side and her sword and gun in hand. Zavryd strode out in black elven robes, soot blackening one side of his face, and a sword made of fire in his grip. They looked around at the carnage, and Val raised her eyebrows when she spotted Starblade poised only a few feet from Arwen with his sword in the air.

She cleared her throat. "Did we come at a bad time?"

Starblade froze. Wrestling to get himself under control?

"I'm sorry," Arwen whispered, making herself hold his gaze, though those glowing violet eyes were so alien and cold that she wanted only to look away. "I didn't want to help them. I never did. I promise."

Starblade lowered his sword, but he said nothing. He turned his back on her and stalked toward the chamber imprisoning his comrade.

Zavryd snarled, using his power to pluck up something on the floor. The broken artifact. It had already stopped working, but he hurled it against a post. Wanting to utterly destroy it? Using his magic, he picked up the cracked husk and bashed it again and again. It shattered into dozens if not hundreds of pieces.

"Feel better now?" Val asked him.

"Odious, vile dark-elven magic," Zavryd spat.

Arwen knew a dark elf hadn't made that artifact, but she didn't care enough to correct him. She slumped to the floor, exhausted.

Starblade might not forgive her, but he hadn't beheaded her. After what she'd done to him, it was more than she could have expected.

"Arwen?" Imoshaun asked in an exhausted voice. "That is you?"

"It's me."

"Oh, the pain was so great. They deemed me important enough to steal my life force for their nefarious plot." Imoshaun flung her arm at the magical capacitor, then peered around. "Is Gruflen still alive? Are we free?" She looked uncertainly toward Starblade, who was clawing the nullifier off his naked body as he attempted to figure out how to free his comrade. Zavryd found more artifacts to destroy while Val headed toward Arwen with her tiger companion ambling at her side. She bled from numerous claw gashes but didn't appear gravely injured.

"We're free." Arwen didn't sense any more dark elves around. Where her mother was and whether Arwen would see her again, she didn't know. All she wanted was to go home. "Or will be soon."

"We'll find and free all the prisoners." Val holstered her gun and offered Arwen a hand. "Thanks for opening the way in for us. That worked perfectly."

Arwen, who knew how it had almost worked perfectly for the *dark elves*, could only shake her head.

"I'll tell Willard. She mentioned she might have a use for you." Val winked.

"I... don't know what to say."

Imoshaun squeaked and ran toward the elevator. Maybe she'd sensed the other prisoners—including her husband—on the level above.

"Yeah, the honor of working for the US government often leaves people speechless," Val said.

With a swell of power, Starblade tore apart the chamber holding his comrade. What had his name been? Yendral.

Without any finesse, Starblade also used fire to incinerate the caked nullifier coating off the other half-dragon. It must not have hurt that much because Yendral threw back his head and roared.

"There's a lot of dragon in those guys," Val observed.

The memory of Starblade standing above Arwen with his sword, not seeming to recognize her, sent a chill through her.

"Yes." She pushed a shaky hand through her hair, hoping she hadn't made herself Public Enemy Number One to whatever dark elves remained on Earth, but she worried she had. "Tracking trouble," she murmured.

"What was that?"

"Just something my father says about me."

EPILOGUE

ARWEN STOPPED BEFORE THE THRESHOLD OF THE BUSY COFFEE Dragon, not certain what to expect. That morning, Zavryd's telepathic summons from the other side of the county had only said that the human military leader wished to see her here and commanded her to arrive at nine.

Since she'd been busy cutting and cleaning produce for the market, Arwen had been tempted to ignore the order, but ignoring a dragon was rarely wise. And she didn't want to find herself on Colonel Willard's bad side either.

Besides, there was something she needed to pick up from the shop. A gift. Not, she told herself, a bribe. Nothing that would create an *obligation*.

Despite her determination to go in, Arwen took several steadying breaths before crossing the threshold. Not only could she hear the chatter and laughter of a crowd, but she sensed all the magical beings inside. That familiar feeling of panic seeped into her.

"You only need to stay a minute," she assured herself, attempting to will the tension out of her neck and shoulders.

LINDSAY BUROKER

She'd survived battling dark elves. She could survive a crowded coffee shop.

Inside, there was no sign of Zavryd, nor did Arwen sense the dragon's aura, but she spotted Val, Matti, and Willard sitting at a table in a corner with an empty chair waiting. Val and Matti had carbonated waters before them, while Willard nursed a mug of coffee so black it looked like it could fuel a rocket ship. Val smirked and made a comment that might have been snarky, because it prompted Willard to scowl at her, but as soon as the colonel sipped from her mug, contentment replaced the facial expression.

Arwen had only taken a few steps toward the table when two goblins carrying what looked like components for a siege engine staggered inside, almost bumping her when they passed. She skittered back, resisting the urge to flee out the door. She had a mission.

"Once we have our super automated drink mixer assembled," one goblin said, "we're sure to win the cocktail-creation competition."

Ah, a drink mixer, not a siege engine. Her conversations with Starblade must have lingered in her thoughts.

Arwen hadn't seen him for three days, not since he and his rescued comrade had freed the rest of the captives, then left the building, departing without a word to her. Given that she'd *shot* Starblade, she hadn't been surprised, but she had been... disappointed.

Sadness crept into her at the thought that she might not see him again, that he wouldn't forgive her for betraying him. It hadn't been her fault, and she hoped he'd gathered that, but she didn't know if that would make a difference in how he felt toward her.

When she'd woken up the morning after the battle, the dragon tattoo on her arm had been gone. She'd never wanted it. She'd even resented it. But now... she missed it. Strange.

"There's no doubt." The other goblin nodded toward a corner that held a bar and bottles of alcohol on shelves, though a sign said the area didn't open until lunch. "The half-blood bartender uses only that silver container and her own arm muscles to shake drinks. Can you imagine a goblintini being satisfactorily stirred by such anemic means?"

"Absolutely not. The special ingredient would *never* be sufficiently pulverized to mix in with the vodka and shots of goblin-fuel espresso. Work Leader Nin, where can we set up our mixer?"

The part-gnome lady expertly making lattes and macchiatos while also expertly scowling at the goblins said, "In the alley behind the shop."

"The *alley*? Oh, no, someone might steal the very valuable parts."

"Or copy our design. Intellectual-property theft is rampant among goblins!"

They scurried behind the bar with their loads, then started whispering and pointing furtively. Val waved for Arwen to join them, so she didn't catch Nin's response.

"Should I ask what the secret ingredient for the *goblintini* is?" Willard asked.

"No," Matti and Val said together.

"My assistant, Gondo, is working on a recipe to enter into your competition. I understand it will pair delightfully with his clan's ten-pound cakes."

"It's not really *our* competition." Val pointed Arwen to the empty seat. "In fact, I believe Nin shredded all the signs that kept appearing on the bar, announcing its approach. She even asked Zav to incinerate one of them. It's possible she meant for him to incinerate the goblin that kept putting up the signs, but he only threatens to flame those who snip trimmings from the dragon topiaries guarding our yard. I understand someone at the goblin sanctuary down the street is trying to grow topiaries of their own and believes it might be achieved by using cuttings from ours."

"I thought those topiaries could defend themselves," Willard said. "Don't they spit fire?"

"At anyone who passes in front of them and tries to go up the walkway to our house, yes, but, as we learned last Halloween, they're not that good at protecting *themselves,* especially if you go at them from behind."

"Ah, yes, I recall you mentioning the toilet-papering incident."

"*Incidents.*"

"Don't forget the shaving cream," Matti said. "Arwen, you were called in to help deal with the miscreants responsible for that, weren't you?"

Arwen nodded. "Lord Zavryd asked Sigrid to track them down, and I did go along to assist her."

Sigrid had been willing to humor her daughter's mate, but neither she nor Arwen had wanted to *deal with* the twelve-year-old boys who had been at the end of the trail.

"See?" Val thumped Willard on the shoulder. "Arwen has been helpful to our missions for a long time. You shouldn't have hesitated to hire her."

"I *didn't* hesitate. She never came to me to request a job." Willard arched her eyebrows at Arwen.

"*I* never came to you to request a job either," Matti said. "You strong-armed me into joining your league of independent contractors."

"I did, and it was an impressive feat, if I do say so myself, to *strong-arm* someone with dwarven blood."

Maybe because it was the weekend, Willard wore exercise clothing instead of her Army uniform, and it was easy to see that her arms were quite muscular. Had Arwen sensed any magic about her, she would have believed that Willard *also* had dwarven blood.

"I wasn't aware that you were hiring," Arwen said. "My last job interview didn't go well."

"I don't know about that. It led to you finding a way into that building when the rest of us couldn't and weren't even sure yet that we wanted to."

Technically, Arwen had only found some keys. It had been Starblade who'd burned a hole through the foundation wall into the parking garage. Again, she thought wistfully of him, wondering if he and his comrade were lounging in their rejuvenation pool, recovering from their ordeal. Her ribs and shoulder still ached from having been hurled against a post, making her wish again that *she* had a rejuvenation pool.

Val raised a finger. "I'm sure Zav could have found a way in if we'd been more certain that we wanted to get in. While we were waiting for Arwen to open a door for us, he was pointing out that incinerating the ten-block radius around the building might effectively take out its magic."

"Dragons do have a singular method for dealing with their problems," Willard said.

Arwen smiled sadly.

"It's why I've never attempted to hire one of them," Willard added.

"They're too powerful and important to work for humans," Val said, "as Zav has told me numerous times."

"*Self*-important, maybe." Willard pushed a manila envelope across the table toward Arwen. "For your assistance with the dark elves. I understand we could have to deal with them again?"

Arwen grimaced. "I'm not sure, but Zyretha mentioned others before she, uhm, passed."

She'd *mentioned* Arwen's mother. Unfortunately.

Arwen eyed her sleeve. The spider tattoo had stopped itching, glowing, or doing anything else ominous, but now that she knew her mother's people could control her through it, she had much stronger feelings about it than before. She vowed to find a way to have it removed. How, she didn't yet know, but she would figure it out. Until she did, she wouldn't be free.

"Passed?" Val asked. "Wasn't she beheaded?"

"Which caused her to pass," Arwen said, "yes."

"Well," Willard said, "you're the perfect person to go on missions to thwart the dark elves since you know more about them than any of my other operatives."

Arwen couldn't keep her grimace from deepening. The last thing she wanted was to cross paths with her mother's people again, but now that she was on their radar, she feared it would be inevitable.

"Don't worry." This time, Val gave *Arwen* the thump on the shoulder. "Willard is sure to throw in some missions tracking down yetis, rogue assassins, marauding orcs, and krakens. You know, fun stuff. Hm, can krakens be tracked?"

"It's hard to trail something through the water," Arwen said.

"I suspect you have ways." Willard's gaze was more knowing than Arwen would have liked, and Arwen suspected she was aware of soul tracking.

"Before you say yes to signing over your life to the Army," Matti told Arwen, "let me tell you that my real-estate-agent friend did some snooping around in regard to your farm's taxes. It seems that the designation was changed by a clerk who no longer works at the county office. A bribe might have been involved. Or maybe those shifters leaning on someone. They might have guessed you wouldn't be eager to work for them if you didn't need money for some reason. Anyway, when Zadie called up the county and pointed out that you guys are an active farm, the new clerk agreed and changed the designation back. They *want* to encourage people to farm out there."

"Meaning my father's taxes will go back to normal?"

"Yup."

Arwen wondered what had happened to the remaining shifters. She hadn't been quite sure if they'd been after her from the beginning, or if they'd been after Starblade, as they'd said, and had only later gotten orders from the dark elves to collect her. Someone had tried to pay those ogres to get her, and the shifters had those stacks of hundreds.

"I guess I don't need extra money then," Arwen said, relieved.

"No, *but*—" Willard patted the envelope, "—it's a good idea to increase your earnings and put some money away for your retirement. Or random life expenditures. You never know when an unexpected emergency will crop up, like a dragon dueling with an elf on your property and charring all the grass and leaving a *crater* in the lawn."

"You didn't have to pay for that out of your pocket, did you?" Val asked her dryly.

"I have limited funds that can go toward maintaining the landscaping around the office," Willard told her.

Arwen eyed the envelope, the bulge promising a stack of bills inside. Apparently, independent contractors, at least contractors for Willard's magical-operations Army office that didn't technically exist, were paid in cash.

She opened it and counted out ten thousand dollars in hundreds. She'd never seen that much money in one place before. She and her father were lucky to make a few hundred in a weekend at the farmers market, and a lot of that went toward maintaining equipment, buying supplies, and paying for their business and commercial-kitchen licenses so that everything was on the up-and-up with the county.

"That's more than you pay me." Val must have watched the counting closely. "And Matti. Really, Willard. Are you going to play favorites with your operatives?"

"I'm giving her a combat bonus. She limped out of that

building grabbing her ribs, and she had to deal with that uptight half-dragon. That's above and beyond the call of duty."

Another twinge of regret went through Arwen, and she was tempted to defend Starblade. If he was uptight, which she didn't think he was, it was because the Cosmic Realms had treated him poorly since he'd woken from stasis. Maybe since he'd been born.

"I have to deal with Zav all the time," Val said, "and he's three times as uptight as Starblade."

"Yes, but you *married* him. You must like that."

Matti nodded at Val.

"I accept your offer of work, ma'am." Even if the taxes would be less onerous now, Arwen admitted that it would be good to earn a little extra so the farm had some padding if anything came up. Their tractor, her father's truck, and a lot of their equipment were decades old. Besides, as much as she hated to admit it, she was better qualified than most to deal with dark elves.

Arwen counted out ten hundred-dollar bills and slid them across the table to Val. "Will you give that to Amber? I owe her ten percent." She hesitated, then added another hundred. "And a new leopard-print briefcase."

"What happened to the other one?"

"I needed it to club a half-orc."

"You might pick up a hammer," Matti said, "not just a bow. Something for close-range battles."

"I have a foraging knife." Arwen showed them the blade.

"It has a fluffy brush on the end," Matti said, as if that disqualified it as a weapon.

"Those are boar bristles. They're for dusting off mushrooms."

"That'll be handy against a kraken." Val swept up and stacked the hundreds, though she shook her head. "I'll give this to Amber, but it seems like a lot of money to pay a sixteen-year-old for work. For *anything*."

Matti and Willard nodded in agreement.

"What did *you* make at sixteen?" Val asked Matti.

"My grandpa paid me four dollars an hour to help put up drywall and learn plumbing and tile work."

"That was less than minimum wage then, wasn't it?" Val asked. "You're not that old."

"As I recall, it was the wage my grandfather believed my experience, work ethic, and mouthiness deserved."

"So, *not* minimum wage."

"I gained in experience what I lost in dollars." Matti nodded sagely, though a smirk teased the corners of her mouth.

"I'm glad I never worked for your grandpa," Val said.

"When I was a girl," Willard said, "I only made two dollars an hour loading sacks of Vidalia onions into freight boxes after the harvest."

"Yeah, but that was back in the 1800s, wasn't it?" Val asked. "That was good money then."

"Ha ha, we're almost the same age, and you know it. Not everyone has *elf* blood that makes them look hot and young into their forties and beyond." Willard curled a lip at Val, then decided to include Arwen in the gesture, though Arwen didn't think anyone had ever accused her of excess hotness.

A goblin in an apron came over—one of the staff? She held a pen and notepad and looked more reputable than the scheming inventors behind the bar.

"Would you like to place an order?" Since the others already had drinks, the goblin looked at Arwen, though she also cast a speculative glance at the money on the table. "Tips are appreciated."

"Do you have change?" Arwen held up one of the hundreds.

"Nope." The goblin smirked.

"*Yes*," Val said firmly.

"Yes," the goblin sighed reluctantly and dramatically.

"I'd like a coffee and..." Arwen's original reason for wanting to visit the shop came to mind. "Would you be able to bag up your used coffee grounds for the day and sell them to me? I have a friend who's getting into gardening and needs soil amendments."

"Yes, we can do that. One hundred dollars a bag."

Arwen stared. "That seems steep." She was certain she'd heard of other coffee shops giving the grounds away for free.

"No charge," Val said in her firm tone.

The goblin sighed dramatically again before heading to the kiosk.

"It's hard to find good help," Val said.

"I've heard that," Willard said, deadpan.

Val and Matti squinted at her.

"You'd better be careful what grounds you give your gardener friend," Willard told Arwen. "Amending soil with the remains from the goblin-fuel blend might kill whatever you're trying to grow."

"Or result in a Jack-and-the-Beanstalk situation," Matti said.

"My, ah, friend has some mushrooms in need of a lot of help."

"Mushrooms, huh?" Willard glanced at Arwen's foraging knife. "Well, I'm not an expert on those. The Army frowns against the consumption of psychedelic substances. Though they might make my workdays seem less odd."

"Not having a goblin for a secretary would make your days less odd," Val told her.

"Gondo is my best informant. Who do you think found the link between the shifters and the missing people?"

"He managed that while he was busy plotting drinks to win the cocktail competition?"

"He's a goblin of many talents."

When Arwen received the bags of grounds, she stood, intending to flee the increasingly crowded establishment.

"One more thing, Forester." Willard lifted a finger.

"Yes?"

"Get a phone."

"A what?"

"You've seen them before, I'm sure. When I have work, I want to be able to call you, and I don't mean telepathically via Val's dragon."

"Zav *would* appreciate not being the messaging service. I have to bribe him to get him to perform such menial tasks, as he calls them." Val opened her duster to show a folded manila envelope sticking out of an inside pocket. "*My* earnings go toward paying for his meat requirements, plus tasty extras that I pick up for when I need favors."

"Being mated to a dragon sounds challenging," Arwen said.

"Fortunately, I like challenges. It's why I keep contracting for Willard, who is grouchy and demanding."

Willard folded her arms over her chest. Grouchily.

"Maybe you're just not properly respectful toward her," Arwen suggested.

"That's the truth," Willard said. "And respectful subordinates get phones."

"I'll... look into it."

"Do you know where to go to get one?" Matti asked.

Arwen hesitated, wondering if that was a trick question. "A phone store?"

"Maybe Amber can go with her to help her pick out something sufficient," Matti suggested to Val.

"If she takes Amber, she'll get all the accessories too. And bling."

Arwen curled her lip, though it was less at the thought of bling and more at the idea of being in the middle of tracking in the woods and having a phone ring.

"Just get connected, Forester." Willard flicked her fingers toward the door.

"And let us know how your mushrooms react to *goblin-fuel* grounds," Val said.

Arwen waved and left, not correcting them on who the grounds were for. Assuming he would accept them. Would he?

Since the goblin sanctuary northeast of Arlington was a long hike from the farm outside Carnation, Arwen asked for a ride. Normally, she wouldn't have presumed to make such a request of a dragon, but when Val had flown over on Zavryd's back to fulfill an order of *ten* jars of pickled cherries for Amber, Arwen had asked them, saying she would throw in two extra jars. Since Zavryd had no interest in cherries or fruit or vegetables of any kind, the negotiations hadn't been as simple as Arwen had hoped, but Val had thrown her weight behind the request, promising to make a batch of bacon-beef meat loaves for her mate.

Thus Arwen found herself on the ridge opposite the hill where Starblade made his home, the foliage in the lush gully in between covered in water droplets from a recent rain.

The magic of the place kept her from sensing if he was inside. If he was, he had to be aware of her presence. Zavryd hadn't been camouflaging himself, so Starblade would have detected his approach.

She waited a few minutes to see if he came out or spoke telepathically to her. He didn't.

Sighing, Arwen picked her way across the gully, the leaves dampening her trousers. She carried the bags of used coffee grounds as well as her last three jars of pickled cherries. As soon as the fruit trees on the farm ripened, she would make more. She might have to trade with the neighbor who also had a cherry orchard so she would have extra to work with this year.

When she reached the top of the hill, the bench empty, she

eyed the little keyhole she'd used before. It had been filled in with a silvery substance. Access denied, it seemed to say. Not that she would have gone in without an invitation, not for a second time anyway.

As she set the jars and bags on his bench, Arwen spoke, just in case Starblade was nearby monitoring her. "I'm sorry again for what happened. I hope you don't believe I intended to betray you all along. I understand why you might think that, given the tracking and the shifters, but... that was before I knew you. And found out you're... well, you seem decent and like you've had a rough life. I'm glad you were able to free your friend. I hope he recovers and isn't too traumatized by... Well, memories of time spent with dark elves can leave a mark on the mind. Trust me; I know."

A part of her was tempted to point out that *Zavryd* wasn't holding a grudge about being lured into the building, but he also hadn't walked into the dark-elf lair at her side and believed she would be an ally. And he hadn't been tormented. Besides, Starblade didn't like Zavryd, and she didn't want to irk him by mentioning the dragon.

After arranging the items neatly on the bench, Arwen reached into a pouch tied to her belt and retrieved the gold coins Starblade had given her, their weight heavy in her palm. Since Willard had paid her, and Matti had gotten the tax problem resolved, Arwen didn't need his money. And, given that she'd almost been the death of him, she didn't feel right keeping it. She stacked the coins beside the other items.

If you want a return ride, came Val's voice from the goblin village where she and Zavryd waited, *you'd better come back soon. A little boy is reciting historical trivia about how dragons once enslaved the lesser species, and Zav is getting a touch exasperated.*

I'll be right there. Thank you.

"If we don't cross paths again," Arwen said aloud, though she had no idea if Starblade was listening, "I hope you'll have a good rest of your life on Earth and succeed in figuring out how to blend in. Or at least how to avoid being reported to the Dragon Council." More softly she added, "Goodbye," then headed back down the hill, trying not to feel disappointed that he hadn't come out.

He might, she reminded herself, not be home at all.

But a whisper of magic came from behind her as she walked across the gully. *His* magic.

Arwen turned to look. At first, she didn't see or sense what had caused it, but she soon glimpsed something floating toward her. An... empty jar?

She lifted her hand and caught it as it floated into her grasp. It was one of her pickling jars. The three new ones she'd brought remained on the bench, so this had to be the first one she'd brought, cleaned and ready for use again.

It wasn't quite the response she'd hoped for, but Starblade could have used his magic to bash her in the head with it, so maybe this was a way of saying that he forgave her. At the least, it didn't seem to forbid her from ever returning.

"Thank you." She nodded at the hill before heading into the woods.

THE END

Thank you for reading! If you enjoyed the adventure and would like to continue on with the series, *Bound by Blood* is next up!

Made in the USA
Middletown, DE
13 June 2024

55711715R00203